DAUGHTER OF EDEN

Chris Beckett is a university lecturer living in Cambridge. He is the winner of the Edge Hill Short Story competition, 2009, for *The Turing Test*, the prestigious Arthur C. Clarke award, 2013, for *Dark Eden* and has been shortlisted for the British Science Fiction Association Novel of the Year Award, 2015, for *Mother of Eden*.

ALSO BY CHRIS BECKETT

The Holy Machine
Dark Eden
Mother of Eden

CHRIS BECKETT

DAUGHTER OF EDEN

CORVUS

First published in hardback in Great Britain in 2016
by Corvus, an imprint of Atlantic Books Ltd.

This paperback edition published in 2017 by Corvus,
an imprint of Atlantic Books Ltd.

10 9 8 7 6 5 4 3 2 1

A CIP catalogue record for this book is available
from the British Library.

Paperback ISBN: 978 1 782392 41 5
E-book ISBN: 978 1 782392 40 8

Printed in Great Britain by
CPI Group (UK) Ltd, Croydon CR0 4YY

Corvus
An imprint of Atlantic Books Ltd
Ormond House
26–27 Boswell Street
London WC1N 3JZ

www.corvus-books.co.uk

To my two daughters,
with much love and great pride

Part I

One

I look back through all the things that have happened since, and it's like looking out through the trees and lanterns of a forest. So many things in between, but there, far off in the distance, is me as I once was, Angie Redlantern, walking along the cliff path to Veeklehouse with my little Candy hopping and skipping and dancing along beside me. On our right is the glowing water, pink and green, stretching away to World's Edge. On our left is the humming forest: dark trunks, shining lanterns, glittering starflowers, on and on blueway as far as the slopes of Snowy Dark. Above us, the huge spiral of Starry Swirl fills up the whole of the black black sky. I am carrying a bag of bone tools to trade. 'Twinkle twinkle little star,' Candy sings, and gives a little twirl. She is four years old: five wombtimes we'd have said when I was a kid, but that Angie back there on the cliff has been living so long among Davidfolk that she's become used to thinking in years.

Ahead of us is Veeklehouse, the Davidfolk's biggest trading place, sitting there on the clifftop in the spot where John Redlantern once stood long long ago, wondering whether or not to throw Gela's metal ring out into the water. Veeklehouse is bright with firelight – though it's a rough dirty dangerous brightness, completely different from the soft light of forest – and it sits under a flat cloud of smoke that's pretty much always there, glowing a faint dirty orange against the starry sky.

That's me and Candy, long ago: little dots on the clifftop, between the shining water, and the shining forest, and the high cold light of the stars.

'Look, Mum,' says Candy. 'Lots of boats!'

I'd first seen Veeklehouse some ten years previously. A bunch of us came down in a boat from the little sandy grounds I grew up in, way up rockway from Veeklehouse and ten miles out into the water. Me and my friend Starlight were so excited we ran up the cliff like little kids, leaving the older grownups behind us to follow the best they could. Gela's heart! The colours, the people, the things they traded! It all seemed wonderful to us. And that was before we'd even seen the Veekle itself behind its high fence, that huge mysterious metal thing, steeped in the strangeness of Earth.

But that later me, the me walking along the cliff path with Candy, had lived near Veeklehouse about eight years. I came along this path every couple of wakings back then with a bag of the little things that my bloke Dave carved out from buckbone – knives, scrapers, earrings, beads – and Veeklehouse had come to be something ordinary. Things always do, I've found: you grow tired of the ordinary things and long for some bright and wonderful thing that you can't reach, and then you find you *can* reach it, and it turns out to be just another ordinary thing. I never gave a second look at the buckfat lanterns any more, though their restless light had once seemed so strange and dangerous and full of possibilities. I didn't look at the earrings made of coloured feathers, or the bats waiting in cages to be done for and cooked on the spot. I just went straight to the traders who would take the things I had to trade, and give me sticks in return, on to other traders who would swap those sticks for things we needed, and then back again to Michael's Place.

As to the metal Veekle behind its fence, well, aside from taking my kids to see it – as well as Candy, I had my big boy Fox and my baby boy Mehmet: Metty as we usually called him – I never even thought about it. Yes, the Veekle was huge. Yes, it was made using skills we couldn't even imagine. Yes, it came from Earth, and three men died in it. But all that was long long ago. I had people to look after now who were still in reach, real living people who needed me. And, when it came to people who'd gone, well, I had plenty from my own life to grieve over. There were three other kids for one thing, little Star, and Peter, and Happy. They all died a few wakings after they were born.

'Mum, *look*!' Candy said again. 'Lots lots lots of boats.'

'Yes, sweetheart,' I said. 'There *are* lots of boats here, aren't there?'

I didn't bother to look. Boats were always coming back and forth between Veeklehouse and the rest of Eden. My little Candy always *always* pointed them out and usually I obliged her by looking and making surprised or amazed or impressed sounds at what she'd spotted. But sometimes, when I was thinking about the past and the things I'd lost, it made me sad looking out over the water, and I preferred to keep my eyes on the things near me, the shining trees, the stones on the path, the waves right below us splashing on the rocks, with the supple branches of the shining watertrees, green and pink, swaying this way and that beneath them. It just seemed to make sense to keep my attention on the things that were nearby, not the ones that were far away and out of reach.

Out there on the bright water was where I'd last seen my friend Starlight. I'd stood crying down there on that rocky ledge and watched her boat, dark on the bright water, until World's Edge swallowed it up. And out there too – out there and behind us, way, way up rockway – I'd said goodbye to everyone else I knew, in little peaceful Knee Tree Grounds in its little patch of water forest, far out in the bright water.

'Come on, *look*, Mum!' my little girl called out again, tugging impatiently at my hand. '*Lots* of boats! One-two-three-four-five boats! And they're all together. You haven't even looked *once* yet.'

So finally I looked, and I saw five boats side by side, strung out along World's Edge: five dark shapes with their windcatchers changing from pink to green to pink in the waterlight shining up from beneath them.

'So there are, Candy. Five boats. Clever girl. You're getting *good* good at counting.'

It wasn't at all unusual to be able to see five six boats all at once out there. Often there were more than that. Veeklehouse was a busy place, and boats came from all over Eden, but I'd never before seen five all together like that, all heading the same way. I wondered where they were from. Time had been when you knew that any boat with a windcatcher must have come from New Earth, but everyone was making them that way by then, and no one bothered with log-boats any more, or with the little bark Knee Boats we used to make back on Knee Tree Grounds. Once again, I guess, the Johnfolk had led the way.

'I wonder what they're bringing,' I said.

'Metal,' said Candy. 'Or colour-stones. Or buckfat. Or bark.'

She knew these were things that pool-traders brought to Veekle-house, because me and her dad had told her. Metal came from New Earth. Colour-stones came on boats from Brown River (though I'd heard that the stones themselves came from Half Sky, over on far side of Snowy Dark). Buckfat was brought in every waking from up and down poolside, wherever there were still fatbucks left to be hunted, to feed the hungry lamps of Veeklehouse. Bark came once in a while from my old home, Knee Tree Grounds, out there up rockway across World's Edge. No one made boats with it any more, but it was pretty good for roofs.

'I guess so, sweetheart,' I said.

A nagging worry was beginning to stir inside me, like a tube-slinker inside a tree, scrabbling up an airhole with its hundred hard scratchy little legs. Why would five boats arrive all together and side by side? And why, I wondered, as they drew closer and I could see them more clearly, were there so many people standing on each one, looking out towards us across the bright water? So many people, and so little in the way of a load.

'Look!' cried Candy excitedly. '*More* boats.'

Oh Gela's heart. There were another five of them behind the first lot, another row of five, appearing from across World's Edge. My hand tightened round my little girl's, and she glanced up worriedly at my face.

'What's the matter, Mum?'

'Oh, probably nothing, dear,' I said, 'but let's go and find your dad and your brothers.'

'But we're going to Veeklehouse!'

'Another time, sweetheart.' I pulled her back the way we'd just come. 'I just need to... well, talk to your dad about those boats.'

'Ow, Mum, you're hurting me.'

I glanced back at the Pool. I could see the faces of the men on the first five boats now, lit from below by the waterlight, and I could see they *weren't* faces, but metal masks.

I snatched Candy up and started to run.

Two

When I went to Veeklehouse that first time with Starlight and the others, I thought it was just for fun. We'd do a bit of trading, have a look at the Veekle, and then go proudly back again to tell the story to all the folk in Knee Tree Grounds who'd never been further than boring old Nob Head. That was what I thought would happen. Nothing would really change.

But in fact *everything* did. When we were there, Starlight met a strange, beautiful, powerful man called Greenstone. He was one of the Johnfolk from New Earth across the water and he talked English in such a weird way that at first it was hard to make out what he was saying. He had a brooch made of metal, and men with metal spears who followed him round and did whatever he asked of them. It was obvious from the beginning that he was a high high man, and it turned out that he was as high as could be, the son of the Headman of New Earth. Like all high men, he was used to getting what he wanted, and as soon as he saw Starlight, well, he wanted her. She was pretty pretty and smart smart, and, now I think about it, she was kind of used to getting what she wanted too, especially from men. She went away with him, far far away across the water, and the rest of us returned to Knee Tree Grounds without her.

I had lost my best friend. I had learned that there were things in the world that my best friend valued more than my friendship, and I had seen for myself that there were things that could happen to someone beautiful like Starlight that would never never happen to me. Because I am a batface. I can't properly close my mouth because it's joined up with my nose in a single messy hole that's lined with twisted gums and twisted teeth. If I worked hard at it, people liked me when they got to know me, but no one was ever ever going to fall for me as Greenstone fell for Starlight, or as she fell for him. (Greenstone himself could barely bring himself to speak to me or look me in the face.)

And now Starlight was going to a new and wonderful place where they'd found how to make metal, and boats that blew with the wind – Greenstone said it would make bright Veeklehouse look small and dark – and I was going back to a little patch of sand to cut bark and gather waternuts with the same bunch of people that I'd known all my life. Good old Angie: she's not much to look at, but she works hard and she has a kind heart.

Oh I felt sad sad, like a big aching hole had opened up inside me. But I still thought that life on Knee Tree Grounds would carry on as before.

I was wrong wrong wrong. The ripples from what happened in Veeklehouse were still moving outwards across the world. They would break over New Earth, they would reach Brown River, and along Brown River right through the mountains and into the ground called Half Sky. And one of the things they did was make the Davidfolk look at us Kneefolk in a different way. That changed Knee Tree Grounds for good.

You see, the people in Veeklehouse were Davidfolk, as were the people nearest to Knee Tree Grounds at Nob Head, along with all the other people along poolside from up Rockway Edge, down through Veeklehouse, and on until the edge of Brown River Ground, way down alpway. But of course the people from New Earth were Johnfolk. And yes, okay, the Davidfolk at that time were letting the New Earthers come to Veeklehouse and trade their metal, but that didn't change the fact that the Davidfolk would never forgive them for stealing Gela's ring, or for breaking the Circle, or for splitting up Family, or for bringing killing into the world. And nor did it mean that the Johnfolk had forgiven the Davidfolk for driving John Redlantern out of Family, and trying to do for him and his people. Never mind that all these things happened long before anyone still living was born, long before the *parents* of anyone still living were born, long before even their great-grandparents. That made no difference. The Johnfolk and the Davidfolk still hated each other.

We Kneefolk, in our quiet little grounds, ten miles out from Nob Head, weren't on either side. We didn't actually use the word when we spoke about ourselves – we just called ourselves Kneefolk – but, if the others were Davidfolk or Johnfolk, then we were Jeffsfolk. Our great-great-grandparents had followed not John Redlantern or David Redlantern, but Jeff Redlantern, and Jeff always said there was no point in fretting about the past, and arguing forever about which story was the true one. He and the people with him came to Knee Tree Grounds so they could get away from the fighting that was going on back then between the followers of David and the followers of John, and live their lives in peace.

When I was born, of course, that fight had been over for generations. There were still Johnfolk living way down alpway at Brown River, and we knew that John himself and some of his followers had disappeared over Worldpool with the ring, but when we paddled across to Nob Head to trade, the only people we ever met were Davidfolk. (Except for once twice, when there was a trader there from Brown River: 'Look!' someone would say. 'That man is one of the Johnfolk,' and we'd all stare at the guy in amazement, like he had two heads, or wings sticking up from his shoulders like a bat.)

So we Kneefolk were the odd ones out. The Davidfolk knew this, and sometimes they teased us for the funny way we talked, or for following someone like Clawfoot Jeff, but we were no threat to them out on our little patch of sand, and they liked the bark boats we brought them. They'd let us alone for generations.

She didn't mean to, of course, but Starlight had changed all that. A lot of people in Veeklehouse had seen what was going on between Greenstone and our Starlight – well, of course they had: they'd watched the Headmanson of New Earth like a leopard watches a buck, they'd taken note of every little thing he did! – so the Davidfolk knew that one of our people had gone with Greenstone. And that reminded them that we Kneefolk *weren't* Davidfolk but Jeffsfolk, and that actually Jeff was John's cousin, and had taken John's side when Family first split in two. So now they asked themselves whose side we were really on, and what it was that New Earth wanted with us. Among the Davidfolk, you see, the high men chose their shelterwomen from the daughters of men they wanted to have as friends.

What was more, the Davidfolk had learned that the Headman of New Earth was thinking of attacking them – some of the New Earth traders had boasted as much when they'd drunk too much badjuice in Veeklehouse – so now they wondered whether the Headmanson had chosen Starlight because Knee Tree Grounds would be useful to New Earth. A little place like Knee Tree, far out in the bright water: their ringmen could gather there, couldn't they, after crossing Deep Darkness, before they pushed on into the Davidfolk Ground with their metal spears?

So Starlight going with Greenstone had moved the pieces on the chessboard that lay, so to speak, between the Davidfolk in Mainground and the Johnfolk over in New Earth. Suddenly Knee Tree Grounds had become an important square and the Davidfolk started to take an interest in it. They sent guards over with their big blackglass spears, they sniffed round, they asked us questions. Of course we tried to tell them that we really *weren't* on the Johnfolk's side. After all, whether or not Jeff had sided with John all those generations ago, we had far less in common these wakings with the New Earthers, who'd lived for generations on far side of the Pool, than we had with the Davidfolk, our trading partners, who lived just ten miles away. We pointed out to the guards who came over that Starlight was the only one of us that had ever *ever* gone to live in New Earth, while many many Kneefolk had crossed to Mainground to live among the Davidfolk.

The guards listened to all this. They smiled and nodded and agreed it was all true, but they still kept coming. And not just guards, but guard leaders. Traders came too when, up to now, we'd always crossed over to Mainground to trade.

And then one waking a shadowspeaker came.

Three

Michael's Place, our little sheltercluster, was set back just a little bit from the Pool, so as to keep out of the way of the people who went back and forth along the cliff path on their way between Veeklehouse and all the other little poolside clusters up rockway. The guy it was named for had died before I ever came there, and the top people there now were his grandchildren and great-grandchildren. It was in the ground of Leader Hunter who was the guard leader at Veeklehouse. He was our high man, and in fact he was one of the highest, for he was the third son of David Strongheart, the Head Guard of the Davidfolk Ground, and the many-greats grandson of Great David. As a trade for living there under his protection, we had to give him so many skins each year, so much dried meat, so much buckfat, so many bundles of dried starflowers. And, as was the case all up and down the David-folk Ground, we had to send all our boys, when their new hairs had fully grown, to go and be guards for him whenever he asked for them.

Michael's Place didn't look so different, I guess, from where I used to live on Knee Tree Grounds, with its bark shelters arranged round a circle of open space where we lit our fires and sang our songs. I guess that's how low people live all over Eden. But the ground it stood on was black dirt instead of pale sand, and the trees shining round it were Wide Forest trees – whitelanterns with their pure white shining globes, redlanterns with their long tubes of glowing pink, and spiketrees with their little bright blue flowers – and not the knee trees with their drooping branches and yellow-green flowers that grew out on the Grounds. And another thing that was different was that, right there in middle of the circle of open space the shelters stood round, there was another circle, a little circle of small round stones gathered from poolside, which no one ever stepped inside. Every Davidfolk cluster had one of these, even if it was only tiny. It was a copy of the original Circle of Stones, over there across the Dark, in Circle Valley, which marked the place where people from Earth had first come down to Eden, and to which, so the Davidfolk believed, Earth people would one waking return. About thirty of us lived there round that little ring of stones, including grownups, newhairs, oldies and little kids, and it was my home now. It was the new family I'd found, after I'd lost the one I had before, and after a lonely time with no one to be with at all. I'd become one of them, one of the Davidfolk, who believe that nothing is more important than family, and nothing matters more than keeping family together.

I was gasping for breath as I ran into the cluster, Candy still squirming angrily in my arms: 'Let me go! Let me go! Let me *go*!' Ten eleven grownups were sitting there peacefully working on this and that – Tom, the head of our cluster, was slowly chopping up a buck with his one hand, Lucy was sewing wraps, Kate was grinding up starflowers – and little naked kids were playing round them or helping with small jobs.

'Dave!' I screamed, as soon as I had the breath to speak. 'Dave! Quick! Get the boys and the buck!'

Dave turned his long grey face towards me. He'd been sitting by the fire – he always seemed to feel cold – whittling away at buckbone, while Metty played nearby. Now he climbed uncertainly to his feet and took a couple of hobbling steps towards me, like he still hadn't quite figured out what it was I wanted from him.

'Kate! Davidson! Lucy!' I screamed. 'Get your kids! Blow the horn! They're coming now! *Now!* Ringmen in masks! Johnfolk from across the water!'

What was wrong with them all? How could they be so slow?

'The Johnfolk?' asked Tom.

'Yes, the Johnfolk, ten boats of them, with metal masks on their faces and metal spears in their hands! Come on, everyone, *move!* We need to get away from the poolside.'

Tom stood up. He was a big big man with a loud voice, and could hardly have been more different to his brother Dave. He'd been a guard for a long time until he lost his hand, and he was used to bossing people about.

'Right everyone, pack up whatever you can carry, and we'll head for Davidstand.'

Davidstand sat at the foot of Snowy Dark, and it was where David Strongheart himself lived when he wasn't travelling about his ground, along with all his shelterwomen and most of their children and grandchildren and great-grandchildren. There were many guards there, and if there was any place in Wide Forest that was going to be safe from the Johnfolk, Davidstand would surely be it.

'Oh Gela's heart!' Dave groaned. 'I just sent Fox to Veeklehouse to get some glue. I'd better go after him.'

Fox liked to go to Veeklehouse along the little path that went through the trees, rather than the one along the cliffs. He liked to imagine he was a hunter, out by himself, far out in the depths of forest.

'No you hadn't, Dave,' I said, 'not with those clawfeet. You get the buck loaded up and the other kids ready, and head straight towards Davidstand. I'll go after Fox.'

Kate's man Davidson started blowing our old hollowbranch horn to bring in the people who were out scavenging or hunting in forest, and everyone began fretting about people they couldn't get back, such as sons in the guards, and daughters who were the housewomen of guards.

'They'll know we'd go to Davidstand,' Tom said. He had four sons in the guards himself. 'They'll be able to come and find us there if they need to. But I reckon that won't be necessary. We'll be back here soon. Our guards are more than a match for a bunch of ringmen.'

'Dave, take Candy and Metty,' I said. 'I'll go and get…'

But right then Fox came running back into the cluster: my own little Fox with his thin little arms and legs and his big big eyes.

'Oh thank Gela!' I murmured, grabbing him up with tears of relief welling from deep inside of me. Fox wriggled free. He was past the age where boys liked to be babied, and anyway he had news.

'Everyone's running away from Veeklehouse, Mum.'

'I know, Foxy, I know,' I told him as I let him go. 'Your dad's getting the buck ready, look, and then we're all going to Davidstand. It'll be safe there.'

Dave had thrown dried meat and bags of flowercakes over the back of our old smoothbuck, Ugly, and now he lifted up Candy and Metty onto its back before hauling himself up there behind them. He wasn't being lazy. He knew that his clawfeet would hold us all back if he tried to walk.

Waves of grey were rippling across Ugly's flat black eyes and its four mouth feelers were sniffing and snuffling at the air, like it was trying to figure out what all the humans were so agitated about. Then it tipped back its head and gave one of those little shrieking sounds that bucks make when they know they're in danger.

A few of the other dads or mums had gone off to look for missing people, but the rest of them had loaded up bucks like we'd done, with dried meat, trading sticks, wraps, sleeping skins, spears and bundles of arrows. I scooped up some embers in a pot, so we could cook along the way.

As we set off towards Davidstand, we heard a huge roar rising up from somewhere in the distance, down alpway and towards the Pool. Tom nodded wisely, like he was the only one who could tell what that sound could possibly be.

'That's the guards on the cliff,' he said, 'shouting and yelling to ready themselves for a fight.'

It was strange to think about. At that moment every single one of those guards at Veeklehouse was still healthy and whole and strong, and so was each one of the ringmen on the boats from New Earth. But soon the arrows would be flying back and forth across the water: metal-tipped arrows one way, glass-tipped arrows the other, and then people would start to die, and bodies that now were fit and whole would be torn and broken. There would be fire arrows too. Our men would shoot them to set their windcatchers alight, and their fire arrows would come flying back in answer to burn the shelters in Veeklehouse.

Fox was terrified, but he was trying hard not to show it.

'I wish I could watch the fighting, Mum,' he shouted out in an odd, loud, excited voice, though I was standing right by him and would have heard him quite clearly if he'd simply spoken. 'It would be exciting exciting, and I know our blokes are going to win.'

On Ugly's back, little Metty cried in Dave's arms, sensing the fear round him, while Candy frowned out from Ugly's back and said nothing at all. Dave tried to catch my eye so he could give me one of his worried looks, one of those looks that grownups give each other over the heads of their children, but I avoided it. Gela's heart, I thought, it's not as if all of us don't already know how bad things are.

As we started to walk away from Michael's Place, we looked back one last time at the shelters we'd built for ourselves, the fence of branches we'd worked on for wakings and wakings, so as to make sure it was strong enough to keep out leopards.

Four

I was telling you about that shadowspeaker who came over to Knee Tree Grounds.

We'd never had one there before – Jeff didn't believe in clinging to the past or talking to the dead – but we'd seen shadowspeakers from time to time when we went to trade over in Nob Head. They would cry and wail in middle of a circle of silent, troubled David-folk, or even have a kind of fit and roll on the ground with spit bubbling from their mouths. Sometimes, they'd pick out people in the crowd and tell them, in front of everyone, the bad bad things they'd done. We'd seen big grownup Davidfolk hanging their heads and crying like little kids who've been told off.

'Mother Gela is reaching out to you!' the shadowspeakers would wail. 'But how can she help you if you don't reach back? How can she guide you home through the emptiness between the stars?'

Sometimes they'd suddenly stop and listen, holding up their hands for quiet, so they could hear the voices of the dead loved ones of people in the crowd.

'It's… Yes, it's your little boy, my dear, the one who died. He's telling me his name – I can't quite hear him. David, is it? Yes, I thought so, David – he's begging me to tell you to be true to our Mother. He's afraid that otherwise you'll never find your way back to him.'

The Kneefolk grownups always kept out of the way of the

shadowspeakers. If we were over in Nob Head and came across a shadowspeaker giving a show, our grownups would go and sit on the cliff and talk among themselves until the shouting and crying was over and the speaker had collected her presents. This was Davidfolk business, they said, and nothing to do with us. But newhairs like to be different from their grownups and me and Starlight and our friends would sometimes sneak off to watch the shows. We were careful to keep a straight face, and avoid looking at one another – we understood that we were among the Davidfolk and on their ground, and mustn't give them any reason to be upset with us – but afterwards we'd all go off along the cliff together and, as soon as we were alone, we'd burst out laughing.

'Mother Gela is crying!' Starlight would wail through her own tears of laughter. 'She's crying crying crying!'

'You'll all be lost in the cold cold darkness!' our friend Poolshine would sob.

'The starship will never come back for us,' I'd moan, 'unless you listen to our Mother and look after her family!'

We laughed and laughed. How could those stupid Davidfolk be so easily fooled, we wondered? Wasn't it obvious that the speakers told people whatever they thought would either please them enough or frighten them enough to get good presents out of them?

But of course this was only obvious to us because our grownups had told us what to look for, and how to explain what we saw. It was only obvious to us because they'd told us, as Jeff had taught, that a single life was like a wave moving over the surface of the Pool – the wave disappears completely, but the Pool remains the same, shifting this way and that in its enormous bowl – and that Mother Gela was long dead, and that even when she was alive, she'd just been a person like anyone else, nothing more and nothing less.

Yes, and even though we told ourselves it was obvious that what the shadowspeakers said wasn't true, I think one of the reasons we laughed so loudly was to shut out the little secret doubts that came to each of us. What if the Davidfolk were right? What if it really *was* true that when our bodies died, our shadows lived on, to wander through the emptiness between the stars, and maybe get lost there forever, all alone, with no hope of company or warmth?

After all, the Davidfolk were many and powerful. They'd built Veeklehouse and Davidstand. Their ground stretched from World-pool to Circle Valley, and from Rockway Edge down to the White Streams. They had the Veekle, the Circle of Stones and all the other things from Earth except the ring. Their Head Guard was such a high man that he had seventeen shelterwomen and more than a hundred kids. Who were we to say that they were wrong and we were right?

So we'd seen shadowspeakers before, but when that shadowspeaker came over to Knee Tree Grounds, it was a different thing. This was our ground, not the Davidfolk Ground, and yet here she was. And there were guards with her too, guards who had suspicions that we Kneefolk were really Johnfolk in disguise, and who were watching us carefully to see how we'd behave. We gathered unhappily. Most of the grownups felt we had to go along so as not to upset the David-folk, but it felt all wrong that she was there.

'Remember, no laughing and no smiling,' mums and dads warned their children, just as our mums and dads had done when we went over to Nob Head. 'Not unless the speaker smiles herself.'

There she was, the shadowspeaker, standing right in middle of our own Meeting Place, the same place where we Kneefolk met every waking to listen out, not for some long-dead person, or some far off voice calling out to us from Earth, but for the Watcher who was as close as can be, the secret awakeness that looks out from the eyes of everyone. I could see the tree right behind her where Jeff Redlantern's own words were carved. WE ARE REELY HEAR, he'd written.

I heard one of the older grownups mutter that the shadow-speaker was trampling on purpose on the things that mattered most to us, trampling on the story that made us Kneefolk into who we were, and I must say it felt like that to me as well. But I'd decided the best way of dealing with this was to see the funny side of it. Just like we'd done at Nob Head, I'd listen politely, and then have a good laugh when she and her guards had gone.

But now we were actually faced with the shadowspeaker, things felt different. This woman wasn't really ridiculous at all. You could see she was smart smart. You could see her studying our faces with her sharp sharp eyes, and it was like she could see right through us. Her name was Mary. She was a short, solid, fierce-looking woman, with a big square face, reddish hair that she'd cut short so it stuck out in little tufts and spikes, and small piercing grey eyes. She wore a longwrap made of fakeskin, woven from crushed starflower stems, much as the high people wore on Mainground, though without the fancy colours or the feathers and beads and dried batwings. We Kneefolk just wore little buckskin waistwraps, with bare feet and bare breasts.

Mary stood there waiting until we were all silent, and then, with-out speaking a word, she took a stick and drew a circle in the sand, the way that Davidfolk always do when they find themselves in a place where there isn't already a circle of stones. Then she stood up straight again and looked round at us. She'd made the Davidfolk sign, right there in middle of the place where we met to tell our own stories, and it was like she was daring us to object. None of us did – we knew better than to do anything that might upset the Davidfolk, and in any case, Mary wasn't the kind of person you'd want to argue with – so then she stepped inside her circle, which was something that only shadowspeakers and Head Guards were supposed to do.

'Do you know what the Circle stands for?' she asked.

No one wanted to answer, but she just waited, knowing quite well that sooner or later someone wouldn't be able to bear the silence any longer. And sure enough, a woman called Fire finally spoke.

'The Circle of Stones,' she muttered.

Mary nodded.

'Thankyou. You're right. It stands for the Circle of Stones, where the Veekle from Earth landed and where one day people from Earth will come again. But it doesn't just stand for that. It stands for the one True Family of Eden, and how we're all linked together. John Redlantern tried to break that Family but, though he stirred up trouble among us, it's still one Family. *Jeff* Redlantern tried to break up that Family.' She paused to look round at our faces, daring us to rise to this challenge to our precious Jeff. 'And *he* stirred up trouble among us too. But it's still one Family all the same, one Family with one Mother. And our Mother still loves us all.'

Again Mary paused, the stick still in her hand, searching our faces, figuring out who would be easiest to reach and who would be hardest. Then suddenly she took up the stick, snapped it in two and flung the pieces out at us to her left and right.

'Oh you foolish, silly people! You babies!' A little bit of spit flew from her mouth. 'Hiding away out here in the bright water! How do you think that's going to help you, eh? What do you think it's going to save you from?'

She paused just for a moment while the questions sank in, and then she carried on. 'Oh you can hide away from trouble out here, I'll give you that. You can hide from playing your part. But do you really think you can hide from death?'

I could see some angry faces round the Meeting Place. I could see people who were fighting back the desire to shout out in our defence. But I could see many faces that were scared as well. Not just the kids who were there but grownups too looked like children who had been told off. I was close to tears myself. Mary had made me ashamed of being one of the Kneefolk.

'You're lucky lucky,' she told us. 'Your Mother still loves you. In spite of everything. You might have turned your back on her.

You might have stamped on her face. You might have stood back and let her precious ring be taken from her. But she still loves you. She still...'

Mary broke off, like something inside herself had interrupted her, and suddenly she began to shake all over. At first we thought she was having some kind of fit, but then we saw in amazement and horror that she was shaking with sobs of grief.

'I can hear her,' Mary said, struggling to get her voice under control. 'I can hear her now. Mother Gela is crying, but... but – oh our dear good Mother! – she's not crying for herself, however much you've hurt her. She's crying for you. She's crying crying crying for her foolish children. And she'll never stop crying until every single one of you turns away from wicked John and foolish Jeff, and comes back to True Family of Eden.'

I could feel my own tears running down my face now, and I could see others crying all round the Meeting Place. Well, we *had* been hiding out here, hadn't we? We'd been hiding out here for generations! The world went on without us across the water, Eden grew and changed, but we refused to be part of it, staying here on our own, cutting bark and fishing just as our parents and their parents had done, and turning our backs on everything else.

Mary walked over to a girl called Brightwater and asked her name.

'Do you know why our Mother cries for you, Brightwater?' she said.

Brightwater had been crying and crying. 'Because...' She sniffed. 'Because we're bad!'

Mary shook her head, half-smiling through her own tears.

'No, it's *not* because you're bad, Brightwater. It's because if you don't reach out to her, she can't reach back to you. And do you know what will happen then?'

Brightwater shook her head. Wiping the tears from her own face with the back of her hand, Mary strode back into her circle in middle of the Meeting Place.

'I'll tell you what will happen, Brightwater. You'll die one waking, as we all will, and your shadow will fly out from your body, and from our poor dark Eden, into the blackness between the stars. It's cold cold out there, with no trees to warm you. You'll be shivering, you'll be lonely and scared, and you'll search and search, as all our shadows must do, for the brightness and warmth of Earth. But look up at the stars, Brightwater. They're like a forest, aren't they? They're like a huge huge forest, full full of lanternflowers. We know little Earth is hiding out there somewhere among all those thousand thousand stars, but do you know where to find it? Look up at the stars, Brightwater, and tell me. Do you know the way back to Earth?'

Brightwater glanced fearfully upwards at the vast wheel of Starry Swirl, where the stars were packed so tightly that most of them were just a blur of light. She sobbed and shook her head.

'Mother Gela will be calling out to you,' Mary said, 'but what use will that be if you've never got to know her, and never learned to hear her voice? You'll have no one to guide you. And so you'll wander, you'll wander forever, out there where it's a hundred times colder than Snowy Dark, a hundred times darker than Deep Darkness far out there in middle of Worldpool. And you'll be all on your own, shivering, lonely, lost, forever and ever and ever.'

Brightwater covered her face with her hands and sobbed. Again, Mary looked round at all of us, searching our faces, sizing us up.

'You silly, foolish people,' she said again. 'Do you think you can hide from death? Do you think that Watcher of yours is going to show you the way home? The Watcher who looks out of your eyes? The *Watcher*! How could it find the way anywhere, when you yourselves admit that it's only inside your head? Only Gela can help you, and if you want her help, you need to reach out to her. Turn away from the ringstealers, turn from the ones who brought killing to Eden, turn away from John and his clawfoot cousin Jeff, and come back to the people of Gela and her son Great David, strong strong David, who held Family together when John and Jeff tried to break it apart.'

She fell to her knees and again she began to shake. She wasn't faking it, you could see that. She was really hurting, and at the same time she was listening listening listening to some faint voice that she could hear but we couldn't.

'Our Mother is begging me,' she said. 'She's *begging* me. "Please, Mary, do your best," she's saying. "Please please do everything you can to bring these poor people back to me before it's too late."'

Perhaps we'd got it all wrong, I thought. Jeff used to say (or so we'd been told) that the only place that was important was the one we were in right now, but maybe the opposite was true? Perhaps this wasn't the real world at all, and the world that mattered, the world that would last, was out there somewhere across the stars, far far away from this dark sad place? Maybe that's why this life seemed so empty, so full of sadness and disappointment. We were on a sort of journey, and hadn't yet arrived at where we were going. The David-folk knew that, but we Kneefolk had huddled together out here on our little patch of sand with our backs turned, telling ourselves that we were already there.

And as these thoughts were going through my head, Mary suddenly looked straight at me, like she'd noticed me for the first time. She stepped out of her circle again and walked right up to me. I was scared scared, thinking she'd be angry with me and tell everyone about some bad and shameful thing I'd done, but her face was kind and concerned. She took my hand in one of her own, and with her other hand she reached out gently and stroked my face, touching the edge of the ugly ugly hole where a proper face should be. She spoke to me softly softly.

Five

We'd heard screams in the distance, screams of terror and agony. We'd heard terrible roars of rage and triumph, rising and falling and rising again, without knowing if it was our people or theirs. Without being there to see it, we knew that there were dying men all along the clifftop at Veeklehouse, men with their arms hacked through to the bone, men with arrows sticking out of their faces, men with guts spilling out of their bellies onto the blood-soaked dirt. And we knew some of those men were boys from Michael's Place.

We sank deep into ourselves as we headed away from those dreadful sounds, far far too slowly it felt, though we were going as fast as we could with our little kids clinging to us and our oldies and clawfeet perched on the backs of bucks so loaded up with pots and bags and skins and knives and spears they looked more like walking piles of stuff than living creatures. It seemed strange that Starry Swirl still shone down, the same as ever, and starbirds still shrieked and boomed to each other through the trees. Our whole world had changed completely this waking, but all round us, bats looped and dived, just as they always did, among the bright lanterns. We passed three huge nightmakers pushing through the trees off rockway to our left, cracking off branches as they pulled the shining flowers to their slowly chewing mouths, and far off alpway to our right, a leopard sang its sweet sad treacherous song. Eden didn't care what was happening at Veeklehouse. It carried on its own life, just like it always had done, since long long before any human being had ever heard of the place.

All of us were *scared* scared. The little kids kept crying. The older kids were silent and pale and grey. Young or old, we'd all heard the stories about the last time the Johnfolk and the Davidfolk fought. We all knew how cruel the Johnfolk had been. We knew they'd stolen children from their mums and dads to be ringmen for them, and the mothers of ringmen. We knew they'd done for dads in front of their own kids, and sons in front of their mothers. We knew they'd laid traps with long spikes inside them, and dipped the tips of their spears and arrows in human shit to make sure the wounds would go bad. Even back on Knee Tree Grounds, where the Jeffs-folk had hidden away from the fight, I'd heard these stories. The Davidfolk told them and retold them all the time.

At least I had Dave and all my kids with me, though. Tom and Clare had four boys in the guards, two of them at Veeklehouse. They knew quite well that either those two were fighting right now with their glass-tipped spears against enemies with metal spears and knives, or they were already dead. It was same for most of the older parents who were with us.

'Even if my boys live,' Clare kept worrying, 'how are me and Tom ever going to find them again if we can't go back to Michael's Place?'

One time, some traders from Veeklehouse came past us. I knew them slightly because they'd sometimes had some of Dave's bone tools from me, when I took a batch into Veeklehouse to trade. There was a man, his two shelterwomen and nine of their kids, all packed onto four big smoothbucks. They were headed to David-stand too, but having no one among them who had to go on foot, they could travel much faster than we could.

'We've lost everything,' the man told us. He was a big guy with a black beard, and he always wore a long red fancy wrap like he thought he was one of the high people. 'They burnt down our shelter, and smashed up every single bit of our trading stuff that they didn't take for themselves. But we're lucky to be alive. Bloke who traded next to us – you remember old David with the bald head? – well, he tried to stop them from taking his stuff, and ended up with a spear through his belly.'

'They were like starbirds crawling over a dead buck,' the older of his shelterwomen said. Her name was Kindness, which always made me smile, because she never seemed to smile and was hard hard hard when it came to trading. 'They took all our food and our badjuice, and when they'd had enough, they flung what was left at one another and trampled it under their feet.'

'Yeah, and then they propped dead guards up against the posts of shelters,' the man said, 'and pranced round them laughing, in women's wraps and feathers. You'd never see our men behave like that.'

Later, when Clare was busy with her little ones, her daughter Trueheart came to walk beside me and Fox.

'I guess you've been to Davidstand before, Auntie Angie?'

Trueheart was about fourteen fifteen years old, counting ages, as she did, in the Davidfolk way. I wasn't *really* Trueheart's auntie – I left my brothers' and sisters' kids behind me when I left Knee Tree Grounds – but Clare had always been like a sister to me, even since her bloke Tom brought me back to Michael's Place, and there'd always been a special connection between me and Trueheart because she was a batface like me. It's not so easy being a batface. That's as true among Davidfolk as it is among the Kneefolk, even though Great David himself was a batface. We're teased as children, mocked as newhairs, passed over as grownups, and so of course we tend to stick together.

'Yes, a couple of times,' I told her as we plodded through the trees. 'Back when I used to help that shadowspeaker Mary. We travelled all over the Davidfolk Ground back then. Way further than Davidstand. We even went as far as Circle Valley.'

Trueheart had never been further than Veeklehouse herself, just a few miles from where she was born, and in her longing for new and exciting things, she reminded me of myself and Starlight when we were kids. Except that for us it was Veeklehouse itself that had been the wonderful far off place that we longed to see, while for her it was the boring ordinary place she longed to get away from.

'I never get how come you were with a shadowspeaker, Auntie Angie,' she said. 'You don't seem the type to go for all that.'

'Well, there were a lot of reasons I went with her. I've told you before about how my friend Starlight went away across the Pool.'

'With that handsome guy with the metal brooch?'

I wouldn't have expected it, but when Trueheart said that, my head was suddenly full of tears, so that I knew if I spoke at all they would all come bursting out. It was a long time since Starlight had gone away, and many years had passed since I'd felt the pain all raw like that, gaping and bleeding like a new wound. I guess it had felt so sad and scary leaving Michael's Place, that one more bit of sadness was all it took to open everything up all over again.

'You're upset, Auntie Angie!'

I nodded, still not daring to speak. Trueheart studied my face in silence for ten twenty heartbeats as we trudged on through the shining forest.

Hmmmph hmmmph hmmmph went the trees all round us, just as they always did.

'I guess you knew a thing like that would never happen to you,' she finally said, pointing at her own face. Trueheart had a lovely strong supple body, she could run fast, she could throw a spear further than many men and swim faster than any of the other newhairs in Michael's Place, whether boys or girls, and, what was more, she was smart smart as could be, but her face... well, it was like mine. Her mouth opened up in a twisted scrunched-up gash into the place where her nose should have been, her top teeth stuck forwards and sideways out of her face, and when she said 'upset' it came out more like 'uffthet' because her mouth just couldn't form itself into the shapes you need to make the word sound right. There are lots of batfaces in Eden, of course – maybe one out of every ten people – but no one thinks we're pretty, and no one chooses a batface to slip with, if they can find someone halfway as nice who's got a proper mouth and nose.

'Yes, that's right,' I said, getting a grip on myself once more. 'I didn't think anyone would ever come along and single *me* out. And then, all of a sudden, shadowspeaker Mary arrived and chose me out of all the people on Knee Tree Grounds.'

Trueheart gave a scornful snort. 'I can't stand those women.'

She got into a lot of arguments with her mum and dad for saying things like that, sometimes making her dad so angry that he'd take a stick and beat her until her mother Clare begged him to stop. Like all the other grownups from Michael's Place, Tom and Clare feared and admired shadowspeakers. Like all the others, they would take presents to them when they came to give their shows in Veeklehouse, and then come back to Michael's Place with tears in their eyes, and messages from Mother Gela and their dead. They were all Davidfolk, after all, and Tom especially, who'd lost his own right hand in the guards, was proud proud of being so.

I looked round to see where Tom and Clare were, and saw they were some way behind us. 'Well, just make sure you don't say things like that in the hearing of any guards,' I said. 'They're going to be touchy about that sort of thing, now that the fight with the Johnfolk is on again.'

'I *know*, Auntie. I'm not a kid, remember, and I'm not stupid.'

'Stupid is one thing you're *certainly* not, Trueheart, my dear.'

'So this shadowspeaker – Mary – came, and...?'

'Mary came out to our grounds, and in middle of her show she noticed me there among the people listening to her. She came right over to me and touched my face and...' I broke off, once again finding myself suddenly so badly shaken that I was afraid I was going to cry. 'Well,' I said, 'she said a few words, just to me.'

Trueheart's eyes narrowed as she examined my face. She really *wasn't* stupid.

'Yeah? So what *did* she say exactly?'

'Well...' Those tears were pushing pushing against the back of my eyes, trying to get through. 'Well, okay then... What she said to me was "You're beautiful!"'

Trueheart went quiet for a few seconds. She understood, better than anyone could with an ordinary face, the huge power of those words.

Then she snorted angrily. '*Bloody* shadowspeakers! They always figure out the one thing you most long to hear.'

I shrugged. She'd just said exactly what me and Starlight used to say when we saw the shadowspeakers at Nob Head, but these wakings I didn't think it was that simple.

'Well, I don't know about that. But I do know that no one else had ever said those words to me before. Plenty of people had said the opposite, and plenty, wanting to be kind, had told me it didn't matter how I looked—'

'Oh Michael's names, Mum does that and I really *hate* it! One moment she'll say looks don't matter and she loves me just as I am. Next she'll come back from Veeklehouse all excited about how she saw Leader Hunter's new shelterwoman and how she is pretty pretty *pretty*.'

'My mum was the same.'

Gela's heart, *I* was the same. I told myself that it didn't matter what my kids looked like, I would love them just as much, but when my Fox was little I couldn't stop stroking his beautiful face, with its perfect nose and its perfect little mouth that made my heart ache with love.

'So the shadowspeaker said you were beautiful...?'

'Yes. She was looking straight into my eyes, and it was like no one else was even there as far as she was concerned, no one else but me. "Mother Gela loves batfaces especially," she told me. "Not only because Great David was a batface, but because all batfaces suffer, and all batfaces have to dig down inside themselves and become wise.""

Trueheart glanced at me, and decided not to speak the thought that had come into her mind. But I knew what she was thinking. She was thinking how easy it is for anyone to get round a batface, or a clawfoot, or a slowhead, or anyone else who wasn't so sure of themselves, by telling them how special they are.

But the fact was that when Mary went back into middle of the circle and carried on with her show, the words she spoke from then on didn't seem so silly any more, and they *still* didn't seem silly now, walking through forest with Trueheart, even though I'd since fallen out with Mary. Of *course* Mother Gela didn't want her family to break up. What mother would? And why shouldn't it be true, just as Mary and all the Davidfolk said, that Gela herself had come alive again back on Earth, and was reaching out to us through the emptiness between the stars? Earth people could do all kinds of wonderful things, after all, and we ourselves were proof of it. For wasn't it amazing that human beings from across the stars should be here at all, living among creatures with green-black blood and flat flat black eyes, who are kin to one another but not to us at all? If Earth people could find a way of crossing that cold black sky, who was to say they couldn't bring someone's shadow home and give it flesh?

'Well, I know you don't like shadowspeakers, Trueheart, but I liked Mary. She taught me things. You've got to remember that I didn't grow up with the True Story as you did, so some things that seem obvious to you were fresh and new to me. We Kneefolk were Jeffsfolk, remember, not Davidfolk.'

'So she said you were beautiful and she asked you to go with her?'

'That's right. At first I couldn't believe she'd chosen me. After all, she travelled all over the Davidfolk Ground, including the big clusters like Davidstand and Veeklehouse, and every few wakings she stood in front of a different crowd of people. But yet out of all those hundreds of people she'd met, it was me she'd picked out and asked to be her helper. Of course, my mum begged me not to go, all my friends told me I was crazy, everyone was angry angry angry. And of course, when I sat in Mary's boat, heading to Nob Head, I began to have doubts, wondering if I'd been a fool and done the wrong thing. But then I remembered how lonely I'd felt when that handsome man from across the water had asked my friend Starlight to go with him, and I felt a bit better. "Now it's happened to me as well," I told myself. "Someone has chosen me. And I'm doing as Starlight did, leaving everyone else behind for the sake of that someone who sees something in me that no one else has ever done. Starlight was scared as well – of course she was – and she must have had doubts too, but she didn't let them stop her. And I'm going to be brave as her." That's what I said to myself, whenever I began to panic.'

Trueheart glanced at me again, not speaking her thoughts, but thinking them so loudly I could almost hear them.

'How far is Davidstand now, Mum?' my Fox asked.

'Too far to walk in one waking, my love. We'll rest soon and have something to eat.'

Presently Metty began to wail, and Dave gave me one of his long looks to let me know that he thought I should carry the boy for a bit and give him a break from the crying. Poor little Metty didn't know what was happening, but he could feel the fear, and he could tell that this was different from any other waking he'd ever known. I held him to my breast while we walked.

'You guys alright?' asked Tom, striding up to us. Straight away Trueheart fell back, to be out of the way of her dad.

'Yeah, we're okay. You must be worried about your boys at Veeklehouse.'

'Clare's worrying, but I'm not. Okay, some guards have been killed by the sound of it, but it won't be many. When I was in guards, we planned for this over and over. Our leaders always told us that we'd fight just for a short time and then back off. The Johnfolk were bound to be in a strong position when they first grounded, because we'd be spread out all along poolside, and they'd all be in one place. No sense in losing a lot of men fighting them when they were at their strongest. But it'll be a different story soon, I promise you, now that we know where they are.' Tom laughed grimly. 'It'll be a different different story.'

'Still,' said Dave, looking round at his brother from Ugly's back, 'what a terrible thing to happen, eh, just before the four hundredth Virsry?'

Of course we didn't know exactly when the Virsry would be. It was a bunch of old people far away over the Dark in Circle Valley who decided that, counting their sleeps and wakings until they got to three hundred sixty-five. But we knew it was about now, and we knew there were supposed to be special celebrations up in the Valley, to mark those four hundred years since Gela and Tommy first laid out that Circle of Stones.

'No, mate, this is a *good* way,' Tom said firmly, rubbing the stump of the right hand that he'd lost in a fight with a thief. 'It's a good good way to celebrate. Teaching those bloody Johnfolk a lesson for once and for all! What better way could there be to celebrate the Circle than to kick those circle-breakers back into the Pool?'

Behind me, I heard Trueheart give her scornful snort, but quietly quietly, so that, if her dad took her up on it, she could deny it had happened at all.

'And believe me, Dave,' Tom went on in a loud firm voice, either not hearing Trueheart or choosing to pretend he hadn't, 'we *will* kick them into the Pool, every single one of them that we don't do for first with our good blackglass spears. There'll be fast riders heading to Davidstand right at this moment to give old Strongheart the news, and – trust me! – as soon as he hears, he'll be on to it, him and Leader Mehmet, they'll be onto it like a leopard that's seen a buck. I've met them both, you know, Strongheart and Leader Mehmet, and I'm telling you those two guys aren't just tough, they're smart smart as well. No way will these Johnfolk get the better of them, not when they're on our ground, and so far away from the place they know. Strongheart will beat them, don't you worry. He'll smash them into little pieces.'

Six

Myself, I'd only ever seen David Strongheart once back then. It had been eight years before, after I'd parted with Mary up in Circle Valley. I'd made my way back over the Dark and down into Davidstand. I was tired and cold and hungry, and I didn't know who to turn to.

When I finally reached Davidstand that time, I discovered that just about everyone was gathered together in the big Meeting Place there, between the Great Shelter and the L-shaped pool. Strongheart had just got himself a new young shelterwoman, and there was a celebration. At one end of the Meeting Place there was a raised-up floor of wood, where a man was twanging the string of a little guitar while a woman sang and another man tapped on a drum. But when they finished their song, a guard leader came out and spoke to us:

'People! People! The Head Guard of all Eden, David Strongheart.'

Everyone knelt and bowed down their heads, and a fat old man with white hair came waddling out onto that wooden floor in a long blue wrap, with a young newhair girl on his arm. We'd heard stories about him out on Knee Tree Grounds: how harsh he was, how cruel, how he tied his enemies to hot spiketrees and left them screaming there until all the skin and flesh on their backs was blistered off. But this old guy looked so friendly and kind that it was hard to believe that this was the same man, the three-greats grandson of Great David. He looked more like some nice old uncle, who'd save bits of stumpcandy for you, and carve you toys out of bone.

More of Strongheart's family came out to join him on the wooden floor: his oldest son Leader Mehmet, who'd be Head Guard after he'd gone, a bunch of grownup daughters and sons, four five of his other shelterwomen, and twenty or more of his kids and grandchildren and great-grandchildren. Strongheart put one arm round his pretty new shelterwoman and the other arm round one of his grownup grandsons, and had all the little ones gather in front of him in their fine fakeskin longwraps, sewn with feathers and batwings and coloured stones.

'Stand up, everyone!' he called out to us. 'Dance! Have a good time! This is a celebration, a celebration of my family. And I don't just mean my family that you see here round me with my lovely new shelterwoman, but my *big* family, True Family of Eden, which is every one of you.'

Everyone cheered at that.

'We're Davidfolk,' the old man said, 'and there are two things that Great David taught us, two things that I want you to remember and never never forget. The first is that there's only one True Family in Eden, and we're all in it, and we must hold that Family together no matter what. The second is that sometimes that means being tough. Back when Great David was young up in Circle Valley, all the people in Eden lived together by the Circle that our Mother and Father made. They understood the first part of what I've just said, about family being important, but they stumbled badly on that second point. And that meant that when John Redlantern started his nonsense, way back at Virsry One Six Three, Family couldn't bear to be as firm with him as they needed to be. Only Great David saw that this wasn't a time for kindness. Only he saw that it was one of those times like when you get a boil on your neck, and you've just got to take a knife to it. But the rest of them faltered – Oh! Oh! Oh! Not a knife! A knife will hurt! – and that meant that when they *did* finally come to their senses, it was too late: Juicy John had split them in two. Which is how we got to the situation we're in now: two grounds facing each other across Worldpool, hating each other. None of it need have happened, none of it, if only Family had listened to Great David.'

He took his arms from the shoulders of his young grandson and his even younger shelterwoman, and picked up one of the little kids in front of him.

'Isn't she beautiful, people?' he asked, and everyone cheered. 'I've got eighty-two kids, nine hundred forty-one grandchildren, and… well… more great-grandchildren than I can count, and – do you know what? – I love every single one of them. You're all good Davidfolk out there, I can see, and I know you'll understand.'

Again everyone cheered, while Strongheart looked round for one of his women to take the little girl from him.

'What makes me madder than anything about the Johnfolk,' he told us, 'is how they claim that, if it wasn't for them, everyone would still be living in Circle Valley. Of course not! Tom's dick and Harry's, we Davidfolk would have found our way across the Dark in our own good time, without any help from Juicy John. Of course we would! But we would have done it when *everyone* was ready. And that's the difference between us and them. We look after everyone. We make sure everyone is ready before we move.'

I looked round at the people round me. I badly needed someone's help, but whatever old Strongheart said about us all being one Family, they all looked like strangers to me. I noticed a guard nearby, though, who seemed to have noticed me. He was maybe twenty years older than me, and was holding his spear with one hand because his other hand was cut off at the wrist. He saw me look at him, and I guess he could tell how scared and desperate I was, because he beckoned with a sideways movement of his head that I should come over and talk to him.

'You look a bit lost, my dear,' he said.

I told him I was. I'd fallen out with the shadowspeaker Mary and she was the only family I had left. I didn't know where to go, and I was hungry hungry.

'Here,' he said. 'I've got a couple of flowercakes, and when this is over, I'll sort you out with some more.'

It was Tom. He was still in the guards back then, but his guard leader was about to send him back to Michael's Place because of his hand, and because he wasn't so young any more in any case. Later on he found me food to eat and let me sleep in his shelter, and I let him have a little slip with me because I was grateful. He had me turn my back to him – men often did that – and grunted away to himself for a bit. I just went away into my own head until he'd done.

During the eight years I lived since then at Michael's Place, this was to happen from time to time. Tom would follow me when I went out into forest, and have me bend over for him, and afterwards he'd just carry on like nothing happened, heading back to our cluster, or going off hunting by himself. We never spoke about it, but somehow it was as if we'd agreed that this was the trade for him letting me come back with him to Michael's Place. If I'm honest, I guess I also hoped that maybe it would mean that fewer of my kids would have clawfeet.

Anyway, that first time at Davidstand, in his rough little shelter, he just lay down afterwards, said, 'Sleep well,' and then, almost at once, began to snore. But he was friendly enough when we woke again. He told me he was going to leave the guards and go back to Michael's Place to be with his shelterwoman and kids.

'I know when I'm not wanted,' he said.

He said his dad had been head of the cluster but was too old to carry on, so he was going to take over.

'You should come with me,' he said. 'My brother Dave is looking for a shelterwoman. He's a clawfoot and he's a bit slow, but he's alright. I reckon you and him would get on.'

Seven

Whatever was happening in Veeklehouse had long ago been buried by the hum of forest all round us, the pulsing of the trees, pumping their sap down to find the heat of Eden's core, and pumping it back up again.

Too tired to speak, we walked in silence. We wanted to get as far away as possible from the Johnfolk, and so we pushed on for much longer than a normal waking, though our feet were sore and tired, and our kids were worn out. In the end it was our bucks that made us stop. Loping along in that strange way they have, with their backwards bending knees and their splayed feet, and their six legs that each move in turn, they began to stumble under their heavy loads, and to pant and groan and ooze green froth from their mouth feelers.

Well, we recognized the signs and we did *not* want bucks that couldn't go any further and would have to be done for. Not only did we rely on them to carry our stuff and our clawfeet and old people and our little kids, but each one of them was a few wakings' meat for us if things ever got hard and we couldn't find anything else to eat. So we finally stopped, and ate some flowercakes, along with a slinker that Davidson and Tom had managed to do for along the way, tearing its tough muddy-tasting meat from its bony shell and hoping it didn't give us a bellyache. Then Tom drew a circle on the ground and called out to Gela, as all Davidfolk do at the end of a waking, asking the Mother of us all to look after all until the time came for us to return to Earth:

'Keep us safe, Mother! Keep us strong! Help us hold together and help one another! Help us be patient until the time comes, just as you were patient patient in all your time on Eden. Help us beat the Johnfolk and drive them back into the water.'

He got out the little guitar that my Dave had made for him from the hard grey shell of a groundrat, and started to twang out a tune on its string. It was a song from Earth, one of those songs that were so old that half the words don't even make sense, but we still sing the sounds anyway so as to keep the song as close as possible to how it was sung on Earth. We used to sing that same song back on Knee Tree Grounds, and quite probably the Johnfolk sang it too, but it was surely the Davidfolk's favourite song:

> Come Tree Row, take me home
> To the place I come from
> Wister Jinyer, mountain mother,
> Take me home, Come Tree Row.

We sang it slowly, standing together round that circle that Clare had scratched on the ground, bringing the song round not just once but many times to the place where it came slowly to rest on that final note. Oldies sang, and little kids. Candy belted it out, beating time with her little strong arms. Everyone joined in, even Trueheart. She might think she'd seen through shadowspeakers, but she still liked the story the shadowspeakers told about going home to Earth. So did I, so did pretty much everyone on the Davidfolk Ground, and though we didn't understand all the words of that song, we knew it was a song about home. You could tell that even just from the tune, the way it comes to rest on that last note.

We were scared scared – scared for our missing friends and sons and daughters, scared for ourselves – and we were grieving for our life at Michael's Place. Tom's dick, that life had seemed hard in its own right when we were living it, what with worries about finding enough stuff to satisfy Leader Hunter and still feed ourselves and our kids, worries about how it was getting harder to find meat, worries about sick kids, and births that go wrong, and so many other things, but it had seemed happy and peaceful and safe compared with now. So we needed home right then more than ever, the true home that we all long for, where Johnfolk wouldn't come and smash our shelters, and leopards wouldn't sneak through the fence, and death itself couldn't reach out its cold cold hand and snatch away our babies and the ones we loved.

Everyone needs a home, even people like my friend Starlight, or old Juicy John Redlantern who set himself against whole of Family. People like them might seem to be turning their backs on their homes, but really they're just looking for a better home, one that goes deeper, one that's stronger and truer than the little flimsy things that most of us try to cling to. They're looking in the wrong place, though, that's what I learned from Mary. We human beings are just passing through this world, so of course it feels flimsy, of course it never quite feels like a proper home. And it's no good trying to find one either, because it's just not here to be found. We need to be patient and look after each other, and not ask too much, and listen for our Mother, and then we *will* go one waking to our real true home. Either a starship will come and take us back when we're alive, or our shadows will fly there after we're dead, and come alive and solid again in the warmth and brightness of Earth's star.

Where I grew up we followed Jeff of course, and we used to just laugh at ideas like that, but Mary said the Kneefolk were like people who sit and shiver in some cold place, secretly wishing they were warmer, but telling themselves loudly all the time that they're warm enough already and that anyway there's no such thing as fire. 'Doesn't the fact you long for a thing show that it's out there somewhere to be found?' That's what Mary used to say. 'If we feel cold, there's fire. If we feel hungry, there's food. If we want a man and his dick, well, there are men with dicks who want us too. It's the same with the true home we all long for. It's there, if we can just find our way to it.'

And that's what the Circle was, Mary taught me, a way home. So I tried not to think of people who stayed hungry, or people who died of cold, or people who longed for someone to hold them but never found one all their lives, and I stood by the Circle with the other Davidfolk, and sang 'Come Tree Row'.

Afterwards I laid out a buckskin on the ground for my kids, and another for me and Dave, up beside the trunk of a redlantern tree.

'How do we know the Johnfolk won't come?' Fox wanted to know, looking up at me with his big big eyes.

For my kids, *I* was home, like mothers usually are for little kids. I was the safe warm place they knew they could come back to. But that was a hard part to play when I was scared scared myself.

'They won't come, darling. They're too far away and they've got our guards to fight. And anyway, we've got Strongheart, don't forget. He's strong and smart and powerful and he'll know exactly what to do. We're going to Davidstand where he lives, so he can look after us.'

Poor Fox was so tired from all that walking that, frightened as he was, he still sank straight down into sleep. Candy was the same. 'I saw the boats first,' she said as she closed her eyes, and then she was gone. Metty took a bit longer to settle, but eventually his eyes closed, and I kissed his twisted little face and laid him carefully down. Dave put his arm round me as I stretched out on the ground beside him. He'd been on buckback all waking of course. He hadn't had the exercise that I'd had. All the muscles in his body were taut with fear, and I knew he wouldn't sleep, just worry worry worry, eating himself up inside.

'What are we going to eat at Davidstand? That's what bothers me,' he muttered. 'There's no hunting round there any more – they've done for all the bucks for miles: it's even worse than round Veeklehouse – and what have we got to trade with?'

'No point in worrying about that now.'

I turned my back to him and settled myself down. I did not love Dave that much: there was no fun in him, no joy, and he had almost no curiosity about anything. I loved the kids we'd had together – I *think* they were all his, though Fox might possibly have been Tom's – and he loved them too, but the truth was that I'd just made do with Dave because I wanted to be able to stay in Michael's Place and not have to be on my own any more. I guess he'd made do with me as well. No one chooses a batface if they can avoid it.

I lay listening to the pulsing of the tree beside us – *hmmmph hmmmph hmmmph* – and watched the flutterbyes flapping round the redlantern flowers shining above me. I saw they were beautiful things, those shining pink tubes, curving upwards at the end so the flutterbyes could find their way in. Swaying slightly slightly in the breeze that came from across the Pool, they were beautiful beautiful. But it was a beauty that made my heart ache, almost as if they weren't really there at all, were just a memory from some far off time, long long ago.

Eight

So I said goodbye to Knee Tree Grounds and crossed over to Mainground with Mary, sitting behind her in middle of an old log boat with four guards to paddle us across the bright water, two in front of us and two behind. Three other women had chosen to come with Mary too: Sue, Janny and Watershine. All three of them had been made pregnant by visiting guards and Mary had told them they should try and find their babies' fathers, and let their children grow up as part of True Family. They sat in front of me, silent and tense, but I hardly to spoke to them at all on the way across, and I never saw them afterwards. I don't know if they stayed on Mainground or went back again to Knee Tree.

Mary leaned forwards so she could speak only to me.

'I know we'll work well together, Angie,' she said, 'I just know it. We're two of a kind.'

Two of a kind? I'd have been proud proud to think I was like her, but that wasn't how it seemed to me. She was so strong and smart and certain. I didn't feel alike to her in any way. And I was waking up now to just how much I'd left behind in Knee Tree Grounds: all my friends, my brothers, my sisters, my mother and my mother's men, Starlight's sister Glitterfish and her little boy, all the familiar places and things… And here I was, with this scary stranger, so smart and grownup and fierce, with nothing round us but glowing water, and Knee Tree Grounds just a patch of yellow-green light disappearing behind World's Edge.

'You've got sharp eyes,' Mary told me. 'I saw that at once. You'll be able to notice the things I miss when I'm in middle of it all. You'll be able help me, I know, even while you're still learning. One waking you'll come back to that little grounds of yours as a shadowspeaker yourself, I'm sure of that. And let's hope you manage to bring all of your friends over there back to our Mother, and back to the real world.'

I was terrified that she'd made a mistake, that she'd seen something in me that wasn't really there at all, and that soon she'd find out the truth. I tried to think of an answer that wouldn't show her how ordinary I really was.

'What's it like to hear the voice of Gela?'

Mary turned to look at me. Most people's eyes are brown but hers were grey, and that made them seem extra fierce and sharp, as they looked out at me from that big square face of hers. Those small sharp eyes could bore through stone! I was quite sure that if she hadn't seen right through me already, she soon soon would.

'You have to learn how to hear her, Angie. It's hard to explain, but I'll teach you, and when you're ready, you can go up and stand in the Circle of Stones, and call on her to speak to you, so you can be a shadowspeaker too.' She reached back and squeezed one of my hands in her own big mitt. 'I'm sure she will speak to you, Angie, I'm sure our Mother will love you. I'm sure she'll see your beauty just as I do.'

'Stand in the Circle of Stones?' I was trembling. We Kneefolk lived way out in the Pool, and none of us had been as far as the slopes that led up to Snowy Dark, never mind *across* the Dark to Circle Valley, but even we knew that ordinary people were forbidden to stand in the Circle. Even we knew that the punishment for anyone who stepped inside it was death.

'That's right. Shadowspeakers have always been allowed to stand there, going right back to the first shadowspeaker, Lucy Lu. Apart from the Head Guard and his family, we're the only ones who can go into the Circle on our own. But we're allowed to take others in there with us, if we think they're ready to become shadow-speakers too.'

She was still looking into my eyes and holding my hand in her own. Now she gave it a squeeze.

'Our Mother's voice is quiet quiet,' she said. 'She doesn't shout at us. She speaks so softly you might think it was just your own thoughts. But if you try, if you really concentrate, if you shut out all your own worries and problems, if you live your life like she would want you to, then slowly slowly you'll learn to hear her.'

When we reached Nob Head, Mary put on another show. It was different to the one she'd done out on the Grounds, because these people were already Davidfolk. They knew the True Story as well as she did, and they believed it too (or at least if they didn't, they kept that to themselves). So, instead of telling them they needed to come back to Family, Mary told them the ways they were letting Family down.

'You lie and trick each other,' she said, with tears running down her face. 'You slip with the shelterwomen of other men. You hide things from the guards, and hold back from your guard leader the things he needs to keep you safe. How you hurt your Mother! How you disappoint her, when she worked so hard to make Family kind and strong, and works hard still, reaching out to you from across the stars.'

She looked round at the circle of Nob Head people who were watching her.

'I see good people here,' she said. 'But I see foolish people too, who've forgotten to listen out for their own Mother, forgotten the sound of her voice.'

She moved restlessly back and forth across the small circle of round stones laid out in middle of Nob Head, which, of all the people present, only she was allowed to enter. And in the light of the whitelanterns, her grey eyes searched the faces watching her, sizing up their fear and their desperate hope.

'You've suffered a terrible loss,' she told a short plump woman. The woman nodded, and tears flowed down from her big sad bulgy eyes. 'A terrible loss, and not so long ago. A child of yours, maybe?'

The woman sobbed.

'My little boy, Davey.'

'Davey,' repeated Mary, her tear-filled eyes gazing at some distant place that no one else could see. 'Davey. I see him now. He's in the arms of our Mother, home and safe, happy and warm, waiting for the waking you can be with him again.'

The woman grabbed hold of her hand, pressed trading sticks into it, and then squeezed it closed, so Mary couldn't return them. 'Thankyou thankyou thankyou.'

Mary crossed the circle, stood in front of another woman, tall and slender, and looked up into her eyes.

'But you, my dear, our Mother can't reach. She calls out to you, but you turn away. She cries out to warn you, but you act like you don't care. How you hurt poor Gela. She's crying crying. But she doesn't cry for herself, you know. She cries for you. She cries because she knows you have forgotten how to hear her, forgotten even that she was ever there. "Reach out to her, Mary!" she begs me. "Please reach out to her and teach her to listen, or her time will come and her shadow will be alone out there in the blackness, and I won't be able to call her home."'

The tall woman looked down at her, her face unmoving. You shouldn't have taken that one on, Mary, I thought to myself. You really shouldn't have. No way will she bend for you, and now you'll just look silly in front of everyone. But Mary didn't look worried at all.

'You're hiding something,' she told the tall woman. 'You and I know what it is. Our Mother knows what it is. Do you want to tell it to everyone, or do you want to make peace with your Mother on your own?'

Still the woman stared down at her coldly, and Mary's big square face stared straight back up. It made me think of two men having an arm-wrestling contest, each one straining against the pressure of the other's muscle. You've taken on more than you can handle, Mary, I thought again. But then quite suddenly the tall woman broke, covering her face with her hands and shaking with sobs. Mary put her arms round her.

'It's okay,' she murmured, holding the woman tightly. 'It's going to be okay. You're back with your Mother again, and she'll help you home.'

People all round the circle were crying as they watched this, and some threw down trading sticks and blackglass arrowheads. It was part of my job to gather up these presents.

'It isn't just shadowspeakers who can hear Mother Gela,' Mary told her listeners. 'We hear her more clearly because we're the ones she's chosen to bring back the ones who are lost, but everyone can hear her if they let her in. If only everyone would remember that. If only. Because when we all listen to our Mother, Family will be one again, and then we won't even have to wait for our deaths to be able to go home, we won't have to become shadows to return to Earth. No, when that waking comes, a starship will come and fetch us all.'

The Kneefolk thought that the shadowspeakers were liars, just like Trueheart did. They thought shadowspeakers were just tricking people so as to make them hand over sticks and presents, sometimes by frightening them and sometimes by telling them things that they longed to hear. Well, I think there *are* some speakers out there who are like that, and Mary herself thought the same. 'That woman's only interested in how many presents she can get,' she'd say of one two of the others. But I know Mary wasn't lying. When she finished a show, she was shaking shaking all over. She couldn't eat, she couldn't keep still, she couldn't attend to what was going on round her. Each time it was like she'd stripped off her own skin, so there was nothing left between her and the people of Eden, nothing to protect her from their loneliness and fear, their greed and their stupidity.

'How did I do, Angie?' she'd ask me when we were on our way to the next cluster. 'Do you think I got through to them?' And some-times: 'Just hold me a moment, could you, Angie? Just hold me.'

As she stood there in my arms, I could feel her heart pounding, I could smell the fresh sweat on her hot hot skin, I could feel the trembling in her limbs. It seemed strange that she asked me for comfort, when she seemed so much more grownup than me, like a mother asking for comfort from a child, but I felt proud that she wanted it from me, and I gave it as best I could.

'It's like beating and beating on a cliff of stone,' she said, 'trying to get through to these people, trying to get them to see.' And I could see it was so. To Mary, putting on a show wasn't just telling a story, or playing a part. It was a mighty struggle. It was a strug-gle against lies, a struggle against forgetfulness and laziness and selfishness, and it was hard hard work, because in her struggle she opened herself up to all the things that people normally want to push away from themselves.

And as for the sticks and presents, well, she traded them for food for us, and for things we needed, but how else could she keep herself going? It wasn't like she had a big shelter, or coloured wraps, or lots of helpers to run round after her. I was her only helper and she treated me as a friend.

We travelled to Davidstand, and then along the little clusters along the bottom edge of Snowy Dark, where the paths go up to the High Valleys. All the way Mary talked about what she'd learned in her years of shadowspeaking, and answered my questions, and probed me again and again with questions of her own about my life among the Kneefolk. What was it like, she wanted to know, to be among people who pretended to themselves that they had everything they needed already, and that they didn't need a mother or a home, except for the mothers they already had, and the little patch of sand they lived on?

'So many people are like that,' she said. 'Not just your Kneefolk, but people all over the Davidfolk Ground. They've stopped believing there's anything in the world but the things they see round them every waking. But those Kneefolk of yours – those Jeffsfolk – are the only ones who've made that into a story in its own right.'

'It's not quite like that,' I tried to tell her. 'I know you don't like the idea, but we had the Watcher.'

She wouldn't have that, though.

'But the Watcher was just something inside you,' she'd say. 'That's the story you were told, isn't it? Just something in your head. It was like you were trying to be mothers to yourselves.'

We turned peckway about a waking short of the so-called White Streams that mark the end of the Davidfolk Ground and the beginning of the Brown River Ground, making our way through forest to the Pool, and then heading slowly slowly up rockway towards Veeklehouse, sometimes along poolside, sometimes turning away from it so as to take in tiny clusters back in forest, so that we wandered back and forth, blueway and peckway, blueway and peckway, while gradually moving rockway all the while. Guards always rode with us to keep us safe, but when we stopped to rest, they made their fire apart from us, and me and Mary were alone.

'You and me are two of a kind, Angie,' she told me again and again, as we cooked up our meat and flowercakes at the end of a waking, though I still had no idea how someone like her, so strong and certain and afraid of no one, could see any of herself in me. And then she'd put an arm round me as we lay down to sleep, so we'd lie together looking up at Starry Swirl and listening to the sounds of Eden.

She wasn't the shelterwoman of any man, and, as far as I know, she never slipped with a man, whole time I was with her. I decided after a while that she was probably one of those that prefer other women, like Julie Deepwater back on Knee Tree Grounds, though she never allowed that to herself either. In fact she would often warn people at her shows that it was bad bad for two women to go together like that, or for two men to do it, just like it was bad to slip the back way, or for a woman to say no to a man if she was his house-woman, or for a man to pull out of a woman before he was done. If Mother Gela or Tommy had done any of those things, she'd point out, none of us would even be here.

There were times I wondered if she'd chosen a batface like me to be her companion, so I wouldn't be too much temptation for her. Sometimes, when she hugged me, she would press her body up against mine, and then suddenly she'd pull back and look me straight in the face, look at the hole between my nose and my mouth and at my twisty gums and my teeth that stuck out all differ-ent ways. And it was like it calmed her down, turned her back into a shadowspeaker and me into her helper.

'You are beautiful, Angie,' she'd say. 'You are beautiful beautiful.'

I liked her saying that, of course, but it seemed to me that it was a kind of discipline for her. Like she was making herself say what her head believed to be true, even though her body doubted it. I guess it was a bit like what mothers of batfaced kids have to do as they force themselves through the disappointment and grief, so they can give their ugly babies the love they need. I was to go through it myself, years later, when Candy and Metty were born.

One time, in a little cluster on poolside, a trader came up to Mary after she'd done a show, a man who took bracelets and necklaces made with coloured stones from one cluster to another, and asked her if she could help him. He was a big guy with a big black beard that came halfway down his chest, but it was obvious he was full full of tears. His little daughter back home was sick sick, he said, and he couldn't bear the thought that when she died she'd be lost forever among the stars and never have anyone to care for her.

'Where do you come from, dear?' Mary asked him gently, taking one of his hands.

'Brown River, mother,' he told her, as his tears began to flow.

I could see Mary tense slightly, but she didn't let go of his hand. 'So you are one of the Johnfolk?'

'Yes, mother, and I know you think that's wrong, but we love Mother Gela too, you know, in our own way. It's just that we don't have shadowspeakers as you do here who can help us to reach her. Only storytellers that wander round and remind us of the old stories. I thought perhaps you could—'

'My dear, I can't help you unless you turn away from John the ringstealer. I know you Johnfolk think you love Gela as we do, but you really don't. What you love is John's *idea* of Gela, his childish dream of a mother who will tell him that whatever he chooses to do is right, and that whoever tries to stop him is bad and wrong. That's not really Gela at all. It's just something that came from John's head.'

'But I live in Brown River. If I was to follow David, I'd be driven out. Surely I can—'

'Unless you turn away from John, I can't help you. If you want your little girl's shadow to find her way back to Earth, you need to teach her about the true Gela, and not the Gela that John dreamed up to make it seem alright that he stole the ring from True Family.'

The man became angry then. 'Tom's dick, it was hard enough for me to speak to you at all!' He pulled his hand away from her. 'Have you got any idea what people at home would say, if they knew I'd asked the advice of a shadowspeaker? But I came to your show, and I thought you were a wise kind woman who could see past all those old stories. I guess I was wrong.'

Mary just shrugged. 'Unless you turn away from John, I can't help,' she told him as he turned his back and walked away.

I was shocked by this. The man had been so desperate, and it seemed obvious to me that it must have been hard hard hard for him to approach her at all.

'He can't help coming from Brown River, Mary,' I said. 'He can't help it that he grew up with the Johnfolk stories. Surely we could have helped him just a bit?'

Mary snorted. 'I *did* help him, Angie. I told him exactly what he needs to know. What else could I have done?'

'But he *can't* do what you said, Mary! Someone in Brown River can't follow David, any more than someone in Davidstand could follow John.'

Mary studied my face for a moment with her small grey eyes. 'Suppose someone was to come up to us now and ask the way to Veeklehouse,' she said, 'what would we tell him?'

'We'd say to head rockway along poolside.'

'And what if he said he didn't want to go rockway because all his friends would be angry with him, and he'd prefer to get there by going alpway?'

'Well, we'd tell him...' I laughed, seeing how her story had trapped me. 'I guess we'd tell him he could go whichever he liked, but if he went alpway from here he'd never get to Veeklehouse.'

'Exactly,' said Mary.

'Please don't be angry with me, Mary, for saying this, but how can we be sure it works like that? Surely the way to Gela depends where you start from, doesn't it? I mean...' I struggled to think of a little story to explain what I meant that would be as smart as hers. 'I mean, if you started off from Nob Head, you *would* need to go alpway to get to Veeklehouse. And don't the Johnfolk start in a different place from us? Yes, and anyway, please don't be angry with me, Mary, but you said the Gela the Johnfolk believe they love is just an idea in their heads. But how can we be sure that the Gela we think *we* know isn't just an idea in *ours*?'

Mary laughed. 'You mean like that Watcher of yours on Knee Tree Grounds?' She reached out and took my hand to show she wasn't cross and was only teasing. I didn't try to tell her that the Watcher wasn't supposed to be in our heads, but behind the whole world, looking out at everything through our eyes, because I knew she'd say, as she always did, that that came to the same thing.

'Listen, Angie,' she said. 'We know our Gela's not just an idea in our heads because she speaks to us. It's difficult for you now to understand this, I know, it's difficult difficult, but I promise you, my dear, when you hear our Mother's voice more clearly, you'll know exactly what I mean.'

Eventually we came to Veeklehouse. It was the first time I'd been there since I said goodbye to Starlight, and it was strange strange to be back again, in that place where me and her had seen all the wonders and possibilities that lay beyond our home, and she'd gone after them, and I'd just paddled back home again. All those old feelings were still there, it turned out, waiting for me just where I'd left them. Grief, loneliness, jealousy, anger: they all welled up inside me again, as if no time had passed at all since I was last there. And as they welled up, they stirred up newer feelings that had been building up since I'd been with Mary: mixed-up feelings about leaving my home behind out in the bright water, and spending all my time with no one but Mary to be my family and my friend.

Soon after we arrived, a guard came to bring some meat and flowercakes for Mary, and to ask her to come and meet the guard leader so he could discuss with her the messages she was going to give to the people in Veeklehouse. This had happened a couple of times before when we arrived in a new place: guard leaders wanting to discuss what the shadowspeaker was going to say in her show. After all, it was their guards that kept us safe when we were travelling round. And this time, of course, it was Leader Hunter, guard leader of Veeklehouse and Strongheart's third son: the same one who received our buckskins and starflowers and boys when I came to live at Michael's Place.

Mary told the guard that me and her had just arrived after travelling all waking. Would it be alright if he came back for her a bit later when she'd had a chance to wash her feet and put on another wrap? As he headed off, she glanced round at me, and seemed to see something in my face that made her uneasy.

'I'm not here to speak for the high people,' she told me. 'I hope you know that, Angie. I'm here for everyone, but I do need the high people's help and support, and if they want things from me that Mother Gela wants too, there's no harm in helping them out. Meet me in a half waking by the Veekle Gate, and we'll get ready for our show.'

I wondered what expression she'd seen on my face. All I'd really been thinking at that moment was that I didn't fancy being on my own in Veeklehouse just then. It was only now she mentioned it that it struck me as interesting that the guard leaders thought they could tell the shadowspeakers what to talk about. And it was interesting too to discover that Mary imagined me watching her and judging her, when I still saw her as the teacher who knew almost everything and myself as the helper who knew hardly anything at all. I really hadn't noticed that before. Yet now I *had* noticed it, I remembered a few other times when she'd glanced at me uneasily in that same way, like she thought I wouldn't approve of what she was doing.

While Mary was busy with Leader Hunter, I walked round the trading shelters for a while, looking at the feather hats and the earrings, the wraps and rings and spears and boats. Then I went to see the Veekle, and after that, I filled in some time by watching a little group of guards and traders playing a game called toss-up that men like to play right across the Davidfolk Ground, where they all chuck trading sticks into a heap, and then throw little wooden dice to decide who gets the lot.

After a while, I walked to the cliff and down the path to the ledge below, where traders from other places pulled their boats out of the water. I hadn't set out on that walk with any clear plan, but now I was there I knew exactly what I was looking for, and it wasn't hard to find. The boats from New Earth were easy to spot back then, when the rest of Eden still hadn't yet figured how to copy those smooth bodies made of planks of wood, or those windcatchers hanging from their poles. I found a couple of New Earth guys who were sitting down there drinking badjuice from a jug, and got talking with them. They were just paddle-men, blokes that came across with the New Earth traders to pull their boats back home for them against the wind. They wore simple skin wraps like I used to do back on the Grounds (I wore plain fakeskin now I was Mary's helper) and the older one of the two was a batface like me. I think he was the dad of the younger one, or maybe his uncle. They both had arms like tree branches and massive shoulders, from all that paddling paddling paddling, waking after waking, across the Pool.

'A friend of mine went to New Earth,' I told them. 'My best friend.'

'Oh yeah?'

'We grew up on a little grounds far out in the Pool – a waterhill, I think you people would call it – but when we came down here to Veeklehouse once, she met your Headmanson, and crossed over with him.'

The men looked at each other, half-impressed, half-disbelieving.

'What?' exclaimed the younger one. 'You're saying you knew the *Ringwearer*?'

'Ringwearer? Is that what you call her now? Her name's Starlight, and the Headmanson was called Greenstone. I was with her when she met him. He had red hair tied up in a hundred little bows.'

Again the men looked at each other. 'Well, they do say she came from a little waterhill,' the older one said. He laughed, and the guy laughed with him. 'Tom's dick! Who'd have thought we'd meet a friend of the Ringwearer!'

'Do you know her then? Can you give her a message from me?'

They laughed even louder at that.

'What? *Us?* Us know the Ringwearer?' the younger one said. 'Some chance. If we're lucky, we'll see her in the distance some-place one waking, with people crowding round her to kiss the ring.'

'What ring?'

'What ring?' The younger one glanced uncomfortably at his companion. 'Well... a special ring that the Headman's house-woman wears.'

'Not the ring in the story? Not the one that John found and—'

'Let's not go over all that,' the old guy said. 'It's always made trouble between us Johnfolk and you lot.' He smiled, and reached out to shake my hand. 'A pleasure to meet you, though, my dear, a pleasure to meet a friend of the Ringwearer. She's pretty pretty, so they say, and all the small people love her.'

'Small people?'

'You call them low people here,' the young guy said. 'It means regular people like us. The ones that do the work, in other words. The ones that take all the crap. We all love her. Everyone says she's as kind and gentle as Gela herself.'

❦

I loved Starlight, but kind and gentle wouldn't be the words I'd have used to describe her. Determined, yes. Tough, yes. Smart, yes. But not kind and gentle.

Never mind that, though. What I was thinking about right then was this ring the men had spoken about. They didn't like to say so, but it was obviously Gela's ring, the one that Gela lost and John Redlantern found, the one that John had worn on his finger when he set out across Worldpool from the Brown River Ground, all those years ago.

Tom's dick, I thought, imagine that! My best friend was wearing that ring from the old story, the ring that was made on Earth, the ring that was the cause of all that fighting! It was almost like Starlight was in a story herself. In fact never mind almost, she *was* in a story. A young girl from a place no one had heard of, putting on the ring of the Mother of us all: if that wasn't a story, then what was? Starlight had become a story, and I was there when it all started, so I was kind of in it as well.

As I made my way back to meet Mary, I was bursting bursting to tell her this exciting news, but I knew I couldn't. She hated the Johnfolk. She hated them for breaking up Family, and destroying the Circle (though of course the Circle had been put back again by Lucy, the first shadowspeaker, with Gela herself guiding her hand). And, like all the Davidfolk, she hated the Johnfolk especially for stealing the ring, which Gela had been given by her mum and dad, and which ought to belong to all of us. Ringstealers, she called the Johnfolk. If I told her, she'd be angry angry with Starlight for wearing that stolen ring. And she'd never rest until she was sure I was angry about it too.

But I knew I couldn't be angry about it. I loved Mary for choosing me, and I respected her, but I couldn't help myself from loving Starlight as well, and I couldn't help myself from being proud of her. So, bursting though I was to tell someone, I said nothing about what I'd heard. When Mary came back, we talked about this and that as we began to get ourselves ready in the place that was set aside for shows, but I didn't mention Starlight at all. In fact I'd never spoken to Mary about Starlight. I hadn't mentioned her even once.

Nine

Fox slept for a couple of hours, but then woke up.

'Mum! What's that sound?'

'What sound, darling?'

Dave sat bolt upright beside me.

'*What?* What is it? What can you hear, Fox?'

'Oh *shhh*, Dave. Don't wake everyone up. It's just forest, Foxy. It's just the trees and the animals.'

It was my job, I figured, to be a home for my children, even when they had no home, and to try and make them feel safe, even when there was danger. But the truth was I'd been lying awake myself, listening to rustlings in the starflowers and cracking branches, imagining the Johnfolk creeping up on us with their metal masks and spears. They were near near. Even if they'd stopped right there on poolside where they'd grounded and not moved into forest at all, they were still only a waking's walk away. And who was to say they *had* stopped? Who was to say they weren't heading straight for Davidstand just as we were? *Hmmmph hmmmph* went the trees, *hmmmmmmmm* went forest, and I wanted to yell at it to shut up and be quiet for once so I could listen out properly for danger.

No one had been sleeping deeply. Foxy and Dave set off a whole string of other anxious voices round us: grownups muttering to other grownups, kids calling out to their mums or dads. A baby started to cry – it was little Suzie, the daughter of Tom's new young shelterwoman – and that woke up Metty, so he began to cry as well. So much noise! The Johnfolk could have crept right up to us and we still wouldn't have heard them.

'We'll carry on,' Tom decided. 'Seeing as we're all awake, we'll get the bucks loaded up and get going again.'

As we set off again with our bucks, Clare came to walk with me: Trueheart's mum and Tom's first shelterwoman. She was older than me, old enough to be my mum, but she'd been my friend since I came to Michael's Place. A big solid woman with big long breasts and broad hips, she plodded along beside with three of her smallest kids. She'd had seventeen children, as she liked to tell people often, and fourteen of them had lived. But now she'd reached the end of her childbearing time, and Tom had got himself a second shelterwoman called Flame, who was barely older than his daughter Trueheart, and given her a baby. He'd told Clare that he was cluster head, and so it was only right that he have two shelter-women, just as it was right that guard leaders often had five or six. Strongheart had twenty-three by then.

'It's not like you can give me any more babies,' Tom had said to Clare.

Clare hated that and, though she was usually a kind woman, she couldn't stop herself from muttering about Flame and her baby Suzie.

'She doesn't know how to handle that kid,' she grumbled, look-ing back at Flame, who was riding on Tom's buck and trying to get little Suzie to suck from her. 'She's only a kid herself, and all she cares about is herself.'

Poor Flame. I don't suppose she'd have gone for an old grand-dad with a missing hand if she'd had a choice in the matter. But she was the daughter of another cluster head further up poolside who'd been in the guards with Tom, and Tom had gone up there to collect her in his guard's fakeskin wrap, carrying a whole big bag of trading sticks.

'I mean, what was Tom thinking of?' Clare muttered. 'It's like he thinks he's some kind of high man or something, not just a bloody old cluster head who was chucked out of guards when he lost his hand.'

'Mum, my feet are sore sore,' said Fox.

'Oh poor love. Walk a little bit more if you can, sweetheart, and then we'll let you have a go on the buck with your dad. I can carry Candy for a bit.'

He was a good boy. He didn't argue, just picked up a stick as he carried on and began to slash out at flutterbyes that came too close to the ground, stamping on them as they flapped about on the dirt with their broken wings still shining, waving their tiny legs and arms. Poor little man, he had dark rings under his eyes from lack of sleep. Presently Clare's kids joined in with the flutterbye hunt. Little bits of shining wing flew this way and that through the air, as they let out their anger and fear.

'We're taking too much stuff with us,' Clare said, after a bit. 'That's the problem. I told Tom, but he wouldn't listen. Kids their age can't walk for wakings on end like this. It's all well and good carrying pots and jugs, but we're going to need these bucks to carry people. Especially if we have to move on from Davidstand.'

I looked down at Fox.

'Well, we *will* have to,' I said. 'We're not going to be able to feed ourselves at Davidstand.'

'Where do you reckon we should go then? We need a plan, don't we? I need to start working on Tom now, so it'll be there in his head when we need it to be.'

'Well, I think we should…' Then I stopped. 'Oh Gela's heart!'

There were men coming towards us through the shining trees, men on the backs of bucks, in front of us, behind us and on either side. The bucks were a strange new kind with bluish skin and tough lean bodies, and the men's faces were hidden behind metal masks.

Ten

That first time Mary took me back to Veeklehouse, Leader Hunter himself came to watch her show, bringing three of his shelter-women, and six seven of his kids. Mary cried and rolled on the ground. She begged and wept and scolded. She warned some folk that they must come back to Gela or it would be too late, and gave others news of their loved ones who'd died and crossed the darkness between the stars. One of Leader Hunter's women began to cry and cry, and Mary spoke gently to her about her little daughter who'd drowned in a pool.

Then, after a while, Mary began to speak of problems and difficulties that were happening in Veeklehouse.

'How is it for you here,' she asked, 'now these Johnfolk are coming here to trade: the ones from New Earth as well as the ones from Brown River? Do you worry your children are listening to their stories, or that they might go back with them across the water?'

'My boy *has* done,' called out one woman. 'The silly kid crossed the Pool as a paddle-man with one of these New Earth traders. What will happen to him if he stays over there, among the people who turned their back on Family? Where will his shadow go when he dies?'

Mary took the woman's hand and held it tight.

'What a worry for you, my dear. What a big big worry. I'm so sorry to say it but not one of those Johnfolk will ever find their way home, unless they first come back to Family. Just as John Redlantern tricked those foolish newhairs long ago and led them up into the darkness and snow, so he leads the Johnfolk even now into the icy blackness between the stars.'

The woman sobbed. 'But my boy Luke? He's not so bad really. Surely there must be some hope for him?'

Still Mary held her hand tightly. 'Gela is reaching out for him now,' she said, her own eyes filling with tears. 'She's whispering to him, she's begging him to come back home to his mother and his True Family, the people of David. Let's trust in Gela, eh? She's a *true* mother, my dear. She'll never never give up.'

What would Mary think, I wondered, if she knew my friend Starlight was living at that moment with the high people in New Earth, and wearing the stolen ring on her finger?

But Mary had moved on to something else.

'Gela wants me to warn you about a bad bad thing that's happening right here in Veeklehouse,' she said. 'It's as harmful in its own way as the Johnfolk are with their lies. In some ways it's even worse, because it's secret and hidden away. I'm sure some of you already know what I'm talking about. Gela needs your help to make it stop.'

And now she started talking about some secret words that certain foolish mothers passed on in secret to their daughters, claiming that the words came from Gela herself.

'What could be worse?' asked Mary, walking round the circle of people, peering one by one into women's faces. 'What could be worse than pretending to speak for our Mother?'

She stopped in front of a young batfaced woman, about the same age as me, and stared intently into the woman's eyes.

'You've heard it, haven't you, my darling? You've been told the Secret Story yourself?'

The batface girl began to sob. Mary threw her arms round her.

'You're not in trouble, my dear. You're not in trouble at all. No one can blame you for hearing it. And as for your mum – was it your mum?' The girl nodded, still in Mary's arms. 'Well, she's been foolish, but now she's been found out, and we can help her to see sense again.'

She looked round at the other people, over the weeping girl's shoulder.

'This brave young woman has done the right thing. If anyone's told you this so-called Secret Story, or if you know of anyone that's telling it, then you should talk to your guards and get their help in having it stopped. Because it's all wrong! It's all nonsense. Mother Gela is alive right now, alive and speaking to us! She talks to you directly and she talks to you through her shadowspeakers. What need could she possibly have for whispered stories that are supposed to come from the past?'

And straight away, four five women came forward sobbing, to kneel on the ground to say they'd heard the Secret Story too, and beg for Mary's forgiveness.

🌿

'Did Leader Hunter ask you to speak about the Secret Story?' I said to Mary, when we were some miles rockway of Veeklehouse, with our two guards far enough behind us for me to be sure they couldn't hear. It had taken me some time to pluck up the courage to speak. 'Only you haven't spoken about it before.'

Mary had pulled up a dead starflower as we walked and was picking at something between her teeth with its dry stem.

'He mentioned it, yes.' Suddenly she stopped dead, taking hold of my arm to make me stop as well, and looking straight at me. 'But what are you trying to say, Angie?'

'I don't mean to criticize, Mary. Please don't think that. But what you said before the show about helping out the high people ... well, it kind of made me think. And I wondered if it's possible to speak for Mother Gela and the high people both?'

Mary frowned. I thought for a moment she was going to shout at me, and I felt scared and ashamed like a naughty child. But then she laughed and gave me a hug.

'Oh Angie! Angie dearest! Do you know why I love you so much? It's because your heart is pure! It's pure and clear as the light inside a whitelantern flower. I saw that from the moment I first spotted you, out on that little grounds of yours. I just knew you would help me to see clearly. I knew you'd help me stay on the path I've chosen, and not wander off. Because even shadowspeakers can wander, you know, and sadly there are some that have done just that, like bloody old Suzie Batting, for instance, who only pretends to hear our Mother's voice, but really just thinks about the pile of presents she's building up, and the fancy shelter she's having built for her at Davidstand.'

She took my hand, leading me forwards again.

'Listen, Angie. Of *course* I have to listen to the high people. The guards and guard leaders are part of Gela's plan. Their job is to protect Family and keep it whole. And of course, if they're worried about something that worries Gela too, then I will happily speak out about it. But I've never...'

Again she stopped and turned to face me, still holding onto my hand.

'I would never never say anything at a show, Angie, unless I knew for certain, for *certain*, that it was Mother Gela I was speaking for.'

I nodded and smiled. It was my turn to hug her. 'You are good, Mary,' I told her. 'You're good good.'

She'd said my heart was pure as a whitelantern flower, and I knew that wasn't so. But I also knew that Mary's *was* pure. It wasn't like a whitelantern flower, not gentle and white, but it was pure pure like a flame. Of *course* she'd never say anything she didn't believe herself. Of course not. Of all people on Eden, Mary would be the last to do that. Anyone who knew her could see that all that mattered to her was speaking for Mother Gela and bringing Family back home. She'd given her whole life to that. Of all people, she could be trusted to speak the truth.

And yet I still didn't tell her about Starlight, and nor did I tell her that I myself had heard the Secret Story.

Eleven

They were right round us, their cold metal faces all alike, staring down at us from the backs of those strange blue bucks. The bucks shifted restlessly from foot to foot, snuffling with their mouth feelers and scratching at the dirt with their claws. We Michael's Place folk formed a kind of circle, and some of the men pointed their spears out towards the Johnfolk. But we knew there was no point in fighting them. There were thirty of us, but most were oldies or little kids, and only a few of us had anything to fight with. There were about thirty of them too, but every one of them was a strong grownup man, and all of them carried either spears with long long metal tips, or bows and metal-tipped arrows.

I looked round for my kids. Dave, still on Ugly's back, was shielding Candy and Metty in his arms. Fox had come to stand beside me. His face was blank, but he silently reached up for my hand. How could I protect him? Yet even now he took some comfort from my being near.

Trueheart had come over to be with her mother. We watched the metal faces of the ringmen, waiting for them to decide what they were going to do. Every grownup, and every kid who was old enough to talk, was thinking of the old stories about how cruel the Johnfolk had been, all those years ago, in their last big fight with the Davidfolk. We remembered how they'd taken children from their mothers: boys to raise up as ringmen, and girls to make into the mothers of yet more ringmen. That was how they built up their numbers when once they'd been so few and Davidfolk had been so many. We remembered how they'd burnt down whole clusters, how they'd done for young men, and forced their dicks on women and young girls.

We had no young men with us: they were all in the guards. But we had young women. I thought of young Flame with her little baby. I thought of Trueheart. You might think an ugly batface like hers would give some protection, but I knew it didn't always work that way. There were plenty of men who saw batfaces as being so damaged already that they might as well be damaged some more.

'There are two three good glass knives in that bag on our buck,' I hissed to Trueheart. 'If they come for us, run over and grab them for us. We may not have metal but we can give these blokes a fight.'

One of the bucks came forward, a second following straight after. Their riders wore coloured longwraps, rather than the plain ones that the other ringmen wore, so we could see they were the high men in charge. The first one's wrap was blue, the second one's white but sewn with big writing. They stopped side by side and the first man reached up to his mask. It seemed to be fixed to his metal hat, for when he pushed at it, it folded upwards and forwards, so we could see his face underneath. He was a young young guy, no more than twenty, I'd say, with long black hair. His wore his beard tied in little bows, and though he had a proud face like high people often have, he smiled. And it wasn't a cruel smile, but a smile like he wanted to reassure us.

'My name is Luke Johnson,' he said. 'My father, Dixon, is the Headman of New Earth.'

A little shiver ran down my spine. I knew Dixon. Dixon had been with Greenstone when me and Starlight first met him in Veekle-house. He'd been Chief Dixon then, a tall, cold, proud man with thick grey hair, who'd done his best to stop Greenstone from taking Starlight with him across the water. I remembered how he wouldn't so much as look at me, not just because I was a low person, but because I was a batface. And I could see Dixon's face now in this young guy who was talking to us. Luke Johnson was a younger version of that tall grey man. But, if it wasn't just my wishful thinking, he also seemed kinder, and friendlier, and less proud.

'My father, Dixon, is the Headman of New Earth,' he said. 'My mother, Lucy, wears Gela's ring. We are *not* your enemies, and you don't need to run from us. You've been told a lot of lies about us Johnfolk. You've been told that we steal and are cruel. But you need to remember it was Johnfolk who first found this forest that's all round us and gave it its name; Johnfolk who found the Veekle; Johnfolk who first saw Worldpool and stood at the top of the cliffs. So-called Great David had forbidden John to come here. He sent guards to do for John. He threatened to tie him to a spiketree and let him burn. And yet you'll notice that when John had found the way for him, David was happy enough to follow him across the Dark.'

Again he smiled, and I noticed for the first time that it wasn't just his dad he reminded me of, but Greenstone too. This guy's mum was Greenstone's cousin, from what I'd heard. And it occurred to me now that my friend Starlight would almost certainly have met him, though he would only have been a kid when she went over to New Earth. It was strange to think that she would have met him, not as a low person meeting a high one, but as one high person meeting another. Not that that would help us now.

'Well, I *say* it was us Johnfolk who found Wide Forest,' Headmanson Luke corrected himself, 'but actually there was no such thing as Johnfolk and Davidfolk back then. John Redlantern didn't want to split Family in two. That's another lie you people get told. He wanted *everyone* to follow him. He wanted to find a way for everyone to spread out from Circle Valley into all the rest of our beautiful Eden. I know you've been told that John was the disobedient one, the one that turned away from Mother Gela, but think about that for a moment. How come Gela guided him to the ring? Don't tell me it just happened! It had lain on the ground for generations since she lost it, remember, but John was the one who found it. And do you know what? That isn't the only time that Gela brought the ring to us. Just thirty forty hundredwakes ago – ten *years*, I guess you guys would call it – a wicked woman stole that ring and brought it right across the Pool to Old Ground here. We thought we'd lost it then. But it still came back to us. Gela brought it to us again!'

While he'd been speaking, the rider behind him had also lifted up his mask, the guy with the letters sewn on his wrap. He was young young too, and he had one of those faces you can't help liking at once: kind and smiley, beaming out at us delightedly like we were the most interesting people he'd ever met and all he wanted was to be friends.

'Hi, I'm Teacher Gerry,' he said. 'You probably don't know what that means exactly, but in New Earth, teachers don't just teach, we also learn and figure things out. Do you see what it says on my wrap here?' He pulled his wrap straight so we could see the words. Out of all of us, only Tom and Trueheart could read, but Teacher Gerry saw our puzzled faces and read the words aloud for us. 'It says "Become like Earth". Because that's what our Mother and her Father want us to do. They don't want us to waste our time repeating the same things over and over, but to learn and make things better. Otherwise why did our Mother guide John here across Snowy Dark? Why did she lead him across the water to New Earth? Why would she help us find metal, and not the Davidfolk?'

'That's right,' said Luke. 'Like I said, John was Gela's true son and he was trying to help whole Family of Eden. And that's what we want to do too. We've not come here to hurt you people or drive you off your ground. Not at all. What we've come here to do is to bring the True Story of Eden back to Old Ground – Mainground, as you call it – and to drive away the false one. We've come to make your lives better. We really have!'

I looked round at my Davidfolk companions. Tom's face was stiff and cold, and Clare's lips were tight. What these men had just said was all just typical Johnfolk lies as far as they were concerned. That had been confirmed for them when the Headmanson told us his mother was wearing the ring – Gela's heart, they were thinking, how could this wicked man sit there and say that without shame! – but whether he'd spoken of the ring or not, they'd still have dismissed everything these two men said, and so would Davidson and Kate and all the other grownups there from Michael's Place. The Headmanson and the Teacher might as well had said 'la la la' for all they'd heard and taken in. Only Trueheart seemed to be really listening, her eyes darting between the two men like she wasn't just hearing them out but trying to weigh up what they said.

As to me, I was more familiar with the Johnfolk way of seeing things than any of the others, because I came from the Kneefolk, and our Jeff had sided with John. But that didn't mean I liked what they said. All this talk of new ground, and metal, and becoming like Earth, all this pushing forwards no matter what! How about the other side of all that, I wanted to ask? How about the fighting, the killing, the cruelty? How about the dividing up of one Family into Johnfolk and Davidfolk, high people and low people, men and women? Was it really possible that our kind gentle Mother could have wanted all that for her children?

'So what do you want with us?' Tom called out, his voice tight with cold cold rage.

The two men on buckback looked at each other. Two good-looking high men, used to being listened to and having their own way, they smiled like they were sharing some private joke.

'We want to be your friends,' said Luke Johnson. 'It's as simple of that. Of course, if your guards come and fight us, we'll fight them back – and we'll beat them too, because our spears are ten times better than their spears, and our knives ten times sharper – but we don't want to fight, and we don't want you to feel you have to run away from your homes. We want you to stay with us. If you do, we'll send underteachers who'll show you how to read and tell you about the True Story, and all we'll ask of you is that you accept me as your chief, and ringmen as your protectors, instead of the guard leaders and guards you have now. But it's completely up to you.'

Tom looked round at the men who were his closest friends: Davidson, Little Harry, Blackknife. Then he looked at Clare in a certain way that he had, half-hoping she'd know better than he did what to do, half-resenting the fact that this really did quite often turn out to be the case. Harry's dick, how dare she have good ideas? Wasn't he the man, and wasn't he supposed to be the cluster head? This time, though, she had no more of a plan than him. No one did. Well, why would we? Nothing like this had ever happened to any of us before.

Tom ran his tongue round his lips. 'Okay,' he said to the Headmanson, 'well, if we really have a choice, we'd like to go to Davidstand. Will you let us through?'

Again the two high men looked at each other with that private smile. The two of them were close close, I suddenly thought, closer than just friends. That look that passed between them was like the one you sometimes see in the eyes of men and women who have recently started slipping together, and they're giving each other more pleasure with their bodies than the rest of the world together could ever hope to give.

'Alright,' said Luke Johnson, 'I'll let you through. I can see that most of you are too old or too little to fight us, and I can see that you, my friend, have lost your fighting hand. I don't think you've got anything much we're likely to need on those bucks of yours, either.' Someone among us must have looked surprised at that, because then he laughed. 'Oh I can see you've got blackglass spears and leopardtooth knives, but believe me, dear people, we really aren't bothered by those one bit. You can keep them. They're no match for metal. Keep them by all means. And, if that's really what you want, we'll let you go on to Davidstand.'

'Bear in mind, though,' said Teacher Gerry, 'that in a few wakings, Davidstand will be ours as well, just like Veeklehouse is now.' He laughed. 'Ours *again*, I should really say, because John was the one who first found the place. I wonder if you knew that? John called it Ellpool and he and his people lived there for some time.

Soon it will be Ellpool again. Your guards fight bravely enough, there's no denying that, but they're no match for us. The Veekle is ours again already, and before long we'll have whole of Wide Forest in our hands and be crossing Snowy Dark to take back Circle Valley.'

'That's right,' said Luke. 'But still, we'll let you through if you're sure that's what you want.' He watched Tom's face, his eyebrows raised, waiting for our cluster head's final decision, and then another thought occurred to him and he spoke to us all. 'Just one thing, though. Just one favour. I'd like you all to ask yourselves, as you carry on, whether your guards would be as generous as us in the same position? I know you've been told how bad and cruel we Johnfolk are, but would bad cruel people just let you go like this?'

'We want to go to Davidstand,' Tom repeated, and then just stood there with his face all tight and closed up, waiting to see if they really were going to let us carry on. It didn't seem likely. And the ringmen showed no signs of moving out of our way.

'You know what,' Teacher Gerry said to us. 'I'm sad that you won't stay with us because there really are things we could teach you. You Davidfolk just pass on the old stories from Old Family, and you don't think enough about where they came from or how the women that used to run Old Family might have changed them when they had the chance. Me and the Headmanson here know you're not bad people. We know you love Mother Gela in your own way, and we respect that. But there's a lot you don't know. For example, you know nothing about President, Gela's dad, not even that he *was* her dad. Or even that President was a man. And that's a big shame because, important as our Mother is, wonderful as she is, kind friend that she's been to all of us, her power comes from her father President. He was the Headman of all of Earth. He had the starship built, and the other sky boats, and it was him that made lecky-trickity and telly vijun and all the wonderful things we know they had on Earth. And of course it was him that told the Three Disobedient Men to return to Earth, and him that sent his daughter Gela to fetch them back. In fact he's behind the whole story, when you think about it. He might *seem* to be on the edge of it, but really he's out there all the time, looking in, reaching in himself only when he has to, so as to make the story go the way it needs to go. I believe he even meant for Gela to come to Eden, and that he arranged everything to make that happen, just so his children could have another whole world to make their own.'

We just stood there, enduring this weird nonsense, waiting to learn if we really could carry on towards Davidstand, unharmed, with all our bucks, and all our kids, and all our stuff.

'So tell me,' said Teacher Gerry. 'Who made the world? Who made the stars? Who made Eden and Earth?'

We looked at each other. What a thing to ask us now! And what kind of crazy question was it, anyway? No one made the world. How could anyone have made it? The world was what people were *in*.

'You don't know, do you?' said Gerry. 'And why should you? It's not like it's obvious. But we teachers, we think and we write down our thoughts, we read what teachers wrote who came before us, going all the way back to John, and slowly slowly we figure things out. And you know what, we're starting to understand that President wasn't just a man. He was there from the beginning. He made the world. He made all of this. He made Eden and Earth and all the stars.'

We stood there staring at him, some of us with our mouths wide open. Teacher Gerry laughed.

'You look pretty surprised!' he said, like he really believed that, right then, when we were frightened for our lives, we would be interested one way or the other in his weird ideas. 'But what's your explanation, eh? How did bats get here? Or trees, or woollybucks, or people? They can't just have made themselves. No, President made *everything*. It all began in his head.'

Again he laughed cheerfully. He genuinely seemed to have no idea how scared we were. He was one of those people who likes everyone and just assumes that everyone will like him back. It didn't seem to even occur to him that we might not feel too friendly towards ringmen who'd forced their way onto our ground, and driven us from our homes. It didn't seem to strike him that some of those guards these ringmen had done for at Veeklehouse might have been the sons and dads and brothers of the people standing here in front of him now.

'But you don't have to take it from me,' Teacher Gerry said, 'because if you listen hard enough, President will speak to you himself. You can hear his voice, I promise you, if only you make your mind quiet enough. And if you think about it, that isn't even surprising. It's him that's telling this whole story, after all, and if he fell silent, there'd be nothing left: no you, no me, no Eden, no Earth, no stars, no anything at all. Think about that. President is speaking all the time, but it's like the pumping of the trees, the humming of forest round us. We don't notice it because it's always there.'

He smiled at us, and then glanced back at Luke, who smiled back at him yet again like they were remembering some private joke they'd shared lying side by side, when no one else was there.

'But that's enough from me, eh?'

'More than enough, I'd say,' said Luke, 'if the faces of these poor people are anything to go by!'

Gerry laughed merrily at that, while Luke called out to his men. They backed away to the left and the right so as to open up a path between them.

We looked at each other, wondering if this was a trick, a weird cruel joke. Maybe they were just waiting for us to make a move, and then they'd laugh and take our bucks and our meat and our sleeping skins and knives, steal whichever kids of ours took their fancy, force their dicks on whichever women they liked, and do for everyone else. It seemed quite likely.

But what could we do? Tom looked at Clare again, and she shrugged. So then he shrugged too and began to walk. We all did – grownups, kids – pulling on the strings of our bucks to get them moving. Hardly daring to breathe, we passed in between those two high men with their happy smiles and then on through the ring-men in their cold shiny masks, which you couldn't read any more than you could read the faces of bats, or leopards, or slinkers. In fact they could have been skulls, so empty were they of any sign of feeling, though sometimes we could see their eyes glinting in the treelight.

No one spoke a word, until suddenly little Candy called out.

'Mum! Why have all these men got two faces?'

Twelve

After Veeklehouse, Mary and me headed up rockway with one smoothbuck to carry us both and all our stuff, while two guards rode with us to keep us safe and show us the way. We didn't go along poolside this time, but went back across to Davidstand and turned up rockway there, zigzagging between the little forest clusters along the folds and slopes that slowly climb up to Snowy Dark, and from time to time swapping one lot of guards for another as we passed between the grounds of different leaders. Sometimes the guards rode with us and talked to us, but usually they went ahead of us, or hung back, so they could talk more freely to one another. The Davidfolk respect shadowspeakers, but they don't feel at ease with them, and, though guards are men, and men usually enjoy the company of young women, they weren't quite so keen when the young woman was a batface like me.

Mary worked hard hard. I wished the Kneefolk who laughed at shadowspeakers could have seen that. Even in the smallest clusters, places where as few as ten grownups came to hear her, and there was no way she was going to get a pile of presents or impress any of the high people, she worked every bit as hard as she'd done at Veeklehouse. To her, even one person brought closer to Mother Gela was worth her trying for with all her might, whether that person was high or low. And, just for that one man or one woman or one newhair, Mary was willing go right down to those lonely, scary places that made her weep and sweat and tremble. She made me feel silly and selfish by comparison, like she was a real grownup and I was only a child. For what had I done in my life except to try and keep on the right side of people, and have as much fun as I could?

One time we met a little group of Hiding People, people who didn't even live in a cluster but just wandered naked through the trees like animals do, eating whatever they could find, resting wherever they were when they felt tired, and hiding away from guards and Davidfolk. There were just five grownups and a bunch of kids, but Mary sat down with them for the rest of the waking, finding out what stories they told one another, so she should figure out how to talk to them and what it was that they needed to know. They spoke about a great Leopard Man they must feed with burnt meat to keep him happy, and a Slinker Man with a thousand bony claws, who'd crawl into their dreams and steal their shadows if they didn't repeat certain words at the end of every waking, and rub ash into their skin.

'Who looks after you, then?' asked Mary. 'If Leopard Man and Slinker Man are after you, who's there to care for you in this dangerous world?'

'The Great Mother,' said the oldest of their women.

'She's like a bat that's as big as the sky,' a younger woman explained. 'Sometimes she flies across the stars, but mostly she lives deep down under the ground, using her big big wings to fan the fire.'

Their stories seemed so weird and childish that I had a job not to laugh at them, but Mary didn't so much as smile. 'What fire is that?' she asked, like she really wanted to understand.

'The one that warms the roots of the trees, of course,' the old woman said. 'The one that makes them grow. Without the Great Mother there'd be no heat or light. There'd be no food. There'd be no animals or starflowers. There'd be nothing alive at all.'

'And where do your shadows go when you die?' asked Mary.

The old woman laughed. 'When we die, this dream ends and

we wake up. No one knows in their dreams where they'll be when they wake up. If they knew that, they wouldn't really be dreaming in first place.'

As we travelled round the Davidfolk Ground, I'd heard folk laughing at Hiding People and saying they were no better than animals. I'd even heard of guard leaders who rounded them up like bucks, and made them work for them. Certainly the two guards who were with us now couldn't believe we were wasting our time on these people. They didn't even try to hide their feelings, sometimes sniggering, sometimes sighing with boredom, and one of them made the other laugh by pulling scary faces at Hiding People who looked in his direction. But Mary insisted we stay with those folk for two whole wakings, while she patiently taught them the True Story, and warned them about false stories they might hear: the stories of the Johnfolk who said that President was a man, and claimed that Gela had chosen John over David, and the so-called Secret Story, which women whispered because they didn't dare speak such nonsense out loud.

Their own stories, though, she listened to carefully and with so much respect that I felt ashamed for wanting to laugh at them.

'Who knows?' she told them. 'You may well be right about some of this stuff. But the thing you've got to remember is that there are two kinds of life in Eden. There's the life that came up from the warmth of Underworld, like trees and bats and bucks and leopards, and there's the kind that came down from the stars, which is us human beings. Maybe there *is* a Great Mother in Underworld – I don't know – but if so, she's not *our* mother, she's mother of the bats and leopards.'

She drew a circle on the ground. 'This is the way back to Earth,' she said. 'It's all you need. You mustn't step inside it until you're called, but draw a circle like this at the end of every waking, and you'll be able to go to sleep knowing that your true home is near near, close enough for your true Mother to whisper to you and for you to hear.'

When we were on our way again, and the Hiding People were out of hearing distance, I asked Mary how come she'd paid so much attention to their strange stories.

'Well,' she said. She was riding at the time, and I was walking beside her. 'We don't know how life began on Eden, do we? We know it came from Underworld, as Michael Namegiver taught us – and you notice the Hiding People knew that too – but we don't know how it came into being down there in first place. So who am I to call those people liars?' She laughed, and pointed out two little sweetbats watching us from the branch of a tree. 'And if there *was* a mother of all the creatures in Eden, I reckon it would be a bat, don't you? I'm sure they're the smartest of the animals. I mean, look at those two. It's like they're curious about us, isn't it? It's like they're trying to figure us out. None of the other creatures are like that.'

'I've heard there are bats in New Earth that can be trained to speak.'

Mary shrugged. 'Well, maybe, but you've got to bear in mind that those Johnfolk are liars. Did you know they even claim to have real *cars*?'

Presently the path became strangely dark, and we knew there must be nightmakers not far ahead of us, reaching up with their long black necks to bite the lanternflowers from the trees, and bending down to chew up the starflowers.

'Why did you warn those people about the Secret Story?' I asked.

Mary turned and looked back the way we came, though the Hiding People had been out of sight for a while. 'Well, I reckon people like that are easy easy to fool, and I just don't *want* them to be fooled like that. Like I said in Veeklehouse, Gela is alive. She speaks to us now. So, even if the Secret Story *was* true, even if it really was a thing Gela said to her children long ago when she was young, why would we need to pass it on when we can still hear her now? What would be the point?'

The nightmakers had done a thorough job. With no starflowers or lanterns left along the path, all the light that was left to us came from *behind* the trees along the path, instead of *from* them or from beneath them. I could see the big square shape of Mary's head, but I could barely make out her face.

'And of course it's not true, anyway,' she said. 'Gela hates it. You can't yet read our Mother's heart like I can, Angie dear – though you will one waking, and you'll be brilliant at it – but take it from me that Gela hates it that people can speak that nonsense in her name.'

We rode for a while in silence beneath those strange dark trees.

'I suppose the high people must hate that story especially,' I said, 'because it says that women are as good as men, and—'

I couldn't see her clearly in the darkness the nightmakers had made, but I could see enough to tell she'd grown suddenly tense, and had turned to peer in my direction.

'How do you know what it says, Angie?'

Tom's dick and Harry's, I was glad of that darkness right then! 'Oh you know, people talk about it sometimes, don't they? It's never been *completely* a secret.'

She relaxed and turned away again. 'Well, you shouldn't listen to them, dearest. It's just stuff some silly woman or other made up long ago, wanting to make herself feel important. No doubt some of it makes sense: well, of course it does, or no one would believe it, would they? Any story that lasts at all has some truth in it some-where. But that doesn't change the fact that it's a big big lie, or that it's wicked for people to pretend to speak for our Mother when they really don't.'

I didn't argue any more, but it stuck in my mind what she said about stories and how no one would believe them unless they made some sense. I'd never thought about it that way before, but it seemed to me that what she said was true. The stories that lasted had to fit in in some way with what we knew the world was like, or at least with what we longed for, otherwise why would anyone listen to them, or bother to pass them on? But I couldn't help myself from thinking that the stories that could be spoken out loud had to fit in with something else as well: they had to fit in with what the high people wanted.

Presently we caught up with the nightmakers. There were four of them, huge huge creatures tall as trees, with four thick legs the height of men, and skin that was black as a forest leopard's, black like the sky between the stars. Three of them were reaching high up into the treetops with their long long necks and noisily gulping down the lanternflowers, pulling the branches towards their mouth feelers with those thick muscly arms. The fourth one was lying comfortably on the ground, its neck half-hidden in a big drift of twinkly starflowers that it was pulling up in great big armfuls and cramming into its mouth. It lifted its head above the flowers to watch us as we passed, and rubbed its face with its hands, but it still kept munching all the while. So did the other three, peering down at us from above with their big flat flickering Eden eyes as they crunched and chewed.

And then we were past them, and back under trees that gave out light.

'They were named after a place on Earth, apparently,' said Mary, her face friendly and familiar once again. 'A place called Night. The light of Earth's star never shines there, and there are no lanterns or flowers either, so it's dark dark.'

'I guess the Earth people have lecky-trickity to help them, don't they?' I said. 'They use it to make light of their own.'

Out on Knee Tree Grounds, where there were only water creatures and bats, we used to love hearing stories about the big animals on Mainground, like nightmakers and leopards and woollybucks. We were always told that nightmakers were named by John Redlantern, and that he'd named them, not after a place, but after a kind of enormous shadow that swept across the Earth each waking, hiding it from its star for a while. When the shadow passed, the light came back again, pouring down from the sky like it does on Earth. And weren't nightmakers just like that? They made a big shadow as they passed through forest, but then new lanterns grew in a waking or so, and the shadow passed.

But I didn't talk about that to Mary. Any mention of John Red-lantern or the Johnfolk always made her cross, and I didn't like it when she reminded me that my old friends were Johnfolk too.

I remembered when I was first told the Secret Story by my aunt Sue back there on the Grounds. She was a bit embarrassed about it, not because she thought it was bad in any way, but more because the way we lived back then, a lot of it seemed so obvious:

'Always remember that women are just as good as men... Just because someone thinks they're special doesn't mean they're really better than anyone else, and nor does having a big shelter, or a fancy wrap... Don't treat people like they're things that belong to you...'

Obvious obvious all this had seemed back then! Who could possibly disagree? But there were also odd bits that made no sense at all, like: 'Don't ever treat someone differently because of the colour of their skin.'

The colour of their skin? If you really thought about it, it was true that some people's skin was a lighter shade of yellowy-brown than others. But who would ever think of making something out of that?

Thirteen

'I'm just saying, Dad,' said Trueheart, 'that if the Johnfolk are really as wicked as you've always said they are, how come they let us go without hurting us or even taking any of our stuff?'

The two of them had been arguing for some time, and Tom had been getting crosser and crosser. Now his face was red, his breathing fast, his eyes bulging. He was almost too angry to speak.

'I can't believe you could even think of saying a thing like that,' he spluttered, 'when your own brothers are fighting them right now. Tom's dick and Harry's, girl, for all we know your brothers are dead – have you thought of that? – and one of those slinkers back there in metal masks may have been the ones who did for them!'

'I love my brothers, Dad, but they might equally well have done for some of those guys' brothers or those guys' mates.'

'So you take the side of the Johnfolk, do you? I can't believe it! Gela's tits, I never thought I'd *ever* hear my own daughter taking the side of the ringstealers, but least of all when those slinkers are over here, doing for our young men, and wrecking our clusters.'

'I'm not taking their side. I'm just saying that maybe they aren't quite as bad as we think. Those guys were fair with us, weren't they? And one of them was the son of their Headman.'

'What do you mean *fair*? They came here for no reason but to wreck our clusters, and to—'

'But we'd wreck their clusters, wouldn't we, if we had the

chance? And anyway, maybe that wasn't the real reason they came over here. Those men said, didn't they, that they'd come over to tell us their story.'

'Oh and that makes it okay, does it? The fact they came here to spread their lies and their filth makes it okay that they fight and do for our boys?' Tom wasn't much of an actor, but now he put on a silly voice and a silly face, and tried his best to say his words in something that sounded a bit like New Earth speech. '"President is rarly a marn,"' he squeaked. '"Gela gave Jarn the ring."'

'I'm just saying—'

'You're not *just saying* anything, girl, if you've got even a bit of sense left in you.' He'd turned his big thick guard's spear upside down and was waving the blunt end of it in his daughter's face. 'You're not saying anything else at all, if you don't want *this* across your back.'

He looked round for support and straight away spotted me watching them.

'*You* tell her, Angie. She won't listen to me. You were with that shadowspeaker all that time. You talked with her about the mind of our Mother. *You* tell this dumb dumb daughter of mine what Mother Gela thinks about the Johnfolk!'

'I don't want to get involved in this, Tom,' I told him. I was worried for my own kids as much as anything. Fox and Candy were watching Tom and Trueheart with big scared eyes as round as a bat's. They'd been through so much already that waking, but they knew as well as I did that Tom might suddenly decide at any moment that it was time to give Trueheart a beating, and they always dreaded that. 'We're all tired,' I said to Tom. 'We're all tired and scared, and—'

Clare came striding in between her daughter and Tom. 'You're as bad as each other, Tom and Trueheart. Just shut up both of you, and think of the rest of us for once.'

'You shut up!' Tom bellowed at her. 'You will *not* talk to me like that! I'm the cluster head of Michael's Place, and you're just one of my shelterwomen. No wonder Trueheart behaves like she does, the example you give her!'

'One of your shelterwomen! Listen to yourself! Harry's sister-slipping dick, Tom, who do you think you are? David Strongheart?'

'As to those shadowspeakers, Dad,' Trueheart said, 'doesn't it ever strike you as funny that whenever they tell us something Mother Gela is supposed to have said to them, it's always exactly what the high people say as well? They know where their meat comes from, that's pretty obvious; they know who to please if they want to keep their fancy wraps!'

Tom didn't answer her in words. He just kind of roared, and, pushing past Clare, he began slashing down at his daughter with the end of his spear, not just across her back, but onto her face, her belly, anywhere at all that he could reach. Trueheart screamed, holding her arm in front of her face to shield it, and sinking to the ground. Four five littles started to cry, including my Candy. And everyone else, weary from walking and lack of sleep, and just from being so scared for so so long, either simply turned away from them and began to trudge on, or yelled at the two of them to stop.

'Gela's heart, Tom, just leave her alone for once, can't you,' some folk shouted, 'and let us have some peace?'

Others told Trueheart to apologize. 'Why have you always got to be so bloody stubborn, girl? Just say you're sorry for once, and he'll let you be.'

'Yes, that's right, say you're sorry,' bellowed Tom, still trying to hit her with his spear, while Clare and Kate and Davidson grabbed hold of his arm to stop him, and dragged him slowly away from his cowering daughter. 'Say you're sorry, you bad bad girl.'

Trueheart climbed to her feet again, though she was bleeding from the side of her mouth and had a big red weal across her arm.

'Say you're sorry,' Tom kept shouting. Clare and the others were still holding onto him but they could tell that the fight had gone out of him, and they were beginning to loosen their grip. 'Or would you prefer to run after your darling Headmanson back there, and his pretty slip-buddy Teacher Gerry?'

Trueheart didn't answer him. She was close to tears, but she refused to let herself give way to them. She just turned away from her father and carried on walking towards Davidstand, clutching her hurt arm with her hand. The rest of us walked on as well, almost in silence, except for the mums like me who were murmuring to our tired scared crying kids to try and calm them down again. Wearily wearily we trudged on towards Davidstand, though we had no idea what we'd do there, or how we'd put food in our mouths.

I didn't say it aloud, but I thought to myself that it might have been better to have taken the Johnfolk's offer and gone back to Michael's Place to live under their protection. We knew how to feed ourselves there, after all.

But then again, we had to think about what the guards would say about that, if they managed to drive the Johnfolk out again. We had to think about what they would say, and how they'd treat us, if they thought we'd gone over to the Johnfolk in any way.

Fourteen

Way way up rockway, me and Mary came to the ground called Rockway Edge, where Wide Forest and Worldpool come together like the fingers of two hands sliding in between one another, so that forest and water lie side by side in narrow bands: forest, water, forest, water, shining, glowing, shining. The guards that had been with us since we met the Hiding People turned and rode back into their ground and new ones from Rockway Edge began to ride with us. I rode our buck while Mary strode along beside me to stretch out her legs.

Long ago, Mary told me, the people in Rockway Edge used to be Johnfolk. There'd been a little group of them up here, as far rockway as you can go, a bit like the other lot way down alpway at Brown River, at far end of Wide Forest. But there hadn't been so many up here as there were down there. So, while the Brown River lot had managed to keep their own Headman and their own ground and their own story, up here at Rockway Edge, Great David's son, Harry Stonehand, had been able to surround the Johnfolk with so many guards that they had no chance of either beating him or getting away from him. Stonehand had given them a choice. Either their blokes could fight him until none of them were left alive – in which case he'd take all the women and kids to be helpers and bedwarmers for him and his leaders, and send good Davidfolk up to live on their ground and in their shelters – or they could agree to turn their backs on John and come back to True Family – in which case they could keep their shelters and carrying on living here as they'd done before.

'He gave the Edgefolk two wakings to decide,' Mary said. 'He even had horns blown to mark the time. One blast at the beginning of each waking, two in middle, and three when the waking was done. The whole first waking went by and nothing came back to him. Then the second waking came. The first horn blew. Nothing. The two blasts blew. Nothing. But right at the end of that second waking, just as Harry's guard was blowing the third of the three horn blasts, the Headman of Rockway Edge came and knelt down in front of Harry and told him his people would come back to the Family of Gela.'

Mary'd had enough of walking now, so she climbed up on the buck behind me, and we began to ride out onto one of those narrow fingers of ground, in between two fingers of water. There were strange creatures here. Three small bucks ran across our path and dived into the water, heading down into the shiny wavyweed, as easily as if water was where they always lived. Their four hind feet had skin stretched between their toes so they could use them like paddles as well as walk on them, and they didn't use their front legs as legs for walking or swimming at all, but held them out before themselves, like the arms of a fish.

'The wonderful thing,' Mary said, 'is that the Edgefolk have ended up truer and better Davidfolk than anyone. As best they can when they're so far away, they try and mark the Virsry every year at the time it's marked at Circle Valley, and at each Virsry they have a special way of remembering how they were Johnfolk in the past and how they used to follow a story that was a lie. Every one of the young men whose new hairs have finished growing since the last Virsry lets himself be tied to a spiketree, just as Great David always said should have happened to John. Every single one of them! They're tied to the hot tree for a whole minute – the people count out the sixty heartbeats – long enough for most of the skin to be burnt right off their backs. Imagine the courage to do that! Imagine the love they must feel for Gela and her True Family! But for the rest of their lives, the men carry those scars with pride.'

'We surely do,' said one of the two young guards who were riding with us. With a big smile, he proudly pulled his wrap down off his shoulders so we could see the pink twisted skin on his back. His mate did the same, both of them beaming happily.

Mary laughed loudly. 'I *love* these guys, Angie! Down in Veekle-house, a man would be ashamed of scars like that because it would show he'd done something wrong and been punished, but up here, they're proud proud of them. And quite right too! What could be better proof that they've turned away from John and back to Gela? Let's just hope that one waking, all the Johnfolk in Eden will be as brave as them.'

It didn't seem possible to me that these people could have changed in two wakings from believing one story was true, to believing another. I thought it was pretty obvious that they'd just pretended to change their minds so as to save themselves, and I was kind of surprised that Mary couldn't see that, seeing as she was older than me, and so much smarter, and so much wiser about people. In fact I wasn't just surprised. I was actually a bit shaken by her saying something so silly and dumb. I'd given up my old friends and family for this woman and, as long as I travelled round with her, there was little chance of my making new friends or finding a new family. I'd shut away a whole big part of my life that I knew she wouldn't approve of. I'd set aside all the old stories I'd grown up with. And all of that was based on her being smart smart, and seeing things I couldn't see.

'We humans are clever, aren't we, with the stories we tell our-selves?' I finally said, when the guards were up ahead and out of hearing distance. 'Harry Stonehand shamed those people, beat them, made them feel small small. But, even though they *were* beaten, they found a way of turning that round, and making them-selves feel big and strong all over again.'

There was an uncomfortable silence for a moment. I'd come at this from a direction Mary wasn't expecting, and she wasn't sure what to make of it.

'Yeah,' she finally answered, a little doubtfully. 'Yeah, I guess so.' Then she smiled. She *was* smart, and she too had figured out a way of turning a story round. 'And quite right too,' she said happily. 'Because of course it's *not* being beaten when you come back to True Family. It's winning. It's always winning. Because it's joining the side that's bound to win in the end.'

She leaned forwards, put an arm round me to pull me against her and kissed my cheek from behind. It seemed like I'd worried her a bit for a moment there, but now she felt as sure and confident as ever. 'What you've got to remember, Angie dear, is that when people are wrong, they know it deep down. It's hard to admit to being wrong of course, but it's always a relief as well.'

Well, that shut me up, because I knew it was true only too well. I knew I had things that I ought to tell her about, and I knew it was wrong that I didn't. So I felt badly about that, as I always did, whenever I thought about it. And yet in a funny way, I was *pleased* I felt bad, because it meant that Mary was right, and that what she'd said about the Rockway people made sense after all. And *that* meant I didn't have to have doubts about the reasons for my choosing to be with her.

We came to Harry's Rest, which was the Edgefolk's biggest cluster. Everyone seemed pleased pleased to see us – I guess they didn't have many visitors up there – and after we'd been given a big meal and had a good long sleep in one of their shelters, Mary put on a fine show in front of one of the most excited crowds I'd yet seen. Mary was quite right about the Edgefolk. Whatever their reasons for giving up John and turning to David, they didn't seem to have any doubts about it now.

As usually happened when we put on a show in the main cluster of a guard leader's ground, the leader himself came along. He was a man called Mike and it so happened that we'd heard from two three of the women who'd fed us when we arrived that he was a cruel man. Out of the hearing of guards, they'd told us that he expected any girl who took his fancy to come to his shelter and take his dick, and he didn't take it well if any woman tried to say no. The women took a risk telling us that, seeing how shadowspeakers were often close to the high people, but Mary had a reputation for being honest, and I guess they hoped she'd say something in her show about how high men should behave, seeing as shadowspeakers always spoke about things that people were doing wrong.

But Mary didn't speak about it in the show. She spoke about how she admired the Edgefolk, and she picked out a few of their lower people for a telling-off – there was a young woman who slipped with more than one man, a man who held back from giving his share to the guards, an old woman who, so it was said, had told her granddaughters the Secret Story – but she said nothing at all about the guard leader who, so it seemed to me, had behaved much worse than any of them.

'Mary,' I said to her later, when we were riding on to another cluster, and the guards were too far ahead of us to hear, 'can I ask you about something I've noticed? How come when you speak to people about the bad things they do, you only ever pick on low people? High people do bad things too, don't they? That Leader Mike isn't the only one. And surely Gela doesn't like high men who behave like that any more than she likes low ones?'

Mary laughed. It was a special loud bright laugh that she used – or so it seemed to me – when I said something that was kind of smart, but at the same time kind of showed up the things that I still didn't understand. There was a little bit of annoyance in it, I could tell, but then it wasn't really surprising that she'd sometimes be irritated by my slowness, or cross with me for questioning what she did.

'You *do* have sharp eyes, Angie, and you're quite right too. Often high people do the *worst* things. Of course they do, because there's no one there to stop them. And Gela cries for them, she really does, but at the same time she tells me to be careful, because if I criticize them they may send me away from their ground, and then I won't be able to help *anyone* there at all. It worries me and it worries our Mother, but of course it's the high people themselves who lose out in the end.'

She was sitting in front of me on our buck, but now she looked round and took one of my hands in hers.

'Don't ever think I'm on the side of the high people against the low ones, Angie, because you couldn't be more wrong! Really you couldn't! Gela cares most about the people whose life is the hardest: low people, women, batfaces, clawfeet.'

I smiled and nodded. I was reassured. It kind of made sense what she said, and I accepted that she understood these things much better than me. And, like I said before, no one could accuse Mary of not believing in what she did.

After we'd been round the clusters of Rockway Edge, we turned alpway again and made our way slowly back towards Veeklehouse by another path, down through middle of Wide Forest, once again zigzagging back and forth to take in as many clusters as possible.

One of the clusters was called Hot Pools, because it was near to a place where water came bubbling up from Underworld into strange yellow pools that were boiling hot, so that the people who lived there could cook their meat without even needing to make a fire: they'd just wrap it up tight in a special greased skin and lower it into the water on a string. These pools had no life or light in them at all, apart from a kind of wobbling jelly that grew round their edges and, with no wavyweed growing in them, they were only lit by the trees round them. Yet they seemed to have a life of their own, bubbling and roaring and pouring out clouds of warm steam that rose up to the black sky with a strange, slightly rotten smell, like nothing I'd ever smelled before.

Hot Pools was a sad sad place when we arrived. Just two wakings before, a little girl, two three years old, had wandered off and fallen into one of those boiling pools. Of course, when the people heard her scream, it was already too late, and by the time they'd managed to fish her, or most of her, out of the boiling water with sticks and hooks tied to strings, her poor little body was already cooked and falling apart, not a child any more, or a human being, but just a mess of flesh and hair and bones. Although I didn't know back then, as I do now, what it was like to lose your own child, I did have some idea how this must have felt for the twenty thirty people who lived at Hot Pools, because I could remember how it had been back on Knee Tree Grounds when someone drowned, or (as happened to my friend Starlight's mother when we were little children) was taken by the spearfishes that, once in a while, would wander in from the deeper water and grab people who were cutting bark or gathering waternuts. It's like the whole world has been poisoned when something like that happens. Nothing means anything any more, and you hate and hate this miserable dark dark Eden where people should never have come.

Mary decided straight away not to put on one of her usual shows. She just sat down in middle of the cluster, with her arm round the mum of the little girl – the woman was scarcely more than a kid herself – and talked to the Hot Pools people like a friend. She told them how Mother Gela never let go, however bad things were. She told them how that little girl's shadow had flown to Earth and come alive again, as alive as she'd ever been. She told them Gela would look after that little girl, and dry her tears, and make her forget those few dreadful heartbeats between her fall into the boiling water and her death.

'This whole world is a story,' Mary told them. 'And just like in any story, everything has a purpose, even the sad things. Everything's connected to everything else. It really is, my dears. As long as you keep your heart open to our Mother, you will be holding a string that stretches off into the future, on and on, through times and places you can't yet see, some of them happy but many of them sad, until at last it reaches your true home, where bad things won't happen any more and the happiness is there for good. Remember that. Of course it won't take away your sadness now, but it will remind you that sadness doesn't go on forever. Hold onto that string, however bad things are, and there will always be a way back home at the end for all of Gela's true children.'

Judging by their faces, they didn't fully understand what she meant but they could tell that Mary believed it completely and they could see, as I'd seen myself when I went to that show of hers on Knee Tree Grounds, that she was smart and strong and brave, and had driven out all the weak little doubts and fears that most of us have inside ourselves. And so they believed her, or believed her enough at any rate to get some sort of comfort from her words, some sort of sense that the world did still have some point even if they couldn't quite understand it themselves.

Again and again, I saw Mary do that for people: bind the world together again for them when it had broken apart, give them something to hold onto when things were empty and pointless and cruel, lay out for them, like she said, a kind of string to hold onto. It wouldn't change how things were right now, it wouldn't take away their pain, but it led to a far off place where the pain would be taken away.

It's no good pretending that I didn't sometimes have doubts about the things that Mary said and did. Well, how could I not, when I'd grown up with people who thought the whole shadow-speaker thing was a trick to fool people? But again and again, when I had those doubts, I'd see her helping people, like she helped the people at Hot Pools, and the doubts would just blow away. Doubts were a kind of weakness, that was all.

'When your stomach is sick,' Mary would sometimes say, 'the sickness seems to fill up the world, and it's hard to hold in your mind that you'll soon be well again. When you're cold, it's hard to believe you'll ever be warm. When you're lonely, you feel like you'll never have friends. But these things do pass, and so will the sadness of Eden, just as long as you stay strong, and believe in Mother Gela.'

By the time we reached Veeklehouse, the better part of a year had gone by since we were last there. It was still only the third time I'd ever visited the place, but I knew from the last time that when you went away from a place, it stored up all the feelings you had when you were there before, and gave them back to you again when you returned, all at once, all wrapped up together. And they were lonely feelings that Veeklehouse had been keeping for me, not just from the first time when Starlight left me there, and all the excitement we'd shared about going there had all turned to grief, but from that time a year ago, when I'd got that news of Starlight and then had no one to share it with. Here was the shame I'd felt about not being truthful with Mary. Here was anger at Mary – I'd hardly noticed it at the time, but here it was – for not being the kind of person I could just talk to about Starlight, without it being all complicated and hard. And here was doubt and worry too, about whether I'd done the right thing to leave my home and give up all my family and friends for the sake of this one single person who I was afraid to share things with that I'd happily have shared with anyone on Knee Tree Grounds.

Mary was tired tired from travelling, and from a long string of shows with hardly a break between them, and she lay down for a rest. Straight away I hurried to the cliff as I'd done last time. I knew I'd never tell Mary where I'd been or why – she'd have seen no good reason for talking to Johnfolk, unless I was trying to persuade them to come back to True Family – and I felt badly about that, but I went anyway. There was a part of me, it seemed, that just didn't fit in with how Mary wanted me to be. There were hungers that Mary couldn't feed, and wouldn't even recognize as being real.

I soon found some traders over from New Earth, and I got talking to one of their paddle-men. He had clawfeet, like my Dave, but his arms were thick and strong. Being a paddle-man is a good job for someone who can barely walk.

'I used to be friends with a woman called Starlight,' I said. 'She crossed the water to New Earth. Last time I was here, one of you blokes told me she was the Ringwearer or something...'

I was looking for the nice warm feeling I got last time from hearing about my friend and seeing how impressed the New Earthers were that I knew her. But, before I'd even finished speaking, I could tell that it wasn't going to be that way this time round. The clawfoot man was quite friendly at first, but as soon as he understood that I was a friend of Starlight's he became hostile and harsh.

'The *False* Ringwearer, you mean? The one that came over from here and tried to steal our ring? The one that told wicked lies, with our Mother's ring on her finger?'

I was so shocked that at first I just gaped at him, not knowing what to say.

'What do you mean *wicked lies*?' I asked at last.

'Have you heard of the Secret Story?'

I did my best to look like I hadn't.

'Well, maybe you don't have it over here, but it's a pack of lies that silly women whisper to each other. If they get caught they're sent straight to the fire, and serve them right. But your Starlight seemed to think she was above all of that. She didn't just tell a girl or two, like other whisperers do, she shouted it out to whole crowds of people, up and down our ground: men, women, children, everyone who came to see her. But she got what was coming to her in the end. You won't be seeing your little buddy again, I'm afraid, holeface. No one knows for certain what actually did for her, but she washed up way down alpway from here near Brown River with her lungs full of water and a big old spear hole through her.'

'What? Starlight, you mean? You mean she's—?'

'That's right, holeface, I mean she's dead. Looks like she had a quarrel with one of her stonehead mates, and either died from the wound or drowned.' He'd been avoiding looking at me, but now he gave me a little sideways glance to see how I was taking it. He spat and shrugged. 'I guess it's hard to hear if she really was your friend, but I'm afraid it served her right, the little slinker.'

'But Greenstone—'

'That weak fool of a Headman who brought her over? He got what he deserved as well. He should never have been Headman in first place and nor should his dad either. Greenstone ended up in the fire, that's what happened to him. The big big fire that no one ever comes out of. It's Headman Dixon in charge now, and quite right too. He's a good strong man, and a proper Head. And his woman Lucy's a proper Ringwearer as well.'

The man stood up, turned his back to me, and hobbled over to talk to a friend of his. He didn't want anything more to do with a friend of the False Ringwearer.

I made my way slowly back to Mary. I felt like my whole body was packed as tightly with tears as a spiketree is packed with boiling sap. And yet I couldn't talk to Mary about it. She'd have no sympathy with someone who went over to the Johnfolk and wore that ring for them, let alone someone who spread the Secret Story. I remembered how Mary had given comfort to the people at Hot Pools whose little girl had died, how she'd comforted grieving people in little clusters right up and down the Davidfolk Ground, but I knew she wouldn't be able to give that comfort to me. That wasn't because she'd want to be unkind to me. It was because Mary knew without any doubt that anyone who'd turned away from Gela's True Family would never find their way home. Starlight would wander forever through the dark icy forest of the stars.

Daughter of Eden   99

'But perhaps Starlight was bringing the ring back for True Family?' I whispered to myself. 'Perhaps in the end she saw what was right, like those people did up at Rockway Edge?'

But, however hard I tried, I couldn't persuade myself that this was true. It wasn't just that Starlight had had no time in the past for shadowspeakers, and had laughed loudly at the stories they told. After all, the same had been true of me. No, it was because I knew Starlight was way too firm and strong to ever change her mind about a thing like that.

And that was a strange thought, because what was I really saying? Was I saying I only believed this stuff because I was weak?

Mary saw I was sad, of course. She'd had a lot of practice of spotting people who were sad or uneasy in themselves, and she was good good at it, even when the people were complete strangers to her.

'You're sad, aren't you, my dear?' she said. 'Coming to Veeklehouse has made you sad sad.'

I nodded, and then I couldn't help myself any more and all those tears came pouring out as Mary took me in her arms. But I didn't tell her about Starlight. I told her instead that coming back to Veeklehouse made me sad because it reminded me of my friends from Knee Tree Grounds who'd been with me when I first came here, and it made me miss my old home and my family.

'Of course you miss them, my darling one,' Mary murmured as she gently rocked me in her arms. 'Of course you do! And I promise you we'll go back there to see them. But let's wait for a while longer, if you can bear it. If you can hold on that long, I'd like to go back there when we've done that trip up to Circle Valley, and you're a shadowspeaker in your own right. And we're not quite ready for that. You're learning fast, but you're still learning, still full of worries and doubts, though I know you're working hard hard hard at sorting them out. If we do another round of shows in Wide Forest,

I reckon when we come back here again we'll be ready to go up to the Circle. We'll go across the Dark, and when we come back over, you'll be a shadowspeaker like me, and we can go over the water to that pretty grounds of yours as two shadowspeakers together.'

I nodded through my tears, and she reached up and kissed me on my tear-stained cheek, pressing me close against her short solid body.

'But that's only if you can wait that long, my darling,' Mary asked me. 'Do you think you can? Do you think you can leave it that long before you see your people in Knee Tree Grounds? If you don't think so, just say, and we'll go up there now.'

'Let's go now!' I longed to say. Why not now? Why did I have to be a shadowspeaker first? But I felt guilty because I knew I was hiding things from her, I knew I was only telling her a small part of the real reason for my tears. And for that reason alone, knowing I was letting her down and wanting to make up for it, I said the thing that I knew would please her.

'Yes, of course, Mary,' I said. 'Of course I can wait.'

Fifteen

Davidstand was taut and jangling with fear. All of that big square space between the L-shaped pool and the L-shaped fence was packed with people who'd come, like us, from poolside. They were crammed in under the trees between the shelters of the people who normally lived there, some of them with eyes screwed up, trying to sleep, some talking together in tense low voices, some hunched over fires as they cooked up slinkers and bats and ants and whatever other scraps they'd been able to find to eat. They eyed us warily as we came through. Who were we? Where did we come from? What had we seen? Why had we chosen to come here when each new arrival just made things harder for them?

The first place we tried to stop, a bunch of Davidstand men came over with big sticks in their hands and told us we couldn't stay there, it was their ground. So much for the Davidfolk being one big Family. The exact same thing happened the second time round, just as Kate and Clare had finally managed to get a fire going. Tom and Davidson picked up their spears and began to growl that they'd been guards here for years, and deserved some respect, but Clare and Kate pulled them away from the Davidstand men. We abandoned our fire and found yet another patch of ground, right under the fence, to put down our babies and our loads, hand out small bits of dried meat to our kids to chew on, unpack our bucks, and start the business of firelighting all over again with those little pots of embers that had to be gently gently coaxed into glowing and smouldering again before they would make flames. All round us other small fires were crackling under the trees, and other low tense worried voices were asking the same questions that we asked ourselves: What were we going to eat? How far away were the John-folk? Where would we go when our meat ran out?

When my kids were as settled as they could be, I walked over to some people nearby. They told me they'd come from near David Water, a fishing cluster on poolside, some distance down alpway from Veeklehouse, where I'd been a couple of times with Mary. The Johnfolk had attacked there too, it seemed, as well as Veeklehouse. Twenty boats, they said, had grounded there. Last they'd seen of David Water was the smoke rising from their burning shelters.

'And the worst part is that Strongheart doesn't know about it!' one of them said, a clawfoot woman about the same age as Clare.

'He doesn't *know*?'

'He doesn't know about any of this at all. He's not here.'

Gela's heart, that was a big shock. I felt sick and empty inside. All of us had imagined Strongheart and his sons here in Davidstand, figuring out how to drive the Johnfolk back into the Pool. We'd talked about it on our long walk over here. We'd comforted ourselves with the thought that, even as we trudged along, our Head Guard was working out how to get us back home again. We'd told one another, over and over, that the place we were going was the one place, more than any other, that Strongheart would keep safe.

'He's gone to the four hundredth Virsry at Circle Valley,' the woman told me, watching my face with that funny pleasure people take in giving bad news. 'He was long gone by the time we arrived here. Guards have been sent after them, of course, on fast fast bucks, but they can't possibly have reached them yet.'

Strongheart had taken Leader Mehmet and Leader Hunter with him as well, she told me, his first and third sons. They'd be on their bucks now, up on Snowy Dark, making their way to Circle Valley to join Strongheart's second son, Leader Harry, who was guard leader up there and was getting things ready for the Virsry. So it wasn't just Strongheart who didn't know. All four of the highest men in the Davidfolk Ground knew nothing at all about the Johnfolk attacking us.

A whole crowd of people had gone with them, so the woman had heard. The four hundredth Virsry was a big big thing, and, for the first time ever, the Headman of Brown River and the Head Woman of Half Sky had been invited to come to it. Strongheart had taken his two newest shelterwomen, Jane and Flowerlight – Jane was pregnant, and Flowerlight had a small baby – and Mehmet and Hunter had each brought one of their women, along with about thirty helpers and forty of the guards that we'd been thinking would be here to protect us.

'They went off as happy as anything, apparently,' the woman said, 'with horns blowing and drums thumping. The high women chucked out handfuls of stumpcandy for the kids to run after. The high men chucked out trading sticks. And all the while those ringmen were coming towards us across the Pool.'

I dreaded bringing this news back to the others so much that I put it off for a bit by walking to see what other news I could gather. It was a strange thing. I'd been brought up on the Grounds to think of Strongheart as a cruel man who would willingly do for people if they so much as questioned him or criticized him or stood in his way. And he really was. Even the Michael's Place people, and the folk I talked to when I was in Veeklehouse, would complain about how much stuff he took from them and how little he let them keep, even though they were Davidfolk. 'Those high people are all the same,' they'd say, 'they just look after themselves.' And yet still, in a time like this, we all looked to Strongheart to protect us, like he was some kind of kind wise granddad, and we were little kids.

More little fires, more scared exhausted faces. Guards were riding about on bucks, trying to look important but not really knowing what to do. Davidstand people were frightened that all these strangers from poolside would try and take what was theirs, and so their men clutched sticks and spears and glared out at us from their solid shelters whenever we went too near to them. Poolside people were worried that the Davidstand folk would throw them out, and so *their* men clutched sticks and spears too, daring the Davidstand men to even think about it. And everyone, from Davidstand or poolside, worried that no one was in charge, no one was telling them what was happening, or what was being done, or what they were supposed to do.

When I spoke to other poolside people, I heard stories about the Johnfolk. We'd been lucky lucky it seemed. The ringmen hadn't been as kind with others as they'd been with us. One time, in a cluster near David Water, a bunch of them had caught some guards trying to sneak up on them, and tied them to spiketrees to scream and burn. And when a woman in the cluster had run forwards to untie them – she was the granny of one of the guards – they'd pulled off her wrap and tied her to a tree as well. In another cluster, just alpway of Veeklehouse, the people had foolishly refused to bow down to the Johnfolk, and the New Earthers had done for everyone they could get their hands on, cutting the throats of oldies and little kids with their long cruel metal knives. And in not just one but many clusters the ringmen had gathered everyone together and made them watch while they pissed and crapped over their precious circles of stones, and then danced in middle, where no one was supposed to go except high people and shadowspeakers, lifting up their fakeskin wraps to show their arses and their dicks.

'So what's our plan?' Clare asked, when I got back to the others.

I hadn't passed on all the stories I heard – Candy had run to me and climbed into my arms as soon as she saw me, and Fox was right beside me, listening listening listening – but I'd told her that Strongheart and his sons were up on the Dark, heading for the Virsry at Circle Valley, and that they were going to meet the high people from Brown River and Half Sky.

'We're not going to find any food round here,' my Dave fretted, tugging anxiously at his straggly grey beard. 'And now it looks like we won't be safe from the ringmen here either.'

'The guards will still fight, won't they,' said Clare's sister Kate, 'even if Strongheart isn't here? Maybe they'll feed us too?'

'Don't think there's much chance of that,' said Kate's man, Davidson. 'They've got a fight on. They need the food for themselves.'

'So what are we going to do then?' asked Little Harry. (We called him that because he was tall tall tall.)

We all looked at Tom. He was our cluster head, after all, even if he didn't know any better than anyone else what was happening, or what our options were.

Tom passed the stump of his right wrist over his mouth. He gave a little sideways glance at Clare in that funny furtive way he had, half-hoping she'd make a suggestion, half-warning her not to. But Clare's face told him nothing at all.

'Well…' he began, and then hesitated. 'Well, I reckon we should go on to Circle Valley.'

It was the obvious choice. Where else was there to go? But Kate was appalled.

'*What?* Take our kids across the Dark? No way! There's snow there, and ice, and big white leopards that sneak up and eat people. You can't even see them coming!'

'I've been across it before,' I told her. 'It's different these wakings from how it used to be. The guards have put up big poles in the snow to show the way across.'

'Yes,' said Tom, who'd been there too when he was a guard. 'And so many people go back and forth that the path is clear to see anyway, even without the poles, except when there's been a new fall of snow. There are even little shelters every few miles, with guards on watch, and fires.'

'That's true,' said Davidson, who'd also been there as a guard, 'but it's still as cold as it ever was, and cold like that will do for you if you're not prepared for it.'

'We've got some woollybuck skins,' Clare said. 'We can make

some bodywraps and headwraps and footwraps. I know how. I made them for Tom when he was a guard. We just need some grease for the footwraps.'

'What about snowleopards?' asked Trueheart, who'd been standing on the edge of this talk between the grownups, not quite part of it, but not quite outside of it with the kids either. She came to stand beside me. She had a cut in the corner of her mouth where her dad had hit, a big dark bruise round her left eye, and an ugly weal on her arm, with the skin split open along most of its length.

'Honestly, Trueheart,' I said, 'they're hardly any danger.' As I spoke I was aware of my Fox's big scared eyes, waiting desperately to be told why he should not be scared of snowleopards. Gela's heart, if only it was just snowleopards he had to fear, I thought, and not ringmen with metal knives and heads full of hate. 'I never saw even one leopard when I crossed with Mary. She'd been that way many times herself and she told me she'd never seen one once.'

'Yes, they keep out of people's way these wakings,' Tom said, 'now there are men up there who trap them and hunt them for their—'

'And anyway, they're afraid of loud noises, aren't they, Mum?' Fox interrupted in that funny false shouting voice he put on when he wanted to show he wasn't scared. 'If I see one, I'll just chase it away!'

'Okay.' Kate frowned. 'So the leopards don't do for us, and nor does the cold. But suppose we get to Circle Valley, and then the Johnfolk follow us there as well? They wanted the Veekle. Won't they want the Circle too?'

'John didn't like the Circle, though, did he?' began Dave. 'He destroyed it, remember, and Lucy Lu had to—'

'Oh Gela's heart,' muttered Trueheart, 'not *more* old stories.'

No matter how often her dad hit her, she would not give up.

'Perhaps we should wait here for the Johnfolk,' Little Harry said. No one had yet spoken that thought among us, though I'm sure I wasn't the only one who'd had it before. Yes, the ringmen had been cruel, but wasn't that only to people who tried to stand up to them? 'Or even go back to Michael's Place and accept that Headmanson Luke as our new leader. They can't do for *all* of us, can they? And at least we'd have enough to eat.'

Several people had tried to interrupt him angrily while he was still speaking, and now they began talking all at once.

'Have you gone mad, Harry?' shouted Davidson. 'Have you forgotten we're Davidfolk?'

'No way!' growled Tom. 'No way will I ever live among ring-stealers!'

'Yes, and didn't you hear what the ringmen did at David Water?' demanded Kate. 'Men, women, newhairs, kids… That woman just over there told me she'd heard they chucked babies in the air for a game, and caught them on the end of their spears.'

Oh well done, Kate, I thought, as Fox and Candy turned to me in terror. That was a smart smart thing to say!

Squatting on the ground in the background, Flame gave a little gasp and clutched baby Suzie against her tiny breasts. She never spoke when the whole family was together. The older women always talked over her, and she'd learned that if she ever did manage to get a word in, they'd just pour scorn on what she said.

'And they're cruel to low people,' Davidson said. 'They're cruel even to their *own* low people. I spoke to one of their paddle-men once, when he'd had too much badjuice. He said the low people over there have to dig for metal all waking long in little holes deep under the ground, too small to stand up in or even to sit up straight. You need big big fires, apparently, to burn the metal out of the rock, so they cut down all the trees, all the trees in a whole valley, until the only light and warmth comes from fires and lamps. It's almost as dark and cold in the clusters round those holes, this bloke told me, as it is up in the ice and snow, but they still have to live there when they're not underground, never seeing proper treelight from one waking to the next.'

'I bet those are just stories,' muttered Trueheart, but so quietly that only I could hear. 'I bet they say things like that about us as well.'

'We're going to Circle Valley,' Tom decided. 'Not now, but in a couple of wakings, when we've have time to make ourselves some warm bodywraps.'

'Quite right, Tom,' Davidson said. 'It's the only way we can go. And if the Johnfolk do follow us over there, I've heard there's a path over the Dark on the other side of Circle Valley too, over the Blue Mountains, to Half Sky.'

Tom snorted. No one ever mentioned Half Sky in Michael's Place without one or other of the men snorting like that and making some kind of joke. I knew hardly anything about the place, but I'd heard you got there by going down to Brown River, and then paddling up the river itself right through middle of Snowy Dark and round the other side. Only other thing I really knew about it was that it was Tina Spiketree who first took people there, about the time that Jeff and his followers came out to Knee Tree Grounds, and for the same reason: to try and get away from the fight between the Davidfolk and Johnfolk. Sometimes you heard the Half Sky people spoken of as the Tinafolk. Not that people spoke much of them at all.

'What?' said Tom. 'To the Women's Ground? To let women boss me round? You must be joking! No way would I—'

'They have Head Women and Headmen both, from what I've heard,' Clare said, 'and a Council that has men and women in equal numbers. And anyway, if it's such a stupid useless place, how come Strongheart himself has invited their high people to the four hundredth Virsry?'

But Tom took no notice of that. 'No way am I ever going to live in a Women's Ground,' he repeated firmly, glancing half-angrily and half-guiltily, first at Clare, and then at Trueheart, daring them to argue.

'Me neither!' said his brother, my Dave. 'We get bossed round by women way too much already if you ask me.'

'Okay, okay,' Clare soothed them. 'But if we don't like their ground, we could find our own place over there. There's lots of space, so I've been told. There's a whole big forest on far side of the Dark that's every bit as big as Wide Forest. We could find ourselves a new Michael's Place, with no high people there to tell us what to do. Whether men *or* women.'

Flame giggled, that poor lonely girl. She might be Tom's second shelterwoman but she was squatting there on the ground behind the rest of the grownups, almost like she was just another kid. 'No high people,' she said. 'That sounds good to me.'

'It does, doesn't it?' I came in quickly, mainly to stop one of the other women crushing her as they often did. 'The trouble with high people is that they think the story is all about them.'

Tom frowned at me, not quite sure what I meant, but not liking the way this was going. 'Anyway,' he said, 'that's something to think about another time. For now, we're going to Circle Valley.'

He brightened up a bit. 'Maybe it's good that Strongheart is going to meet the guy from Brown River. Those Riverfolk play a clever game, you know. Sometimes they offer their friendship to the other Johnfolk in New Earth, and sometimes they offer it to us Davidfolk. You can't trust them of course – you can't trust anyone that follows John – but maybe if Strongheart talks to their head guy, he can persuade him to line up with us and not with New Earth.'

He gave that snort again. 'Same for the Women's Ground, I guess. Whatever we might think of that place, we certainly don't want the New Earthers getting round there.'

Sixteen

Me and Mary set out from Veeklehouse and did another big loop, over to Davidstand, and then back to poolside and down alpway again towards the White Streams. In each little cluster Mary would walk out into whatever kind of circle they'd laid out on the ground – it might be six yards wide and made of rocks as big as heads, it might be a little ring of pebbles just big enough for one person to stand in – and speak to however many people were there. She'd sense their mood, pick up the things they were worried about and feared, the things they felt guilty and ashamed about, the things they loved or longed for. She'd let those feelings build inside herself: one woman holding all the hopes and fears of a whole cluster, and then, so she explained to me – and I saw it happen for myself – she let their feelings wake up her *own* longings and fears until she was so full of all those powerful feelings that she couldn't hold them inside herself any more and they came bursting out. And that meant everyone could see that what came pouring out of her was real. Everyone could see she wasn't acting or playing a part, but living out for all of us the way we felt.

And yet, even though she wasn't acting, she was riding those feelings skilfully, like some of the kids back on Knee Tree Grounds used to ride the waves that came rolling in from Deep Darkness when a storm was coming, to break on the edge of our little water forest. She would pace about, fall to her knees, stand up again, cry, laugh, and then look into people's eyes and, without even hesitating, boldly tell them what was going on inside of them. Words would pour from her: warnings, bright flashes of truth that suddenly came to her, words of comfort, tellings-off, messages of hope. Just as the kids who rode the waves would turn their little bark boats first this way and then that so as to keep the force of each wave behind them as long as possible, so Mary would move quickly from one thing to another, from grief to joy, from one person to the whole group and back to another person, somehow sensing the exact heartbeat when it was time to change. It was wonderful to watch. You couldn't help but be moved by it. You couldn't help admiring her smartness and her courage and her skill. And you couldn't help admiring how much she gave of herself, so that at the end of it, when we'd left the cluster and moved on, she'd be pouring with sweat, trembling, dazed. I just had to hold her sometimes, like you'd hold a child. I had to cook for her. I had to rub her shoulders and her neck to loosen her tense tense muscles. Sometimes I even had to feed her and make her open her mouth to take a drink.

I liked doing all that for her. I still couldn't believe that of all the people she could have chosen to look after her, from all across the Davidfolk Ground, she'd picked ordinary old me: batfaced Angie from Knee Tree Grounds. I was proud proud of that, desperate desperate to live up to it, afraid afraid that I wouldn't. But it was a strange life for me, all the same. The guards that rode with us came and went, changing over whenever we passed from the ground of one guard leader into the ground of another, and there was no one I could grow to know and feel at home with apart from Mary herself. It felt lonely lonely sometimes. I missed my family and my old friends. And sometimes, however much I tried not to, I couldn't help thinking of my friend Starlight and imagining the horror of her last moments, and it was like someone had shoved a spear through *me*, and I was writhing round on the tip of it, with no one anywhere to help me. But I still loved Mary, I still respected her, I still admired how hard she worked to hear what Mother Gela wanted to say and pass on her messages to the Davidfolk, I still liked how she hugged me and kissed my cheek, and told me I was beautiful and smart.

And yet I held things back from her. I didn't tell her I'd heard the Secret Story. I didn't tell her about Starlight and what she'd done. I didn't tell her I was proud of Starlight for becoming the Ringwearer of New Earth, even if that did mean wearing the stolen ring. I didn't tell her that I even felt proud of her for speaking the words of the Secret Story out loud. (How brave that had been, when the Johnfolk hated those words every bit as much as the Davidfolk, and you could be thrown into a fire for saying them!) I didn't tell her about Starlight's death, or about how I grieved for her.

I was often angry with myself for not telling her these things. I often told myself I was a coward, and that I was a fool to myself. I told myself I should trust Mary. I reminded myself what she'd said about how, deep down, we always know when we're doing the wrong thing and always feel relieved when we do the right thing, however scary it might be. I even told myself that holding these things back from her was like holding them back from Mother Gela herself.

'Of course you feel lonely,' I whispered to myself when I was alone, 'if you can't even share things with your closest friend.' But I just couldn't bring myself to tell her. I was afraid that if I did, she'd ask things of me that I didn't know how to give. And then she'd think less of me, and maybe decide I wasn't good enough after all to be a shadowspeaker like her, or not even good enough to be her helper.

The worst of it was that she kept praising me for my honesty.

'I've had helpers before,' she'd tell me, 'but never one like you. The others just wanted to learn shadowspeaking like it was some kind of trick, a bunch of things you had to remember to do in the right order, like building a shelter, or cooking a sweetbat with candy, or making a string for a bow. But you know it's nothing like that, don't you? That's why you ask questions, isn't it? That's why you tell me your doubts and your worries about what I do. Because you know it's not about doing this thing or that thing, it's about opening yourself up completely.'

I'd smile and nod, and tell her I did know that, and that I admired her courage for doing it so well, and she'd grab my hand and pull me towards her so she could look straight into my eyes.

'But you're like that too, Angie!' she'd say. 'That's what I keep telling you. You open yourself up as well. I spotted that straight away, as soon as I saw you. I saw you'd be more than a helper. I saw you could be my friend, my sister, my equal.'

🌿

We went right down to the White Streams this time, right to the edge of the Brown River Ground. There are many many shallow streams there, running side by side, joining each other and then branching away again. They run over beds of round white stones, with whitelantern trees hanging over them and making their white-ness shine up at the black black sky. All round is stony ground with white cliffs, and strange-shaped lumps of white glittery rock that stick up from forest, and here and there are dark dark patches, some of them half a mile wide, where this hard rock completely covers the ground without so much of a crack in it for trees to push through from Underworld, so there's no light at all, like that place called Night that Mary spoke about.

It's a long journey for the people down there to get to the rest of the Davidfolk Ground, but it's easy easy for them to go back and forth across those shallow streams to the Brown River Ground on the other side. So the Davidfolk cross the streams to trade with the people of the Brown River Ground – the people down there always just call them the Riverfolk – and the Riverfolk come back over and trade with them. In fact some of the Riverfolk have come to live among the Davidfolk, and some of the Davidfolk have moved the other way, and they all wear the same kind of wraps, and talk with the same kind of speech, so that I couldn't tell one from another.

But of course the Riverfolk people were Johnfolk. It was true they were different from the Johnfolk across the Pool. It was true that they'd been separated from those other Johnfolk for such a long time that their speech sounded more like Davidfolk speech than like the speech of New Earth, and it was true that they had their own Headman and their own stories, which were sometimes more like the Davidfolk stories than they were like the New Earthers'. But still they were Johnfolk. Their stories still said that John was the good guy in the Breakup, and Great David the bad guy, and that Gela was on the side of John, and led him to the ring.

'These people down here get muddled up sometimes,' Mary told me. 'They truly think of themselves as good Davidfolk, and they are at heart, I know. They're good good people. But living alongside Riverfolk all the time, they get muddled up and sometimes they tell stories that really come from John, without even knowing it. Part of our job here is to set them straight.'

To confuse things even more, there were a lot of Hiding People down there as well, people who'd slipped away into forest long ago, to keep out of the way of guards and ringmen, always on the move, hunting and scavenging among the shining trees without any clusters of their own. Mary said Hiding People was a good name for them. They were hiding away from the world, 'a bit like those Kneefolk of yours on their little grounds.' But, whether or not they were hiding from the world, when there were no guards round, the Hiding People came into the White Streams clusters to trade, just as the Riverfolk did, and brought in their own stories about giant bats and leopardmen to mingle with the others.

None of this stopped the White Streams folk from loving Mary's shows, though. Just like the Edgefolk up at Harry's Rest, they were excited excited to have her there. They shouted and cried, they fell to their knees, they raised their hands up to the black sky and thanked Mother Gela for bringing us to them, tears streaming down their faces. There was no doubt they loved Gela and wanted to hear from her, even though, when it came to the True Story, they had it all wrong in so many different ways.

One time, when we'd done a show right next to one of those white white streams, an old woman came up to Mary afterwards and asked her if Mother Gela would make her go to Earth when she died, even if she didn't want to go.

'Only I'd prefer it if my shadow could stay here,' she said, 'in some quiet place by the White Streams where it's peaceful, and I can stay near my family.'

'*Earth* is peaceful, my dear,' Mary told her. 'It's our true home. It's the place where all our troubles end.'

'Well, that's not what I've heard,' the old woman said. Her whole face was covered with wrinkles so deep that you couldn't see right down into them, and her breasts were like two little empty skin bags that have been soaked in water for way too long and then left out to dry. 'What about all those stories about trouble on Earth? Like the story of the white and black people, for instance. You know that one? About how the white people tied the black people up with ropes and made them work like they were bucks? Or the one about Hurter the Germ Man and how he killed the Juice People. They say he took their leader Jeez and hung him up from a—'

'My dear,' Mary gently interrupted, reaching out and touching the woman on the back of her spotty old hand. 'Those *are* stories from Earth, it's true, but they're only meant for fun. They're just silly stories for telling to children. I mean, white people and black people! Think about it. Have you ever seen anyone that was either white or black?'

The old woman considered this. 'But don't they say our Mother had black skin?' she asked.

Mary smiled. 'Her skin was dark, and Tommy's was light. But that doesn't mean that she was black like the sky or that he was white like these stones, and it doesn't mean there were two different kinds of people. I mean, look…' Mary held her arm against the old woman's. 'My skin is a bit lighter than yours, and Angie's here is darker. But you get that everywhere, don't you? The same as you get people with different colour eyes and hair. My eyes are grey, look, and yours and Angie's are brown. Everyone's different, but that doesn't mean there were ever black people and white people living apart from one another!'

She gave the old woman a friendly, teasing prod. 'What an idea! Next you'll be telling me there are green people and blue people!'

The woman giggled at that. Mary had shown her how she'd got the story wrong, but done it without shaming her or making her feel small or bad.

'You're so good at that,' I told her afterwards when it was just the two of us again beside our fire, the guards a little way off through the trees. 'You're so angry with people sometimes, but then with someone like that you're kind kind. You always seem to know which way will work best.'

'I only get angry with people if they ought to know better,' Mary said. 'I get angry if they know quite well what Gela wants from them but pretend they don't. But I can't blame people if they've been told the wrong stories and just don't understand. They're doing their best with what they've got, the same as you and me.'

'But how can you tell whether someone knows but pretends they don't, or whether it's just that they don't understand?'

'It's just practice, Angie, practice and hard work. You'll be just as good at it as I am one waking, or most likely even better. I'm so looking forward to that. I'm so looking forward to you and me being shadowspeakers together, talking about our work, trying together to understand the mind of our Mother.'

I don't know why, but I clearly remember that when we lay down to sleep that waking, I couldn't settle. I just couldn't stop myself from thinking about the people I used to know at Knee Tree Grounds and how far they were away from me, and I missed them so much I ached inside.

A tubeslinker stuck its head out of the airhole of the whitelantern tree above me. There were two bats hunting for flutterbyes round the tree's lanterns, and the slinker watched them as they dived and swooped. As it watched the bats, the slinker swayed from side to side, following their movements. And then suddenly one of the bats came too near and it sprung outwards. Two three feet of thin bony body came shooting out of that hole as it grabbed the bat in its jaws and held it tight. The bat thrashed about with its wings and waved its little arms about, but none of that stopped the slinker from dragging it back down into the hot sticky darkness inside the tree, crushing its wings as they were tugged inside the hole.

Eventually we came back to Veeklehouse again, my fourth visit this time, about a year on from the third. As she always did after a journey, Mary lay down for a rest and, once again, I walked over to the cliff. That's how it is, I've noticed, when you come back to a place where you've been before. Unless you make an effort to avoid it, you find yourself doing the exact same things you did last time you were there.

I went back to the cliff, but I wasn't looking for New Earthers this time. What would be the point of finding New Earthers to hear them mock my old friend, and laugh about her death? But since that time by the White Streams when I couldn't sleep, I'd been missing my home a lot. I knew it was going to be a long time yet before we went back there, but I thought that if I could at least have some news of Knee Tree Grounds, it would make the place feel a bit closer again. So instead of trying to find New Earth paddle-men, I sought out the Davidfolk paddle-men, the ones who took the traders from Veeklehouse up and down poolside to places like Rockway Edge, and David Water, and Brown River.

I must have spoken to twenty men on the ledge under the cliff where the boats were, but most of them hadn't even heard of Knee Tree Grounds, and the few that had heard of it had never been there. I knew I'd been away from Mary too long – she'd be waking up now, wondering where I was, and wanting me to help her get ready for her show – but I just couldn't bring myself to go back to her without having some news, so I kept on asking, until at last I did find a bloke who knew something.

'Knee Tree Grounds?' he said. He was an old guy with a long white beard. 'You're one of the people that used to live there, are you? I wondered what happened to you all.'

'What do you mean *to us all*? They're all still there apart from me!'

'They aren't, you know. You can see the remains of shelters, and the stones and ashes where the main fire used to be, and some writing on a tree. But the people have all gone.' He chuckled. 'I can't read myself but apparently the writing says: "We're really here", which is kind of funny when you think about it, seeing as there's no one there at all, unless you count all those fatbucks lying round on the sand. That's why I went there, in fact: to do for fatbucks and melt them down. These Veeklehouse lamps are always hungry. You wouldn't believe the amount of buckfat that's needed just to keep them all burning. Just as we were paddling out of the place, I remember, another bunch of guys came over to cut bark from those funny trees that bend over in middle. But apart from them, we didn't see anyone at all. There are a few guards over there, but they have their own camp they've made out on the peckway edge of the water forest. My boss paddled out to them with a couple of guys just to let them know who we were, but the rest of us didn't see them whole time we were there. Well, they're there to watch out for Johnfolk coming across Deep Darkness, aren't they? There wouldn't be much point in them sitting on the sand with the fatbucks, because you can't see anything with those big droopy trees in the water all round you. The guards have built a little grounds of their own out there out of sand and wood, my boss said, where they can look straight out towards Deep Darkness, and watch and wait. Of course, they've got a fast boat waiting ready all the—'

'Where have the people gone?'

'No one knows. I thought you'd—'

'Do you think someone has done for them?'

'I don't think it's that. The guards told my boss that they all just went, just disappeared for some reason, not telling anyone where they were going.'

Well, there was just one good thing about hearing that my home was no longer there, and that my mum and brothers and sisters and friends had all gone off somewhere where I might never find them. There was just one single good thing. At least this time I could tell Mary all about it, and not have to keep it a secret inside my head.

Mary was kind kind of course. She'd been about to put on a show, but now she told the Veeklehouse guards that it couldn't go ahead for another waking and they should send the people away. And then she held me curled up against her while I cried and cried.

'Mother Gela is watching you, remember,' she said, 'and she's watching all your old friends too. Never forget that. Just because they turned their backs on Gela doesn't mean she loves them any less. She's a mother, isn't she? And what mother loves her children less just because they're naughty and run away from her? You need to trust Gela, my dearest. When you trust her, that's when she can help you. Trust her, and I promise you she won't let you down.'

'Please forgive me for saying this, Mary,' I said, 'but I can't see Mother Gela, and I can't touch her. But I *could* touch those people, I could talk to them, I could see their faces.'

'I understand, dear one,' said Mary, still holding me close to her and gently gently rocking me. 'Of course I understand. We all need people we can touch.'

For a moment I felt grateful with Mary for understanding that we needed real people more than her precious Gela, but then I felt angry with her instead. It was all well and good her being nice and understanding now, but if she hadn't insisted that I stay away from the Grounds until I was a shadowspeaker, I would have gone there much sooner, and I might have got there in time to learn what the Kneefolk's plans were, and why they were leaving, and where it was they were all going to.

I didn't speak my anger out loud and if Mary had noticed any change in me at all, it would have been me suddenly tensing for a moment in her arms, arching my back away from her touch. But I quickly realized it wasn't really fair to blame Mary and pushed the anger out of my mind. She couldn't have known that the Kneefolk were suddenly going to leave a place where they'd lived for over two hundred years, any more than I could have done. And she hadn't really *insisted* that I didn't go back yet, either. She'd just suggested it. She'd just given it as her opinion that it might be better to wait, and asked me if I'd agreed. She'd even offered to go there sooner if I couldn't wait, and I knew quite well that she'd have done just that if I'd asked her. The only reason I *hadn't* asked her was that I'd been feeling guilty about things I hadn't told her.

'It just makes me feel so alone,' I told her. 'It makes me feel I'm all alone in Eden.'

'You're really not, you know. You have me here with you, for one thing, and you know I love you. And you have our Mother, the best person there is to have on your side, even if you can't yet touch her, watching every moment of every waking and every sleep.' I'd relaxed in her arms again now, and she bent over to kiss me on my head.

'I'm glad I've got you, Mary,' I told her, 'I really am, but it seems you're *all* I have now.'

'Well, you're all *I* have too, you know, Angie, apart from our Mother. My mum and dad are dead, and I never see the friends I used to have when I was kid. Not that I was ever *that* good at making friends. I always knew I was going to be a shadowspeaker, even when I was little, and the other kids thought that was weird. My mum thought so too, actually. She kept telling me that I should let my dad find a man for me, like the other girls. People were talking about me, she said, and making her look bad, people were saying I wasn't a proper girl at all. My dad was proud of me, though, and I do miss him. He was...'

It was strange to think of Mary as a child somehow, Mary with a mum and a dad.

She gave a little laugh. 'I'm sorry, dear. I don't know why I'm going on about my people when you're sad about yours! I guess I just wanted to show you that I do know something about how you feel, and that I'm not so different from you. I'm so so sorry we didn't go back to see your people sooner, Angie. If I'd had any idea this was going to happen, I promise you I wouldn't have asked you to wait.'

'I know that, Mary.'

'I reckon you'll find them one waking anyway,' she said. 'The good part about being with me is that we travel all over. We're sure to hear some news of your people somewhere. And of course when you're a shadowspeaker yourself, everyone will know your name, right across the Davidfolk Ground, and so your people will hear news of you as well. And you'll be closer to Gela too, you'll be able to hear her voice better, and then she'll help you too.'

I nodded, wiping the tears from my eyes.

'It's time to go to Circle Valley, isn't it?' said Mary. 'I'm sure you're ready now. It's hard to say this, dear, but suffering is part of it. We need to know what it is to suffer. It teaches us how to help people from sad sad Eden to get back to our Mother on Earth.'

Seventeen

When the Michael's Place people left Davidstand again, our bucks were carrying even more stuff than when we'd arrived because we'd loaded them up with our new, hastily made wraps tied up in rolls. There were bodywraps, headwraps with holes for eyes and mouth, footwraps with three layers of skin and grease to keep the snow from soaking through, big ones for the grownups and little ones for the kids. We hadn't had enough skins with us to make them all, but I'd managed to get a few more as a trade for some metal cubes that I'd carried with me ever since I left Knee Tree Grounds. (They'd been a present from Greenstone to the Kneefolk when he took Starlight away with him across the Pool.) No one in Davidstand would give food in exchange for anything – they knew they'd need it themselves – but people were happy enough to trade their heavy buckskins for things that were easier to hide and lighter to carry.

The path soon began to climb, though the slopes ahead of us were still warm and shining and covered in trees. We were all afraid of crossing the Dark and we didn't talk much. Whatever I might have said to try and calm the fears of the others, I knew how dangerous it was up there. Sometimes the snow fell so heavily that you couldn't see through it, or cloud came right down from the sky and wrapped the mountains up in a mist so thick you could hold out your hand in front of you and not be able to make it out. Poles stuck in the snow weren't much use if you couldn't see them, and nor were guards' fires. People often got lost when when the mist was like that and were never found again; experienced people who knew the Dark well, never mind folk like us. And of course it was in those times when the path was hidden by snow or cloud that the snowleopards still felt safe enough to come back down from their hiding places up in the high cold places where people had never been, and hunt for human meat. In normal times, few people crossed the Dark without a guide, even if they'd crossed it before. But darkguides now were asking for more sticks than we Michael's Place people had ever had.

Not that we were the only ones taking the risk. Each time we came round one of the folds of the mountain and the view opened out, we saw people ahead and behind who'd also decided the risks were worth taking, and were trudging slowly upwards through forest. The Dark might be dangerous, but it wasn't as if Davidstand was safe. There were already groups of Johnfolk down there, on their fast, blue-skinned bucks, who were sneaking right up to the outside bank of the L-shaped pool and shooting arrows over the water.

'I'm really worried, Angie,' said Dave, clutching little Metty in his arms as he bumped and jolted along the stony path on Ugly's back. 'Look at all those people ahead and behind! Circle Valley's going to be packed. There wasn't enough to eat in Davidstand, but what are we all going to eat up there? The Valley can't feed itself even in the best of times. They have to bring food over from Wide Forest.'

'Dave, there's no point in—'

'Watch out!' somebody yelled. A couple of stones came rolling down the slope that we were skirting round. And then two three bucks came into view, scrambling straight downhill and towards us, fast fast, with men on their backs in metal masks.

'Quick, Dave! Get out of their way!'

Those of us near the front ran or rode or stumbled ahead.

Those at the rear turned and hurried back, so that the Johnfolk could cross the path and carry on straight down the slope, as we hoped they wanted to do, without having to get mixed up with us.

We were lucky, I guess. The ringmen *did* carry straight on. I guess they weren't interested in a bunch of low people like us – what use to them were women and kids and guys who were too old to fight in the guards? – but as they passed through one of them put an arrow on his bow. Turning his empty metal face towards the half of our group that were out in front, he shot it among us. And then, without waiting to see whether he had hit anyone or not, he went crashing on down the slope with the others, giving an excited whoop as he disappeared under the shining trees. We heard a starbird screeching as it blundered off through the branches. And then we heard a terrible scream that came, not from forest, but from right up close.

'*Suzie!*'

It was Flame, that thin little girl that Tom had got with trading sticks to be his second shelterwoman. Clare always refused to speak to her and, out of loyalty to Clare, none of the other women had really befriended her either, but right now it was impossible to ignore her. She was standing there screaming and screaming with her little baby clutched in her arms, and the child was pouring with blood.

Clare got to her first.

'Hey, hey,' she soothed, taking Suzie from Flame and laying her gently on the ground. 'It's not so bad. It's not so bad. She's been lucky, look. The arrow just grazed her shoulder. We just need to stop the bleeding and she'll be fine.'

I had a little bit of fakeskin that I carried for things like this – it's much better than buckskin – so I knelt beside the little screaming child and pressed it firmly against the wound.

'There, you see.' Clare seemed to have forgotten for a moment that she was angry with Flame, and she put one arm round the shoulder of Tom's other shelterwoman. Truth was, Flame was

younger than five six of Clare's own kids. 'She'll be fine, look, she'll
be fine. Angie will stop that bleeding and she'll be fine.'

Tom was boiling over with rage. He looked round him to find
Trueheart.

'So what do you say to that, eh?' he demanded of her. 'What do
you say about your friends the Johnfolk now? That's your little sister
there, in case you'd forgotten! That little child there that couldn't
harm anyone! What kind of man shoots an arrow at a tiny baby?'

Trueheart turned away from him and wouldn't answer, though
her eyes were shining with angry tears. She was standing under a
whitelantern tree, and you could still just see the fading bruise next
to one eye from that last time he'd beaten her.

We stopped to sleep less than halfway up, and then it was another
whole waking after that before we reached the place where the
trees started to get thinner and smaller, so that the light was much
dimmer and the air much cooler than it was down in Wide Forest.
There were monkeys up there, those weird creatures that have
six arms sticking out from their body in all directions, with hands
on the end of each, so it's hard to say sometimes which is top or
bottom, or which is front or back. We'd seen them sometimes in
cages in Veeklehouse but this was the first time most of our group
had ever seen one moving freely. We managed to shoot a couple
of them to cook over the fire we made, after much puffing and
blowing, with the embers we'd brought with us from Davidstand.

Starry Swirl shone down cold and bright as we munched the
tough green meat, without a proper forest to steal away its light.
Another bunch of people came past us as we were eating and
pushed on towards the Dark. We called out to ask them where they
came from and why they'd left, and they told us they were from a
place in forest called Tomsneck, halfway between Nob Head and
Davidstand. They told us that New Earthers had grounded at Nob

Head too, as well as at Veeklehouse and David Water. I thought about Nob Head and how we used to visit it when we were kids, with its high cliff and its little circle of stones, and the batfaced trader in bowls and pots called Met who always used to give us a bit of stumpcandy.

Again we rested up for a few hours, and then began to climb once more. The air was getting much colder now – or at least it seemed cold then: it was nothing compared to what lay ahead – so we put on those bodywraps and headwraps and footwraps. This took a while, because the little kids didn't like them and some of them kicked and screamed to stop us from wrapping them. Metty managed to tear his bodywrap with his kicking and struggling, so I had to mend it, and Candy kept pulling off her headwrap: 'I don't *want* it, Mum. It stinks! It makes me feel sick!' When we finally set off again, we didn't look like people any more, but strange furry creatures, strange even to themselves, that walked on their back legs and smelled of wet fur and sour stale meat.

We had nine bucks, all told, but only one of them was a woolly-buck with a headlantern to give us light. It belonged to Tom, and he led it out in front with two of his boys beside him. Dave followed behind his brother on his buck with Candy and Metty. (Our Ugly was a smoothbuck, of course. It didn't like the cold. It kept snuffling and spluttering with its mouth feelers and trying to turn round and go back down.) I walked further back with Trueheart and Clare, while Flame rode another buck next to Clare, holding little Suzie tightly in her arms. Clare seemed to have decided to be nice to her, at least for the moment. We were all worried worried about the nasty cut that arrow had made on Suzie's shoulder, although we tried to tell Flame that it would be alright. It wasn't just a graze, whatever Clare had said. That metal arrow had made a deep cut as it passed, and there was a redness round it that we didn't like, though there was nothing we could do about it except wait and hope. Flame whispered to a little wooden doll of Mother Gela that her mum had given her when she first came to our cluster.

It was the kind you could get for three four sticks in Veeklehouse, carved, so the traders always said, from wood that came from Circle Clearing.

Time came when the trees were barely taller than a man, and stood forty fifty feet apart from each other. There were no bats and flutterbyes any more, and the ground was mostly stones. It was almost dark but not quite. Here and there we could just make out a monkey or two squatted on the ground, turning over the stones in search of bugs. The place was quiet quiet, without a proper forest pulsing away round us, but from every side came the tinkling trickly sound of the little cold streams that brought water down from the big snowslugs above us, joining together into bigger and bigger streams as they tumbled towards Wide Forest below. We saw pale blotches round us in the dimness here and there, and realized that they were patches of snow.

We came to a big square rock that had been set up beside the path. It had writing on it, letters that had been scratched deeply into its surface with a leopardtooth knife or piece of blackglass, and then stained with red dye. I couldn't read – all letters were just marks to me except for the ones in my name – but I'd been this way before and I already knew what these ones said, even before Trueheart had read them aloud. They said: 'DAVID'S PATH'.

'Funny, isn't it?' said Trueheart, or rather the furry creature said it that spoke with Trueheart's voice. 'We call it David's Path, yet it was John Redlantern who first found it.'

And that was weird because I'd said the same thing last time I'd come this way. I'd been with Mary, of course. It had been some eight years before, when I was only five years or so older than Trueheart was now. I'd changed since then, so many things had changed, but the stone looked just the same now as it did then, exactly the same, almost as if the time in between had never really happened. The darkguide had read out the words to us, and straight away I'd turned to Mary and said exactly the same thing as Trueheart had just said now.

It was the same place, the same stone, the same feeling of dread at the thought of snowleopards and getting lost, and at the thought of wakings of coldness and darkness ahead. And this time, just as last time, there was a young batfaced woman to speak those same words. It felt to me as if two separate streams of time had somehow come together and were flowing in a single bed.

'Hey! Look round!' said Clare suddenly, and we turned and saw far far below us the hundred thousand lights of Wide Forest, stretching away alpway and rockway, to our left and right, and peckway ahead of us, until they met the soft soft glow of Worldpool.

Eighteen

There were five of us altogether back then, the darkguide, two guards and me and Mary. The guide and the guards all rode their own woollybucks. Me and Mary shared the same big smoothbuck, with a woollybuck skin draped over it to keep it warm. She was riding in front.

'It's funny when you think about it,' I said, 'that it's called David's Path, yet it was John Redlantern who first found it.'

Mary was silent for some time. She was silent for so long, in fact, that when she did finally speak, I assumed at first she was talking about something completely different.

'A bunch of people were walking through forest,' she said, 'heading for a pool to have a swim. They were all sorts – grownups, kids, newhairs, oldies – and because of the oldies with them, and the clawfeet and the little kids, they were moving slowly slowly. But one young newhair boy grew bored of going slow. "I want to see the pool *now*," he complained. "Why can't we walk faster?" The grownups scolded him. "Be patient," they said. "Think about the ones who can't walk as fast as you." But the boy didn't listen and ran on ahead, ignoring their shouts. Well, of course, when they'd seen him get away with it, a bunch of other kids decided to run on ahead as well. And soon as they all reached the pool, they dived straight in without bothering to wait for the grownups, even though some of the kids couldn't swim too well. If the grownups had been there, they'd have told those silly newhairs to be careful, and been there to help if there was a problem, but there weren't any grownups. The poor swimmers dived in with the other kids, and a couple of them got caught in the wavyweed and drowned.'

She turned round and looked at me.

'So what do you reckon, Angie? Should that pool be named after the silly boy who ran on ahead and got those kids drowned? He was the first one there, after all.'

'No, of course not. They were all going there. He just ran on ahead.'

'Do you know who first told that story?'

I told her I'd never heard it before.

'That story was told by Wise Mehmet, way back when this stone was first set up, two hundred years ago. It was a few years after Great David died. David's son Harry had asked Mehmet to set up the poles and the guard fires that mark the way across the Dark between Wide Forest and Circle Valley, and when he'd finished doing that, Mehmet came here and put up this stone. As you know, Wise Mehmet himself was one of the group of silly kids who followed John – he was called Mehmet Batwing then – but, unlike most of the others, he had the sense to realize he'd made a mistake and he came back to David. He made up that story about the pool and the swim as his way of explaining what John had done wrong. Okay, John didn't drown anyone, as far as I know, but there's no doubt that many people died, thanks to him, who would have lived otherwise.'

'But what happened back then with John wasn't quite the same as the story, was it? It wasn't as if everyone agreed it was a good idea to try and cross the Dark, and John was just rushing ahead. Everyone told him it was a bad idea. In fact he was told he mustn't even *talk* about it.'

Again Mary turned to look at me.

'How do you know he was told that, dearest? It was – what? – two hundred forty years ago, near enough, and you weren't there!'

'No, but I thought that…'

But of course, I *didn't* know. There was no way I could know what really happened all those years ago. I just *felt* like I knew because I'd been brought up with a certain story about those times, a story that Jeff and his followers had told their kids long ago, and their kids had passed on to us through the generations. And of course Jeff was one of the ones who'd chosen to go with John. He wouldn't be likely to say that it had all been a silly mistake. There really was no reason why his version should be any truer than Mehmet's.

❧

'Are you angry with me, Mary?' I asked her later, after we'd been riding in silence for some time.

The last tree had been left behind us now, and the only light came from the headlanterns of the four woollybucks, lighting up the strange furry forms of the guide and the two guards.

'Why would I be angry with you, sweetheart?'

'For asking why this is called David's Path?'

Mary gave that loud bright laugh. 'No of course not, darling. I like the way you ask questions. That's good in a shadowspeaker. We have to work with people who don't understand the True Story and help them understand it. Remember those Hiding People and their giant bat woman? Remember that sweet old woman by the White Streams with her children's stories about Earth? We need to think of all the questions that people might ask and wonder about, and learn to answer them without getting upset.'

❧

She liked the way I asked questions: Mary said that again later on when we were in Circle Valley, the first time I went into the Circle by myself to listen for the voice of Gela. 'Let your mind go quiet,' she said, 'and then ask questions. You're good at asking questions, after all! You know how much I like that. Ask questions and listen for our Mother's answer. And, whatever you do, don't go worrying about whether you're good enough, because that will just get in your way. You *are* good enough, Angie, remember that! I know you are, and what's more I know for certain that Mother Gela thinks the same.'

There was a fug coming on. The air was warm and wet, and the cloud had come down from the sky and was seeping through the trees. I walked into the Circle. How strange! How scary! To walk by myself into the Circle of Stones, where so few were allowed to go. I walked to the five stones in middle that are supposed to remind us of Tommy and Gela and the Three Companions who died in the Veekle: Michael, Dixon and Mehmet. I stood there and looked out. The fug made the edge of the clearing look blurry. Mary was waiting out there, near to one of the guards who are always there watching the Circle, but they were both like blobs of darkness in the mist. All the lanterns on the trees were blurry too, with rings of light round each of them, white or pink or blue. It was only close to me that things were clear. Each one of the white stones in the circle that surrounded me was separate and solid, and inside the Circle I could see every grain of dirt on the ground.

I squatted down. It was quiet and still. The fug seemed to muffle sound as well as light, and there were no flutterbyes round the lanterns as there would be normally, and no bats to hunt them. The trees were still going, of course, they *never* stop – *hmmmph hmmmph hmmmph* – and I could hear voices and other sounds from the cluster round us beyond the trees, but they seemed far far away from me, like they were in another world. Only inside the Circle seemed completely real, and even that was a weird kind of real that felt more like a dream than ordinary waking life.

I squatted down there by the stones in middle and tried to settle my mind as Mary had told me to do, and not to fill up my head with worry. It wasn't easy to do. Mary had said she knew I was good enough, but there were things that Mary didn't know. I hadn't told her I knew the Secret Story or who I heard it from. I hadn't told her that my own best friend had gone over to the Johnfolk and put on the stolen ring. I hadn't told her that, no matter how I tried, I couldn't help feeling proud of that, even though poor Starlight had ended up dead, which sort of proved that what she'd done was bad. Mary didn't know these things and she loved me and wanted to think the best of me, so of course she believed I was good and pure. But Gela would know better. She could see into the hearts of all her children and would know all of my secrets, and all of my doubts.

I remembered that Mary had told me to ask her questions.

'Mother,' I whispered. 'My mum and my brothers and my sisters. Are they alive? Are they well?'

I waited and listened. I listened for a long time, but there was no answer. All I could hear was the pulsing trees, and the sounds of people out there somewhere in the fug.

But I'm listening to the wrong kind of thing, I said to myself, wiping the sweat from my face. Gela's voice wasn't going to be a sound out there like the *hmmmph hmmmph hmmmphing* of the trees, it was going to be inside my own head, like a voice in a dream. So I tried to shut out all the sounds that came from the world beyond my skin, and concentrate on the sounds inside me. But all I could hear was the racing of my thoughts, and my own blood pounding in my ears, like there was another tiny forest inside my head: a tiny forest, hot and fuggy like forest outside, but with no one living in it but me.

I could still see Mary out there, or at least I could still see the blurred shape in the fug that I knew was Mary, patiently waiting for me to hear what she could already hear herself. 'I so look forward to when we're both shadowspeakers together,' she often said, 'and can talk between ourselves about our Mother and what she wants for us. It's lonely doing this on your own, it really is. Everyone is a bit scared of us shadowspeakers. No one wants to come close, and no one really understands what it's like for us.'

I'm going to let her down, I thought. After all her patience and all she's done for me, I'm going to let her down!

But then I told myself firmly to stop all this. It was just worry and fretfulness, and Mary had particularly said there was no point in that, and that it would only get in the way. So I pushed thoughts of Mary and whether I was good enough out of my mind and tried again to hear our Mother. Still nothing came. Still there was nothing at all beyond my own thoughts, my own pulse, and the sounds coming in from outside.

I wondered if my question was too selfish? After all, Mother Gela didn't speak to shadowspeakers for their own benefit, she spoke to them so they could pass on her messages to all her children. I must try again with another question that wasn't about me.

'Mother,' I began again, 'what should I do so as to be able to help your daughter Mary as best as I possibly can?'

Tell her everything, of course, came the thought straight away. Don't hold things back from her. Tell her everything and accept whatever it is she has to say. Why even ask the question, when you already know what to do?

I was just pushing this thought to one side when it struck me that maybe this *was* my answer, that maybe this was Gela speaking to me right now? That was a scary scary moment, but it quickly passed. This couldn't be Gela, I decided almost at once. Whether or not they were right, these weren't new thoughts. I had this same conversation with myself every waking. And this wasn't a new voice either. It was just the same soundless muttering that went on inside me all the time. It was just me, talking to myself. Maybe I should pay more attention to it, but not now, not when I was trying to hear our Mother.

'Mother,' I tried again, 'I'm not even sure what I should ask you. I want to be a good daughter to you, though. I really do. Please could you just tell me what you want from me?'

Nothing came back. I waited and waited, trying to persuade myself that this thought or that was different from normal, but each time I really knew that wasn't true. These were just thoughts, ordinary thoughts, just like the ones that went through my mind every waking. Eventually I stood up and walked out of the Circle and back to Mary.

'I'm sorry, Mary,' I said, looking into that big square face of hers, full of passion, full of certainty, full of trust and confidence in me. 'I know I've let you down and I've let our Mother down, but I can't hear anything at all.'

'Oh darling, darling.' Mary laughed and threw her arms round me. 'You're so hard on yourself. It takes time, of course it does. I couldn't hear her at first either.'

I pressed her against me, sobbing with relief as I felt her warm solid body, all sticky with fug just like my own.

Nineteen

Nothing but ice and darkness. People say that all Eden was like this once, before the trees came up to the surface: a huge frozen ball of ice. But there was fire deep down in Underworld, the same fire that sometimes comes bursting out from volcanoes. In hot caves deep down near the fire, rock twisted itself into strange new shapes as a lanternflower will writhe and twist if you hold it in a flame. Some of the new shapes that came from that twisting were the first trees. They only grew far underground at the beginning, but then they began to climb up to the surface, melting the ice with their hot hot sap as they reached out into the air. The lowest parts of Eden's surface filled with water and became Worldpool, and the trees that grew there became the shining watertrees that I used to see beneath me when we went out on the bright water from Knee Tree Grounds, their soft branches waving back and forth. Middle parts of Eden were opened up to the air as the ice melted and flowed down to the Pool, and so the trees there became forest, lit up by their lanterns, and filled with the constant sound of the muscles pumping inside their trunks, bringing up the heat that kept the ice at bay. But in the highest parts of Eden, the parts that were closest to the cold black sky, the ice never melted, and light never came.

We trudged through the snow, warmed ourselves beside the little fires at the guard camps, and trudged on again in the little pool of light from the headlantern of our only woollybuck. Outside that pool was darkness, but in the distance there were other little patches of light, ahead of us and behind us, with little shadowy groups of human figures inside them. Like a necklace of glowing white beads laid out over the dark ground, these patches of light wound their way along the side of a mountain and up to a crossing place ahead of us where there glowed a single red bead of fire.

I walked up beside Ugly to check the two little kids were okay, and found both of them asleep in their father's arms, far away from all of this, at least for a little while. Dave himself stared out miserably over their heads at the mud and the snow and the darkness. Fox was walking up in front beside the woollybuck with his uncle Tom, who sometimes liked to tell him stories about his time in the guards.

'I'm really not sure this was a good idea,' Dave muttered. 'We're already cold cold and there's a long way to go. Plus, I don't care what you and Tom said about snowleopards, they're still up here. What chance would we have against them if one came?'

'I'm sure we'll be fine,' I said with a little sigh. 'Try and keep cheerful for the kids, eh?'

Because he was riding on the buck, he wasn't really aware of the biggest danger we faced, which was that our footwraps would fall apart or get soaked through. That's how people got the black burn. Your toes and feet got so cold that they died and turned black, rotting away while they were still on you. You had to cut them off if you were going to have any chance of living, or the black rot would spread right through you. My footwraps were already worryingly wet, and so were Fox's. And we had only a little bit of buckskin left to make new ones.

But I didn't say anything about that to Dave, just moved away again, and walked on ahead through the muddy snow of David's Path. Dave was hard to be with when things were difficult. Even back in Michael's Place, he worried worried worried. Even down there in forest, with the warmth and light of the trees all round him, Dave behaved like he was up here in the Dark, with danger all round him. That's why he always looked half-starved. It wasn't that he ate any less than anyone else. It was just that worry sat inside him like a slinker and stole away the food that should have made him strong.

I supposed in one way he was right, as well. We *were* always in danger, even down in forest. Warmth and light and life were such little fragile things, like the necklace of little lights laid out through the blackness in front of us; and darkness and coldness and death were so big and strong. But still, I didn't like to be with Dave when there was stuff to worry about. He made it worse, and he made me feel angry angry. Darkness was real of course, you couldn't deny that, but surely we could choose what story we told ourselves about it? Surely there was no need to *always* tell the story in which the darkness won? After all, it *hadn't* won yet, not in all the time people had lived on Eden. Here we were, look, as proof of that, with our wraps and our embers and our bucks, our blood still warm and our hearts still beating, making our way across the Dark.

Presently Trueheart came up to walk beside me.

'Auntie Angie,' she said, when we'd been trudging along together for a while in silence. 'You know how you said that high people think they're in a story that's all about them, but low people know they're not? What did you mean by that?'

However many times her dad beat her for questioning the things she wasn't supposed to question, however much her mum scolded her for making trouble, however much the other newhairs mocked her – 'Batfaced *and* mouthy. Who's going to want a girl like her for a shelterwoman?' – Trueheart would not stop trying to understand things, figure things out, make sense of them.

'Oh I don't know,' I said. 'I was talking nonsense probably. But I sometimes feel like the high people think we're here just to help them act out their stories, even if that means us doing for each other and burning down each other's clusters, and it never seems to occur to them that we might have stories of our own. I mean,

Johnfolk wouldn't be coming across the water at all, if it wasn't for the old fight between John and David. Yet they were just two guys who somehow managed to draw everyone in Eden into their quarrel.' I sighed. 'But then again, who knows? David and John wouldn't have become high men in first place unless other folk let them, so maybe people *needed* their stories.'

An idea came to me then, seemingly from nowhere, that made my heart beat more quickly all of a sudden. I looked round us to see if anyone was near, and found there wasn't. We were all walking in a long straggly weary line behind Tom and his shining woollybuck up front. Fox was some way back now, having a little ride on a buck with his friend Brightspear and Brightspear's old granny. There were twenty feet, in front and behind, between the two of us and the next nearest person.

'Trueheart,' I began, my heart now absolutely pounding, 'there's something you might like to—'

But that was far as I got, because right then a bunch of new buck-riders appeared over the ridge in front of us, heading towards us fast. There were twenty of them at least, with spears, and each one was riding a proper woollybuck, so that the ground all round them was white white, and the snow their bucks were throwing up glittered and sparkled like little stars.

Some of our group began to blunder sideways into the deep soft snow to the side of the path, remembering the Johnfolk who'd come crashing across our path and shot that arrow at poor baby Suzie. Pretty soon they were in up to their thighs. (Tom's dick, did they *want* the black burn? That was exactly the way to wreck your footwraps or even lose them!) But of course these men riding towards us were going the wrong way to be ringmen. These were guards, Davidfolk like us, returning from Circle Valley to join the fight down below in Wide Forest and round Davidstand.

As they came nearer, we saw there were two high men in middle of them, with fancy coloured fakeskin draped over the backs of their bucks. When they were up close to us, one of them pulled off his headwrap to scratch his face, and we saw it was Leader Hunter, Strongheart's third son, and our own guard leader. At once, whether we were on the path or standing out there in the deep snow, all of us knelt and bowed. The two of them waved in acknowledgement as they hurried past, in that almost lazy way that high people wave to low ones. Then they were gone in their glittery cloud of tiny stars, and we all got busy dragging people out of the snow who had got stuck, and retrieving footwraps that had been pulled off.

We only found out later that the other high man was Leader Mehmet, Strongheart's oldest son, and the one who would be Head Guard after him. The two of them and their dad had got right down into Circle Valley and had been making their way across it when the news reached them about the Johnfolk coming from across the Pool. They'd talked it over, the three of them, weighing up the different alternatives, and in the end they decided it was best that Strongheart carried on and went to the four hundredth Virsry, while these two came back to lead the fight.

Strongheart and his sons had never before invited the heads from Brown River and Half Sky to come to the Virsry, but they'd done it this time in the hope of building stronger links between the three different lots of people that shared Mainground. And right now, they'd figured, that was more important than ever before. The Riverfolk had always played that game of sometimes leaning to their fellow Johnfolk in New Earth, and sometimes leaning to their neighbours, the Davidfolk, on Mainground. But with the New Earthers attacking our ground, they were going to have to come down on one side or the other, and which side they chose would depend a lot on who they thought would win. And so the most important thing right now – or so Strongheart and his sons decided – was to seem confident and to celebrate the Virsry exactly as planned.

'You were going to say something, Auntie Angie,' said Trueheart, when we were all finally moving again.

'Was I? I've quite forgotten if so. It was probably nothing much.'

But I hadn't really forgotten and it certainly hadn't been nothing much. Truth was, I was badly shaken by the thought of what I'd been about to do. For if those high men hadn't interrupted me, I'd have started telling Trueheart about the Secret Story. *Women are just as good as men… Having a lot of stuff doesn't make you more important… Don't trust a man who thinks the story is all about him…* I'd been about to tell her all of that, along with the story that came with it about how our Mother Gela herself had told it to her daughters and asked them to keep it secret and pass it on to their daughers in turn through the generations.

How could I have even *considered* doing that, I asked myself now, when I'd have been giving Trueheart the burden of a secret that she'd have to keep forever, unless she wanted to get me thrown out of Michael's Place and sent away from my kids and my friends? How could I have put her in the position of making that choice? It wasn't as if I didn't have my own daughter to pass it on to if I really had to tell it to someone. And it wasn't as if I didn't know that Trueheart *hated* secrets. For hadn't she always refused to divide her heart in the way that I'd done with Mary, showing one part of myself but holding another part back? Trueheart was braver than me and more honest with herself. She refused to hide, she refused to pretend to believe something that she didn't really believe. That was why she kept saying the things she did, however many times her dad hit her. There was no way it would have been fair to have told her the Secret Story, and put her in the position of either wrecking my life, or having to keep a big big secret. I felt myself shaking just at the thought of what I'd been about to do, shaking like I shook once long ago when I was a kid, when I'd slipped and nearly fallen down the high steep cliff at Nob Head.

And never mind Trueheart, I asked myself, how could I think of passing that story to *anyone*? After all, I myself believed, didn't I, that the Secret Story wasn't true? I myself believed, didn't I, that at best it was something from long ago that hadn't been remembered properly, and that at worst it was a lie? Gela's heart, I might not be with Mary any more, but I was still one of the Davidfolk! And if I believed in True Family, believed that Gela was still watching over her children, believed that Gela could still reach out to us, why would I want to tell anyone a thing like the Secret Story?

But, even as I asked myself these questions, I knew quite well why I'd nearly told Trueheart. The things she said and thought were *like* the Secret Story and for a moment there I'd thought she'd like to know that Gela had been on her side.

Twenty

After that first time in the Circle, Mary got a good big meal for us from a trader, and took me to a pool she knew of where the water wasn't too warm, so we could wash away that sweat that clings to you when there's a fug in forest, and refresh ourselves with a bit of coolness. And then she made me lie down to sleep, sitting beside me and stroking my hair, like a mum or dad does with a little child who's tired and troubled, and needs help with letting go of wakefulness.

'Dear sweet Angie, why do you worry so much? You of all people! Of *course* Gela will speak to you. Our Mother loves you so much! You're so pure, Angie, you're so honest, you're so careful not to mix up in your mind what you want for yourself with what's important for everyone. I think of all those times you've questioned me – How do we know David was right and John was wrong? How do we know we're not just saying what the high people want us to say? – and I know you do it because you don't want to say anything unless you're sure sure it's true. That's exactly what our Mother wants: someone who'll listen carefully, someone who'll never confuse their own selfish thoughts with our Mother's voice from across the stars.'

She bent down and kissed me on the cheek.

'Now get some sleep, my dear, and we'll try again next waking. Not many speakers get to hear our Mother the first time they try.'

I slept. I dreamed. I wandered through a forest. Everywhere I looked, there were objects lying on the ground: stones, fruitskins, fallen branches, dead starflowers, broken seedgrinders, buck-bones, ratshells, feathers, leopards' teeth, coloured beads, lumps of stumpcandy, old stone spearheads. I was searching searching but, however hard I tried, I couldn't remember what I'd been sent to find.

'I want to show you something,' Mary said, when we'd both woken again.

We bathed in that pool again, to wash away the sweat of the night, and then she led me along a path into forest beyond the fence of Old Family cluster. The fug still hadn't lifted. The ground was wet with its moisture, the mist still made rings of colour round the lanterns, and everything further away than twenty thirty feet was a blurry shape that didn't seem quite real.

We came to a place where the trees opened out. It was another clearing like the one where the Circle was, but this one wasn't empty. From one side of it to the other and even under the trees all round it, dark shapes loomed up in the fug like silent, watching creatures, some no higher than my knee, some much taller than I was. Actually, they were simply piles of fist-sized stone. When one of them was near enough, I could see that perfectly well. Yet I still couldn't quite get the idea out of my head that the other ones, the hundreds of others that I couldn't clearly see, disappearing into the fug, were something more than that, something alive and listening. Even when we'd walked up to one, touched its stones, felt their hardness and coldness, it still seemed to change back into one of those silent, listening beings when we'd moved on and I looked back at its blurry shape.

Mary didn't need to tell me what this place was, because I knew it from stories. I recognized at once that it was Burial Grounds, where everyone who died in Circle Valley was buried, along with high people from across the whole of Davidfolk Ground.

'Tom's dick,' I said. 'There must be more dead people here than there are people still alive in Veeklehouse and Davidstand together.'

'But this isn't anything like the true number of dead people,' Mary said. 'When no one remembers or cares any more about one of them, they take the stones to use again and bury the bones in a pit. Most people only lie here for a generation, or two at most. There are only a few who never stop being remembered and loved, so that their piles just get bigger and bigger.'

The biggest pile of all was right in middle, and of course it was the pile that covered the bones of Gela. It was like a little hill, twice as high as me, and Mary and I made it a little bit bigger still by laying two more stones on it that we'd brought down specially from the edge of Snowy Dark. Not far away from it, there was another smaller pile for Tommy, with the words 'Tommy Schneider: Astronaut' scratched on a flat stone in front of it. He'd once lain next to Gela, Mary told me, but her pile had grown so big that it had begun to bury his and he'd had to be moved. At far end of the clearing there was another big pile over Great David, which also rose well above my head, though it still wasn't anything like as big as Gela's.

We walked round for a bit and Mary read out some of the names and words scratched on flat stones that were propped in front of the piles. The fug was round and above us, and we could see nothing at all beyond these dark piles that waited there silently in every direction, some of them close and clear, some further away and pale and shadowy. We were in a peaceful little world all on its own that had been set apart for the dead.

'This is Wise Mehmet,' said Mary, stopping in front of a middle-sized heap. 'A lot of people love him, especially in Tall Tree Valley and up at Rockway Edge.' She bent down to look at the small writing: '"Mehmet Batwing," it says. "He showed the way back to Family."'

She had a soft spot for Wise Mehmet, and liked to tell people when she got the chance that she was his great-great-great-great-granddaughter. I guess it's not surprising that Wise Mehmet would be a favourite for a shadowspeaker, whose work was all about finding the ones who'd wandered away and bringing them back again into True Family.

'And look,' she said. 'Over here is Strongheart's dad, Harry.'

But though there were many dead people from generations ago who were still remembered, Gela's pile rose high above them all. When we'd walked round all the others, we came back to it, and Mary read out the writing that had been scratched on her flat stone by Gela's son, First Harry. 'Angela Young,' it said. 'Orbit Police'. Mary took my hand and we both stood quietly looking at that great hill of stones.

'You get back the love you give, don't you?' she said. 'You only have to look at the size of this pile compared with all the others to see that our Gela is still pouring out her love, still reaching out to everyone, still making herself heard.'

She gave my hand a squeeze. 'And right now, my dearest, she's reaching out specially to you.'

She led me along the side of Longpool, where a couple of jewel bats were out hunting fish in spite of the fug, and back again to Circle Clearing. Mary asked the guard there to keep people out of the way for a while, because I was going back into the Circle and needed quietness. I was more scared this time round than I had been the first time, but Mary told me there was no need to worry, I should relax, I shouldn't think of this as something I had to work at, I should just let it come.

I nodded, and she hugged me, and then I made my way out into middle, stepping between the stones into that special place and squatting down once more by the five stones at the centre of the Circle.

Round me the fug was thickening once more. At first the edge of the clearing was blurred, and the lanterns had rings of colour round them, but soon I couldn't see the lanterns any more, just patches of different-coloured light, and I couldn't make out the tree trunks at all. I couldn't see Mary either. Even the stones of the Circle were half-hidden from me, though I was right there in middle of them. I was all by myself and no one could see me.

'Mother, are you going to speak to me?' I whispered.

There was no answer. Nothing at all. Nothing that wasn't either my own thoughts or the muffled sounds from the cluster and forest round me.

Well, of course she doesn't answer! I suddenly heard myself thinking. She's dead, isn't she? I've just been where her bones are. She's just an old skeleton under a heap of stones!

That was what the Kneefolk thought, after all. That was what we were always taught that Jeff Redlantern had said: Gela was simply a human being called Angela Young, who died a long time ago.

As soon as I'd had that thought, I felt so ashamed that I felt the red blood rushing into my face. How *could* I? After seeing that huge pile of stones, that pile of love, bigger even than the pile over Great David himself, how could I come into middle of the Circle, this special special place that was closer to our home on Earth than anywhere in Eden, and think that thought? I'd been so so lucky – most people were never allowed to come here from the moment they were born to the waking they died – and this was how I showed my gratitude!

I reminded myself what Mary had taught me about the Kneefolk. 'Well, I suppose at least they're harmless,' she'd once said, when we were riding back to Veeklehouse from Rockway Edge. 'They keep out of the way of the rest of us, I'll give them that. But they're over-grown babies really, aren't they? They're like silly newhairs who don't want to grow up. They tell themselves they know everything already when really they know nothing at all. It's quite funny, when you think about it. All they've ever seen is their little bit of sand, and those trees of theirs that bend over in middle, and maybe a few bats and fatbucks, and yet they say *there is nothing but this*.'

And she was right. I remembered how ashamed I'd felt that time when me and Starlight and the others went down to Veeklehouse from Knee Tree Grounds. The flamelight, the trading sticks, the traders with all their wonderful things spread out in front of them, the people with bright feathers in their hair, and coloured fakeskin wraps, and batwings dangling from their ears... The Davidfolk had done *so* many things there, had learned *so* much, had been *so* busy. And what had we done out on Knee Tree Grounds meanwhile, other than catch fish and gather waternuts, and cut bits of bark from trees?

'Mother, please, I'm sorry,' I whispered to Gela. 'I *know* it's only your bones under those rocks. I know it's only the old bones you don't need any more, like an old wrap that's worn through. I know your shadow flew to Earth, and put on new bones and new flesh and new skin. I know you're alive. I know you speak to Mary. I know...'

Tears were running down my face, along with the sweat and the moisture from the fug.

'Please, Mother, I beg you, speak to me. Just tell me you're there, and then I'll be able to reach out to you better, and get to know you, and learn what you want of me.'

But still there was nothing. I couldn't hear Gela, I couldn't feel her presence at all. In fact quite the opposite. Out there in that strange little patch of ground, surrounded by softly glowing fug, Gela's absence sat beside me like a big cold person-shaped hole.

There's no such thing as a shadow that leaves us when we die, Jeff Redlantern had said. We *are* the shadows. We're the thin flimsy things that fade away. What carries on after us is the thing that's always there, deep down inside us: the secret awakeness, the Watcher, looking out of our eyes, as we'd look out through the eye-holes of a buckskin headwrap, or through a mask.

Gela's heart, how awful if that was true! One set of eyes, one single being, all alone, picking up one mask after another, putting it on for a while, then throwing it away again to try another.

I ran out of the Circle.

'Mary? Mary? Are you still there?'

'Of course I am, dearest, I'm right here.'

And there she was, her solid shape appearing out of the fug.

'I'm so sorry, Mary, but I still can't hear her, and I don't dare stay there any more because all kinds of bad thoughts are coming to me. All kinds of bad thoughts and doubts.'

She didn't hug me this time, but she took my hands and stood there for a moment looking into my eyes: me and Mary alone there, surrounded by nothing but the softly glowing fug.

Twenty-one

Once we saw a single tree with shining white flowers, much much taller than the whitelantern trees you see in forest. It was standing by itself at the bottom of a valley of snow, and steam was rising from its airholes towards the stars. It was the only tree we'd seen the whole way across.

'That's the Crying Tree,' said Tom, and I remembered Mary telling me the same. When John Redlantern's people came this way, the story went, they'd seen a big bat the size of a child, standing right at the top of it. As the bat looked around and cooled its wings, the way bats do, a long long slinker had come out of one of the tree's airholes and begun winding up round the trunk towards it. But suddenly, for no reason, John Redlantern had started to shout and cry out, and the bat had heard him and jumped into the air to fly away just before the slinker reached it.

We had a similar story on Knee Tree Grounds, but our story came from Jeff, while it was Wise Mehmet who told the story to the Davidfolk. Mehmet always said, apparently, that this was the moment when he first properly admitted to himself that he'd been a fool to put his trust in Juicy John.

We looked down at the tree, alone in its bowl of light, and carried on back into the darkness, baby Suzie's thin weak cry carrying on all the while.

Tom was out front as usual with the woollybuck, and he saw Circle Valley first. 'There it is!' he yelled out, and the rest of us hurried to join him, our cold cold feet sloshing in the trampled snow that had been seeping through our footwraps more and more over the last waking, in spite of all their layers of greased skins. We were tired tired, we were cold all the time, and all the grownups had been worrying for miles that the cold would get too much before we reached the warmth of trees again. A couple of our oldies had completely shut themselves down, like they were giving up the fight to stay alive, and getting ready to merge themselves back into the coldness and darkness all round us. Little Suzie's shoulder was badly swollen now. She was hot hot to the touch, and she kept up a continuous crying for hours and hours, while Flame wept and Clare muttered little gruff reassurances, which she herself didn't really believe. All of us, including Flame, knew how dangerous the poison fever was.

But still, we'd made it across. There it was below us, the shining forest, surrounded on every side by the huge black shadows of mountains against the stars. We could even just make out smoke in the distance. Lit by the flames, it rose up from the fires of Old Family cluster, the first home of people on Eden.

I pulled off my headwrap to get some air. At once the icy coldness hit me. We might be able to see the light of forest down there, but up here it was as cold as ever.

I'd been in this place before, of course. I'd stood in this exact spot with Mary – 'There it is, dearest,' she'd said. 'Just think! When we come back this way, we'll be two shadowspeakers together' – but most of the Michael's Place people had never seen Circle Valley until now. They'd heard story after story about the place. In stories and songs, and acted out in shows, they'd heard how the Veekle had first come down there and how Tommy and Gela had laid out the stones in Circle Clearing. Over and over, they'd heard how Juicy John threw the stones into a stream, and how Great Lucy, the first shadowspeaker, had found them and put them back. But now the real thing was right in front of them. It wasn't in a story any more. It didn't lie on far side of the mountains. It was right in front of them, right there where the smoke was rising.

Trueheart's eyes were dry, I noticed, peering out of the holes in her headwrap, but most people's eyes were shining in the light from our buck's headlantern. One guy called Big Dixon – he was wide as two of me – pulled off his headwrap so as not to soak it with his tears. All their lives, these people had lived beside circles on the ground that were copies of that Circle down there in forest. Every guard they met had a circle of dots painted on his forehead in memory of it. Each time they went into Veeklehouse they'd seen the traders offering those little bags of dirt, which were supposed to have been scraped up from the ground of Circle Clearing. ('Only ten sticks,' the traders would call out, 'for a whole lifetime of health and good luck!') In the minds of Davidfolk just to be near that special Circle that they weren't allowed to step inside was like being a bit nearer to Earth. They might never have been there but the Circle of Stones was still a kind of home.

That thought brought tears to my eyes too. I'd thought I had a home in Michael's Place, where we'd looked after ourselves and bothered no one, but now the Johnfolk had driven us from it. I'd thought I'd had a home at Knee Tree Grounds far out in World-pool, but no one lived there now but fatbucks. I'd even thought I had a kind of home with Mary, but me and her had fallen out. Deep down I longed, like everyone, for a real home that couldn't be taken away.

So I cried. But Trueheart still held out against tears. She frowned down at the little lights of all those thousands of trees at the bottom of the great bowl of darkness, and refused to be impressed while her dad Tom pointed out to her the Blue Mountains opposite, the Alps to the right, the Rockies to the left. 'And of course the bit of the Dark we've been crossing is called the Peckham Hills,' he said, proud of his knowledge and of having been here before. 'Which is why we say peckway, blueway, rockway and alpway when we're telling people which direction something is in. It all started here.'

'Well, let's keep moving blueway, then,' Trueheart said with a shrug, 'before our feet turn to ice.'

Ahead and below us we could see the light of the first small trees, shining their coloured light over the rocks and the bare ground that was beginning to appear down there from under the snow. There'd been a little group of people ahead of us for the whole of the last waking. We'd seen the light of their single woollybuck as it made its way round rocks and over the crossing places, up and down, left and right, showing us little pale glimpses of the path we ourselves would soon be treading. Now we glimpsed them briefly again among the trees, until they turned a corner and were out of our sight.

Still in the darkness ourselves, we began to move, a straggly line of people and bucks heading down a path that woollybucks had made, long long ago, before people came to Eden. Little Metty needed to sleep and Candy wasn't letting him, so I took my little wriggly daughter in my arms for a while to give Dave a chance to settle him down. My brave Fox walked beside me. He was only seven years old, his feet were cold as anyone's and he was tired tired tired, but he didn't complain or cry.

'There are lots of monkeys in those trees down there, Foxy,' I told him. 'I saw them when I came down this way with Mary. You better keep your eyes open and you might see one.'

He didn't react at first, but after trudging along for sixty seventy heartbeats he asked me how many I'd seen.

'I'd say nine ten at least.'

'That's not lots,' he said, and that was the end of that.

'I'm *cold* cold,' grumbled Candy, still squirming restlessly in my arms. 'I'm cold cold *cold*.'

'I know, darling, but soon we'll be down among the trees, and they'll warm us up again. And perhaps lower down we'll find a nice warm pool next to a tree root.'

In front of us, Tom was talking to Trueheart.

'When I was in Circle Valley before, it made me proud proud to be one of the people who looked after the Circle and stayed by it, not one of the ones who tried to wreck it and then walked away.'

'Yes, Dad, but if you'd happened to have been born in Brown River, or over in New Earth, you'd be telling me now how proud you were of being one of the Johnfolk.'

Tom stopped in his tracks. '*What?*' He just couldn't understand why she kept coming back at him when he'd shouted at her so often, and beat her so many times. How was he supposed to get some sense into her? *Do* for her? 'What are you talking about, girl? How could I *ever* be proud of being one of the Johnfolk? They took the stones from the Circle and threw them in the water! They broke up Family! They stole Gela's ring! How could I *ever* be proud of that? Tom's neck, Trueheart, how could you *think* for a moment I could be?'

'Do you really think all Johnfolk are mean and bad, Dad? Do you really think they don't love their kids like you do? Do you think they don't—?'

'They're attacking us right now, Trueheart! They've driven us from our home! They're doing for our people. Your own brothers are fighting them. How can you—?'

'Yes but be fair, Dad, we would have attacked them if we thought we could win, wouldn't we? In fact we Davidfolk *did* attack them once, didn't we? It was the Johnfolk who first found Wide Forest after all, but Great David wouldn't let them stay there. He came over and pushed them right down to Brown River.'

Tom pulled off his headwrap. 'Because they told lies, because they broke up Family, because—'

'That's our story about them, I know, but I bet they have a story about us too, don't you think? And their own story about themselves? How can we know for sure that our story's true and not theirs? I mean, we can't *know* what really happened all those years ago, can we? All we can know for certain is that everyone born where we come from believes one version of the story, and everyone born across the Pool believes another. In other words, people believe the story they're brought up with. It's stupid saying that people believe such-and-such story because they're good or they're bad.'

Tom was quivering with fury.

'Are you questioning the True Story? You want to be careful careful, girl, or you could find yourself—'

Clare came striding down the path.

'Leave it, Tom!' she hissed. 'I can't believe you're arguing now, when your little daughter Suzie there is burning up with poison fever.'

That stopped him. He turned to go to Flame. But he hadn't quite finished with Trueheart.

'Just remember, girl,' he threw back at her. 'Just remember that Suzie would be fine if it wasn't for that dirty slinker from New Earth, shooting an arrow at her little shoulder.'

Trudging wearily down the wet zigzag path with Candy heavy heavy in my arms, clambering over cold stones, I thought about what Trueheart had said. Stories were important, that was the part she didn't understand. They were so important that we told them to ourselves inside our heads, every time we went to sleep. They were how we joined together all the things that happened to us into a shape that made some kind of sense. They were how we made the best of things in this sad, lonely place, where babies can burn up with fever, and enemies can come from across the water, and people can be born with clawfeet and batfaces, and be teased and left out, and can't do anything about it.

And the Davidfolk's story was a good one. It was a story about keeping family together, watching over the Circle, patiently wait-ing for Earth to come again. It was satisfying and comforting but felt real at the same time, and it had a good ending too, like all proper stories do. The ending was Earth, and the story was about staying together, no matter what, and keeping our way home clear in our minds until we finally got there. The Circle of Stones made us closer to Earth. It was something from the old stories that was still solid and real so we could see it right in front of our eyes. And all those other circles that we made in our clusters, or scratched on the forest floor, or drew in the snow on our way over, *they* made us closer to the Circle of Stones. So the Davidfolk didn't just tell their story, they lived in it. They came back every waking to a circle that marked the end of their whole story. And that meant that, however far away from home they might seem to be, they were reminded all the time that it was still there waiting for them, and that it wasn't so far as it might seem.

Trueheart wanted to scratch away at the Davidfolk story. She wanted to know if it was really true in the way that it might be true to say: 'That's a stone over there,' or 'That's my mum,' or 'Last waking there was a fug.' She wanted to know if it was real like a bat or a tree. She wanted to know what reason there was to think that the Davidfolk's version of what happened at Breakup was *really* any truer than the Johnfolk's.

But no one else looked at it that way. How can you ask if the story is true or not, if you're in the story yourself?

🌿

At last we'd reached the trees, the small trees that grew at the edge of the snow, casting their light over it, white and pink and blue, and making it glitter. We pulled off our headwraps and bodywraps, and our wet wet footwraps, and with our feet and shoulders bare again, we followed a little stream, already shining with waterweed, that was carrying cold water from the melting ice. *Hmmmph hmmmph hmmmph* went the trees all round us, as we walked in the light of their lanterns. There were already bigger trees ahead of us.

'There's a monkey,' said Fox, too tired to be excited, but just interested enough to speak.

We watched it spinning and whirling and wheeling through the warm trees, grabbing branches with whichever of its six hands happened to be in the right place, like it had no sense of which part of it was up and which down, and any way round was fine. Davidson put an arrow on his bow, but it was gone before he'd had a chance to aim.

Twenty-two

'**Y**ou're still trying too hard, Angie,' said Mary, holding onto my hands but not moving to hug me as she'd done the first time. 'You're still expecting too much. Our Mother doesn't shout. She doesn't wave her arms to get your attention. You need to have trust. You need to trust her, and trust yourself. But that's enough for this waking. Some people have asked me to do a little show, so we'll do that now, and then rest and sleep, and then you can come back to the Circle again.'

I noticed she didn't tell me not to worry this time, or reassure me that I'd be fine. And I noticed that I didn't tell her anything about how for a moment there, I'd doubted whether any of this was true. How could I? Mary heard Gela's voice every waking, she cried for Gela in every show, she begged and pleaded and raged for Gela's sake. How could I possibly tell her that, even just for a heartbeat, I'd doubted that voice was real?

We went and did the show. It was in a tiny cluster in forest about two miles out from Old Family and less than twenty people came, but Mary did one of the best shows I'd seen, sobbing, raging, pouring with tears and sweat, with the fug all round and a bunch of frightened low people watching us with their mouths open, and tears and sweat running down their own faces.

'Gela loves you,' she cried out. 'Gela wants to help you more than anything else in the world. But what do you do in return? How do you show your gratitude? You steal from one another! You hold back from the guards the handovers you owe them for keeping you safe! You think bad thoughts!'

She walked up to a pretty young woman. 'You, for example. What's your name, my dear?'

'I'm Gela.'

'Gela. You even carry our Mother's name, but yet look at what goes on in your head! You think angry thoughts. You long for men who aren't your own. That's what our Mother tells me. Is she right?'

The woman lowered her head in shame.

'Of course she's right,' said Mary, and passed straight on to another woman. 'You look guilty guilty. Wait! Let me listen. What's our Mother saying? Is she saying you're one of those that tell that so-called Secret Story? The story about things Gela's supposed to have said to her daughters long long ago? Ah, I thought so. You silly silly girl. Why tell that foolish lie, when Mother Gela herself is alive and calling out to you?'

Many of them were crying now. 'Yes, you might well weep,' Mary told them. 'Because if you don't reach out to Gela, she won't be able to reach you either, and you'll be lost forever. Drifting, drifting, drifting. Shivering, shivering, shivering. All alone forever, all by yourself, in the cold cold blackness between the stars.'

She stood there, trembling and sweating, as she listened to Mother Gela whispering to her inside her head. 'Yes, and no starship will ever come from Earth while you act like this. They'll never come to bring us home. And all our children and our children's children will have to live their lives out here in dark dark Eden.'

By now pretty much everyone was crying, thinking about their hard lives here in Eden, and about our lost home, full of light, far beyond our reach across the stars, where the Mother of all of us was born.

'Gela is pleading with me,' Mary told them, tears running down her own cheeks. 'Our sweet sweet Mother is pleading with me. She knows what it is to live on Eden and long and long for Earth. "*Make them understand, Mary!*" she's begging me. "Please, please make them understand!"'

She raised her hands to the black black sky, where Earth was hiding somewhere, as everyone knew, in the great cold spiral of Starry Swirl. 'Oh Mother, Mother, Mother,' she begged. 'Please don't cry! I can't bear to hear you cry!' Then she fell to the ground, writhing about and sobbing. Everyone was scared and horrified, but of course they were excited too by being so close to our Mother. Earth might be far away but right in front of them was a woman who was hearing Gela's voice.

'Listen to our Mother,' she told them. 'Don't imagine she'll come to you with bright lights and fancy wraps. She is our *Mother*, don't forget. Her voice will be as ordinary and familiar as your own mother's. As familiar as the pumping of the trees.'

She broke off, and for a few heartbeats all we could hear was the sound of the trees round us: *hmmmph hmmmph hmmmph.*

The fug was beginning to clear as we walked back to the cluster again and returned to the shelter where shadowspeakers stayed. Mary didn't talk much. I felt I was getting on her nerves, and she didn't seem to want me to hug her and soothe her down as she usually did after a show. I was sure she was disappointed in me, and I feared she might be angry too, but when I asked her she insisted it wasn't so, reassuring me in a loud bright voice that I'd done nothing wrong at all.

Back at the shelter, I stirred up the ashes and fed the embers with dry twigs, then cooked up flowercakes and a couple of sweetbats whose meat, I knew, Mary especially liked. She rested for a bit after that – she always needed to settle herself after a show – and then went off for a while to see the guard leader, Harry, Strongheart's second son, who'd asked to see her. I walked about a bit by myself, but not for long because I wanted to be sure to be there when Mary came back. I couldn't bear the thought of letting her down, this strong woman who'd chosen me, Angie Redlantern, out of all the hundreds of people who came to her shows in every part of the Davidfolk Ground! She'd always told me she'd seen something in me that was different to anyone else, and I was terrified that she'd change her mind.

It was some time before she came back, but when she did she was in a more relaxed mood. It often cheered her up like that, I noticed, when one of the high people had asked for her. They wanted her advice sometimes about difficult things, like whether or not the baby of one of their shelterwomen was really their own, and it felt good to her that these important people were interested in what she had to say.

'Fug's almost gone now,' she said. 'Good job too. I don't like it when it gets like that. Get some sleep now, Angie, and we'll have another go when we wake.'

I didn't sleep so well, but Mary seemed to, snoring away steadily in her corner. (Mary did everything firmly and loudly: even sleep.) When she woke and we came out of the shelter, the fug had cleared completely, Starry Swirl was blazing down, and bats were once again hunting the flutterbyes that flipped and flapped between the lanterns and the airholes of the trees.

'This is a good waking for you, Angie,' she said, as I brought her a flowercake and some dried fish. 'Everything is lovely and clear.'

She pulled off a strand of the tough green meat and began to chew on it.

'We'll go to the Circle as soon as we've finished eating,' she said. 'And let's see if this time you can get the hang of it.'

Twenty-three

ircle Valley might be small compared with Wide Forest, but it
was still big. The Michael's Place people took another two long
wakings to get down into the Valley and across forest to the big Old
Family cluster that sprawled round the Circle itself. When we did
finally reach it, the place was strangely quiet.

'The Virsry has not long finished,' explained an old guard who
was keeping lookout by the gate in the leopard-fence. 'Everyone's
been keeping the same wakings and the same sleeps, and now
they're all resting.'

I'd heard about this before. During a Virsry, when whole Valley
came together to hear the Laws and watch the Show, everyone in
the Valley had to keep the same wakings, just like people did in
small clusters like Knee Tree Grounds or Michael's Place. That
continued for some while afterwards, because everyone felt tired
about the same time. But, little by little, different families and
groups would begin to follow different rhythms until things went
back to how they were in other big places like Veeklehouse or
Davidstand where, at any moment, there were always some people
sleeping and some waking, some getting up while others were lying
down. And then the time would come round again when the three
oldest people in the Valley – the ones they just call Oldest – decided
that three hundred and sixty-five wakings had gone by (or *days* as
some call them in the Valley) and there'd be another Virsry and

the whole thing would start over once more.

When the old guy and his friends had satisfied himself we were proper Davidfolk, we passed through the gate and found ourselves a place to rest inside the fence in the pink light of a group of red-lantern trees. We were tired tired, but for all our worry and grief about what we'd left behind, it was good to be back in treelight, with starflowers shimmering round us, and the hum of life, and warm trunks to rest our backs against. We lit a small cooking fire with the embers we'd brought with us, and heated some of the few flowercakes we hadn't yet eaten. Flame and Clare bent worriedly over little Suzie. Her whole shoulder was swollen up to double its proper size, and she was still crying weakly all the time.

'Should we go and see the Circle before we settle down?' Kate asked, but everyone was too tired. So we drew our own circle in the dirt like we usually did, as if the real Circle was still far away across the Dark, and sang 'Come Tree Row'. And then we settled the little kids down – they were all so tired that it didn't take long – and most of us curled up to sleep.

I couldn't sleep, though. There was just too much going through my head. Coming back to the Valley had stirred up all kinds of restless and painful feelings, on top of the grief and worry of losing our home and leaving behind so many people we knew. Dave was snoring away as usual, so I checked Candy and the boys were sleeping peacefully, spoke for a little while to Flame who was standing and rocking her poor sick baby, then got up and walked back over to the gate, thinking I'd talk to the guards there for a little while. But when I got there, they were busy with three new guards who'd just come in on buckback from over the Dark.

'They've gone crazy,' I heard one of these new guys saying. 'They're doing for everyone they get their hands on. And—'

He stopped and looked across at me.

'Can we help you?' asked one of the gate guards.

'*Who's* gone crazy?' I asked.

'This news isn't for you,' said the guard who'd been speaking. 'This is guard business.'

'Do you mean the Johnfolk?' I pressed him. 'Have they got Davidstand now?'

'I can't tell you,' the guard said. The three bucks were in quite a state, their eyes rippling constantly, their mouth feelers wriggling and blowing out green foam. They'd obviously been ridden hard hard. But the guard and his friends jumped back onto them and drove them forwards through the trees so as to give their news to the high men further inside the cluster. 'You'll hear soon enough, and you've got nothing to worry about here.'

The Johnfolk in Davidstand, stabbing and burning people we'd only lately been with. I felt sick sick at the thought of it. But of course there was nothing I could do. It was just one more thing to keep me awake. There was no way I was going to be able to sleep now. I decided I'd go over and look at the Circle, the place where my time with Mary had finally ended.

As I was heading off that way, Trueheart came running after me.

'Where are you going, Auntie?'

'I couldn't sleep, so I thought I'd have a look round.'

'I'll come with you.'

'Okay dear, but keep your voice down. Everyone else here *is* asleep. Those Virsries are pretty tiring, from what I've heard.'

We walked through the shining trees until we came to the shelters in the place called Brooklyn where the high people always stayed. They were solid and square like the ones in Veeklehouse, and the biggest one had guards all round it. Strongheart himself was inside, apparently, and so was Headman Newjohn of Brown River and the Head Woman of Half Sky.

Right at that moment, in fact, as I'd find out later, Strongheart and his son Harry were busy talking to those two. Those guards I'd seen at the gate had brought bad bad news. The New Earth

Johnfolk were winning the fight not only at Davidstand but in many different places across Wide Forest. And suddenly Headman Newjohn in particular was finding he had a lot of power, because Strongheart was desperate to persuade the Riverfolk to come over to his side and not join their fellow Johnfolk from across the Pool. He was offering to give Newjohn more ground, including all those little clusters I'd visited with Mary along the White Streams. He was even offering two of his own daughters to be the Headman's shelterwomen. But Newjohn, more than anything, wanted to make sure that he backed the winning side, so he was holding back from choosing until there was more news about the fight.

I didn't know about any of that then, though, and I wasn't much interested in Strongheart's shelter, because we were near the Circle, and that was completely filling my mind. We only had to cross the bridge over the stream and we'd be in Circle Clearing, and it would be there right in front of us.

My heart was pounding pounding pounding. Now I was so close I dreaded seeing those stones again. But I needed to see them too, so I went on anyway, and Trueheart followed after. We crossed the bridge and there it was: the big Circle first laid by our Mother and Father, Gela and Tommy, four hundred years ago, with the group of five stones in middle where once I'd squatted down to listen for Gela. It was hard to believe now that someone like me could ever have been in such a place.

Trueheart stared in silence. Once again, I think, she was trying not to be impressed, but this time she wasn't succeeding. There were so many stories about this place that it was like a hundred different places all packed together into one single spot. And you could feel the pressure of that, you could feel all those squeezed-in stories straining and bursting out. It was a wonder the clearing could hold them at all.

'You can look but you mustn't touch,' murmured a guard with a blackglass spear. He was the only other person in sight, and he was another old guy, like the guard at the peckside gate: I guessed the young ones had been sent to fight the Johnfolk. 'You mustn't touch and you mustn't step inside the Circle.'

I nodded. Only the sons of David could invite people inside the Circle, only them and the shadowspeakers. I'd had my moment there, and it wouldn't come back.

Twenty-four

The third time I went into the Circle there was no fug to hide behind. I could clearly see Mary there waiting at the edge of the clearing. I could see the guard. I could see other people moving round through the trees. And I couldn't pretend that I was in a world apart. I was in Eden, plain ordinary Eden, with its lanterns and its bats and its people. Even the Circle seemed more ordinary than it had done before. It might be a place full of stories, but still, what was it but a bunch of round white stones that you could find any waking in a stream? I remembered how, back on Knee Tree Grounds, I'd been told that these weren't even the original stones laid here by Tommy and Gela. Everyone knew that John Redlantern had thrown the whole Circle into the stream, but only the David-folk believed that Mother Gela had guided the hands of Lucy Lu, so that she found the exact same stones again, and returned them to the exact same places.

I squatted down in middle. I closed my eyes.

'Please, Mother Gela, if you love me, speak to me, or I will disappoint Mary and lose all the trust she put in me.'

I waited for a moment, just in case our Mother was going to answer at once, but of course she didn't. Under the pulsing of the trees, I heard the faint slap and flick of flutterbyes' wings.

'I know I shouldn't keep secrets from Mary,' I whispered. 'Perhaps you can help me figure out the best way to tell her?'

That's easy, I answered myself at once, just as I'd done the first time. Walk over there now and tell her that you have these secrets and you think they might be stopping you from hearing Gela.

Again I wondered if that thought, so clear and strong, could have *been* Gela, Gela herself telling me to go and talk to Mary? Perhaps that's what Gela's voice was like?

But no. I'd said the same thing to myself so many times as we travelled up and down the Davidfolk Ground, and there was nothing the slightest bit new about it this time. If it was Gela at all, it was Gela speaking to me as she spoke to all her children, not Gela speaking to me in the way that a shadowspeaker was supposed to hear her.

But now another thought came to me, one that I'd never had before. Perhaps I should pretend? Perhaps I should go back to Mary and tell her I heard Gela's voice, tell her it was different this time, tell her I've finally understood?

Mary would be so so pleased with me! She would be happy happy! And then we could be shadowspeakers together!

I was so relieved that I actually began to stand up to go and do it, but almost straight away I saw how stupid I was being. Didn't I feel bad enough already about the secrets between me and her? And they were just small secrets. Up to now I hadn't been lying to Mary, I just hadn't told her a couple of things about myself. Pretending to hear Gela would be different. That would be a huge lie, and once I'd told it I wouldn't be able to stop. I'd have to pretend every waking. I'd have to cry and tremble in shows, as if Gela was speaking to me. I'd have to talk with Mary about the things that Gela said, and Gela's plans for us, and what Gela wanted us to do next. (She'd said so often how much she looked forward to that.) And Mary would look at my face and think she could see me, but what she'd really be seeing would be like one of those little wooden people that they have in Veeklehouse: the ones that talk and dance and seem to be alive, but are really just being moved by someone hiding behind them, who pulls them about with strings and speaks their voices.

No, there was no other way. I'd have to go back to Mary a third time to tell her that yet again I'd heard nothing at all.

She didn't hug me this time, or take hold of my hands.

'Still nothing?' she asked as she stood up to meet me.

'I'm so sorry, Mary.'

For a little while she just stood there in front of me, her small grey eyes searching my face.

'You always have to be better, don't you, Angie?' she finally said. 'You always have to be better than me and better than everyone else.'

This was so unexpected that my mouth fell open with the sheer surprise of it.

'*Better?* No, Mary, that's not it! That's not right at all! I don't think I'm—'

'Always questioning, always poking away at what I say, hinting that you think I'm a fool at best and a liar at worst, but never quite saying it.'

'But Mary, you said that—'

'Hinting over and over again that I just say what the high people want me to say, but never coming out and telling me straight that's what you think.' She put on an ugly spluttery voice, imitating my batface speech as cruelly as any kid had done back on Knee Tree Grounds. '"I'm not saying anyfing bad about you, Mawy. I twust you. I juft wondered." Yeah, right, you just wondered. Do you think I didn't notice the expression on your face when I came back from Leader Harry? Oh I noticed alright. And I know exactly what you think. You think I trade with the high people, don't you? You think I trade Gela's truth for their support.'

Sweet Mother of Eden, the poison in her voice! Her face was red. Her spit spattered into my face. It was like she'd been storing up every single little angry thought she'd had about me all these last two years, squeezing them tightly tightly together into some small dark space inside herself, and now the whole lot was coming out at once.

'No, Mary! I *don't* think that. I don't think that at—'

'It's no good, Angie. I know your tricks now. It's always the same. You hint and hint at something, and then you insist you didn't really mean it.'

'But you said you liked me asking questions, Mary!'

She gave a snort and half-turned away from me.

'I was a fool. There are honest questions and there are sneaky questions that crawl round inside the truth like a tubeslinker in a tree. I should have noticed the difference. I should have noticed how your questions made me feel inside.'

She turned back to me.

'Do you know why you don't hear Mother Gela?'

'I'm not sure, Mary, but I guess maybe it's because I—'

'Oh, no need to guess, Angie, I'll tell you why it is. It's because you're *too* good. Nothing is true enough for you unless you can be absolutely certain of it, is it? Good good Angie! Pure pure Angie! You can't take the risk that you might be wrong!'

I was sobbing by then. She was my only friend. My only family. She was my mum, my dad, my sister, my brother.

'Please, Mary, you don't—'

'I'm finished with you, Angie. I've given you two years of my life – two whole years! – and I'm not going to waste any more time on you. But let me tell you one thing before we go our own ways. If you wait to be absolutely certain of a thing before you believe it's true, you'll never know anything, you'll never be with anyone, and you'll never have a home. That's how it is with everything in this life, and that's how it is with Gela. If you want to hear her voice you have to take a risk. You have to be brave enough to take the risk that you might be wrong. You weren't willing to take that risk in Circle, and now your chance has gone. I just hope that sometime you learn to take it in your own life, or you'll have no life at all.'

She wouldn't talk to me after that. She wouldn't look at me. She walked away, back to where the guards who'd come over with us from Wide Forest were playing chess in the blue light and warmth of a big spiketree, on a board scratched into the dirt.

'When you're ready, men, I'm set to go. Angie here isn't coming with us. It seems she's too good for us. It seems she's too good even for Mother Gela.'

And that was it. I tried again to speak to her, but she turned her head and told the guards to keep me away from her.

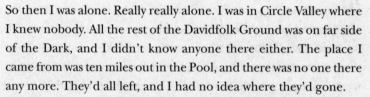

So then I was alone. Really really alone. I was in Circle Valley where I knew nobody. All the rest of the Davidfolk Ground was on far side of the Dark, and I didn't know anyone there either. The place I came from was ten miles out in the Pool, and there was no one there any more. They'd all left, and I had no idea where they'd gone.

I had those metal cubes with me that the Kneefolk had given me when I left them. I gave one of them to a trader to let me cross over the Dark with him and his bucks.

Twenty-five

'Well, I'd say it was obvious,' said Trueheart, as we squatted side by side at the edge of Circle Clearing, pretty much exactly in the same spot where Mary had been waiting for me that third time. 'I'd say it was obvious obvious. She wanted you to fake it, didn't she? She wanted you to fake it like she did, and she was angry because you weren't prepared to do it. It made what she did look bad.'

'I don't think so. You don't know Mary, Trueheart, but I know she believed in what she did. I've got no doubt about that. I was with her two years, remember, and all that time she played the part of a speaker, whether she was doing a show, or whether we were alone. It was all she cared about.'

Trueheart shrugged, looking at the silent Circle of Stones.

'Okay,' she said. 'So she believed in that stuff, but in that case, she'd fooled herself. She'd persuaded herself what she heard was Gela's voice, and now you'd called that into question by hearing nothing. No wonder she was upset.'

'Maybe.' I turned to look at her: strong straight Trueheart with her beautiful shoulders and the ugly hole in middle of her face. 'Listen, dear, you should be careful about mocking people's stories. They're like…' I struggled to find a way of describing the picture that was in my mind. 'They're like the paths in forest that stop us from getting lost. They're… They're like the trunk and branches of a tree.'

She didn't answer me. I thought of all the times I'd watched her quarrel with her dad, Tom, and seen him lash out at her with a stick or the shaft of his spear gripped in his one good hand, and how she *still* refused to shut up, or hide her feelings. And I thought of the things her dad did to me, out in forest, that no one knew about except me and him, and how I told no one, didn't speak about it even to Tom himself. She was braver than me and, because of that, she saw things in a different way, and maybe she was right as well. But still, I could only say what I thought.

'Your dad's wrong to hit you the way he does, but when you make fun of the True Story, I can understand why people get upset. It's like you're covering up the path that will lead them home. It's like they're lanternflowers and you're chopping down the tree that holds them up, and feeds them, and brings them warmth, and connects them to all the other lanterns.'

'Tom's dick, Auntie, I've never said there's no Earth! I've never said there's no Gela! Of course she's there. I know that for myself. I don't need bloody shadowspeakers to tell me. You know how sometimes when Dad's hit me, I have to go out into forest until he's calmed down? Well, I'm all my own then, aren't I? Everyone's angry with me, everyone's wishing I'd just bloody shut up, and I think to myself, well, what am I anyway? Just a batfaced newhair, who doesn't know anything, stuck here in bloody old Eden, where no one else knows anything either. And sometimes Gela comes to me then. I feel her near me. I feel I'm not alone. She comes to me like she comes to everyone. What I hate are the stories that say she only comes to *some* people: only to the Davidfolk, only to the shadowspeakers.'

We sat there in silence under the trees at the edge of the clearing. The old guard had dozed off, his back against a warm whitelantern trunk. All round us, Old Family cluster slept, except over there in Brooklyn where the high people from the Davidfolk Ground and Brown River and Half Sky were still talking talking talking.

'Do you think Suzie will die?' asked Trueheart.

'I think it's quite likely, I'm afraid, dear. Germs must have got into the cut, and now their poison is spreading, and—'

'Germs!' Trueheart snorted. 'What exactly are germs? We say that word like it explains something, but it's just a made-up word. We've got no idea what we mean by it.'

'I guess not.'

'Poor little Suzie. Poor Flame too, I guess. I mean, I don't *like* her because she slips with my dad and that makes Mum unhappy. But I guess she hasn't got much choice.'

I wondered what Trueheart would say if she knew her dad sometimes slipped with me as well?

'I guess we should go back soon,' I said. 'Maybe we could look after Suzie for a bit and let Flame get some rest.'

'Yeah, soon, Auntie. But let's stay here just a little bit longer. I like it here. It makes me feel stronger.'

❦

We looked at those stones out there, all by themselves in the criss-crossing light from the treelanterns round them: white, blue, pink, yellow. Bats and flutterbyes dived and looped round the trees round the edge of the clearing, and sometimes the pattern of light and shadow moved just a little when a wind blew the branches of the trees. But the world was still still.

Forest hummed. Behind the sleeping guard, the little river trickled over its rocky bed where Tommy and Gela found the stones. Jeff's eyes, I thought to myself, if there was anywhere in Eden where you *were* going to hear the voice of Mother Gela – the voices of all the dead, for that matter – it would be here, in this old old place where people first set their feet on Eden's ground. That had been one of the things that made it hard for me to admit I heard nothing. It had felt like I *should* be able to. It had felt like any fool should be able to hear those old voices, if they just sat here quietly and listened.

And now, while I was thinking about that, a weird thing happened. We *did* hear something.

'What's that sound, Auntie?'

Trueheart was younger than me and her ears were sharper. There were a few heartbeats before I could make it out myself, and when I did, I had no idea what to make of it. It wasn't a voice, certainly. It wasn't the sound of trees or of wind. It wasn't the cry of an animal. It was a kind of high-pitched whining sound, almost too high to hear. Neither of us could tell where it was coming from, but pretty much as soon as we heard it, something else began to change.

'Look, Auntie. The clearing's getting lighter!'

'Are you sure? Isn't it just—'

I broke off because, even while I was speaking, the light had become so much brighter that it was simply obvious. There was a big patch of white light that filled up most of the clearing and it was getting so bright that it was starting to blot out the soft and many-coloured light that came from the trees.

I stood up. I was scared scared, but scared in a weird kind of way, because I had no idea what I was looking at, or what there was to be afraid of. I knew this light wasn't anything to do with the Johnfolk. I knew the sound wasn't a leopard, or a crazed buck, or the Johnfolk running down from the Dark, or old Mount Snellins going off in the Rockies, as sometimes happened, and throwing hot ash into Circle Valley.

Trueheart stood up with me, and we reached out to take each other's hands. There was no obvious threat to us. What scared us was just that there was something here we couldn't explain. That light had now reached almost right out to the edge of the clearing, and the whining noise was growing louder: not *loud* loud, not as loud as the trees, not even as loud as the river running over the stones, but still much louder than before.

Where was it coming from? We looked out through the trees all round the clearing, but saw nothing unusual. And then Trueheart looked up at the sky.

'Auntie! It's there!'

Straight away I had to cover my face because of the brightness, but not before I'd seen what it was. We knew that at once, both of us did. Just in that one short glimpse we could see that what was coming down towards us was just like the thing that sat in Veeklehouse behind that high fence. But the one at Veeklehouse was dead, and this one was still alive: a huge dark circle coming straight down towards the clearing, with white lights shining down round the edge of it, brighter than anything I'd ever seen. Michael's names, I hadn't known until then that light could hurt your eyes.

And now I was *in* the light. I could see my own hands like I'd never seen them before, the pale skin, the little chaps and scars, all picked out so sharply that it was like I was seeing them for the first time. I could see the trunks of the trees – I always thought of wood as black, but I could see now that it was a dark bluish colour – I could see the folds and twists of Trueheart's batface, I could see each wrinkle in the buckskin wrap of that old guard, still peacefully sleeping under his redlantern tree. I could even see the hairs on it.

The whining sound the veekle made was almost as loud now as the *hmmmph hmmmph hmmmph* of the trees behind us. We heard men's voices shouting out from the shelters by Longpool. Apart from the sleeping guard, me and Trueheart were still the only one in the clearing but others had seen the veekle too. We peeked upwards again. The landing veekle was right over middle of the clearing, just above the tops of the trees. In the heartbeat before I had to look away, I saw four legs come sliding out from underneath it, spindly and long, like the legs of a flutterbye. The old guard woke up with a cry as the thing reached ground, grabbing his spear and clambering to his feet, his eyes wide with fear. The veekle wobbled, just slightly, on those spindly legs as it settled over the Circle of Stones.

And then suddenly more bright lights appeared all round the side of it, shining sideways out through the trees, filling up forest with a stripy pattern of weird black shadows, sharper than any shadow I'd ever seen. I covered my face and peeped between my fingers. At the top of the veekle was that same round shape there was on the one at Veeklehouse, made of some strange kind of glass that you can see through like water, and I saw the dark forms inside of people's heads.

Me and Trueheart gripped tightly onto one another's hands.

And then suddenly a voice spoke. It wasn't an ordinary human voice – it was so big and strong and metal-like that it felt like the veekle itself was talking to us – but all the same I could tell it was a woman's voice and not a man's. And, though the words sounded strange strange, I found I could understand them.

'Hello there,' the voice said. 'Don't be afraid! We're your cousins. We come from Earth!'

Then the lights became a little less fierce, still bright bright, still picking out every detail and filling forest with black black shadows, still so bright that the lanterns on the trees didn't seem to be shining at all, but not so bright any more as to hurt our eyes.

'I can't believe it!' the voice said, but much more quietly this time, like it was talking to itself. 'Still people here! Still—' It broke off, but after a few heartbeats, it spoke out loud again, talking to us once more. 'Hello there! Don't worry. There's only three of us in here! We're going to come out and meet you in a moment!'

The light had changed in that glass thing on the top, so we could see not just the shapes of their heads but their actual faces looking out. There was a woman, and two others that looked like men except that they were completely beardless like women or kids. All three were staring straight out at me and Trueheart. Trueheart lifted her hand and waved.

I waved too. 'Hello,' I called out. I didn't feel scared any more. Why would I? Hard as it was to believe it was really happening, this was the moment we'd been waiting for these four hundred years. 'Hello, I'm Angie Redlantern.'

Who cared about Johnfolk from across the Pool when there was *this*?

GAIA YOUNG. SUBJECTIVE IMPRESSIONS.
MISSION DAY 20. 20:25 MT.

Far out beyond the orbit of the moon, basking in perpetual noon, we'd turned on the great engine.

Like some kind of prodigious sea-creature, our ship began to heave and strain against the boundaries of space, pushing neither up nor down, neither forwards nor backwards, neither left nor right, but in another direction perpendicular to all of them.

It groaned and shuddered. It threw out purple lightning from its great pylons, only to suck it back in again with equal force, so that it coiled like a fiery whip round the ship's cylindrical core. To fuel its titanic feat of strength, the ship was consuming more energy than would power the entire Earth, and it was eating itself up in the process. When – or if – we ever returned, our engine, that absurdly costly thing that had taken almost a century to fund and construct, would have to be built again, almost from scratch, if anyone was ever going to repeat what we had done.

Metal shrieked. The engine screamed. The panels round us snapped and creaked. It felt like the ship would burst in two. But then suddenly, with a judder, we were through, and the din of the engine dropped to a steady hum. We were outside space now. We were in a miniature universe of our own. We looked out of the little portholes, and there were no stars, no Earth, no moon. We saw the faces of demons peering back at us from weirdly shaped windows set in a kind of silvery, molten wall. But they were only our own faces, distorted and reflected back to us by the tangled space of a miniature universe that our engine had created and now sustained. They were no further away from us than the far side of a city thoroughfare.

The ship turned and twisted, as its drew on the four-century-old records of the *Defiant*, its famous predecessor, and felt about itself for the correct hold, like a climber on a rockface.

The lightning flashed out again, and once more the ship shuddered convulsively and began to groan and roar. Our glowing screens, with their diagrams and numbers, their calm lists of options, told us a story of order and mastery, but we knew this was an illusion. We were like those parachutists who jump off cliffs: there was no margin of error, there was no going back and starting again. A tiny mistake now and we would emerge in some region so remote that we would never be able to find our way home. A slightly larger error and our ship would be crushed like a tin can. It was hard to know which would be worse.

Another shudder that felt like the ship breaking in half, and then we were through again, like a cork released from underwater, shooting upwards to bob on the surface of the ocean. Outside our portholes we could see the great Catherine wheel of the Milky Way.

Hours of anxious searching followed before eventually we found it: sunless Eden, a solitary sentinel, slowly orbiting the galactic disc, one face always turned inwards, the other looking out into the abyss. On its surface were the faint blotches and splatters of light that we'd seen in the images that came back with the *Defiant* four centuries ago, when it limped home broken and crewless.

We were forty thousand lightyears away from anyone we knew. If we'd possessed a radio transmitter powerful enough to send a signal back to our friends on Earth, they wouldn't just be dead by the time it reached them, their whole *civilization* would be dead. An ice age would have come and gone. Their bones, those that were left unpulverized, would be twice as old as the cave paintings at Lascaux.

Still in our tiny metal box, we travelled the slow way now, across ordinary space. More than a week passed before we finally fell into orbit round Eden. Then we climbed into our landing vehicle – our Flying Saucer – fired up its gravitational engine, and set its navigation system to return to the exact same spot on the planet's surface where the *Defiant*'s identical landing vehicle had descended.

And now, dazed, disoriented, exhausted, we stared out at a forest of strange, dark, leafless trees. For four generations my family had been working towards this moment, ever since my great-grandmother first uncovered the hidden story of the *Defiant*'s return, suppressed for so long by the Salvationist authorities. For four generations, we had been leading the global effort to reconstruct the starship and retrace its steps.

But here we finally were. We stared into that strange forest and saw, to our complete amazement, two human beings.

They were funny, wild little creatures, barefoot and bare-breasted, with nothing on them but rough bits of animal skin tied round their middles, and both had the most horrible facial deformities, like great jagged wounds that had destroyed the entire centres of their faces. But they were undoubtedly human all the same. And what was more, they were – they must be – my own distant cousins, descended as I was from a man and woman of Jamaican heritage who lived in London four centuries ago, in the time before the flood, and were the parents of the only woman from Earth to ever come to Eden.

For a few seconds we just looked at them and they squinted back at us through their fingers, their faces screwed up against the light.

We really hadn't expected this. It hadn't been people we'd come to see but the life of Eden itself, the only life known to exist outside of Earth, with its strange geothermal ecosystem that had grown and multiplied and warmed a planet without the help of a sun. As far as human life was concerned, we'd hoped for no more than a few bones, and maybe a clue or two as to what had happened to Tommy Schneider and Angela Young after their decision to stay here by themselves, while their three companions attempted to return to the *Defiant*. For the genetic experts had all agreed that you simply couldn't get a viable human population from just one man and one woman.

Recessive genes. Inbreeding. Even twenty men and twenty women, they'd said, would probably not suffice. But it seemed they'd been wrong.

'We'd better turn off the lights,' I said. 'They're obviously finding them blindingly bright.'

Deep touched his screen. For a few seconds, while our eyes adjusted, the world outside became completely dark and all we could see was the glow from our screens, with their numbers and diagrams, that illusion of order and mastery. But then from the darkness emerged the world that we'd glimpsed in those uploaded images the *Defiant* brought back, and heard described by Eden's five discoverers in those haunting diaries. It wasn't much brighter than moonlight is on Earth, but from all round us a dim light – pink, white, blue and yellow – shone from the strange blooms, some spherical, some elongated and tubular, that dangled from those smooth and fungus-like trees.

Small flying creatures were darting round those lights, as moths and bats might do round streetlights on Earth, and some of these creatures seemed to be shining faintly too. Round the bases of the trees, another kind of vegetation twinkled like the strings of lights we hung up back home to mark the Winter Festival, although very much more faintly. I vaguely remembered that, in the meticulous reports that Michael Tennison uploaded before he died, these lifeforms were called starflowers. He speculated that they were parasites, feeding on the roots of the geothermal organisms he referred to as trees. Mehmet Haribey, who died with him, had discovered they were rich in vitamin D.

But, of course, what held my attention most at that moment were the people. The two harelipped women were the first I'd spotted, and they were still standing there – one of them quite old and wizened-looking, the other more youthful – watching us with their mouths wide open. But there were others too now. Some way over to their left, a very old man with a white beard was clutching a spear like some extra from a movie about the Stone Age, complete with a furry animal-skin garment, and a tribal emblem of white dots on his forehead. And more people were arriving all the time: men with tribal dots and spears, women with bare breasts and skins tied round their middles. We saw two more harelips and a woman dragging herself painfully along on horribly twisted feet. Everyone looked like they were suffering from acute malnutrition. Everyone was shrunken, twisted, gaunt. As you'd expect, they all had Afro-European features, some inclining more to the African side, some more to the European.

'You sure we should go outside now, Gaia?' asked Deep. 'How do we know those guys with spears aren't just going to run us through?'

'We take guns,' said Marius. 'One shot in the air will have them running.'

A group of new people had arrived, wearing not animal skins this time but a kind of coarse fabric that looked like sacking, in various shades of grey and brown. This lot were mostly men – the one in middle was a fat, bald old guy who looked about eighty – but there were several women among them, and one of them in particular caught my eye: she was taller than most of the men, very straight in her bearing and about my own age, and she could have been described as beautiful if she didn't look so wasted and wan.

'Don't even *think* of taking a gun, Marius,' I said. 'If you can't face them without a gun, stay inside.'

'Oh come on, Gaia,' Marius said crossly, 'I wasn't suggesting *shooting* them. But Deep's right, they might attack us. We don't know what they remember about Earth and spacecraft. We could be alien invaders as far as they're concerned.'

'He's got a point,' said Deep. 'Do we really want to be the *second* bunch of explorers who made it here to Eden and never got home?'

'Okay,' I said. 'We need to be careful. But why don't I go out by myself first off? A woman's less threatening, don't you think? No guns, no nothing, but if they attack me, just turn the lights back on at full brightness. I mean, look at the light level they're used to. By the time they can see again, I'll be safely back inside.'

Part II

Twenty-six

I look back through that tangled forest of memories, through the tree trunks and the lanterns, the paths and the pools, through all the many things that happened afterwards, and that time still shines brightly brightly in the dimness, far brighter than any other. In fact it shines so brightly that it can be hard to see, like the veekle from Earth was hard to see when it first came to ground. You'd think a time like that would be easy to remember, wouldn't you, since nothing like it had happened to me before or since? And yet it isn't. It was all *so* so strange that there are whole big chunks of it that I can't properly remember at all, and other parts I remember but don't know when they happened or how they fitted in with everything else. It's the same for everyone who was there. When we talk about it, we can never quite agree what happened, or in what order. And so many stories are told about it that it's hard for us to be sure if we're remembering what we saw, or just remembering a story.

❧

I'm as certain as I can be, though, that after a short time, the lights from the veekle stopped shining all at once. For a moment afterwards – I remember this *so* clearly that I'm sure this is real – everything round us seemed completely dark. Then my eyes got used to the Eden light again, and I could see the treelanterns and the starflowers. I remember how dim they seemed, in a way they'd never seemed to be before. We'd always thought of them as bright, as *shining*, but compared to the lights on the veekle, all they gave out was a dim dim glow.

Mainly, though, we watched the dark shapes of the heads behind the glass, me and Trueheart together, still holding each other tightly by the hand.

More people were running into the clearing now, and there was shouting all round us, in the clearing itself, and back through the trees. A bunch of high people in dyed fakeskin wraps had come over the bridge from Brooklyn. I saw that one of them was David Strongheart, who'd sometimes come to the shows that Mary did at Davidstand. He looked much fatter and older than I remembered him, but he was wearing a fine red wrap that would trade for a hundred sticks at least in Veeklehouse. Normally I would have knelt to show my respect, but somehow that didn't seem to be needed right now: I guess the veekle from Earth was there to remind us that all of us were the children of one man and one woman. There were several other high men with him – one of them I recognized as Leader Harry, who was Strongheart's second-oldest son, and the boss of Circle Valley – and there were also a couple of women, one of them tall and about my own age, wearing a lovely blue wrap.

And suddenly I realized I recognized her as well! It was Starlight, my old friend Starlight from Knee Tree Grounds, whose dead body I'd been told had been found on poolside, full of water and run through with a spear.

A strange dread filled me. Perhaps the visitors from Earth were bringing all the dead people to life again? Perhaps right now, the dead of Circle Valley were waking up over there in the Burial Ground like they'd only been sleeping, pushing aside those stones they were lying under like you'd push aside a buckskin sleeping wrap, and making their way towards the clearing? Perhaps they were waking up all over Eden, swimming to the surface out in the bright water round Knee Tree Grounds, clawing their way out of the ground in forest near Michael's Place? Perhaps bones and scattered ashes were flowing towards each other, up and down the forests of Eden, to join together and rise up again as living human beings? It seemed as if every single thing I thought I'd known up to then had turned out to be completely wrong – the dead were not really dead, lanterns were not really bright, high people were not really high – and now the world was beginning again, or beginning for the first time, or appearing at last as it had always really been.

But then I thought, Wait! If Starlight has come back from death, how come these high people are with her, and seem to know who she is?

'Starlight!' I called out, and she looked towards me at once. I could see she was surprised, and she was about to call something back to me when a sound came from the veekle and we all turned back towards it.

A square of metal swung down underneath it and straight away a kind of ladder came down. We stared and waited and, after a dozen heartbeats or so, we saw feet on the steps. Me and True-heart squeezed each other's hands even more tightly. A woman was climbing down. We saw her knees, her hips, her belly, her chest, and then there she was, standing at the bottom of the steps underneath the veekle. She was smiling. And she wasn't looking at the high people or at anyone else, she was looking straight at me.

I had never seen such a perfect face. Her teeth were white – *white* white, and not a single one missing! – her skin was smooth smooth, and so dark that you could almost call it black, and her eyes were bright and clear. I always thought Starlight was the most beautiful woman I'd ever seen, but this woman was beautiful beautiful in a way I couldn't even have imagined if I hadn't seen it. She was tall too, tall tall for a woman, taller even than Starlight, taller than almost every man I knew. And she was wearing a strange wrap that fitted tightly round her body and arms and legs. It looked like it was made out of some kind of grey metal, but it followed her movements in a way that buckskin and fakeskin never did, almost as if it was living skin.

'Hello there! My name is Gela!'

That's what I heard her say. That's what everyone heard her say. And of course we all knew that all the old stories said that Gela's skin was black, whatever Mary Shadowspeaker might have said. A few yards away from me, an old woman began to scream.

'It's our Mother! Our Mother has come back to us!'

And now, all round the clearing, people began to scream and shout, and some rushed forwards towards the veekle. But then the lights shone out again, all at once, bright bright, brighter than anything any of us had ever seen, scalding our eyes with their fierce fierce whiteness, so that the people stopped running and backed away again, crying out in fear.

But I didn't back away and nor did Trueheart. Something about the woman had convinced us there was nothing to be afraid of and, peeping through my fingers, I could see she was still just standing there like nothing had happened.

'Don't rush her, people!' I called out, and then I heard Starlight call out as well. 'Hold back, everyone! Let her have some space!'

My head was swimming with the strangeness of it all. Here was my friend Starlight, alive and well and wrapped like a high woman, when I'd thought she was dead and lost forever. If it had happened at any time before now, that would have been the weirdest and most wonderful thing that had ever happened to me. Yet right now I could barely give it any attention at all!

'Thankyou,' I heard the Earth woman say. As she came towards me and Trueheart from under the veekle, she raised one hand and the lights stopped shining again. It was as if that whole huge mass of metal was a living thing that she could give orders to as a skilled rider gives orders to a buck.

Again, for a few moments after the lights had gone, whole forest seemed completely dark, like we'd only imagined there was any light there at all, like we'd only imagined this beautiful woman had come back to us from Earth. And then we saw her again, not in the bright Earth light, but in our own dim Eden light that was hardly light at all: Gela, solid and real as anyone you might meet out in forest, standing right in front of me.

'Hello there!' she said gently, speaking kindly and slowly slowly, like I was a child. She held out her hand to me, and I took it. I could feel her warm skin against mine. 'You don't know me of course,' she said, 'but I'm your cousin. One of my ancestors was a woman called Candice Young, and she was the twin sister of a woman called Angela who must be—'

'You're not Gela then?'

She frowned as she looked down into my face. It was a kind, troubled frown, like she pitied me, like she thought I was sick and wished she could help.

'I'm sorry, I didn't understand what you said?'

'You're not Gela?'

'Yes, I'm Gaia,' she said. 'My name is Gaia.'

'Gaia,' I repeated. I looked at Trueheart. I was still confused. Was this a different name, or was it perhaps just a different way of saying Gela? All her other words sounded strange, after all.

Still she frowned, gently and pityingly as she watched my face. 'That's right, *Gaia*. And you are . . . ?'

'Angie.'

'Angie. That was what people sometimes called . . .'

She stopped, and instead asked me something that I couldn't make out at first because she said it too quickly. The way she spoke was far more different to what I was used to than even the speech of people from across the Pool, and that could be hard enough to follow in itself. Every sound seemed to be in the wrong part of her mouth.

She looked at Trueheart, and Trueheart told her her name.

'I'm sorry. Did you say True Heart?' The woman from Earth had that same pitying frown on her face as she looked into Trueheart's eyes. It was like how a mother might look at a sick sick child, or a child who'd fallen and cut herself.

'That's right.'

'Do you know where I come from?' she asked us both, speaking slowly slowly this time to make sure we understood.

'Of course,' I said. 'You come from . . .' It was weird, I was about to say the word when I realized I was going to cry, and had to stop.

'You come from Earth,' said Trueheart, and now my tears did come, and Trueheart's too. 'Are you here to take us home?'

The woman frowned again, kind and concerned.

'I'm sorry,' she began. 'I didn't quite get that. Did you ask if we—?'

'My name is David Strongheart,' said a voice beside me. The Head Guard of all the Davidfolk had hobbled right across the clearing to stand beside me and Trueheart. Now he was bowing deeply to the Earth woman like he was just a small person like us and she was high high. His head didn't even come to her shoulder blade and his red wrap, which would have looked so fine and bright if I'd seen it in Davidstand, looked clumsy and brown and poorly made beside her metal-coloured one. (I couldn't even see the stitches in hers. I couldn't make out the threads in the weave. Perhaps it was the skin of some animal?)

'You're welcome welcome, Mother,' he said. He was crying and stammering like a nervous kid. 'I'm the Head Guard of the Davidfolk, and this is my son, Leader Harry. We Davidfolk have tried our best to keep all of your children together.'

'Pleased to meet you,' said Gaia, shaking the old man's hand with a puzzled look on her face.

'I'm Headman Newjohn,' said one of the other high men, also bowing. He had tight curly grey hair and a sharp pointy face, and he leaned on a stick. 'I'm boss of the Johnfolk from the Brown River Ground, and we're the people who followed John after you led him to your ring.'

The Earth woman was carefully watching his face, frowning with concentration. She was obviously finding it hard hard to make out the words he was saying, let alone what they meant.

Myself, I was finding it difficult to believe that I was there at all, standing right in front of a woman from Earth, and right next to the two highest and most powerful men in all of Mainground: the Head Guard of the Davidfolk and the Headman of Brown River. Yet that wasn't the end of it. The other high people had come over with him, the guards quickly surrounding them and standing ready to hold back the folk all round us. There were screams and shouts of excitement going back and forth through forest round and across the clearing, someone had started banging on a drum, and several people were blowing away at hollowbranch horns: *Paaaaaaaaaarp! Parp! Paaaaaaaaaarp!*

And now, after Strongheart and Newjohn, a third high person spoke. 'Hello,' she said. 'I'm Starlight.'

And here she was, my old friend, stepping forwards from the group of high people to come and stand beside me, reaching out to touch my hand. Ten years older suited her. She'd always been tough, always ready to fight for what she wanted, but now, standing there in her long blue wrap, with coloured stones dangling from her ears and from bracelets round her wrists, she looked like someone who could make things happen without even having to make a fight of it. She looked like someone who could persuade people to do things because they knew she'd know best. She looked gentler, in a way, kinder, and yet still as tough as ever.

'I'm the Head Woman of the ground called Half Sky,' she said, and she didn't bow to the Earth people like the others. She just held out her hand. Gaia reached out and held it for a moment and, as she did so, Starlight put her other arm round my shoulders. 'And this is my old friend Angie.'

Head Woman? Starlight a Head Woman? Starlight a Head Woman of *Half Sky*? It was true that last time I saw her, she'd been heading off far away with the Headman of another ground, but that was New Earth, far off peckway beyond Deep Darkness of Worldpool. And Half Sky was exactly in the opposite direction, blueway even of Circle Valley, across another whole part of Snowy Dark that was known in the Valley as the Blue Mountains.

Twenty-seven

Of course the Michael's Place people weren't the last to come over Snowy Dark to get away from the Johnfolk. All the time we were gathered round the veekle in Circle Clearing, new people who'd crossed the Dark were arriving at Old Family cluster. They were tired, scared and hungry, some of them were hurt, some had the black burn, many had lost people they loved over the other side, along poolside and in Wide Forest, where the New Earth Johnfolk were roaming freely, beating our guards easily pretty much every time they tried to fight back. As these new folk arrived, they wondered why the gates were open and no guards were standing there. Then they heard the shouting and whooping coming through the trees from Circle Clearing. They heard the drums thumping away, and the horns blowing, and voices singing: 'Come Tree Road, take me home...' Yet the shelters nearby were deserted, the fires untended, the trees pumping away on their own as if this was an empty part of forest, not the oldest cluster in whole of Eden. Had the Valley people gone crazy, they wondered? Didn't they know that the Johnfolk were tearing the Davidfolk Ground apart?

Wearily they trudged and limped through the trees towards the sound, past the empty shelters, past the meat that was beginning to burn because there was no one there to turn it, the cooking pots boiling dry, the bucks tied to trees with ropes, sniffling and snuffling because their routine had been broken. They crossed the bridge over the stream and found Circle Clearing packed with people singing and dancing round a veekle like the one in Veeklehouse, but whole and new and alive. The new people looked at each other. The folk who were already there laughed at their bewilderment.

'Earth has come,' someone told them. 'Mother Gela herself has come. She's tall tall, and beautiful beautiful, and her skin is all smooth and black, just like in the stories.'

'And there are two beautiful men with her,' said someone else, 'taller and bigger than anyone you've ever—'

'They've got no hair on their faces,' yet another person shouted.

'We think maybe they're Tommy and one of the companions,' the first one said, 'come back to life like Gela.'

The weary people looked at one another. Up on the Dark all they'd dared hope for was to get across the snow and down where there was warmth again. Walking across the Valley, all they'd dared hope for was to reach the cluster and find something to eat. But now this! Not just those small hopes met, but the biggest hope of all! Our Mother back again to take us home to Earth!

The new people began to laugh, and to hug and kiss each other, and to join in the singing and the dancing. And presently yet more people would come in behind them.

'What?' these even newer people would ask. 'Is that a veekle? Is that really—?'

'Yes!' one of the people who'd arrived before would answer. 'Yes, it's Mother Gela! And she's—'

'Her skin is black black, just like the stories,' one of the others would excitedly interrupt. 'And there's Tommy with her too, and another one they think is Mehmet.'

'Not Wise Mehmet, mind you, but Beautiful Mehmet. You know, the one Gela loved best out of the—'

'They've really come! Just like we've always been promised. All our troubles are over, my friends! They've come to take us home!'

It's hard hard to remember the order of things now. Trueheart ran back to fetch the other Michael's Place people. I felt torn because I wanted to be with my kids at this big big moment. But I was scared of losing my special place close to Gaia and then not being able to get back to her, so I stayed where I was, knowing that Trueheart would bring my children sooner or later. Gaia seemed to like me beside her. I guess with all those hundreds of new people pressing towards her and the two men, it was good to have a familiar face.

'Thankyou, Angie,' she said once twice. 'It's nice of you to stay with me.'

'Keep back! Keep back!' called out the guards. 'Let the Earth people breathe!'

'Don't make Angie move back,' Gaia told them. 'She and Trueheart were the first people we saw here in Eden.'

Later there was a feast. I can't remember exactly how this happened, but I know all three of my kids were with me by then, along with Trueheart, who I guess must have carried Metty, and I remember introducing my kids to Starlight who told me she'd got seven kids herself, and that my kids were lucky because hers were back in Half Sky, missing all of this. I know a big fire was lit over in Brooklyn, because I remember seeing the flames through the trees. And I seem to remember hearing that four big smoothbucks, or maybe it was even five, were done for right there and then and put over the flames to roast. I can certainly remember the smell of the meat, and Starlight laughing – 'Poor Angie, you're hungry hungry, aren't you!' – and Strongheart's helpers carrying wooden plates piled with meat and flowercakes through to Circle Clearing. And I can remember how we all watched closely closely as the Earth people chewed on it, and sipped at the badjuice that was brought to them in mugs.

'Delicious!' they said and everyone cheered, but if you were near to them you could see they could hardly force the stuff down. Food was obviously different on Earth.

The two men were called Marius and Deep. They were both tall tall, taller than any other man there, I reckon, and a whole head taller than most. Deep was the tallest of the two and he was smiley and friendly, reaching out all the time to shake people's hands or pat them on the shoulder. He said hello to Fox and Candy and ruffled their hair. Fox just stood there, staring up at him, stuck to the spot, with the wind blowing in and out of his little nostrils, but Candy ran back to me and buried her face in my wrap. And when Deep tried to tickle Metty under his chin, Metty began to cry. I guess that tall Earth man must have looked pretty scary to my little boy. It wasn't just that he was so big. His skin was pale pale too, like no one we'd ever seen. The story went round the clearing for a while that he was Tommy Schneider, our father, who the old stories tell us was white.

Marius was shyer. He did his best to be friendly too, but he looked like he'd prefer to be alone, and he didn't even try to talk to the kids. His face was less strange to look at than Deep's, though, because it was yellowy-brown like ours. Everyone kept saying that Marius and Deep's faces were as smooth as women's, but they weren't really, not when you saw them close. They did actually have beards, even in that first waking, but they were thin thin, with short short hairs that barely came above the skin. Like Gaia the two of them had white white teeth without a single gap. All three did their best to smile as the people round them cheered, and shouted, and sang 'Come Tree Road', and 'Show Me the Way Home', and 'Swing Low Sweet Cheery Oh'. Gaia and Deep also tried to wave and show an interest when, from time to time, more new people arrived in the clearing, full of trouble and fear, only to find out what was happening and begin to shriek and sob. But all three of the Earth people, I could see, were tired tired tired. Sometimes Marius's head would droop and his eyes would begin to close, and then he'd wake again with a jolt.

Half a waking must have gone by like that at least. At some point, a kind of table was brought into the clearing, and David Strongheart was helped up onto it to welcome the people from Earth on behalf of all the Davidfolk. Then Headman Newjohn did the same for the Brown River Johnfolk. And then, when my friend Starlight had done it for the Tinafolk over in Half Sky, all three of them hugged and shook hands, up there on the table in front of all of us, I suppose so as to show that they were all friends now.

I'm not sure if it was straight after that or later on, but I know Gaia climbed up onto the table too, along with the two Earth men. I remember how the shouting and screaming carried on for a long long time before they got a chance to speak, but eventually Gaia called out her name again and told us that her many-greats grandmother was Gela's twin sister Candice, and the men said they were Deep and Marius, and Deep said his many-greats uncle was Dixon Thorleye. This news made people go suddenly rather quiet. 'So this isn't Gela herself, then?' people were asking one another. 'These weren't Tommy or Mehmet?' But later on, a story went round that the Earth people really *were* those three, but that they'd chosen not to tell their names, like in those old stories that are told about Great David's son Harry Stonehand, and how, when he became Head Guard, he sometimes used to put on a skin waistwrap like a low person, so he could walk round among the low people and find out what they really thought. People were never quite sure who the two men were, but everyone went back to thinking that Gaia was really Gela.

Gaia said some other things too, but she spoke so many words we didn't know that no one understood much of what she was talking about. The starship *Defiant* had gone back to Earth all by itself, from what I gathered, not long after the Veekle crashed with the Three Companions in it. We'd always thought that it was still waiting up there somewhere in the sky! But apparently it could think for itself like a person – or that's what I understood Gaia to say – and it managed to find its own way home. That was how Earth learned that Eden was here, and the way to reach it, though why this had all taken so long, I really couldn't make out.

I think it was some time after the Earth people and the high people had climbed down from the table again that folk started to go up close to the veekle, standing with their toes against the stones of the Circle, and peering up at its shiny metal skin. It was too high up to reach, but four five kids, on far side to where the Earth people were standing, ran right underneath it, even though that meant going inside the Circle, and one of them started to climb up the ladder. Guards shouted after them to come back, but didn't dare follow after them.

'Leave it, please!' called Marius sharply, and as the kid on the ladder jumped down again, and all of them ran off squealing, he pointed at the veekle with a little black thing in his hand and the ladder pulled up inside by itself with a funny whirring sound, and the piece of metal closed up over it until you could hardly make out the place it had come from in that smooth metal skin.

More people were still coming into the clearing. They were given meat and cakes by Strongheart's helpers.

Then Clare came to find me where me and my kids were standing with the Earth people and the high people. With her were Tom and Flame and little Suzie. They were stopped by one guard after another, but they talked each guard round, and gradually made their way forwards. The poisonfever had taken the little girl so badly that she wasn't even awake any more. She obviously didn't have long to live, and the way she flopped in Flame's arms you might have thought she was already dead if it wasn't for the heat of her, which you could feel without even touching her, like the heat that comes off a spiketree.

'Ask them, Angie,' said Tom. 'Ask them if they can help her.'

'Gaia?' I called out. 'Marius? Deep?'

The three Earth people were talking to the high people and they didn't hear me, but Starlight did, and she drew their attention to us, and to the sick child in Flame's arms.

Straight away Gaia and Marius came over, along with Strong-heart's two young shelterwomen, Jane and Flowerlight. I can't believe that those two tough young high women would normally have bothered about the baby of a low girl like Flame. It would be unusual for them ever to be this close to such a child, in any case, because all their helpers had to leave their babies behind when they came to work at the Great Shelter. But now, when they saw how seriously the Earth people were taking this, it was like the two of them were competing with each other to show how much they cared.

'Oh the poor little darling!' cried pregnant Jane, pushing back her hair that helpers had tied for her into hundreds of plaits, each one decorated with coloured stones.

'She's all burning up, the precious one!' cried Flowerlight, reaching out to touch little Suzie with fingers heavy with rings.

'May I have a look?' Gaia asked Flame.

As Flame looked up into the face of this strange tall woman with her black black skin and her pure white teeth, her mouth was hanging open with amazement. But she handed her Suzie meekly over, and Gaia laid the baby girl gently on the ground. All round us people were craning to see what she'd do, but the guards pushed them back, so that we stood in a small half-circle next to the veekle and the Circle of Stones: the Earth people, the high people, me and my kids, Clare, Tom, Flame and Suzie, and Starlight.

Starlight came to stand beside me. She slipped her arm through mine, and I leaned my head to rest it for a moment on her shoulder. We'd been friends since before we could walk. Hardly a waking went by back on the Grounds when me and Starlight didn't cuddle up together, just the two of us.

'Why are you crying, Mum?' Fox asked me, peering up into my face.

'I thought she was dead,' I told him, wiping the tears from my cheeks and forcing myself not to start sobbing. 'I was told they found her body in the Pool, with its lungs full of water and a stab wound right through it. But here she is, look! Here's my Starlight, alive and well!'

Starlight kissed my hair. 'There's a reason for that story, which I'll tell you later. But you can see for yourself that I'm fine,' she laughed, 'and a lot more grownup than when you last saw me. It's good to see you again, Angie. I heard stories about you as well. I heard *you'd* gone off with a shadowspeaker.'

Twenty-eight

That was me and Starlight, I thought. She'd gone off with the beautiful Headmanson of New Earth. I'd gone off with prickly old Mary with her square face and her small grey eyes.

And just for two heartbeats, even with all these other things that were going on, I went right back in my mind to a time when me and Starlight were maybe six years old – eight wombtimes we'd have said back then – and the two of us were alone by that big rock that stuck up out of the beach at Knee Tree Grounds. We'd found a piece of string that someone had dropped there, and we'd hunted round for small things to tie onto it: a stone, a piece of wood, a fish claw, a black bone from a fatbuck. Now the necklace was finished. Starlight held it round her neck while I stood behind her to tie it on, then we ran off together to show it to her uncle Dixon.

'Look at my necklace, Uncle! Me and Angie made it by ourselves!'

Dixon was rubbing buckfat into a new boat. He looked round and laughed. 'That pair!' he said to Starlight's brother Johnny. 'Starlight and Angie! You just can't separate those two, can you?'

I suppose there's always a story about any friendship between two people. It doesn't have to be mentioned out loud, but it's still there every time they meet, tied up tight in a little bundle: a certain particular shape that neither one has to unwrap to know what's inside it. The story about me and Starlight was well known on Knee Tree Grounds. Every one of the Kneefolk knew that the two of us had been best friends since we were babies, everyone knew we were always together. And though we loved each other, and I'm sure we would have been friends anyway, that story bound us even more tightly together. We'd started the story but now we were in it too.

'Here come the two of them again!' people would say. 'Jeff's ride, did you ever see two kids who were so close?'

Of course there were lots of other kids on Knee Tree Grounds who had a special friend, but we were the pair that people noticed the most. Would they have gone on about us so much if we'd been two pretty girls like Starlight? I don't think so. Would they have gone on about us if we'd been two little batfaces like me? Certainly not. Stories catch on for a reason – we Kneefolk loved the story of Jeff's Shining Ride, for instance, because it made our Jeff look good, and he was the many-greats granddad of pretty much all of us – and the reason people liked the story of me and Starlight was the huge difference between the two of us, which made our friendship seem sweet.

Yes, and that wasn't just what made the story work for the Kneefolk. It was one of the things that made it work for me and Starlight too. It helped me because people would have noticed me a lot less if I hadn't come as a pair with her. And Starlight, well, her name was well chosen, she really was bright like a star, and stars look best against the darkness of the sky. Don't get me wrong. The two of us really *did* love each other, really *did* have fun together, really *did* talk to each other about almost everything that happened. But still, when we made a necklace, it was Starlight that put it on and me that ran along behind her to show it to the grownups. She was the star and I was the grateful darkness.

And look at us now! Here she was beside me, tall beautiful Starlight in her blue longwrap, with pretty coloured stones hanging from her ears and her wrists: one of the highest and most powerful people in all of Eden. And here was me in my rough skin waistwrap, a mum of three kids from a little cluster that no one had heard of, the shelterwoman of a clawfoot man I didn't really love.

All that stuff I've just said, I don't mean I went over it all in my mind. Of course not! There was no time. Two heartbeats and it was done. But it was there all the same, that old bundle, and I didn't need to unwrap it to know what it contained. I was happy happy to have Starlight beside me again, happy happy to know she was alive and doing well. But I wasn't so pleased to find that old story still lying between us, that old familiar shape.

And yet having it there close again made me notice something. There was no time to think about it right then, but in those two heartbeats, maybe because those tall and beautiful Earth people made even Starlight shine less brightly, I'd glimpsed something that I'd never quite noticed before. Seeing that old story up close, seeing it there between us in its wrap, made me realize that it hadn't just shaped my life on Knee Tree Grounds, but my life ever since as well. With Mary as we travelled round the Davidfolk Ground, with Tom when I first met him in Davidstand, with the Michael's Place people when I'd come to join them, over and over again I'd played the part of the grateful darkness.

Twenty-nine

arius went up into the veekle to fetch something to help Suzie, while Gaia squatted down and looked at the huge dark swelling that had puffed up the little girl's shoulder and arm to twice their proper thickness. I noticed as she gently touched it that Gaia was wearing a ring on her finger, made of two metals, one white and one yellow, like the one the Johnfolk stole in the old old story. I was about to point it out to Starlight when Marius came back again, carrying a big box made of some hard smooth red stuff, and he and Gaia began to search through the strange things that were packed inside it in neat neat rows.

'Here it is,' said Marius. Whatever he'd found was wrapped up in some kind of thin covering that you could almost see through, a bit like people sometimes wrap up pieces of stumpcandy in the skin of a bat's wing.

Gaia tore off the wrapping and a tiny metal thing flashed. It was white metal, like the white metal in her ring, not red like the metal from New Earth. All round us people pushed and shoved to see, but if anyone so much as whispered, the whole crowd round them hissed at them to be quiet. We wanted to hear every single thing the Earth people said.

'This is a knife,' Gaia said. 'It's completely clean. Will you let me use it to let out the pus?'

Flame nodded, and Gaia, carefully carefully, pushed it into the horrible swollen wound on the little girl's shoulder. The pus came bursting out at once, splattering over Gaia's face, so she had to wipe it off with the back of her hand. And more kept coming, its yellow colour streaked dirty brown and purple with stale blood. A kind of sigh went up from the people all round us, while Gaia carried on prodding and probing with the knife, all the while gently pressing the flesh round the wound to get all the poison out.

'Now I'll clean it with this,' she said, setting aside the knife and taking something else out of the red box: something soft, a bit like a piece of fakeskin, only completely white. She carefully wiped the gash in Suzie's shoulder, pushed more soft white stuff inside it, and then wrapped even more soft white stuff round it and under her armpit, so that her shoulder was covered up.

'And now,' she said, taking another thing out of her box, 'I'll give her…' She said some words that she could see that neither Flame nor anyone else there could understand, so she tried again. 'I'll put something in her blood to make her better.'

Everything in the red box came wrapped in the same strange shiny covering with tiny writing on it. Gaia tore the stuff off and threw it aside (later on, people would fight for a piece of it) and took out a long thin thing with a point on the end, a bit like the needles made from spiketree thorns that we use to sew our wraps. Then she pressed the thorn into the flesh of the little girl's arm. I saw it catch the light as it slid in, and realized that it was made of white metal too. Everyone gasped. After a short time Gaia pulled it out again and wiped clean the tiny hole that it had made with some more white stuff out of yet another shiny wrap.

'Her fever will go down soon,' she told Flame, standing up, and gently placing Suzie back into her arms. 'But we'll need to clean her wound again.'

Flame and Tom and the others stared up at her.

'Are you saying she'll live?' Tom asked, his voice all wobbly and choked up.

'Oh yes,' Gaia said. 'You'll see her looking a lot better quite soon, and she'll be fine in a day or two.'

She said 'day' instead of waking, that old Earth word, like a few old folk still did in Circle Valley.

Tom and Flame were crying, and so was Clare and me and Trueheart. Even Gaia's eyes were shiny, like people's sometimes are when they've done something good. Big grey old Tom fell down onto his knees and pressed her hand against his tear-smeared beard.

'Thankyou, Mother, thankyou.'

Now there was a pause, while the people who had seen all this took it in, and those further back gradually received the news about what had happened. Whole of the clearing outside the Circle was packed with people now, and their excited voices came together in a constant restless clamour that drowned out the sound of the trees. Then people started to shout out.

'Hey, I've got a sore leg,' called out a woman just beyond the guards. 'Can you fix that for me too?'

'My eyes are going,' shouted an old guy. 'Can you make me see again?'

'My little girl has a sore rash on her skin that won't go away!' called a young woman.

'My teeth ache!' a man said. 'They hurt so much I can't sleep.'

'I've got clawfeet.'

'My baby boy has a bad batface.'

'My granddad can't breathe properly. Have you got something in your red box for that?'

More and more voices called out. Who doesn't have aches and illnesses, or at least know someone that does? As Gaia and the two Earth men looked round at these people and then glanced back at one another, I noticed something in their faces that maybe most people couldn't see. I noticed they were scared. And I noticed once again how tired they were, tired tired, like they hadn't slept for many wakings.

I caught Trueheart's eye. She was standing by her mother, Clare, looking at Gaia's face, then down at the red box, then at the two Earth men, then at me, as she took everything in. She could see, just as I could, that there was only so much stuff in there, that there was no way the Earth people were going to be able to fix all the sores and rashes and wounds of everyone here in Circle Clearing, let alone in all of Eden.

'I guess you can't help everyone,' she said.

Marius looked across at her, the shyer of the two men, the one with yellowy-brown skin like we had in Eden, and dark curly hair.

'No, we can't,' he said. 'We just haven't got enough stuff.'

The people standing round us bent towards one another as those who'd understood what Marius had said repeated it to those who hadn't.

'Never mind,' said the woman with the sore leg. 'There'll be plenty for everyone, won't there, when you take us all back to Earth.'

Again, I saw the three of them glance at one another. How strange and scary this must be for them, I thought, to be three Earth people, tired tired by travelling across the stars, surrounded by hundreds of people from Eden.

'Do you need to sleep?' I asked them.

That made them all smile at once. 'Do we need to sleep?' asked Deep. 'I'll tell you what. I could happily sleep for a weak!' No one really knew what he meant by that exactly, but we could tell he meant he could sleep a long time.

'Well, you must come to my shelters,' said David Strongheart at once, 'and I'll have my helpers—'

This was our Head Guard, remember, a man who only had to ask his guards to do it, and people would be speared, or beaten, or tied to spiketrees to die, a man with twenty-three shelterwomen and a hundred kids, a man whose Great Shelter in Davidstand was as tall as a tree and wide as whole of Circle Clearing. This was the great-great-grandson of Great David. This was one of the people who knew they're already in a story, even while they're still alive. But next thing I knew I'd interrupted him!

'Or I could look after you,' I said to the Earth people, 'me and

Trueheart who saw you first, and all our family. If the Head Guard can give you a shelter, we could live next to it and cook for you, and fetch you the things you need.'

'That would be great, Angie,' said Gaia.

No one argued – how could you argue with someone who came from Earth? – and my old friend Starlight spoke out in my support.

'Good plan,' she said. 'Good good plan. I know Angie. She'll look after you well.'

I'm not quite sure, but I think it was just after that when a weird thing happened. Strongheart stepped forward, and, fat and old as he was, high as he was among the Davidfolk, he knelt down in front of the Earth people. It was hard hard for him to do so, but with great difficulty he knelt down anyway, brushing aside his son and his helpers and shelterwomen when they stepped forward to support him.

'I know you must rest,' he said to the Earth people. 'I know you've travelled far far. And I know you can't help everyone here who has a toothache or a bad back. But please please help your Family. The Johnfolk are attacking us right now, they're doing for our people, just over far side of the Dark. They've already taken Veeklehouse from us, and Davidstand as well, and if we don't do something to stop them, pretty soon they'll be coming over here. Please help us to stop them. We're your True Family. We're the ones that stayed and waited for you. If it had been all up to the Johnfolk, there'd have been no one here to meet you at all.'

Trueheart had moved over to stand near Marius – even that early on, there was something about him that interested her – and she heard Marius speak softly softly to Deep about what Strongheart had just said.

'That might have been easier for everyone, actually,' that's what Trueheart heard Marius say. But then, straight away, he stepped forward and spoke directly to David Strongheart, loudly enough for us all to hear. 'You mean you're at war?' he asked. None of us knew the word, so he tried again: 'You mean two whole groups of people are fighting and killing each other?'

'Yes, exactly!' cried Strongheart. 'We need your help to make them stop.'

The Earth people looked at each other.

'We can't take sides,' I heard Deep say to Gaia. 'We don't know anything about the rights and wrongs of this.'

'How far away are these people who are attacking you?' asked Marius.

'Four five wakings across the Dark,' said Strongheart's son, Leader Harry. He was a big man, with thick hair over the backs of his arms and hands, hair poking out of the top of his wrap, and a big thick beard, black but turning to grey.

'We could send them a message,' suggested Gaia. 'We could send the other side a message, telling them to come here and talk.'

Leader Harry shook his head. 'They'll think it's a trick.'

'Even if they can hear my voice?' asked Gaia.

She took a little black square from out of a pocket in her shiny wrap, and spoke softly to it as if it was alive.

'Now touch it here,' she told Harry, handing it over to him.

Harry took the thing from her, carefully carefully like he thought it might be hot, and touched it where she'd told him to. All at once her voice came out of it, as loud as if she was really speaking. The people crowded round gasped in amazement, and Harry almost dropped the thing.

'Hello Johnfolk,' said Gaia's voice from the little black square, 'this is Gaia from Earth. Three of us have come in a starship. Please stop fighting now and come to meet us.'

Leader Harry turned to his father, and then to Headman New-john and Starlight. All three of them nodded.

'I'll get a buck and some men and take it over there right now,' he said. 'I'll bring their leaders back with me.'

Thirty

So Leader Harry and eight of his guards began their journey back towards the Dark and Wide Forest beyond, and the Earth people tried to rest. Strongheart gave them one of his big square shelters in Brooklyn. It had its own fence round it, with guards to watch over it, and inside the fence, us Michael's Place people, all thirty of us, built little shelters of our own round the big shelter where the Earth people slept. So we kind of had our own little cluster again, except that where once we'd had our little stone circle in middle, now we had people: people who weren't just reminders of Earth, but came from Earth themselves.

All round the fence, people stood and stared. They knew to keep quiet, because the Earth people were sleeping, but even so they couldn't help murmuring and whispering, and once in a while even singing, in soft low voices, some old Earth song like 'Come Tree Row'.

Once Marius came stumbling out and squatted down for some time in a drift of starflowers to take a crap. He took a long long time over it, and everyone watched in fascinated silence. Later on, Gaia came out and threw up two three times, and then Deep as well. It seemed our food didn't agree with them. They did their best to smile at us in a friendly way before they hurried back inside the bark walls of their shelter.

Starlight came to see me. The other Michael's Place people watched in amazement as this high high woman, in her blue wrap and her coloured stones, kissed me and hugged me, and then squatted down beside me to talk. They all moved back, bowing, to give us space, and when Trueheart came closer so she could listen, her mother hissed at her to leave us in peace. Glancing at Starlight to check she was okay with it, I told Clare that Trueheart could stay where she was.

'I won't stop long,' Starlight said. 'I need to be there when Strongheart and Newjohn are talking, to make sure they don't do anything that could harm us in Half Sky. But I had to come and say hello properly, and to catch up on your story.'

'Tell yours first,' I said. 'I've heard enough of it already to know it's more exciting than mine.'

Starlight told me New Earth had turned out to be a cruel harsh place. She'd made dangerous enemies over there when she and Greenstone had tried to make things a bit kinder and fairer. It was really true that Greenstone had been thrown into a fire – this would have been more than ten years ago, but Starlight still had to control her face carefully as she told me this – and the same thing would have happened to Starlight if she hadn't managed to escape across the Pool. She and the Kneefolk had put out the story about her body being found with a spear hole through it, so that the New Earthers wouldn't come looking for her. She'd gone to Half Sky so as to be as far away from them as she could.

'I'm so sorry that you had to hear that story, Angie, about me being dead. All I can say, that if we hadn't told it, I think I might *really* have been dead by now.' She laughed. 'But never mind all that, eh? Your mum will be happy happy to know I've found you, Angie! So will everyone. You must come over and see us all!'

'My *mum*?'

'Yes, dearest, your mum! She's in Half Sky now.' She saw the expression on my face – that news was just too much for me, on top of everything else, and my tears were already flowing – and reached out at once to hug me. 'Oh Angie dear, she's there, and so are your brothers and sisters. So are a whole lot of the people we knew at Knee Tree Grounds. Julie Deepwater persuaded a bunch of them to come, when they got tired of the guards from Nob Head bossing them round. Even my sister Glitterfish is there. And you know how she would never go *anywhere*!'

Gela's heart, if the dead really *had* come back to life and health from under the stones of the Burial Ground, it would hardly have been any stranger than what was actually happening. First, the Earth people, then Starlight, and now this! Our home on Earth, my dead friend, my lost family: all of them restored to me in a single waking! I sobbed and sobbed. Starlight hugged me and rocked me. Candy and Fox came running over.

'Why are you crying, Mum?' Candy demanded. Kids do *not* like it, I've noticed, when their mothers are upset. If their mums need looking after, who's going to look after them?

'Don't worry, dear,' said Starlight. As she gently touched Candy's hand to reassure her, I remembered that, when she was younger, she'd never been easy with little kids. 'I think she's crying because she's happy.'

My old friend was still the star and I was still the grateful darkness. She was the high person who surprised and impressed my new friends. And she was the one who'd given the Kneefolk a new home, while I'd just run away from them to live among the David-folk. But right then I didn't care. Candy and Fox squeezed in to hug me along with Starlight, and I felt happy happy happy.

'They left Knee Tree because it was becoming part of the Davidfolk Ground,' Starlight said, 'with guards and traders and shadowspeakers and all the rest. I don't think there's anyone left there now. The ones who didn't come to join us went over to join the Davidfolk on Mainground instead. Like you did, I guess.

You must tell me that story, Angie. I still can't imagine you with a shadowspeaker.'

'Later,' I sniffed, wiping my face and pulling myself out of that little huddle of people that loved me, so I could look at my old friend's face. 'I'll tell you later. Shadowspeakers are different from what you might think. But now I want to hear more about Half Sky. And then I want to hear more about the Kneefolk.'

'Half Sky's a bit like Knee Tree Grounds in some ways, I guess,' said Starlight. 'Like Knee Tree used to be, I mean, when the David-folk left us alone. We don't bother too much with old old stories and we stay out of the argument between John and David. You might think I'm a high person there – a *big* person as people say in New Earth – but I'm not a high person in the way that Strongheart and his guard leaders are in the Davidfolk Ground. I can't make people do whatever I want, I don't get to choose the story that everyone else lives by, and if the Skyfolk decide they want another Head, well, they can have one. So that's a bit like the old Grounds, as well. I guess we *do* more things in Half Sky, though, than we used to do back on the Grounds. It was John Redlantern's friend Tina Spiketree who first brought people to our ground, and all the stories say she liked to keep busy, she liked to make things happen.'

'Just as you do, Starlight,' I said, smiling. 'I mean, look at everything you've done already! You've been right across Eden! You've become a high high person not just in one ground, but in two completely different grounds! You were never one, were you, for just sitting there and letting the Watcher look out of your eyes?'

Starlight laughed. 'Well, believe it or not, I actually think about the Watcher much more now than I used to. I think it's important to remind myself that Starlight Brooking is just a mask the Watcher wears, so as to stop myself from getting to think that the story is all about me. But yeah, in a way I am like Tina. I want Half Sky to get on and *do* things. We're always trying to figure out how to build better boats, for instance, rather than just making them the same way like we used to on the Grounds, and we've found greenstone and are figuring out how to make it into metal. In that way, we're a little more like the Johnfolk in New Earth. We're like those big grounds too, in that we have something a bit like guards or ring-men. But all our young people have to take part, whether they're men or women, and everyone in Half Sky chooses who will lead them. That way they don't end up bossing everyone else round, like guards and ringmen do.'

'Looks like you might not need guards any more,' said True-heart, who'd been squatting there listening all this time, her arms wrapped round her knees. 'Or metal, or better boats.'

Starlight smiled. 'The Earth people have changed everything, you mean? Well, that's certainly true. But as to what we'll need in future and what we won't need, I'm not sure that's something we can tell yet.'

I could see Trueheart wanted to talk more about that, but I needed news first about my mum and all the other Kneefolk who lived in Half Sky. Fox ran off to fetch the chess set that his dad had carved for him out of wood and bone, realizing that this was turning into typical boring grownup talk about people he'd never heard of or met, but wanting to stay in earshot in case it got more interesting again. He drew a board on the ground, and he and Trueheart began to play, Candy cuddling up against her brother and making suggestions for moves that he pretended to think about but hardly ever followed.

Most of Eden still had no idea what had happened, that was the strange thing. Most of Eden thought the world was the same as it always had been. Never mind further away, there were even parts of *Circle Valley* that hadn't heard the story about the veekle from Earth. Hunters over by Exit Falls, for instance, might have seen a strange light in the sky in the distance but there was no way they could find out what had caused it until several wakings later.

The story was gradually spreading peckway, as Leader Harry and his guards rode towards the Dark, shouting out to people as they rode past, but up on the Dark people were still heading our way in that long sad necklace across the snow, not knowing anything about it. Some people up there had decided not to head for Circle Valley but instead go to Tall Tree or one of the other High Valleys, like Steep Shelter or Buck Hole or Snowglass, which meant they wouldn't hear the news for many wakings. On far side of the Dark, all the news that went back and forth through Wide Forest was about the fight with the Johnfolk. Down alpway in Brown River and way over blueway in Half Sky it would be fifteen twenty wakings before anyone knew about the Earth people, even though Headman Newjohn and Head Woman Starlight had already met them in Circle Valley. As to the people over in New Earth, well, if the news was going to get there, it would first have to cross Wide Forest to the Pool, then travel for three wakings across the bright water, and then across Deep Darkness, and then the bright water on the other side before it even reached the outer edge of their ground, let alone their high people who, so it was said, lived in holes in the ground as far back from their poolside as Davidstand was from ours.

The Earth people slept and slept.

'Those were fast bucks that Harry took,' I said to Dave, after Starlight had gone back to join the high people. We all spoke softly softly so as not to disturb the sleepers. 'Do you reckon they'll have reached the path up onto the Dark yet?'

'I don't reckon they can be much more than halfway to the Dark.' Dave glanced up from a little knife that he'd started to whittle from a piece of bone. He scraped away for a bit then looked up again. 'What I worry about is that the Johnfolk won't believe Harry's got a message from Gela, and will just do for him and his guys, without ever finding that… well, that talking thing, I don't know what you call it… That little square thing Mother Gela gave Leader Harry with her voice inside it.'

'Oh they'll find it, alright,' said Tom. 'Even if they do for Leader Harry, they'll see he's a high man and they'll be all over him to find out what he's got on him.'

'She's not Gela,' said Trueheart. 'Her name is Gaia, and she's the many-greats niece of Gela's sister Candy.'

Tom chuckled knowingly. 'Or so she *says*. But look at that dark dark skin of hers. How many people can there be who look like that?'

Marius came staggering out of the shelter, looked at us for a moment, and then hurried off into the starflowers again.

'I'll check they have enough water in there,' I said. 'You need water when your guts are playing up.'

'I never thought, somehow,' said Clare, 'it just never really struck me before that people from Earth would crap and piss and throw up just as we do. It seems odd, somehow, don't you think? And yet, if we need to do those things, I guess it shouldn't be so surprising that they do too.'

Thirty-one

About now, give or take a few wakings, a buck came to the top of the high ridge surrounding Tall Tree Valley, and looked down from the Dark into that little shining forest down there with the darkness wrapped all round it. It was a big old smoothbuck, with a skin draped over it to keep it warm, and on the skin sat a woman, though she was so wrapped in buckskin just then that you wouldn't have been able to tell whether she was a man or a woman, only that she wasn't that tall. With her there were two guards on woolly-bucks, each one holding a spear whose tip glinted in the light of the animals' headlanterns, and two younger women sharing another smoothbuck. She didn't have a darkguide. It was tricky to find one just then, and she and the guards knew the paths pretty well.

The woman pulled off her headwrap. Her face was big and square. Her hair was turning to grey, and there was a stoop in her shoulders that hadn't been there last time I'd seen her, but she looked as firm and determined as ever. She sat there on the back of her buck, looking down into Tall Tree Valley, and then she gave a little nod, pulled the wrap back onto her head, and began to ride forwards again down the steep snow-covered slope.

There are many things I found out later, and had to piece together as best I could with what I already knew, and this was one of them. Mary Shadowspeaker had been over near Nob Head when the Johnfolk came from New Earth, and she'd chosen to head up to Tall Tree Valley to get away from them, going not by the main path – David's Path – that went up from Davidstand, but by another smaller steeper path that climbed up someway rockway from that, called High Valley Shortcut.

🌿

Mary liked Tall Tree Valley and had taken me there on our way over to Circle Valley. Her father had come from there, and she often told people about how one of her own many-greats grandfathers had been Mehmet Batwing, Wise Mehmet, who'd built the first stone shelters there, and been guard leader there when he died.

'And of course, it was Mehmet Batwing who first found Tall Tree Valley all those years ago when he was with John Redlantern and the others,' she'd also told me. 'He saved all their lives when they were lost in the darkness and the cold.'

On Knee Tree Grounds I'd heard that it was Jeff Redlantern who found Tall Tree, that time he rode off bravely all by himself on the back of a woollybuck in search of warmth and light when the others were all stuck on a snowslug and didn't know which way to go. We called the story Jeff's Shining Ride and, as I said before, it was a particular favourite of ours, but I let Mary have her version as I usually did. After all, it was Jeff himself who said that the past keeps changing, and it's the present that always stays the same, so he couldn't really complain that I didn't stand up for him.

We'd had a warm welcome down there in that strange little valley back then. I guess they didn't get so many visitors, and the Tall Tree folk liked it that Mary treated them like they were special. Just about everyone in whole valley came to see her show and, at the end of it, Mary told the people there they were lucky lucky to live in the place that was special to Wise Mehmet, the one who'd turned away from the True Story and then had the courage to come back. Of all the people from the old stories, he was one of the best. Everyone cheered loudly at that.

After the show, I remember, we went for a walk, just Mary and me, along a stream. One of the weird things about Tall Tree Valley is that all the streams there flow not out of the valley, but towards its middle where their water all pours into an enormous hole. We walked right up to the edge of that hole and looked down, with the roar of waterfalls all round us, peering through the spray and steam for glimpses of the warm shining forest of Underworld.

Mary slipped her arm round my waist and kissed me on the cheek. 'Oh Angie, I'm so glad to have you, and I'm so excited we're on the way to Circle Valley. I know you're going to be great.'

She pointed out a kind of ladder made out of rope, which dangled down down down into the hole. It disappeared into the mist so I couldn't see where it led, but apparently it carried right on down to the bottom. Mary told me the Tall Tree people climbed down it to hunt and gather fruit and flowers. Her own dad had often been down in the caves. They stretched away for miles, she said. There were giant slinkers down there, twenty feet long and fat as bucks, that crept along the ground, and there was a kind of tree that didn't stand up by itself but climbed over the walls and roofs of the caves, so the brightness of forest was above you as well as round you. And, if you knew where to go, you could find holes and cracks that dropped down still deeper, with hot air blasting up from yet more layers of Underworld all the way down to the great fire.

I eyed the ladder uneasily, desperately hoping that Mary wouldn't suggest we climbed down it. I wasn't used to heights. Knee Tree Grounds hardly rises above the level of the water, and the cliff near Michael's Place was no more than twenty feet high at most. I found it scary enough just standing on the top there and looking down.

But then Mary laughed. 'The Underworld's for Johnfolk, though, I reckon.' We'd been hearing stories lately in the Davidfolk Ground about how the Johnfolk in New Earth didn't live under the black sky as we did, but under the ground: the high people in big shining caves, the low people in narrow dark holes that the ringmen forced them at spearpoint to dig out for themselves. 'Gela's True Family should be out under the sky, don't you think, Angie, so that Earth can find us when they finally return?'

She stood looking down for a moment, then she turned to wink at me and laugh, pulling me against her again.

'Who am I kidding, Angie? Just the thought of going down that thing makes my hands sweat with fear.'

She could be sweet sometimes. She didn't often make fun of herself, but when she did, it was lovely. And Tall Tree Valley seemed to be a place where she found it easier to be like that. I guess that might have been part of the reason why, when the Johnfolk came across the Pool, Mary headed to Tall Tree: it was a place she felt at home. But maybe she also figured that the High Valleys, which have no Circle of Stones, no Veekle, no mementoes of Earth of any kind, would be too small and unimportant for the Johnfolk to bother about.

And she was certainly right to keep out of the Johnfolk's way. They were especially cruel to the shadowspeakers when they caught them. They showed them no pity at all. All across Eden, people loved Mother Gela, but one thing that Johnfollk and Davidfolk both especially hated were those who claimed to hear Gela telling a different story to their own.

Thirty-two

A long way past the length of a normal sleep, the Earth people were still in their shelter. I think maybe they pretended to still be sleeping, even after they were really awake, just so they could get some peace and quiet for a bit. It must have been hard hard for them, tired and sick in their stomachs, to think of facing all us Eden people.

I sat outside, mending our bodywraps and footwraps in case we needed them again. Helpers came regularly from Strongheart to see if the Earth people were awake yet. The crowd watched and waited, sometimes softly singing 'Come Tree Road' or one of the other old songs about going home to Earth. Over in Circle Clearing, another crowd stared up at the veekle. From time to time that huge metal thing would make a little sound and a light would flash, like it was a living thing that was stirring in its sleep.

Away across the Valley, Leader Harry and his eight guards were climbing up towards the Dark. We didn't know what was going to happen, and everything felt strange, like we were dreaming and awake both at the same time. But this was a happy time, full full of hope.

And good news seemed to keep coming. Little Suzie wasn't so ill now: she cried and squirmed about again, when a waking ago she'd been limp and unconscious on the edge of death.

At last Marius came out. We all knelt and bowed, like people do when a high person appears, and an excited murmur went round the watching crowd outside the fence. He looked embarrassed, waving to us to sit up again and squatting down with us, without even seeming to notice the crowd. He had a stale weary smell to him, and he looked just as tired as he did when he went to rest.

'How long ago was it that you were on Earth?' Trueheart asked him.

'About twenty days,' he said, using that old Earth word again. 'It seems much longer when you're living through it, but I think that's about right.'

We were all amazed. These people were still on Earth, standing under its blue sky, when the Johnfolk set out across the Pool!

'That seems hardly *any* time,' I said. 'We thought Earth was far far away.'

'It *is* far away,' Marius said. He pointed up at the great wheel of Starry Swirl above us. '*That's* far away. All of it. Further away from here than any human being can really imagine. And it's bigger than anyone can imagine too. Earth is deep inside it. We only got here so quickly because we kind of cheat and don't go through space at all, or only a bit of it, anyway, and then take a kind of shortcut. You see, we ...' I was still fixing torn bodywraps, and Marius picked up a scrap of buckskin lying in front me. 'Imagine this is space,' he said, and then folded it over, so that the two opposite ends of it lay side by side. 'We jump across from one side to the other, instead of going through what lies in between.'

That made no sense at all to me, or to Tom or Clare, or to any of the other Michael's Place grownups that were listening. But I noticed Trueheart watching Marius with bright eyes. It was like he was talking about things that she'd never heard named before but had somehow known were there.

'This is ... what? The skin of an animal?' asked Marius, looking at the scrap in his hands. 'What an interesting texture. I'd like to see some animals soon. That's what I study, you see, animals and plants, and—'

'I don't get that thing about cheating and space,' I said, 'but if it only takes you twenty wakings to get here, and if you knew how to find us, how come you've taken four hundred years?'

Behind me, Gaia had just come out of the shelter and it was her that answered me.

'You need to understand, Angie, that for the first three hundred years, hardly anyone on Earth knew that Eden existed, or even that the *Defiant* had come back. It was all kept a secret. My great-grand-mother found out about it and, after a lot of work and a lot of arguing, she managed to find the...' She broke off, and looked at Marius for help. This was going to happen often: one or other of them would be speaking and then suddenly they'd stop and look at one of the other two, realizing that they'd been about to say a word we wouldn't understand and hoping for suggestions for another word to put in its place. 'My great-grandmother found the *Defiant*'s memory,' Gaia said. 'I think that's the best way to put it. She found the memory of where it had been, and the... well, you saw the linkup, didn't you, that black square thing I gave to Leader Harry? So you know we've got a way of saving pictures and sounds and words? Well, my great-grandmother found pictures of these trees you have here, and she found... well... the *voices* of the five people who found this place. And they were... well, I guess you won't know this word, but...'

Marius took over from her. It made me think of kids playing football, and how they pass on the ball to someone else when they're about to be dragged down. 'It's a bit hard to explain,' he said, 'but we can send pictures and voices from one place to another—'

'Don't worry,' said Trueheart. She and Fox were still sitting over their game of chess, but they'd been listening to everything. 'We know about lecky-trickity and telly vijun.'

Marius and Gaia glanced at one another and smiled.

'Well, yes,' said Gaia. 'It *is* like telly vijun. The original land-ing veekle was sending those voices and pictures up to the starship right up to the moment it crashed. The starship... well... it kind of stored them, and when it saw there was no chance of anyone being able to get back up to it from the surface of Eden, it brought them back to Earth. My great-grandmother found out about those pictures and voices and tracked them down. She was a... well, you might not know the word, but she was a *historian*, which means her whole job was to figure out things from the past. She found out about Eden and what happened here, and then she gave all the rest of her life to trying to find a way of getting a starship back here again. Her son, my grandfather, did likewise, and so did my mum and dad. But it's hard to build a starship. It...' Again, like a football player who's been cornered, she passed the ball back to Marius.

Marius rubbed his hands over his tired face. 'Okay,' he finally said. 'Imagine some guy here in Eden wanted to build something that would take a thousand people ten years to make: a thousand people working solidly, let's say, with no time for anything else, with another ten thousand people needed to work alongside them for all those ten years to gather together the things needed to build it with. It wouldn't be easy, would it, for that guy to actually make it happen? How would he persuade all those people to help him? And even if he did persuade them, how would he find enough for them to eat and drink and...' He said some words that we didn't know, but by his actions we could sort of see he was asking how people could wrap themselves or make themselves shelters, if all their time was spent building this thing. 'Do you see what I mean? It would require, well, I don't know, but let's say ten thousand *more* people, just to get food and all of that for those one thousand who were doing the building and for those ten thousand who were getting the stuff together.'

We nodded. It was hard for us to imagine anything that would take all that time and effort, but it wasn't difficult to understand that people wouldn't easily be persuaded to do it. And anyway, that was twenty-one *thousand* people he'd spoken about! Were there that many in all of Eden? I had no idea, but it didn't seem likely to me.

'It's a bit like metal, I guess,' said Davidson after a moment.

'They say it takes hundreds of people to get that special metal stone out of the ground, and heat it up in fires, and gather the wood for the fires. The only way the big people over there can get the small people to do all that is to force them at the point of a spear.'

This interested Marius, tired and ill as he was.

'You're making metal? *Already?*' He seemed quite impressed. 'Where is this?'

'Oh it's far away from here,' Davidson said. 'It's another ground across the water called New Earth, and—'

'But what I still don't get,' I interrupted, 'is why was it kept a secret that the *Defiant* had come back?'

'Well,' Gaia said. 'That's kind of complicated too, but it was to do with the fact that it wasn't supposed to come here in the first place.'

Deep had come out as well now, that tall tall man with his strange pale skin that had so little colour in it that you could see the pink blood beneath it. He smiled at us when we noticed him, a bright warm smile, and raised one big hand in friendly greeting. Their hands fascinated me, I remember. I kept looking at the little marks on their skin, the tiny wrinkles, the uneven edges of their nails. I guess they sort of proved to me that these people weren't shadows or dreams or characters in stories. Only real people, surely, could have wrinkles on their skins you could count?

'The thing is that the *Defiant* wasn't supposed to come here in the first place,' Deep said, squatting down. 'Things were really bad on Earth back then. There were floods and storms in some places and no water at all in others. There wasn't enough to eat. Folk were starving in many different places. Folk were running from their homes in search of new places to live. All over the world, people were fighting for...' He said another word we didn't know but which seemed to mean *ground*. 'And there were fights for water too. I know you have a war going on here at the moment,' at least we knew *that* word now, 'but back then there were *lots* of wars on Earth, all going on at the same time.'

'That's right,' said Gaia. 'That's how it was then. And a lot of people thought it wasn't right that this huge effort should be going into trying to find another world, when they already had all these problems at home, particularly since finding a new world really wouldn't solve any of them. I guess if I'd been alive then, I would probably have agreed with them.'

'I would have done too,' said Deep. 'But anyway, just before the *Defiant* set out – in fact it was when the three astronauts were already inside it – lots of angry people, right across the Earth, started to demand that it shouldn't go, that it should be broken up and brought back down to Earth so its parts could be used for things that would actually help people. It's gen rater, for instance, was more powerful than any—' He broke off, realizing that he'd lost us all.

'Anyway,' said Marius, 'it was decided that the starship shouldn't set out, and that the three astronauts should come back down to Earth. But—'

'But they refused to stop,' said Gaia. 'And that's why *five* people ended up coming here. Only three had set out, but when they refused to come back, two more were sent after them to—'

By now all the Eden folk round them were smiling and nodding.

Gaia laughed. 'Oh I see you know that part already!'

Know about it? Tom's dick, of course we did! Every single Virsry that old story was acted out in every single cluster in the Davidfolk Ground, beside every little circle of stones. Three men were carried about in the Big Sky-Boat, pretending to be Dixon, Mehmet and Tommy, the Three Disobedient Men, and a man and a woman were carried after them in the Small Sky-Boat, pretending to be Gela and Michael Namegiver in the Police Veekle. In the smallest clusters, people might not get round to building those boats, but even they would act it out with little toy ones.

'And when the starship finally came back,' said Deep, 'new people were in charge in the biggest…' He said another word that sounded like 'come trees' but also seemed to mean *grounds*. 'They didn't want people getting all excited about other homes across the stars, because obviously it wasn't going to be possible to move large numbers of folk from Earth to here, and they thought the news would just distract people from what needed doing right there. So they kept it completely secret, so secret that it could have been forgotten if Gaia's great-granny hadn't—'

'How is Suzie?' interrupted Gaia. She'd noticed Flame nearby nursing her baby against her breast. 'I must clean that cut again soon.'

'She's much better,' Flame told her, and then she suddenly thrust the child into Clare's arms and ran over to kiss Gaia's hand. 'Oh thankyou, Mother Gela! Thankyou! Thankyou! Thankyou!'

All this time the people crowded outside the fence had been silently watching us, keeping quiet quiet as they tried their best to make out at least a little bit what was being said. But now, at last, something had happened that they could all understand, for everyone knew by then about the baby and the red box and the metal thorn. They cheered and clapped and began to sing.

They were still singing when helpers arrived from Strongheart's shelter to invite the Earth people to come and talk to the high people. The rest of us settled down to wait for their return, happy happy still, but full of questions, and some of us beginning to sense that, however wonderful this all felt, the ground we stood on was falling away beneath our feet.

I thought about Leader Harry on the back of his buck. He was getting near to the edge of the Dark. The headlantern of his buck was starting to light up the ground round him, and monkeys were jumping and wheeling away from him, and up into those last few trees before the snow.

Thirty-three

Mary probably saw monkeys too as she rode down into Tall Tree Valley with her guards and helpers, but if so they'd have been the special flying kind that you get in the High Valleys, the ones with the flaps of skin that stretch out between their six arms, and let them glide between those big trees as if they had wings. Tall Tree Valley is a little steep bowl in middle of darkness and you can easily see from one side to the other. As her buck climbed down the path, there was a row of little white patches of light moving slowly down far side of the valley. It was more frightened people climbing down from David's Path.

Of course I didn't know until later that Mary was at Tall Tree at that time, but she was in my thoughts all the same. The truth was that, even after eight years, and even though I hadn't seen her once since the time she turned her head away from me in Circle Valley and told her guards to keep me away from her, I still thought about her every waking. And she was particularly in my thoughts when something new happened, something unexpected, because, even after all this time, I would still ask myself, What would Mary say? What would Mary's opinion be? How would Mary sort this out? However unkind she'd been to me, the fact was that her views were much more interesting than the views of anyone I'd met since. I guess that was because she didn't just think about the world we can see with our eyes, like most people did in Michael's Place, but about the greater world that hid behind it, the wider story, in which each person's own little life is only just one thread.

Although I hadn't seen Mary since that time, I certainly *could* have done. In fact I could have seen her at least five times, because that's how often she'd come to put on shows in Veeklehouse while I'd been living at Michael's Place. Each time she came I heard people talking about her a little more excitedly than the last, as Mary became one of the best-loved and best-known shadowspeakers in all of the Davidfolk Ground. 'Some of them just keep on about their presents,' people would say about her, 'so you end up wondering if presents are all that really interests them. But that Mary never even mentions them. Not once. She takes whatever we have to give, of course – well, she's got to live – but you get the feeling she'd put on her shows anyway if we gave her nothing at all.' I felt kind of proud of Mary when I heard people speak of her like that, but I still kept away, afraid of what it might stir up inside me if I saw her again.

I was still angry angry with her for the way she treated me in Circle Valley, turning her back on me after all that time, not even giving me a chance to speak, not even thinking about how lonely and desperate I might feel to be left there alone, so far away from anyone I knew. '*Listen* to me, Mary!' I wanted to yell at her whenever I thought about it. 'Just bloody listen to me for ten heartbeats! You got it wrong. You got it *all* wrong. I *don't* think I'm better than you. Of *course* not. How could you be so dumb? I look up to you! Surely that's obvious! I wasn't trying to say I knew better than you, I was just asking for a bit of the help you happily gave, waking after waking, to everyone who came to your shows.'

But at the same time I could understand quite well why she'd been angry with me. Mary was much braver than me. She dared to believe in something – *really* believe in it, like it was as solid and certain as a rock or a tree trunk – even if she couldn't prove it for certain. And, what's more, she didn't just *say* she believed in it, like a lot of people do, but had given up pretty much everything else for that one thing that she believed in, which is something hardly anybody does at all. It was as if she was playing a game of toss-up, like the one I once watched guards and traders playing at Veeklehouse, and had bet everything she had on one single throw of the dice, so certain was she that she knew which side would come up on top. I've not met *anyone* else who did that, except maybe Starlight, who bet everything on a man she hardly knew from far side of the Pool.

So, even though I was angry with her for the way she'd treated me, I still looked up to Mary. I still loved her in a way. And the truth was that, however angry I might be with her, I was much angrier with myself for what had happened.

I mean, Tom's fat dick, it wasn't as if she hadn't warned me! 'Our Mother's voice is quiet quiet,' those were her words. 'She doesn't shout at us. She speaks so softly you might think it was just your own thoughts.' You couldn't get much clearer than that. And yet, not once but twice, the first time and the final time I went into the Circle, a firm clear voice had spoken to me in my mind and told me exactly what I needed to do, and I'd just ignored it.

Again and again and again, in the eight years since I'd last seen her, I'd gone over that in my mind. How could I have failed to listen to the voice inside my head that told me to go over to Mary and tell her about the things I'd been holding back from her? Could there really have been any doubt at all that telling her was the right thing to do?

And of course the answer to that was no. I should have been honest with Mary. Once I'd done that, once I'd got those secrets out of the way – who knows? – perhaps I *would* have begun to hear Gela herself more clearly, and learned to tell the difference between her voice and my own thoughts. But how could I ever have expected to hear her if I refused to listen even to myself? How could I expect to open my mind to Gela if I closed it up to my best friend and teacher? Over and over, I asked myself these things. Of course, I knew perfectly well that the reason I hadn't spoken to Mary about my secrets was that I was afraid of making her angry, afraid of her asking things of me that I'd find difficult to do. But as it turned out, she couldn't possibly have been angrier if I *had* told her than she was when I didn't, and she couldn't possibly have made things harder for me either.

Sometimes I wondered if she'd known all along that I was keeping secrets. She was so smart about things like that, she had such sharp sharp eyes, and – who knows? – perhaps Gela herself had even told her. It was quite possible that Mary knew everything already and was just waiting for me to figure out what I had to do. It was a test, that was all, and not that hard a test either. If that was really so, no wonder Mary had been disappointed. It wasn't because I didn't hear Gela – she knew that was hard; she knew that took time – it was because I'd let her down.

And look where letting her down had taken me! Look what I'd become as a result. A low low woman who foraged and hunted for her living like a thousand other low people across the Davidfolk Ground, and lived among other low people who knew next to nothing, and didn't matter to anyone except themselves.

And yet I could have been with Mary. I could have been with someone who was known and loved right across the Davidfolk Ground, from Rockway Edge to the White Streams. I could even have become known and loved in the way that she was. (Yes, and how else could a woman be so known and respected among the Davidfolk except as a shadowspeaker? Even the highest of high women had to live in the shadows of their men.) I could have been part of something important, something big, looking after all the people of True Family, helping them understand things, helping them grow, helping them find their way home. I might have come to know Gela, not in the way that everyone can, but as one of her special special helpers, the ones she trusts most, the ones she calls on. And I could have shared all this with Mary, one of the smartest and strongest people I'd ever known, who could have chosen *so* many people to be her helper but had chosen me.

No one was smart like Mary in Michael's Place. Except perhaps for Trueheart, no one was curious about the world in the way she was, no one was quick like she was at figuring things out. The rest of them could talk quite happily all waking about nothing more interesting than the next meal, or their kids, or the trades they managed to get in Veeklehouse, or the scraps of stories they picked up about the high people: 'They say Leader Hunter's oldest boy is in big big trouble with his dad.' 'I heard Strongheart gave his new woman a whole wrap covered in colour-stones, the lucky girl.' 'If we go to Veeklehouse next waking, apparently, we might see Leader Mehmet's daughters. Everyone says they're pretty pretty pretty.'

So I think the main reason I never went to Mary's shows was that I couldn't bear to be reminded of how much I'd thrown away, and dreaded the thought of her seeing me, and having her turn her back on me once more. But a little part of me also dreaded the idea that she might forgive me, as she forgave so many people the stupid things they did, and offer me the chance to go with her once again. Because how could I go with her, now that I had kids to care for?

Mary rode down into Tall Tree Valley, rode in under those huge trees with those long trunks they need to keep their lanterns above the snow when it falls, as it quite often does, right down into the bottom of the valley. She made her way to the Tall Tree cluster – it's not far from the place where the path comes down – and rode in among those strange shelters, different from any other shelters I've seen, with their thick stone walls and their thick strong wooden roofs built to bear the weight of heavy snow. She found the cluster all swollen up, like Davidstand had been, and like Old Family cluster in Circle Valley was now, with scared people from different parts of the Davidfolk Ground who'd come there to escape the Johnfolk.

No one knew how such a small place would be able to feed everyone. No one had a plan as to what to do next. But Mary went to the circle of stones in middle of the cluster – Wise Mehmet had laid it out with his own hands after he took Tall Tree Valley back into True Family – and she put on a show.

She told the people that of course they were frightened, of course they were worried about the Johnfolk. We all knew how cruel they were, we all knew how they forced people to work in holes in the ground, we all knew how they made their low people listen to a false Gela, who told them wicked lies with Gela's stolen ring on her finger.

'But you must remember that Mother Gela's on *our* side,' Mary told them. And she reminded them that, no matter how hard things became for them, if they only remembered that, everything would work out for them in the end. Because Gela was watching them from far off Earth with all the love that a mother has for her children. She was watching them, and she was keeping their home ready for them. And one waking they would all find their way there, just so long as they kept their hearts open to the Mother of us all.

'That's all she asks of you,' Mary told them. 'That you keep your heart open, so she'll be able to reach out to you and guide you home.'

It was one of her best best shows, so people would say later. There was so much grief in that cold cluster, so much fear, so much longing. And Mary had always understood those things. Better than any of the other shadowspeakers, she'd always understood how close those feelings were to the surface of people's minds, even in good times, even in times when there weren't enemies burning down our shelters, and riding through our ground with metal spears. And right then in Tall Tree Valley, those feelings weren't even hidden. Never mind below the surface, they were right on top. Everyone had lost their homes, or was afraid of losing their home soon. Everyone was scared. Everyone longed and longed for something that couldn't ever be found in Eden: a place where things weren't just safe for a waking or two, but were always safe, safe forever and ever.

'It's really there,' said Mary, with tears and sweat running down her face. 'It's really there, waiting for you on Earth, with the lovely light of the sun shining down on it from the blue blue sky. Our *home*! Our real true home, where our Mother waits for us, to take us in her arms, and hold us tightly, and dry away our tears.'

They all cheered and wept and cheered some more. As she often did, Mary went round them, kissing and hugging one person after another, murmuring words of advice. And when people offered her presents, she just pushed them away: 'No, my dear, you need to keep that for yourself and these little ones of yours. Don't you worry about me. I can look after myself.'

Presently she had them all sing 'Come Tree Row' and they went round and round that old song, again and again and again, not wanting to stop, not wanting to bring it to an end. For when they stopped singing it, they knew, the feeling of going home would fade away, and they'd be back in Eden again, crammed into that little bowl of light surrounded by the Dark, with all their fear and grief crowding in on them the same as ever.

And of course none of them – not Mary or any of them – had the slightest idea that only four five wakings away, there was a new landing veekle already standing in middle of the Circle of Stones.

Thirty-four

Two three hours after going to see Strongheart, the Earth people came back to their shelter again. It had been a strange meeting, Starlight told me later. In one way, Strongheart and Newjohn were just as excited as anyone else to have the Earth people among them, and they were proud proud too that it should happen when they were the bosses of their two grounds, because that would help to make sure that they were remembered in the stories of the future. But at the same time both of them were full of worries and doubts.

The Earth people were kind and polite.

'Eden is beautiful,' Deep said to Strongheart, 'and the people are wonderfully welcoming.'

'Thankyou, thankyou!' Strongheart bowed low and gestured to them to sit down on the piles of skins that were arranged under the tall whitelantern tree in middle of his big big shelter. 'We were raised well by our first mother, Gela, who came from Earth just like you.'

'I notice you always talk about Gela here, Head Guard,' Gaia said, when they were all squatting on the skins, by the big warm tree trunk, 'and not so much about Tommy.'

'Well, he was a bad man, wasn't he?' Strongheart said. 'He disobeyed President and brought Gela here against her wishes, when she was only doing what President asked.'

Helpers came with mugs of badjuice and barks piled high.

There were different kinds of flowercakes. There were little sweet-bat hearts, smoked over a fire and stuffed with stumpcandy. There were small strips of dried spearfish.

'Those red cakes are from Brown River where Newjohn comes from, across the Dark and way way down alpway,' Strongheart told the Earth people. 'The white ones are from Rockway Edge. The spearfish comes from way out on the bright water near—'

He broke off. High people always had food that came from far away – it was one of their ways of showing their reach and their power – but it had just occurred to him that, if you came from Earth, the distance these cakes and fish had travelled wouldn't seem far at all, and he didn't want to seem like some silly boasting kid.

The Earth people nibbled at the food and sipped at their bad-juice. It was obvious they didn't like it – last time they'd tried our food it had made them ill – but they pretended they did. Strong-heart only picked at the food himself, and Newjohn selected a bit of dried spearfish and chewed at the edge of it, watching the Earth people with his clever pointy face.

'What we wanted to ask you, Head Guard,' Deep bowed as he wiped his hands and mouth with the strip of fakeskin Strongheart's helpers had given him, 'is if you would mind us spending a couple or three wakings exploring the forest here. We're interested to learn more about the animals and trees. It will help us understand Eden better.'

Strongheart and Newjohn looked at each other. They hadn't expected this at all.

'Animals and trees?' said Strongheart after a moment. 'Of course. But don't you—?'

'If we can learn more about the life on Eden,' Gaia explained, 'we may one day be able to help you with useful things like new...' She stopped, realizing she'd been about to say a word they wouldn't know. 'We might be able to help you find new ways of helping people when they're poorly, like I helped that baby girl with the infected shoulder.'

'Or things that will make you all grow bigger and stronger,' said Deep.

Since neither of the two old men seemed to know what to say about this, Starlight stepped in.

'It sounds a good plan in that case, doesn't it, Head Guard? You can explain to your people that our friends from Earth aren't leaving us when they go out into forest, just trying to understand more about the world we live in. It might seem strange to us that they want to look at animals and trees, but we know, don't we, that on Earth people know much much more than we do? I guess we're learning something now about how they actually find out all that stuff!'

'That's right,' said Marius. 'We call it *science*.'

None of the Eden people knew the word, but he repeated it for them, and told them how it was written, and later on Starlight came back and told it to me.

'*Science*,' she said. (How quickly I'd grown used to the idea that it was Starlight here talking to me, really Starlight, really my old friend!) 'From what I gathered, it's not a thing, exactly, but more a way of figuring stuff out. It's like the world itself has a story – this thing happened because of that, that happened because of the other, and so on – and science is a way of figuring out what that story is, without getting it all mixed up with our own stories.'

Trueheart was listening carefully carefully while Starlight was explaining this. 'That sounds *good* good,' she said. 'Us humans are such babies. Us Eden people are, anyway. We always try and make our stories come out the way we want them to.'

🌿

'Sci-*ence*,' Strongheart slowly repeated, as he sat on his pile of skins in his big shelter, turning the word over, as you might turn over some creature from forest that a hunter had brought in, figuring out what kind of thing it was, what kind of teeth it had, what kind of legs and hands. 'Sci Ence.'

'It means looking at things like animals and trees and rocks,' Deep said. Even sitting down, Deep was big big, but his face was friendly and kind. 'Looking at them in a special way, inside and out, not only with our eyes but with…' He glanced at the other Earth people as he struggled to find words that we'd understand. '…but with different kinds of tools we have for seeing things that are too small for eyes to see, or for figuring out what they're made of.'

Newjohn laughed. 'But we *know* what animals are made of! Meat and bone and blood.'

'Ah, but what are meat and bone made of?' asked Deep with a friendly smile. 'And is the meat and bone of Eden animals made of different things from our own? Why is their blood green, for instance, while ours is red? How come most of them have six limbs while most large Earth creatures only have four? How do their eyes see, when they're so different from ours? And *what* can they see? Do they see the same colours as us, or different ones? Who knows? Perhaps they see heat as much as they see light. That would make some sense, seeing as there'd have been almost no light at all in Eden until life first appeared.'

Again Newjohn laughed uneasily. 'Michael's names, you people say some strange things! How could we possibly know what animals see?'

'Well,' began Marius, 'it's not easy, but we could begin by testing whether they can tell the difference between two colours. It would be a matter of—'

'But that would be for later, Marius, wouldn't it?' Gaia interrupted him with a smile. 'For the moment, if it's okay with Head Guard Strongheart here, we just want to wander out into the forest and see what's there.'

Strongheart looked at Newjohn, who gave a tiny shrug and a nod. When Leader Harry had still been in Circle Valley, Strongheart had turned to him for advice, but of course Harry was crossing the Dark now, and the only other man there who was anything like as high as Strongheart was Headman Newjohn. Starlight found it funny how these two old guys, one fat and round-faced, one thin and pointy-faced, had begun to rely on each other, even though Strongheart was head of all the Davidfolk, and a many-greats grandson of Great David, and Newjohn was head of the Brown River folk, and the many-greats grandson of Juicy John himself.

'Well, if you need to look at the plants and animals,' the old man said, 'then of course you must. I only ask that you come back before the New Earthers get here.'

'We'll be back long before that,' said Deep. 'And when we come back, we thought maybe you'd like us to show you all some pictures from Earth.'

The two old men looked at each other, unsure what was being offered to them.

'If I may, Head Guard, I'll show you an example,' Deep said, and he took out another flat square thing from a kind of bag he was carrying. It was what they called a linkup, much like the one that Leader Harry was carrying to the Johnfolk right at that moment up there on Snowy Dark, with Gaia's voice inside it. It looked like it was made of blackglass, though it was smoother than any blackglass on Eden. 'Here is my little daughter, Avi,' he said, and handed it across to David Strongheart.

Strongheart took the glass from him and looked into it. His eyes weren't so good – many people his age, after all, couldn't see at all – so he held it out at arm's length. Then he, Newjohn and Starlight all peered at it.

'I can see something moving,' Strongheart said.

'It's a little girl!' cried Starlight, whose eyes were still sharp as ever. 'Listen! You can hear her voice!'

'Oh yes, I can see her!' shouted out Newjohn, forgetting for a moment that he was Headman of all the Riverfolk, and acting like an excited child.

Strongheart could hear the little girl, but he still couldn't make her out. 'Maybe you need these?' Marius said, taking out from his wrap another strange new object: two circles of a special kind of glass that wasn't black like most glass, but could be seen through as if it was water, like the glass on top of the veekle. Marius showed Strongheart how to fix them over his eyes and now, when the old guy looked at the picture again, it had suddenly become perfectly clear to him.

'It is!' he cried out, and burst out laughing. 'It *is* a little girl. I can see her wave and smile.'

Tears came to his eyes. Tears came to Newjohn's eyes too, and to Starlight's as well. It was so wonderful and so strange, she said, to think that this little human child was alive right now, far far away through all that cold black empty sky, under the sky of Earth.

'And yet there was something sad about it,' she told me. 'The distance made it sad. Like a happy thing feels sad when you're looking back on it, and it's long long ago.'

'We thought you and your people might like to see more pictures like this,' said Deep, 'pictures of Earth, and maybe pictures of people from your own past, like Gela.'

David Strongheart stared at him. 'Pictures of Gela? Pictures that can move and talk?'

'Yes, I'm pretty sure we can find some,' Deep told him. 'And we have some other screens in our veekle, bigger than this one, which we can take out and—'

'Screens?' interrupted Strongheart. 'Did you say screens? We have a screen here! It's one of the Mementoes from Tommy and Gela.'

'*Really?*'

All three Earth people had spoken at once. It was obvious that they were interested interested. Pleased to have impressed them, Strongheart called out to one of his helpers: 'Go to my store and fetch the Screen.'

'It doesn't show pictures, though,' he warned the Earth people. 'It doesn't do anything at all.'

'Well, it wouldn't,' said Marius. 'It's four hundred years old and its bat-tree would have died long ago.' He looked at Gaia. 'But if the...' he began and then said a whole string of words – *dayter, files, kruptid, coad* – that meant nothing to any of the Eden people. Deep and Gaia nodded, and each of them commented on what he'd said. Starlight recognized many of the words these two spoke, but she still couldn't figure out what they were talking about. But after thirty forty heartbeats of this, Gaia turned back to Strongheart, Newjohn and Starlight, and tried to explain.

'Screens have memories, you see. They have memories inside them: that's how they can show us pictures and sounds. We might still be able to find things in there that Gela and Tommy said after the *Defiant* came back to Earth. Wouldn't that be great? To hear what they were thinking in that time at the beginning when the two of them were on their own!'

When the Earth people finally came back to where we were waiting round their shelter, they had the Screen with them, a grey square, with some crumbling dirty-looking brown stuff round it, which, so the story went, had once been smooth and white. Marius handed it to me to look at, and I passed it on to the others. Only a few wakings ago, the Michael's Place people would have been amazed to see such a thing, and even more amazed to be allowed anywhere near it, let alone touch it with our own hands, but now, as we handed it about, it seemed a rough, broken, tired old thing compared with the new and shiny things from Earth that we knew were in the shelter right behind us.

'When we get back from our trip in the forest,' Marius explained, 'we'll open it up. We're not sure, because it's very old, but we think there's a good chance that we may be able to find words or pictures inside it, or even voices, that were put in here by Tommy or Angela when they were here on their own.'

Trueheart reached out and touched it. 'But how does it work? How can a thing like this hold pictures and voices at all, never mind hold them for four hundred years?'

Marius smiled at her. He liked Trueheart, and she liked him. Not in a man–woman way, I don't mean. They just noticed and liked each other's smartness. 'I'll try and explain it to you, True-heart, but it'll have to wait. Right now we're going to get ready to go out in the forest for a few days. When we get back we're going to show everyone some pictures from Earth, over there in the big clearing with the stones, and then we'll get to work on this thing.'

'What do you mean *pictures*?' I asked.

Gaia laughed. 'I'll show you.' She took out a linkup from a pocket in her wrap, and held it up in front of Trueheart and me and Fox and Clare. 'Speak!' she told us. 'Move about! It'll remember.'

'Boo!' shouted Fox, but I looked at the black square and couldn't think of anything to say. It seemed dumb, somehow, to talk to a thing like that, and I felt myself blush. 'Hello!' I said awkwardly.

Smiling at how nervous we were, Gaia showed us the picture she'd made. Here was my beautiful little Fox, and here was his voice saying boo. Here was Clare – it looked exactly like her – and here was Trueheart with her batface and her smart curious eyes. But next to her was another horribly ugly batface I didn't recognize at all.

'Oh Angie, darling,' said Clare. 'It looks *just* like you.'

The ugly old batface's mouth moved. 'Hello!' it said shyly from inside the glass, speaking in a strange voice I didn't know.

Everyone else laughed and shouted. 'That's her! That's Angie! That's exactly how she speaks!'

After the Earth people had left Strongheart's shelter, Starlight told me that she, Newjohn and Strongheart had sat for a moment in silence.

'Do you think they're really going to take anyone back to Earth?' Newjohn asked after a while.

'Don't see how they can,' Starlight said. 'There isn't room inside the veekle.'

Newjohn nodded. 'That's what I've been thinking too.'

'Perhaps this veekle is just the beginning,' said Strongheart. 'Maybe they'll bring down a bigger one later.'

Newjohn shrugged. 'But would you go? If you could leave Eden forever and live on Earth, would you really want to do it?'

'I'm not sure,' said Starlight. 'They haven't told us enough about Earth for me to say.'

Strongheart thought for several heartbeats. 'We wouldn't be high people on Earth, would we?' he said. 'We'd just be low people like everyone else. Or maybe even lower.'

'I don't reckon it will happen anyway,' said Newjohn. 'I think we'll stay here on Eden.'

Strongheart shook his head. 'Well, let's make sure they don't turn us into low people here as well.'

Thirty-five

Leader Harry and his guards were up on Snowy Dark, their bucks' clawed feet carrying them steadily forwards, their bucks' head-lanterns casting just enough grey light for them to see the bottoms of the steep slopes that rose up round them into unseen blackness far above and the tops of the slopes that dropped down into unseen blackness below. The creatures twitched their mouth feelers this way and that as they sucked in the cold cold air and tested it for the scent of leopards and the whiff of trees and warmth. Sometimes one buck or other would give out a cry, and one or two of the others would answer it – *Eeeeeek! Eeeeeek! Eeeeeek!* – and occasionally the whole herd of them would join in together for a hundred heartbeats or so before they all lapsed back into silence. And then all that could be heard was the sound of their breathing, and the crunching of their feet in the snow.

It wasn't really people who first found the way across the Dark, it was woollybucks. Woollybucks live by moving back and forth between the valleys up in the Dark, as the snow comes and goes. Jeff Redlantern was the one who first understood that, our Jeff, who was also the first to figure out how to get bucks to let people ride them. When John and the others got themselves lost in the Dark, Jeff thought to himself that his buck must know the way to some-place where there was food and warmth, because even woollybucks can't live on ice and snow. So he rode off by himself and let his buck go where it wanted, and in that way he found Tall Tree Valley. Him figuring that was what saved John and his people, and it was what made it possible later on for the other High Valleys to be found, and the other ways across the Dark.

Or that was what we were told on Knee Tree Grounds, in any case. But of course the Davidfolk like to give the credit to Wise Mehmet. Who can say which version is really true? It might even be that several different people figured the same thing out. It was just a case of noticing which ways the bucks were willing to go, after all, and which ways they weren't. And a matter of remembering that bucks had been on Eden long long before people.

Anyway, whoever found it, David's Path is only one of many ways across the Dark. And David's Path itself joins up with dozens of other paths that head off in different directions along the sides of dark valleys, past rock and ice, and above the huge snowslugs. These paths themselves branch, join onto new paths, branch out again, join up again with more paths yet. So it's all one path, really, a path that isn't just a single line but a kind of net. You put your foot on any part of it and you know for sure that all over the Dark there are other feet walking that same path with you: human feet and buck feet, and here and there leopard feet too. Some of those feet are coming towards you, some moving away, others again crossing between two places that you'll never see and have never even heard of. Where human beings have trod is only a small small part of the Dark, and the paths we know of are only a small part of the path.

As Harry and his men rode across the snow, they passed many little groups of people coming the other way. That necklace of shining beads of light was still moving slowly across the snow towards Circle Valley, as the terrified people of Wide Forest tried to get their kids and their bucks out of the way of the Johnfolk. And from time to time Harry came across those little groups of guards who waited at the crossing places by their little red fires. The guards were scared scared too. There were only a handful of them beside each fire. What were they going to do if the Johnfolk came?

When a group of guards saw Harry coming, or a bunch of Wide Forest folk met him in the snow, they saw he was a high man and called out the latest bad news to him in the desperate hope he'd be able to do something about it. The ringmen and their metal spears were winning every fight, they cried. They were taking children from their mums and dads. They were doing for young boys so they couldn't grow up to be guards. They were making people destroy their own circles of stones. The stories were often true, but they'd begun to have a kind of life of their own like stories always seem to, and, just as some stories grow by feeding on hope and longing, these ones grew bigger and more horrible as they spread by gorging themselves on fear.

But Harry's guards put an end to all of that. 'Earth has come!' they shouted back down. 'A veekle's come back to the Circle! Mother Gela herself is there! She's taller than a man and her skin is black black, just like in the stories!'

Fear changed to hope. In middle of the cold and dark, people suddenly felt light and warmth inside them, like they were trees whose roots had found some new warm place deep down in Underworld, just at the moment their lanterns were starting to fade, and their trunks beginning to grow cold.

'It's quite true,' Leader Harry called down to the waiting guards as he hurried by. 'Earth really is here! Tell everyone that passes, but stay on watch here until I come back through.' And to one group of guards at a place where five different strands of the great path all came together, he called out: 'One of you, ride to the High Valleys and give them the news,' and he pulled off his headwrap so they could see his face and know for certain who it was that was speaking to them.

Of course, the guards would have liked to leave their fires at once and head straight to Circle Valley, but they knew better than to go against what David Strongheart's son had told them. One guard from that group by the five paths climbed onto a buck and rode off towards Tall Tree Valley. The rest threw more wood on their fire and waited for Leader Harry's return.

But they were smiling and laughing now. They hugged each other, they squeezed each others' hands, they told each other they couldn't believe that in the generations that had passed on Eden, theirs was the one that had finally heard from Earth. One of them got out a jug of badjuice and shared it round, and presently they began to bellow out 'Come Tree Row' as loud as they could. It echoed off the cold black cliffs that were hidden away in the darkness above them, and a stone broke free, clattering noisily against the rock until at last it hit the snow and fell silent once again.

The path was busy busy. Those guards' friend was riding towards Tall Tree Valley. Harry and his men were pressing on towards Wide Forest. All those little pale beads of grey light were still making their way along that long long necklace that had David's Path as its string. Far off rockway, more beads of light were climbing up onto the Dark on the Shortcut, and over the top, and down again into those little bowls of life we call the High Valleys.

And over above Davidstand, where David's Path came down to meet the many paths that criss-crossed through the shining trees of Wide Forest, a new group of people was starting the climb up to the ice and snow.

Davidstand belonged to the Johnfolk by then. They called it Ellpool, which was the name first given it by John Redlantern. Most of the people there had run away, and those that stayed behind were doing whatever the Johnfolk asked of them. Ringmen lived in whatever shelters they hadn't burnt, wearing the fancy wraps and feather hats that the Davidstand people had left behind. In the Great Shelter, Headmanson Luke and his friend Teacher Gerry drank Strongheart's badjuice and slept on his beds.

It wasn't that Mehmet and Hunter had given up, but they'd

learned that Johnfolk would always win a face-to-face fight because of their metal spears. So instead Strongheart's first and third sons had their men hide in forest and set traps. Sometimes the guards would dig a hole in the ground and fill it with spikes, like buck-hunters do, and then lead the Johnfolk towards it. Sometimes they'd tie thin strings over a path at just the height that would catch a man on buckback and pull him to the ground. Sometimes a bunch of them would scrape away the bark from hot spiketrees, cutting almost right through to the sap. A few of their mates would ride up close to the ringmen and shoot arrows at them. When the ring-men chased after them, they'd lead them to the spiketrees where their friends were hiding, and their friends would take axes and open up the trees, so that as the Johnfolk came by, scalding sticky sap would spray out at them, burning their skin, and making their bucks panic and scream. The guards would pick off the ringmen as they twisted and turned, trying to figure out which way to go.

One waking, about the time that Leader Harry was climbing up onto the Dark from Circle Valley, Headmanson Luke Johnson had gone riding out in forest near Davidstand with his friend Teacher Gerry.

They thought they were pretty safe with their ringmen all round them in their metal masks, and they were chatting away to one another cheerfully, without even wearing masks of their own.

'I'm so looking forward to the waking I can bring my mum over here with the ring on her finger, and bring these people here back to their true Mother,' I imagine Luke saying.

'So am I, Luke,' I imagine Teacher Gerry answering. 'And espe-cially I'm looking forward to—'

Then Gerry stopped, as if a new and interesting idea had suddenly come to him and he was figuring out how best to put it into words. He leaned slowly towards the Headmanson like he was bowing. Then he half sat up again for a moment. He had a strange half-smile on his face. There was blood on his nostrils and on his lips.

'Gerry? Are you okay? What's the—'

Gerry's smile didn't change. It was like it was fixed on his face. And once again he bowed. But this time, he didn't stop. He just bowed and bowed until finally his whole body toppled, slowly and calmly, from the back of his buck. And now Luke saw, for the first time, an arrow sticking out of his back. Our guards had been hiding in the white- and redlantern trees above them. They'd set up ropes from the treetops, so they could shoot off their arrows and then slide quickly down to the ground and run away. Among them, as it happened, were two of Clare's sons, Mehmet and Mike, True-heart's older brothers.

'Father!' the Headmanson's men were calling out to him, for that's how the New Earthers speak to their high people. 'Father! You're in big big danger! Climb down now!'

Several of them had their bows out and were searching the tree-tops round them for targets, as Headmanson Luke jumped down to kneel by his friend. Teacher Gerry's face was empty and white, except for the blood that streamed down from his nostrils and mouth, through his beard and onto his neck. His limbs were trembling, like a sweetbat trembles when you cut off its head.

Luke shook him. 'Gerry! Come on, Gerry! Don't go away from me!' But it was obvious, even to Luke, that his friend had no life left inside him. The arrow had pierced Gerry's lungs and heart, and his wrap was soaked with blood.

Luke had looked up at the ringmen round him. How could anyone have hurt his sweet gentle Gerry? How could anyone harm this man who wished everyone well whether they were high or low, men or women, Johnfolk or Davidfolk? How could anyone shoot dead a man who'd given his whole life to finding out more about the True Story and bringing it to all the people of Eden?

'From now on,' he'd told the ringmen, 'do for every one of

them you find. Do you understand? I don't care if they're old or if they're kids. I don't care if they're guards or flowergatherers. Whenever you find them, cut their throats, string them up like Tommy, tie them to spiketrees and let them burn!'

And then he'd had another idea. 'Yeah. I know what we'll do. They're all running across the mountains to Circle Valley, aren't they? We'll follow them. We'll go after them. We'll destroy that Circle of theirs a second time, and soak the ground beneath it with their blood.'

Thirty-six

Gaia suggested I go with her and the other Earth people when they went out into forest, but Dave objected at once.

'What about your own kids, Angie? You seem to have forgotten you're a mother.'

Straight away Tom backed up his clawfoot brother. 'Dave's right. You should stay here, Angie, and look after your own.'

I felt Gaia and the two Earth men looking at me to see how I'd respond. You never saw Marius or Deep bossing Gaia about: they treated each other like they were all the same. The rest of the Michael's Place folk watched as well: Clare, Davidson, Little Harry, Flame with baby Suzie sleeping peacefully in her arms. Dave and Tom couldn't stop me, after all, and Dave and the others could easily easily look after our kids. But I shrugged and accepted what Tom had said. He was cluster head after all, and I had to live with these people.

The Earth people frowned and glanced at one another, but they accepted my decision. They fetched some boxes made of metal from their veekle, and also a strange big metal thing with wheels, like a child's toy car, though it only had two wheels, big fat ones, one in front and one behind. The *bike*, they called it. They put it together quickly quickly out of several pieces, and it came alive just like the veekle, giving out a little high whining sound, shining out light, and moving by itself through forest, somehow finding its way round tree trunks and rocks and pools. All three Earth people climbed onto its back with those metal boxes and they rode it like it was a buck.

Strongheart sent some guards to keep them safe. There were no forest leopards any more in Circle Valley, but there were still slinkers, which could take off your finger or bite a hole in your face, and lately snowleopards had started to come down sometimes from the Dark.

'I'm sure we'll be alright,' Gaia said, and Deep showed us another new thing that they each of them carried, called a *gun*. He said it could do for an animal, even if it was a long distance away. He pointed it at a dead tree. 'Prepare yourselves,' he said, 'it will make a loud noise.' We thought he was going to throw it like a spear, or maybe put something into it like you put an arrow onto a bow, but he just pointed it and it suddenly went *Bang!* We all jumped, and the tree had a hole going right through it. No arrow could do that. Not even a metal one. Not even a metal arrow shot from a yard's distance. Yet Deep was at least a hundred feet from the tree.

The Earth people were moving off on their bike, and the guards on their woollybucks were getting ready to follow them, when True-heart suddenly spoke.

'I'm going to go with them.'

'You certainly are *not*!' Tom told her, but she ran after them anyway, calling out to them to wait. They stopped their bike and helped her onto the back of it with them, and then the bike rolled off along the path beside Longpool that led out into forest.

Tom watched them disappear through the shining trees, his face dark with anger and shame. It seemed pretty certain that the Earth people would have heard what he said to Trueheart and had chosen to ignore him, taking the side of a newhair daughter against a grey-haired dad. And they'd done so not only in front of all the Michael's Place people, but in front of the crowd that was always waiting round their shelter. Tom was a strong strong man, or at any rate that was how he liked to see himself, he was a guard who'd lost his hand standing up for the laws of the Davidfolk, and he was proud of being cluster head of Michael's Place, but now all these people had seen him failing to control his own newhair daughter. Gela's heart, a batfaced girl was already hard enough to find a man for. Who would want one who hadn't learned to do as she was told?

'What am I supposed to do with that girl?' he bellowed, pretending to be speaking to Trueheart's mother, Clare, though really it was for the benefit of everyone watching. 'It's not like I've spared her the stick when she steps out of line – you know that! – but she still just does what she likes. Anyone would think she was Head Guard of Eden.'

Some people shook their heads and clicked their tongues sympathetically. But no one – not Tom, not anyone else – said a word against the people from Earth.

'I would have gone with them myself,' Starlight said when we met later on beside Longpool. 'But I don't like to leave Strongheart and Newjohn alone too long. They're getting on so well now, you wouldn't believe! If I'm not there to keep an eye on them, I'm afraid they'll start sharing out Half Sky between the two of them. It could double the size of both their grounds.'

'Is it really true that men and women decide things equally in Half Sky?'

'Yes, I'd say it is.'

'How do you stop the men from taking over?'

'Well, they didn't take over in Knee Tree Grounds, did they?'

'No, but…' I laughed. 'But then *nothing* happened there, did it? Nothing happened at all.'

'Half Sky was started by Tina Spiketree, remember. She was with John Redlantern at the beginning, along with Jeff and Gerry, but then she broke away from him, like Jeff did. You don't hear many stories about her in the Davidfolk Ground, or in New Earth either, but of course there are lots of stories about her in Half Sky. The thing she particularly wanted people there to remember was that before John and David came along, men and women decided things equally in Old Family. These Davidfolk like to think they're keeping Old Family as it always was, but really that's nonsense. Actually, Great David turned Old Family upside down when he started the guards and began the fight against the Johnfolk. That was when the men took over. It was the guards and the fighting that did it. It was when power started to come from the point of a spear.'

I thought about this for a bit, looking out over the softly glowing water of the pool. A couple of guys were out there fishing from log boats and, from time to time, there'd be a gentle *splash splash*, as one of them paddled his boat onto another spot to try his luck there. *Splash splash* from the water, and of course the *hmmmph hmmmph hmmmph* of trees round us that never stopped: if I closed my eyes, me and Starlight could have been back on Knee Tree Grounds, paddling through the water forest and gathering nuts.

'If it came to a spear fight between men and women,' I said, 'I guess men would win. Most men are bigger and stronger than most women.'

'Of course. So in Half Sky we make sure that men and woman don't ever think of themselves as two sides of a... what's that word the Earth folk use?... two sides of a *war*. Something I figured out when I was in New Earth is that women might not have so much power as men when it comes to things like spear fights, but they have lots of other kinds of power, and one of them is power over little kids and how they're raised. It seems Tina figured that out as well.' Starlight took my hand and smiled. 'But you should come and see how it all works for yourself, Angie. You can't go back to Wide Forest now, can you, and here in Circle Valley is *not* a good place to stay. Food is running out. If it wasn't for all the flowercakes and dried meat that Strongheart is trading out from those big big stores of his, everyone would already be hungry. And I can tell you for a fact that there's not much food left in those stores.'

'Well, we'll have to go somewhere, it's true. And somehow I don't think we're going to go to Earth.'

'No, I don't think so either. Not more than one two of us at most, anyway, and maybe not even that. The Earth people told me and Strongheart and Newjohn that one of the reasons Gela and Tommy stayed on Eden was that if all five had headed back to Earth together, there probably wouldn't have been enough air and water in the starship to keep them going.'

'So what's going to happen now?'

'I don't know. None of us do, do we? Not even the Earth people.'

Starlight took a stone and chucked it out into the water. There are strange birds called ducks that live on the pools of Circle Valley. You never see them in Wide Forest. They sit on the water and coo, and make a strange rattling sound with their wings. They have a little green light on top of their heads that sometimes flashes, and their hands and feet have flat skin between their toes like some fishes do, so as to help them paddle through the water. The splash of Starlight's stone set off a whole flock of them. Giving low sad cries, they flapped their wings and started to run across the surface with their hands and feet together until they were in the air, then glided off to far side of the pool. We watched the water near us as it became still again.

'Earth didn't come here for us,' Starlight said.

'What do you mean?'

'I heard something when we were going over for that meeting in Strongheart's shelter. I was walking in front with Gaia, and the two of us were talking: you know, comparing how things were on Earth and Eden, stuff like that. Deep and Marius were walking a little way behind us, chatting between themselves. I asked Gaia a question and she answered it. But you know how it is with the Earth people: when they answer a question it just raises more questions. So I was thinking about what she'd said and what I wanted to ask her next, when I heard Marius speaking behind her. He wasn't talking to me and he didn't know I was listening, but I clearly heard him say, "It's a shame there are people here."'

'What did he mean by that?'

'Deep was cross with Marius for saying it. "How can you think that?" he said. "These people are lovely and they're absolutely fascinating." "Lovely, certainly," Marius answered. "Really lovely. But fascinating? I'm not sure. What are we really going to learn from them that hasn't already been learned from…" He said some of those funny words they say that you just can't figure out, and then he said: "Okay, I admit it *is* pretty amazing that they're here at all. It goes against what we thought we knew about…" He said one or two of those weird words – *jenny ticks* it sounded like, but I'm not sure – and then he went on. "And, yeah, it's true, that's going to make a bunch of people scratch their heads. But that's not why we came, is it? This trip took a hundred years to make happen, remember, and we can only stay here so long. I'm just worried that all the stuff we're having to do here to keep these people happy is taking our time away from what we're really here for."'

'So what *are* they here for?'

'Well, Marius more or less answered that question. "I mean, *look*, Deep!" he said. "Look at this incredible life all round us. It shouldn't be here at all! It shouldn't be able to keep this air warm enough to live in! Everything we know tells us that the heat should go straight out into space and the surface of Eden ought to be covered with a mile-deep layer of ice. Yet here it is! Humming away all round us! There is *so* much here to find out and learn, so much amazing science to do. But the way things are going – all these meetings and conversations we're having to have, and this war we're supposed to be helping them stop – we may not have the time left to even begin to answer the questions that Eden raises."'

'What did Deep say?'

'I didn't hear. Gaia asked me something about New Earth, and how far away it was, and why the Johnfolk and Davidfolk were fighting, and I had to pay attention to her.'

'It's forest they came to see, not us? Is that what you're saying? That's why they've gone off on that bike of theirs, to get on with what they intended to do without us getting in the way?'

'That's right. I don't know why anyone would come all this way just to look at bucks and trees, but it seems that's the reason they came.'

'But all the stories—'

'Yes, I know. A lot of stories will have to change.' She sighed. 'Those bloody stories. So many people depend on them in so many different ways.'

Thirty-seven

Every waking of her stay in Tall Tree Valley, Mary did a new show. That was unusual for her. She normally did one show in a place – two at most – and then moved on, but there were new people coming into the valley all the time, desperate people, cold and hungry people, who needed to hear from Mother Gela. And the people who were already there were starting to get scared and angry about their valley being taken over by strangers, so they needed to hear from Mother Gela too. Everyone needed to be reminded that they were all one Family with one Father and one Mother, whether they were the people coming in or the people who'd always lived there.

'Life is hard hard for us at the moment,' she said to a big crowd of people who had squeezed themselves into the space round between Wise Mehmet's circle of stones and those strange stone shelters he'd had built. Like people do in the High Valleys, everyone was wearing bodywraps against the cold. Even down there on the valley bottom, the trees don't give enough warmth to be comfortable with bare skin. 'It's hard hard to have the Johnfolk trampling over our clusters and our forests, and taking away everything we love. It's hard having to cross the Dark. It's hard even to feed ourselves. Your Mother *knows* that. She *knows* how hard it is. Gela lost her own home once, remember? She lost her own family. She lost everything. Now she's back on Earth again of course, far far away, but she still watches you all as closely as any mother watches her children. I hear her right now. "Don't let them fight each other, Mary," she begs me. "Tell them not to fight and quarrel. Remind them that's exactly what caused all this trouble in first place: Family fighting against itself. Please don't let it happen again!"'

She looked at all the tired suspicious faces. The trees pulsed – those strange tall trees whose lowest branches are far above the ground – and the black shadow of the Dark rose up all behind her.

'Remember,' said Mary, 'that it'll only be when Family is together and at peace that Earth will come back from the sky and take us home. Only when Family is one. So please—'

And then a man's voice broke in. 'Oh yeah?' it called out. 'So how come a veekle has just come down from the sky into Circle Valley, eh? How come Gela herself is over there, walking around right now?'

Mary had been the centre of attention up to that moment. Those terrified and grief-striken people had been listening raptly to every word she spoke, hungry hungry for any little comfort the shadowspeaker could give them, however tiny it might be, desperate for any story she could tell that would bind their broken world together again, at least a little bit, and make them feel like there was still a home for them somewhere, and a path that led to it. But in the space of one heartbeat, all that changed. Mary was forgotten and every head turned towards the man who'd called out. They saw straight away he wasn't some crazy guy, but a guard who'd just come down from the Dark. They all began shouting at once.

'What do you mean *a veekle's come down*? What do you mean *Gela*?'

The guard laughed and raised his hands. He'd never had this much attention in his life.

'Whoa, people! Whoa! Listen to me and I'll tell what I know.'

Everyone fell silent, everyone craned towards him. Mary was forgotten.

The man pointed to the circle of white dots painted on his forehead. 'As you can see I'm a guard. Me and my mates were sitting by our fire at Five Ways crossing when Leader Harry came through with eight men, riding full speed from Circle Valley towards Wide Forest. They were in a *big* big hurry, I can tell you. Their bucks were spitting out green froth. If they kept going at that pace much longer, they'd have a bunch of dead bucks on their hands. They didn't stop to talk, but the men shouted down to us that a new veekle had come down back in the Circle, and that Gela herself was walking round. Her skin was black black, they said, just like in the story.'

The guard rubbed his hand over his beard as he paused for breath, looking round all the while at the watching faces to see if he'd been understood. Everyone was silent. The only sound was the pulsing of trees and the tinkling of streams running down from the snow.

'If it had just been the men that told us that,' he said, 'we might have taken it for a stupid joke. You know how blokes like to wind each other up! But then Leader Harry called down to us too. Leader Harry, mind you! Strongheart's second son. Guard Leader of Circle Valley. The third highest man among the Davidfolk, with only Strongheart himself and Leader Mehmet above him. He took off his headwrap so we could see who he was, and he called out to us that what his men said was true, and that one of us should come down here and spread the story among the High Valleys.'

Again, the guard paused and looked round at all the faces watching him. 'So there it is,' he said. 'That's all I can tell you. I know it sounds weird – Tom's dick, it sounds weird to me as well! – but don't tell me Leader Harry would joke about a thing like that, least of all when we're in middle of fight with the Johnfolk. A veekle *has* come down, people, and Mother Gela is alive on Eden.'

I heard about all this later from four five people who were there. Apparently, when that guard had finished speaking, there were two whole heartbeats of complete silence, and then, all at once, the people began to sob and scream, until it seemed that whole of that lonely bowl of rock called Tall Tree Valley was full up to the brim with the sound.

Poor Mary. No one took any notice of her. What news did she have to offer compared with the news that the guard had brought down from the Dark? And anyway, who would believe anything she said? Only just before the guard spoke she'd been claiming to hear the voice of Mother Gela speaking to her, yet she'd obviously had no idea that Gela was actually here on Eden. If our Mother really did speak to her, as Mary claimed, why wouldn't she have told her that?

And Mary was smart smart. If other people could figure that out, then she could figure it out for herself. She'd built her whole life on a story about her being able to hear the voice of Gela, and she'd travelled back and forth, back and forth for more than twenty years, telling people to get ready for Earth to return. She believed in that story more than pretty much anyone, and she'd proved her belief in it by giving her life up to it. But now the thing that she'd looked forward to for so long had happened, the thing that she'd worked and worked so hard for. Earth had returned, Gela had returned, the Circle of Stones had finally done the job that it was laid out to do, four hundred years ago. You'd think she'd have been happy happy, happier even than all the other people who right now were singing 'Come Tree Row' with tears running down their faces. And Mary knew *that* too. She knew she *ought* to be happy. Of course she did. The thing she'd been telling people about for twenty years had finally happened! And yet how *could* she be happy when the news had made her look, not just to others but to herself, like she was either a liar or a fool?

So many times she'd wept and cried in her shows, as she talked about Earth and Gela and home, but now, when everyone else was crying and laughing, dancing and singing 'Come Tree Row', Mary's eyes were dry. She looked round for her helpers and guards.

'Come on,' she told them. 'I'm sure you want to see for yourselves. Let's get the bucks ready and start out for Circle Valley before the paths are so full of people we won't be able to move.'

How can I be so ungrateful? she must have asked herself in her head, as she and the others began to climb the steep path out of Tall Tree Valley. It doesn't matter about me. Why can't I get that through my head? Of course it doesn't matter about me. All that matters now is that Earth has come.

But however hard she tried, Mary just couldn't feel this. She was good good at teaching herself to feel things she knew she ought to feel, and not feeling things that she knew she shouldn't. She was much much better at it than most people. That was where her certainty came from, and her courage. It was how she stopped herself from giving way to doubt. But right now that task, that struggle to make herself feel the things she knew she ought to feel, was too hard even for her.

There are creatures called ants but, apart from being small and living in nests, they're nothing like ants at home. They're like tiny transparent worms with legs and, when they're provoked, they glow a vivid red. There are things called birds but you couldn't mistake them, even for a moment, for the birds we have on Earth. They have arms as well as wings, for one thing, and their so-called feathers are more like scales: long flexible scales that clatter and rattle as the creatures blunder through the branches. There are animals called bats, but they stand on two legs and stroke their wings with strangely human hands. And of course the things called trees have no leaves, and the so-called wood that forms the outer shell of their trunks is smooth and bluish and looks kind of mushroomy, though actually, to the touch, it's chitinous and hard.

The trees are the core round which all of Eden's life revolves, or at least all of the life that isn't under water. The warm moist air round us – I wish I could convey its sweet, damp, very slightly ammoniacal smell – is their creation. The sombre glow of their flowers is what illuminates the stage for everything that happens in Eden. But they don't just provide the light and warmth that on Earth would come from the sun. They're also the food source on which the entire ecosystem depends, from the glittery starflowers that parasitize their roots, to the strange ribbon-like flutterbyes that drink from their flowers and nibble at the sugar that crystallizes round openings in their trunks. Their pulsing sound is everywhere. Whenever we turn off the whiny motor of our bike, there it is: countless iterations of that steady remorseless beat, merging into a hum. It's the heartbeat of the planet itself.

Marius is excited. We've discovered that, in spite of the enormous differences between Eden and Earth, the basic biochemistry is very similar indeed. We've found the same amino acids. We've found something very similar to DNA, and in the animals' blood, a kind of haemocyanin, such as is found in the blood of many invertebrates on Earth, performing a similar function to haemoglobin. All this helps to explain, of course, how the humans here have managed to feed themselves, but what excites Marius most is the contribution it will make to our understanding of the origins of life in the universe. Given that this life has arisen entirely separately from life on Earth, and in an entirely different environment, the biochemical similarities suggest that there may be only one basic template for life, and that any planet that can support life at all is likely to support humans as well.

Speaking just for myself, though, I don't think that's the most exciting thing right now. We have to do this work of course, and it really *is* interesting, but a big part of me regrets the need to turn so quickly away from the mystery in front of us to readings and measurements on our machines. I'm a scientist by training, and I love science, but I still can't help thinking that there is something slightly neurotic about this need to reduce things so quickly to numbers and explanations. I mean, let's face it, we ought to know by now that no matter how far the chain of explanations extends – however far back in time, however deep down into the structure of things – and no matter how many new mechanisms and causal relationships we learn to understand, the essential mystery will always remain untouched. Because it is infinite, like those fractal patterns that re-emerge again and again, at every level of magnification.

Once, some centuries ago, people might still have believed they could get to the bottom of things, solve the riddle of existence, but

I feel we're past that now. Whatever the faults of the Salvationists, they imbued our culture with a healthy scepticism about scientistic hubris. There *is* no bottom, there *are* no final answers. Science will take us all kinds of places, but it will never take us home.

That's not how it seems to Trueheart, though. I watch her over there with Marius, the two of them stooped together over one of his experiments, and she's absolutely *rapt*. She is a truly exceptional girl. We all spotted that very quickly. She's had no schooling, her writing skills are miminal, and she believes, like all the Eden folk, that her ancestor Angela has somehow come alive again on Earth and is preparing a home there. But she's incredibly smart, and her desire to learn is *immense*. I'm still not sure whether we did right or wrong by pretending we didn't hear her dad ordering her back – there's no way we can tell what the ramifications of that might be – but it just seemed criminal to deny her this chance when we know it can never come for her again.

I look at her there now with her strong bare back, her long hair, her athletic shoulders, watching everything that Marius does, listening to everything he says. She's back at the beginning of science, like – oh I don't know – like maybe people were in the eighteenth century on Earth. She's back at the stage when it was possible to believe that this wonderfully powerful tool might one day dispel darkness altogether.

A bat swoops down after a flutterbye not far above their heads, Marius turns his head to watch it, and she looks round with him, so that for a moment she's looking in my direction. It still shocks me when that happens. It's like someone has taken a sledgehammer and smashed it into middle of her face. It's the same with Angie, but poor Angie is so shrivelled and old-looking all over (though from what I can work out she can't be older than her mid-thirties) that the sheer incongruity is a little less jarring than it is with this tough, strong girl with her beautifully made body.

On Earth her face wouldn't have to be like that. On Earth she could study and develop the talents she so obviously has. On Earth, without any doubt, she would *be* someone. But what have we got to offer her here? What have we got to offer any of them, for that matter? They're so excited to see us. They're so hopeful. But, oh precious Earth, when we've gone again, what will we have left behind that will help them in any way with their tough tough lives?

Deep, meanwhile, is chatting to the guards who've come with us. How huge and fair he looks compared with them, standing over there by our unwieldly bike, which all four of them are admiring. As he listens to their questions and comments, he stoops affably towards these small wiry men with their tribal markings, their animal hide kilts, their long beards tied with string. They laugh at some joke he's made, three of them standing, one squatting down to run his fingers wonderingly over the fat rear tyre.

Nearby their so-called bucks are grazing on a pile of waterweed. I'm half-used to these creatures now. I can look in their direction and, just for a moment, think: There are the bucks. Then that moment passes, and I'm overwhelmed by the utter strangeness of these creatures that just can't be squeezed into any earthly category at all. If I look just at their shaggy coats, I might persuade myself that they're a bit mammalian, like yaks or highland cattle, but then I notice those flat expressionless eyes and the tentacles round their mouths and the nearest thing I can think of is something molluscan, like a squid. But then again, the way they stand on their back four legs and use their front pair as arms reminds me more of a praying mantis, while the claws on their six feet are vaguely bird- or reptile-like, and that glowing lump on the backs of their heads makes me think of those weird fish that live in the abyssal depths of Earth's oceans. There is simply no pigeonhole available to put them in. They are themselves. I watch them feeding over there in the eerie glow of the trees, blue and pink and white, and my head swims to the point where sometimes I almost wonder if I've lost my mind.

Thirty-eight

It was a strange time, those three wakings when the Earth people were out in forest. They'd been here, but now they'd gone again. I'd sometimes go into their shelter, pretending to myself that I was going to sweep it or tidy it, but really just to look at the stuff they left behind so as to remind myself it hadn't all been a dream. Or maybe I'd take the kids and walk over to look at the veekle perched there in the Circle on its four thin metal legs. There were always people there looking up at it. Once in a while it would make a sound – *Beep! Beep! Beep!* – and flash its light, and everyone would back away laughing. The children could never get enough of that.

Starlight, Newjohn and Strongheart carried on talking talking talking in Strongheart's big shelter. They weren't talking about the ringmen from New Earth so much now – that would have to wait until they heard news from Leader Harry – but they talked a lot about food. Food was running out quickly in Circle Valley, and yet hungry people kept on arriving from across the Dark. Strongheart had asked the two other heads if they could send to their own grounds for more dried meat and flowercakes, but Starlight pointed out that this would spread the news about what was happening in Circle Valley, and bring hundreds more mouths to be fed from Brown River and Half Sky.

'Yes, and who would we persuade to go anyway?' Newjohn asked with his dry laugh. 'Who's going to leave Circle Valley now?'

'My Harry went,' Strongheart pointed out, 'and eight men with him.'

Starlight thought for a few heartbeats. 'You know what?' she said. 'It may be the Earth people that we have to ask to leave.'

When he'd finally figured out she wasn't joking, Strongheart's face went purple. 'John Redlantern walked away from Circle Valley,' he growled. 'And so did your Tina Spiketree, Head Woman Starlight. But we Davidfolk stayed here by the Circle, waiting patiently for Earth. No *way* am I going to send the Earth people away, now that they've finally come! Tom's dick and Harry's, *this* is what I will be remembered for in stories! Okay, I may turn out to have been the Head Guard who lost Wide Forest to the ringmen, but at least I'll also have been the one who was there to meet Earth.'

'I'm just saying, Head Guard, that the longer they stay, the more people will come into the Valley. Soon there'll be thousands here from all over Mainground with nothing to—'

Strongheart wasn't listening. 'And a bloody good job we Davidfolk *did* wait here! If everyone had followed John and Tina, the Earth people would have come and found nothing here but the remains of shelters, and the ashes of cooking fires, and the skeletons in Burial Ground. They'd have gone back to Earth saying there was no one left alive, and then we'd have been alone forever. Think about that, Head Woman. If everyone had followed your Tina, where would we be now?'

Newjohn watched him with half-narrowed eyes. 'And yet you were grumbling yourself, Head Guard, not so long ago, that they would make us all into low people. The Head Woman has a point. What are the Earth people going to give us if they stay, except for hunger? Hunger and the old stories we live by getting all broken up and confused?'

Strongheart glared at him. 'Well, if nothing else, they're going to stop the fight with your Johnfolk friends from across the Pool.'

The rest of us went hunting and scavenging. There weren't any bucks that we could find, but there were starflower seeds to grind up, and the odd bat or fish or slinker. Davidson shot one of those ducks out on the water, but like most birds its meat was too tough and bitter to eat, however hungry we might be. We eyed the bucks that had carried us across the Dark, and wondered whether to start on them. Sometimes we saw other people eyeing them too.

From time to time a horn would blow to let people know that they could get some food from David Strongheart's stores, and then a long long line would form under the whitelantern trees outside Strongheart's shelter in Brooklyn, a line of thin sad hungry people, and a bunch of guards would hand out little pieces of dried buckmeat and hard hard flowercakes that could crack your teeth, baked that way so they wouldn't go bad. If the people had trading sticks or blackglass, they'd hand them over as a trade. If not, one of the guards would scratch down their names and where they came from on squares of bark, so that Strongheart could come to them later and take something back from them. Maybe he'd take a daughter to be one of his helpers, or a bunch of young guys to build a new shelter for him.

I stood in that line myself one time, waiting for maybe a quarter of a waking for a few scraps, and giving the guard one of my precious cubes of metal. All round me there was a sour smell of fear and suspicion. People accused each other of pushing in. Valley folk muttered about outsiders taking their food. Outsiders snarled back that it was their food in first place: the Valley folk had been living for way too long on meat and fruit and flowercakes brought in for them across the Dark. Once a Valley man and a man from Davidstand started to push and shove each other, and guards had to come over and pull them apart.

'Come on, you guys!' a woman just in front of me called out to them. 'Earth has come, remember! Earth is here! What reason is there now to fight among ourselves?'

I got talking to her afterwards while we waited for our dry scraps of food, and she told me her story. Her name was Treelight. She came from a small cluster in forest towards Nob Head. When the New Earthers who grounded up there came towards her cluster, it was decided that the men who were fit to fight would stand and face them with spears, so as to give the women time to get away with the kids and the oldies. Eight of Treelight's nine sons had been among those men, along with their dad. There was a bit of a hill behind the cluster, and at the top of it there was a crag where the women could look right over the trees on the slope and see what was happening below. Instead of trying to rush the men down there, the New Earthers had ridden round them to make a circle, and now they were shooting arrows at them from every side. Clouds of arrows, it seemed like, cloud after cloud. When the women finally turned away again, most of their men were already dead, and the rest soon would be. But they'd had little kids to look after, so, as best they could, they had to hold their grief inside themselves as they trudged onwards through forest and climbed slowly up onto the Dark.

'But we're all going to Earth now, aren't we?' Treelight said firmly in a bright bright voice, strangely like that one that Mary sometimes used to speak in. 'And I know my boys will be there waiting for me, all healthy and strong and well again. I know that for sure.'

When the Earth people came back from forest, they went straight to their veekle to get those pictures ready that they'd promised, while Trueheart nervously returned to her family. Her dad growled and muttered, but he didn't dare punish her for doing something that the Earth people had offered, especially not when the rest of us were crowding round her to hear her stories about what the Earth folk had said and done.

'They have strange strange tools,' Trueheart told us. 'Little boxes, and tubes, and needles made of glass and metal, and some other stuff they call plasstick that feels a bit like wood. They have tiny screens that tell them what things are made of, and how hot they are, and whether they shine out light that we can't see.'

'Light that we can't see?' I said. 'How could that be? Surely light *is* the stuff we see by.'

'Gaia told me that there are many of kinds of light that we can't see. Heat, for instance. Marius thinks that Eden animals see heat as a kind of light.'

Tom snorted scornfully. 'Heat as light! That's nonsense. You must have misunderstood them. You might be smart, my girl – you certainly think you are – but you need to remember you're not half as smart as them.'

'Well, they said I'm smart smart. They said I'm just as smart as anyone on Earth. I just don't know as much stuff as they—'

'Ha! Well, that makes no sense for a start. How can you be smart if you don't know anything?'

Trueheart ignored her father's jeers. 'Marius told me all kinds of stuff. Like… well, for example, he told me that everything in the world is made up of tiny little things called atoms that are so small we can't even see them. He says once you understand that, you can make all kinds of new things, like… Oh it's too much to explain. Those Earth people are smart, all three of them, but I reckon Marius is the smartest. He's good good at chess for one thing. I tried and tried but I only ever beat him a couple of times… and… and… Oh yes, I must tell you an amazing thing about playing chess with them…' She had so many things to say that her words almost tripped up on one another. 'They don't draw a board on the ground like we do. They play in those glass squares they carry. They show a picture of a board with little pieces on it and you can push them about with your fingers as if they were real. In fact if you want you can even just *tell* them to move and they'll move by themselves. It's hard to believe unless you… All three of them play chess. Gaia is pretty good as well, though I usually beat her. Deep too, but he likes another game better, with pieces that run round like little people. Oh Fox, you should see *that* game! You'd just love it.' She laughed. 'It's weird being with them. It's weird but it's great. They know so so much. And I'll tell you another thing: you wouldn't think it was a woman and two men, because they all treat each other just the same, like they were all men together, or all women.'

Tom glanced at his friend Davidson and pulled a face, but True-heart didn't seem to notice.

'I'll tell you another thing,' she went on, barely even stopping to breathe. 'Deep told me that they can fix batfaces on Earth. He said it happened to his cousin. They've got special stuff on Earth that sends you to sleep, and while you're sleeping they cut open the meat and skin of your face and sew it together again, and when you wake up you don't have a batface any more. You don't feel a thing! It's a bit sore afterwards, but when it heals up you look just like other people. It's the same for clawfeet too, he said… Oh yes, and another weird thing I found out: you know that ring that Gaia wears on her finger, with the two kinds of metal in it, like the one in the—'

Parp! Parp! Parp! Parp! Parp! The sound of wooden horns came from the direction of Circle Clearing, three four of them, summoning us back to the Circle, a new horn blower joining in when one of the others stopped for breath.

Thirty-nine

There were three screens tied with string onto poles in front of the veekle, spaced about twenty feet apart from each other. They weren't like the crumbly old Screen that the Earth people had in their shelter. They were black and smooth all over. The Earth people waited beside middle screen as people came crowding in. Guards stood ready with their spears to hold people back if they pushed too close to the Earth people or the screens.

Gaia had kept a place for me and the other Michael's Place people, right in front of her and the other two by the edge of the Circle. I settled down there with Candy on my lap and Fox beside me. Their bright eyes were darting back and forth as they tried to take everything in. Dave was behind me with Metty. A little further back, tall wooden seats had been set up for the high people so they could look over our heads. Starlight was there, sitting with David Strongheart and his shelterwomen, and Newjohn and a few other high people from the Davidfolk Ground, Half Sky and Brown River.

Someone started to sing 'Come Tree Row' and pretty much everyone joined in, the people already sitting or standing, and the people still squeezing into the clearing. All the arguments and disagreements between Valley and outsiders were forgotten. Men and women sang out happily together, high people and low people, and on those high wooden seats, Davidfolk, Johnfolk and Tinafolk stood singing side by side. Then Gaia stepped forward so she stood in front of the Earth people, and the singing changed into a chant: '*Gela! Gela! Gela! Gela! Gela!*'

'Gela! Gela!' Candy joined in enthusiastically, bellowing as loudly as her small lungs would let her. Fox joined in too until he looked round at me and noticed I wasn't shouting along with everyone else. I knew that Gaia didn't like it that people thought she was Gela, and she'd said many times that she wasn't. But people hear what they want to hear.

When the shouting had quietened down a bit, Gaia held one of those linkups in front of her mouth and began to speak. Everyone gasped – you could hear the sound of that gasp right across the clearing – because, though we could see her lips moving, what we heard was a loud loud version of her voice that came booming down from the veekle, like it was a huge creature that could speak for itself.

'Welcome Head Guard Strongheart. Welcome Headman Newjohn. Welcome Head Woman Starlight. Welcome everyone,' the booming voice said, speaking slowly slowly, so we Eden people would understand.

Then Deep held his own glass square in front of his mouth, and the booming voice changed so that it sounded like his instead of hers: 'Hello there, everyone. Thanks so much for coming.'

Marius said 'Hi' in the awkward way he had when he was faced with a bunch of Eden people. Both Deep and Marius had proper beards now, just like Eden men.

There was another big gasp as a picture suddenly appeared on the screens, exactly the same on each. We all stared at it. How could that happen? How could a picture suddenly be there without anyone to draw it or scratch it or paint it? And of course it wasn't a picture like we might make ourselves on a piece of bark or a stone. It was like the pictures Gaia had showed me and the other Michael's Place people of our own faces: not so much a picture, more a copy of the thing itself.

'Hey! That's Starry Swirl!' someone shouted out.

Gaia's booming voice laughed. 'That's right. Starry Swirl. On Earth we call it the glacksy, though we're right inside it of course back there, so we can't see it so clearly as you can. But look at this! What can you see now?'

There was a tiny black dot against the brightness of the Swirl, and as we watched it, we saw it grow, like it was coming towards us. Worried voices started to murmur. Candy pressed her face into my shoulder. Fox grabbed my hand. People who'd never seen these Earth pictures before jumped and backed away, and some cried out or shouted angrily – 'Hey! Watch out! What's going on?' – like they thought they'd been tricked. But the black dot didn't come out at us. It became a big black circle that filled up most of the screen, but the screen was where it stayed.

'That's Eden,' said the booming voice of Gaia. Now it was so big we could see that the circle wasn't completely black, but covered all over in patches of dim dim light. 'That's what Eden looks like from out in space,' Gaia said. 'And here's the other side. This little black patch here is what you call Snowy Dark. This tiny little patch of light in middle of it is Circle Valley, where we all are now.'

She moved things on too quickly. We could happily have sat and stared at that picture for a long long time, taking it in, and figuring out how it all fitted together. I hadn't even had a chance to work out which patch of light was Worldpool, let alone where Knee Tree Grounds was, before the picture disappeared. And now we saw another circle, but this time not dark at all, but blue blue blue, streaked all over with swirls of white.

'And this is Earth,' Gaia said.

Some people cried. *Really* cried, I mean: I could hear them sobbing round me. But most, like me, were quiet quiet, not knowing what we felt. All our lives we'd dreamed of Earth, each one of us imagining our true home in our own way. But now, quite suddenly, the question was answered. *This* was what it was like. And it wasn't quite what any of us had thought.

The picture changed again.

'And this is me on Earth,' Gaia said.

We could see Gaia in the picture smiling out, and beside her was a handsome young man with dark skin like hers. They were standing in middle of the screen and all round them was a pale blue-grey emptiness.

'That's me and my brother. We're standing beside the See.' She could see we were puzzled, so she explained: 'It's water, a big area of water. Like your Worldpool.'

Everyone frowned at the picture, trying to make it out. Gaia walked up to middle of one of the three screens and pointed with her finger. 'There, look. There's the See and there's the sky.'

I could see now that there was a kind of line behind Gaia and her brother in the picture, a dead straight line like World's Edge, and I could see that the paleness was a bit paler above that line than it was below it. And then I saw that in the darker area below the line there were waves. They were small and blurred and far away, but all the same they were quite like the waves that broke on poolside by Michael's Place, though the colours were all wrong and there was no light shining up from beneath them.

And then suddenly the picture came alive, like that picture had done of me and Fox and the others, where you could see us move and hear us speak. Again, some people yelled out with the shock of it, seeing the waves moving, just like the waves on Worldpool, and hearing Gaia and her brother talking inside the screen, though they were talking too quickly in their strange Earth speech for us to be able to make out a single word. Behind the voices, we could hear the sighing sound the waves made on the beach, and those of us who knew Worldpool – and of course there were many here who didn't – could hear that it was the exact same sound that Worldpool made as it broke on poolside here in our own Eden.

Then the sound stopped all at once, and another picture came.

'This is my house,' Gaia said.

House, we knew that word. A house was a kind of shelter with a door and windholes. Traders in Veeklehouse would give you a toy one for ten sticks, and offer you a car with wheels to go with it. But this was a real Earth house, so big that you could only see a part of it in the picture. It was made of something smooth and white – Earth seemed to be a pale pale place – and in front of it, small like they were far away, stood Gaia's brother and another woman. This second woman had skin like Deep's: skin so pale that you could see the pink blood inside it. Next to them was a big thing that we couldn't figure out at all. It was pale green and many times taller than they were.

'It's a tree,' said Gaia's booming voice, when people called out to ask what it was. 'That's what trees look like on Earth.'

Candy jumped up indignantly from my lap. 'That's not a *tree*!' she shouted out. And everyone laughed, in that way people do when a child says something that grownups think but don't like to say themselves.

It had no lanterns, that Earth tree, and it was the wrong shape, all covered by that pale green stuff that looked a bit like a cloud. Yet when I looked carefully I could see that – yes – hidden under the green was a sort of trunk and branches that were a little bit like a tree. Behind it was a blank pale greyness, almost white, in the place where a sky ought to be.

The Earth people had laughed at Candy's interruption along with the rest of us. 'Well, I'm sorry if we've got it wrong,' said Deep, 'but that's what we call a tree on Earth. I suppose it *is* pretty useless compared to your Eden trees.'

People liked that. It was nice to hear him admit that a thing could be better on Eden than on Earth, even if he was only joking. We smiled at each other, and some clapped.

'*Useless* tree,' Candy shouted, and a little cheer went up from the crowd.

'What sound does it make?' a man called out.

'Our trees don't make any sound,' said Gaia, 'except when the wind blows through them.'

How strange that seemed. In Eden there was no sound that

was more constant in our lives than the sound of trees. They were pumping pumping pumping all round us right now, as we looked at the pictures and listened to the Earth people speak. Even out in Knee Tree Grounds, ten miles away from Mainground, that sound had always been there while we were awake and while we slept, like the heartbeat of the world. How weird it must be to live among silent trees.

'How does it get its heat then?' asked a woman.

'Our trees aren't hot,' Deep said. 'They don't give out heat, like yours do. Or light either. Those green things at the top are called leaves, and they don't give out light, they take it in. They take in the light of the sun, which they need in the same way that we need food.'

People nodded. We remembered that was part of the old stories, that the trees on Earth reached up their branches and drank in the light that came down from the star they called the sun. But I'd always imagined them with little mouths reaching upwards from the tip of every branch, open to the sky. In fact I'd carried a picture of that in my mind since I was a little kid: the trees with their little wide-open mouths that fed on light. In my head, those trees had always seemed kind of friendly, somehow, but this one just seemed strange.

'That little girl was right,' another man said. 'No heat or light. Earth trees *are* useless.'

Several people cheered again.

Then the picture changed once more. There was more colour this time, and at the same time more darkness, which made it seem a little more like Eden.

'Ah,' said Gaia. 'This is another picture from the beach. It's what we call a sunset. It's what happens when the sun goes down at the end of the day.'

The water was dark now, but where the sky should be, above World's Edge, everything was bright and full of colour: pink, blue, green. It was the opposite of our Worldpool, where the sky is dark and the water shines. In middle of this strange sky, there was a small round circle of bright bright yellow. A long line of light stretched down from it across the water, broken into pieces by the waves.

'This is the sun,' Deep said.

We stared. How small it seemed, when all the stories said the star was many times bigger than whole of Earth or Eden.

'That's the sun?' a man said. 'It's *tiny*!'

'Oh it *is* big,' Deep's voice boomed out. 'But it's far far away from Earth, so looks small in the sky.'

'I thought Earth's sky was blue,' said Clare.

'It is sometimes,' Gaia said, 'but it can be many different colours, and every night it's black just like the sky here.'

So 'night' *wasn't* a place, whatever Mary had said!

'Look,' said Gaia, as the picture changed again. 'This is my brother's dog. It's a kind of animal.'

It was another moving picture. A strange brown creature was running about in a pale place full of strange square-shaped things that it kept banging into. It was hard to make out its shape properly, it was moving so much. And it was shouting shouting shouting all the time.

'Rough! Rough! Rough!' the dog creature kept yelling, like it could speak but there was only one thing it wanted to say.

'Rough! Rough! Rough!' a boy about Candy's age called out and began to laugh. Candy looked across at him interestedly for a few heartbeats and then joined in loudly: 'Rough! Rough! Rough!' she hollered. And then *everyone* joined in, the whole big crowd, laughing and shouting at this silly creature from Earth: '*Rough! Rough! Rough!*'

The Earth people smiled uneasily, glancing at one another. There was an edge in our laughter and it was obvious that they could hear it.

'Now,' said Deep, 'we thought you'd like to see some pictures of people from the past. We didn't bring many, I'm afraid, because...'

He didn't finish. I reckon he'd been about to say they hadn't expected to find anyone here, but had then thought better of it.

Never mind that, though. Now there was a face on the screen: a young woman, maybe twenty twenty-five years old, with black skin like Gaia's, though her face was narrower and sharper. She was smiling faintly as she looked out at us. It was a wary smile, like she'd felt she had to put it on but didn't really feel like it. She looked kind of tough. You wouldn't want to argue with her, I thought, or say something dumb when she was listening. You wouldn't want to take anything that she thought was hers.

Don't tell us this is Gela, I said inside my head to the Earth people. Please don't tell us this is Gela!

'This is Angela Young,' boomed out the veekle in Gaia's voice. 'This is the woman you call Gela.'

There was another big gasp that filled up whole of the clearing, then, for a few heartbeats, a strange stunned silence followed by muttering and murmuring, as we all stared at this stranger. She was completely different from what any of us had pictured when we'd listened to the stories. And she was different too, in spite of having the same dark skin, from the Earth woman standing in front of us.

This time the Earth people had the sense not to move the picture on so quickly. We needed to study this picture, we needed to absorb it, we needed to weigh it up in our minds, like a Veekle-house trader weighs a lump of blackglass in his hand, turning it this way and that, looking for cracks and blemishes. More than a hundred heartbeats passed in which all the grownups who could see at all, and all the newhairs, and all the kids who weren't too small to understand, were staring staring staring, some in silence, some whispering to one another, as they tried to figure out what this picture meant to them.

Off over to the left of where we were, there was a bunch of people who were standing because there was no room left to sit. And from over there, another small child suddenly spoke out loudly as little children do. 'Who's that, Mum?' the child asked. But this time no one laughed in the way that they'd laughed when Candy spoke, and her mum stooped down and whispered the answer in her ear.

'It's Mother Gela, apparently,' I guess the mother said to her little daughter, 'but now be a good girl and be quiet.'

The kid wasn't having that, though. 'I thought you said that was Gela over *there*!' she said, still in the same loud voice that everyone could hear.

'*Sssssh!*' her mother told her, looking anxiously round. I'm sure most grownups there were every bit as confused as that child was, but no one else spoke out, no one else asked to have the confusion cleared up, even though not long before they'd all been shouting: 'Gela! Gela! Gela!' Partly because they were embarrassed, I guess. But mainly because people didn't really want to hear Gaia answer the question as to whether or not she was still Gela in some way – Gela born in a different body, maybe, Gela changed by being made new again – or whether she was someone completely different. They preferred to leave that unexplained.

Presently Strongheart spoke from his high seat behind us, his voice gruff and choked up. 'Make her talk and move like the other pictures.'

'I'm sorry,' said Gaia, 'but we've looked and looked and it seems we've got no moving pictures of Angela with us, and we don't have her voice either. We're hoping that when we get a chance to look inside that Screen of yours we'll find some ...' She said some words we didn't recognize: *ord yohs*, they sounded like. 'But until then, I'm afraid a few still pictures are the best we can do.'

'Another picture then,' said Strongheart.

The next picture was cloudy, like we were looking at it through fug or muddy water. There were three young young men sitting behind a kind of table. None of them had beards, which made them look even more like kids. In front of them was a big crowd of people, some sitting, some standing, so we saw the three men over the backs of their heads.

'This is Tommy Schneider, Mehmet Haribey and Dixon Thorleye,' said Gaia. 'I know a lot of you are named after one or other of these three guys. Tommy, your ancestor, is the one on the left.'

The three of them seemed so small, somehow, and so so young. And they were kind of... well, ordinary. It was hard to believe that guy on the left was the father of *anyone*, let alone the dad of all the people of Eden, the one we spoke of when we said, *Tom's dick*, or *Tom's neck*, the one someone in every cluster acted out each Virsry when the old story was told. He was barely more than a newhair, and he had a kind of silly nervous smile.

Then the picture started to move. We heard the sound of an angry crowd, everyone shouting out at once. We saw Tommy raising his hands to ask for quiet.

'Hey guys,' I think he said, though it was hard to make out, 'we don't make the decisions, we just—'

But the crowd in the picture wouldn't let him finish. Their shouting rose up again and drowned out whatever he'd been about to say, and then the picture stopped moving.

'Why were those people yelling at them?' someone called out.

'They didn't think Tommy and the others should go up to the starship,' Deep said. 'They thought they should stay on Earth.'

'Here's Angela again,' said Gaia as another picture appeared, and we saw the young woman with black skin. She looked even younger here, and she was holding out her hand to show off her two-coloured ring. 'That's her coming-of-age ring!' said Gaia. 'I hear you have lots of stories about it. I've got one just like it here on my finger, look. It was given to Angela's sister, Candice.'

Then the picture changed and Gaia moved on, like what she'd just told us was nothing much at all. Like Gela's ring was just some ordinary thing you saw every waking, and not the cause of fighting that had done for hundreds of people and was doing for even more right now, just across the Dark in Wide Forest. 'And here's another picture of Tommy,' she said. 'He's meeting the Presid—'

But before she could even finish saying the word, Strongheart had stood up and started to bellow.

'No more pictures! Do you hear me? Stop the pictures now.'

Forty

Not feeling like talking with her helpers or her guards, Mary had ridden out in front of them, and now she'd pretty much forgotten they were even there, plodding along behind her. She was struggling struggling inside herself as she turned the news from the Valley over and over in her mind. She was trying to figure out how to be happy about it, as she knew she should be, working with all the huge energy that she possessed to find a way of understanding it that wouldn't mean throwing away everything she'd done in her life so far.

Could she really have been mistaken all that time, she wondered, when she thought she'd been listening to Gela? And if she'd been mistaken, then who *had* she been listening to? Whose voice had that been that seemed so strong and so clear? Yes, and why had the true Gela not reached out to her and put her straight, when Mary had always tried so hard to be true to her? It just didn't make sense.

The cruel part was that, for all these years, making sense of things was what Mary had done for other people. All that time, she'd travelled back and forth across the Davidfolk Ground, from blueside to peckside, from rockside to alpside, giving up the chance of any sort of home of her own, any sort of family, so that she could tell people a story that would tie things together for them, giving meaning to their lives, however hard and sad, and give them a way to follow, like a string laid out through forest. So many times she'd helped people deal with grief and death and pain. So many times she'd gone down with them into their saddest and loneliest places, crying alongside them but then showing them a way to move forwards. Yet now she couldn't do it for herself.

'I'll tell you something,' she'd said to me once. 'If we shadow-speakers didn't keep up our work, the Davidfolk would forget they had a Mother called Gela, or that they came from Earth, or that Earth and Gela will return again to the Circle of Stones. They'd end up like those Hiding People we met with their Leopardman and their Great Bat Mother.' And in one way the arrival of Earth people in Circle Valley proved that she'd been right. Earth *had* returned, it *had* come back to the Circle, and, or so it seemed, Gela really *was* alive! And yet, in the moment of being proved right, she'd been proved completely wrong as well.

'I can't figure it out,' she muttered. 'There's something missing here. It makes no sense at all.'

Ahead of her a guard fire was a flickering point of red. In the distance behind her, beyond her helpers and guards, a long line of beads of grey bucklight and shadowy people were following after her to Circle Valley.

Meanwhile, Harry was riding in the other direction with his eight men. They had already passed Tall Tree Valley, and were riding as fast as they could go towards Wide Forest. Sometimes Harry felt with his hand to check for that little black square of glass with Gaia's voice inside it that he carried in a pocket in his wrap. Once twice he even took it out and touched it so he could hear her speak, and remind himself this wasn't all some kind of dream.

'Hello Johnfolk,' it said, each time in just the same way, 'this is Gaia from Earth. Three of us have come in a starship. Please stop fighting now and come to meet us.'

And still further across the Dark, another high man was riding towards Harry with another bunch of men with spears. They were climbing up the mountains from Wide Forest, and they were angry angry. They were going to do for every guard they met.

Forty-one

The Earth people stopped showing pictures as soon as Strong-heart told them to. The screens went black. All three of them looked worriedly at the old man. They had no idea what they'd done to offend him. Most of the people watching had no idea either. Myself, I'd got used to Earth speech, but most folk could only barely make out what the Earth people said, so that if something made no sense to them, they just assumed they must have heard it wrong. Some folk even began shouting angrily at Strong-heart, upset that their show of Earth pictures had suddenly come to an end. It was a strange thing to see: before the Earth people came, no low person from the Davidfolk Ground would ever have shouted like that at any high person, no matter how angry they might be.

With helpers standing anxiously round him, and his two shelter-women Jane and Flowerlight gripping his hands, old Strongheart climbed down slowly from his seat and made his way towards the Earth people. Us Michael's Place folk pulled back to let him through.

'President was a woman!' Strongheart hissed, when he was close enough to speak to the Earth people without shouting. Most people there wouldn't have been able to hear him, but of course, we Michael's Place people were right there at the front.

The Earth people stared at him for several heartbeats, while forest pulsed round us – *hmmmph hmmmph hmmmph* – and Starry Swirl blazed down from the black black sky.

'The President of Merka, you mean?' Marius asked. 'There *have* been women presidents of course, going well back before then, but at that particular time—'

Old Strongheart shook off his two shelterwomen. His face was purple with rage, but at the same time he looked like he might be about to cry.

'*All* our stories say President was a woman.'

'Like Marius said,' Gaia soothed him, 'many presidents *were* women but—'

'But at the time of the *Defiant* mission, President was a man,' Marius said. 'His name was Rivera, and—'

'All our stories say it was a woman,' Strongheart repeated stubbornly – he didn't look so much like a Head Guard right then as a scared and wobbly old man whose life would soon slip away from him, 'and it was her that called the three men in the starship and told them to come back down from the sky.'

'She called the three men?' Marius smiled. '*Ah!* I think I can see what's happened here! You're thinking of Kate Grantham, the Drektor of the Glacksy Project. It was her who called the three of them to say the mission was cancelled, and her that ordered the Orbit Police – you know them as Angela Young and Michael Tennison – to go after them when they ignored her. Grantham *was* a woman, but the President was a man. I reckon you've got the two of them mixed up somewhere along the line.'

All round us, people were watching the conversation intently, trying to make out what was being said. Far off in forest, a starbird called: *Hooom! Hooom! Hooom!* And just when you might have expected another starbird to answer it, the veekle answered instead. *Beep! Beep! Beep!* It was pretty funny, but only a couple of people laughed.

'I'm not sure you've even mixed it up all that much,' Gaia said kindly. 'It's more like you've made it a bit simpler. You've just combined the two characters into one. Not surprising after such a long time. It *was* a woman that called them back, you're quite right about that, and she *was* a very powerful person, just as you remember in your stories, but she wasn't the President of Merka.'

They could tell our pride was hurt, but I don't think any of the Earth people really understood how much this mattered to us, or why. The Davidfolk said President was a woman, so did the Tina-folk at Half Sky and the Jeffsfolk from Knee Tree Grounds, and so, even, did the Johnfolk down at Brown River. The only people whose stories said President was a man were the Johnfolk from New Earth. And they were our enemies, they were the ones who were over in Wide Forest right now, doing for our people, burning our shelters, mocking our precious circles. More than half the people here in the clearing had had to leave their homes to escape them. Almost everyone, including Strongheart himself, had boys and men over there in the guards, or members of their families who hadn't yet crossed the Dark when they last heard of them, and could be alive or dead. It was hard hard to bear the thought that the New Earthers' story might be the one that was right.

'But how *could* we have got it wrong?' croaked old Strongheart. He seemed to be finding it hard to breathe. It was as if this single bit of news had finally pushed him, in a few heartbeats, from being the tough old guy who still ran the Davidfolk Ground, and had got both of his new young shelterwomen pregnant, to a weak pathetic little oldie on the edge of death. 'We tell the story over and over! Every single Virsry we act it out! If someone had changed it, every-one would have noticed and put them right!'

He looked like he might fall over, and his shelterwoman Jane took his arm to support him. The other shelterwoman, Flowerlight, had turned to say something to his helpers, so Starlight took his other arm. (My old friend, taking the arm of the Head Guard: any other time that would have been a story good enough for me to tell for all the rest of my life!)

'I don't really get this either,' she told the Earth people, as she helped hold the old guy upright. 'It's true that in New Earth they say President was a man, but that's only because they've decided to change the story. Believe me, I know. Even *they* admit there was a time when everyone in Eden believed President was a woman.'

'And they say President was Gela's dad,' Strongheart said wearily. 'I suppose you guys are going to tell us that's not true as well now?'

Gaia burst out laughing. 'Angela's *dad*? The President of *Merka*! Certainly not! Angela's dad was a *postman*! He lived in London and his family were from J'maker. As far as I know, he never even visited Merka! As to the President, well, there's no way he would even have heard of Angela until the men in the *Defiant* made her famous by taking her away!'

None of us knew what a postman was, of course, but the Earth people explained later it was a guy who took messages from one cluster to another. J'maker was a little grounds like Knee Tree, far out in the pool called See, and was where all the Black People came from. And as to Merka, well, it seemed that President wasn't boss of whole Earth as we'd always thought, but only of one big ground. Merka was sort of like the Davidfolk Ground of Earth.

'I don't understand,' Strongheart complained miserably. All our stories were unravelling, like an old fakeskin wrap, and a cold wind was blowing in through the holes where the wrap had once kept us warm. Strongheart's pregnant young shelterwoman, Jane, held on grimly to his arm, glaring at the Earth people like they'd insulted him on purpose.

'What they're saying,' Starlight told him, 'is that our story here in Mainground is wrong about President, but—'

'But the New Earthers haven't got it right either,' interrupted Jane. She wasn't going to have some jumped-up creature from the Women's Ground taking it upon herself to explain things to the Head Guard of Eden. 'And that's something, isn't it? At least they're wrong as well.'

Strongheart looked at her uncertainly. 'The New Earthers too?'

'That's right, Head Guard,' said Marius. His voice was weary weary now, like he wished this could be over and he could be somewhere else. I guess he was missing his animals and trees. 'If those New Earthers think President was Gela's dad, they're absolutely and completely wrong.'

Headman Newjohn had been fiddling with his beard and quietly watching all this. Now he cleared his throat. 'But wait a moment,' he said. 'I don't want to be rude, but who's to say that you Earth people have got the story right any more than we have? These stories are way more important to us than they are to you. *Way* way more important! Surely we're the ones who'd remember them best?'

It seemed like a good point to me, but Marius obviously didn't think so. He looked round at Deep and Gaia, as if to say, You deal with this. I'm fed up with trying to explain things to these dumb Eden people.

'The thing is…' began Deep. 'The thing is that you people rely on stories that one person passes on to another, and of course, no matter how careful you are, they're bound to change over time. But we've got these pictures and clips and—'

'Deep means we can make copies of voices and words that don't change in the way that stories do,' Gaia said.

The people round us were getting bored.

'Show us some more pictures!' a man shouted out.

'I want to see Gela again!' called out a woman. 'I want to see Gela and her ring!'

'How can it matter so much to them who the President of America was four centuries ago?' Marius grumbled. The three of us had returned to the landing vehicle so we could talk without being overheard. We'd turned the lights down so as not to feel like goldfish in a bowl. All round us, our softly glowing screens offered us information about the world we were in, beautifully organized into diagrams and tables. 'I mean, it's not as if they've got the slightest understanding as to what a President *was* – or what America was, for that matter!'

I like Marius a lot, but I think he suffers from a common delusion of very clever folk. Since he's much better at reasoning than ninety-nine point nine per cent of the people he meets, he's prone to assume that his way of thinking about the world is the only one that makes any sense at all.

'It's an article of faith,' I said. 'It's just one of the things that binds these people together and defines who they are.'

'That's right,' Deep said. 'Come on, Marius, it's not that hard to get! The President thing is a little part of a larger story. And the story means a lot to them.'

'It's a powerful story,' I said, 'about how Angela was brought to Eden against her will, and suffered here, and longed for light and Earth, just as they all do, and eventually found it again after her death.'

Marius snorted. 'Which of course is nonsense. If we try and protect this belief system, we're essentially denying them access to the truth.'

'Which is what?' I asked.

'That Earth isn't a paradise. That Gela isn't waiting there. That there's no life after death. That no more than a handful of people from Eden will ever visit Earth. Yes, and that the universe doesn't work in the way they think it does. It isn't a backdrop for human stories. It's—'

'What gives *your* life meaning, Marius?'

'Science, I guess. Getting to the truth. Peeling away the surface and figuring out how things really work.'

'And why does the truth matter?'

'Because... Well, for lots of reasons, but for one thing it's only if you know the truth about the world that you can really understand it and make it different.'

'And why would you want to make the world different?'

'Well, to make life better, and richer, and—'

'And why would you want to do that?'

'Because... Sacred Earth, Gaia, why the interrogation? What point are you trying to make?'

'That even supersmart, superrational Marius has things he just *believes* in.'

He half-smiled, like he was conceding I'd very nearly got one over on him, even if not quite. 'I guess. In a *sort* of way. But come on, be honest with me, Gaia, what would you prefer: to have the intellectual vistas that are available to us, or to be stuck inside this infantile story that the Eden folk tell each other? I mean, look at Trueheart! Look at that sheer hunger she has for knowledge.'

'Fair point. Though most people aren't like Trueheart, here or on Earth. But we can't give Trueheart or anyone else here the knowledge *we* have, however much they might want it. We can't build universities for them. We can't teach them the whole of science, or even the beginnings of it. Yes, we can easily destroy their old stories if we choose to, but we've got nothing to give them to put in their place.'

Marius shrugged. 'Well, that's up to them, isn't it? They're not kids, Gaia. It's not our business to protect them from the truth. It's up to them what they do with it, but it's our job to give it to them as best we can.'

Deep nodded. 'Marius is right about that, Gaia. We don't have a right to hide things from them.'

'I know,' I said. 'I accept that. But their beliefs *aren't* nonsense, Marius. I'm not having that. They're not literally true, I grant you, but that doesn't mean there's no truth in them. Truth isn't some binary yes–no thing, as you seem to think. All kinds of wisdom can be wrapped in old stories. Throw away the story and you throw away the wisdom as well.'

'I agree with you, Gaia,' said Deep, 'but you need to remember that whatever we tell them or don't tell them, their beliefs will still have to change, just to cope with the new situation the three of us have created simply by being here.'

I stood up and looked out through the clear dome of our flying saucer, at the people out there in the eerie glow of the trees round the clearing, waiting for a glimpse of us. Such a tiny outpost of humankind, they were, and so incredibly far away from everyone else. No wonder they were excited to have us there.

'You're right,' I said, waving back to a small child who'd spotted me and was pointing in my direction. 'The fact that we can't live up to their expectations means that a large chunk of their belief system no longer works.'

'It'll be painful for them,' Deep said. 'But it's always been hard, hasn't it, throughout human history, when new realities come up against old certainties? It was hard when Earth society had to adjust to the ecological problems in the twenty-first century, and the Salvationists came along. It was hard when the Salvationists were overthrown. There was a lot of blood spilt each time, a lot of cruelty. But then again there was bloodshed here too, wasn't there, before we even arrived?'

I looked down at the people below us, with their bare feet, and their animal-skin loincloths, and their crude spears tipped with shards of volcanic glass. The little girl's mother was standing beside her now, and both of them were waving and smiling, trying to get my attention. The woman was one of the people who had twisted feet – clawfoot, to use the Eden word – like Angie's Dave. A bunch of other people round them were waving with them, all of them beaming delightedly up at me, now that I was looking their way. There was another clawfoot among them, and a couple of batfaces. I waved quickly back and just managed a smile for them before I had to turn away with tears in my eyes, unable to bear their hope. Marius had stood up to come and join me, and he too smiled and waved at the folk outside.

'You know what would really help these people more than any-thing else we could do?' he said. 'It would be if Deep and I were to go out there and get as many women pregnant as possible. We could double Eden's gene pool at a stroke.'

I studied his face for a moment. 'You are joking, right?'

'Of course I am, Gaia, but it happens to be true all the same.'

Forty-two

Leader Harry and his men met a guard riding at full speed towards them on the back of an exhausted woollybuck, its mouth dripping with green foam. He pulled up in front of them in a cloud of snow that glittered in the light of the headlanterns.

'The Johnfolk are right up on the Dark already, Leader!' the guard said, jumping down and bowing to the high man. 'I was watching the fire with my mates two crossings away from here, and we saw their lights coming towards us. They've only got a few woollybucks, but we could see the shadows of the men against the snow, and the light on the metal spears, and I can tell you there were a whole lot of them. They'll have reached my mates by now, I reckon. I guess they'll have done for them.'

Harry nodded. 'I'm sorry about your mates, my friend, but it's actually good the Johnfolk are on the Dark already.'

The poor guard was amazed. 'It's *good*, Leader?'

'We're looking for them. We've come to tell them that Earth has come! There's a new veekle standing in the Circle right now, and a new Gela.'

The guard – he was a friend of our Tom's – stood there beside his exhausted buck and watched Harry and his men riding on towards Wide Forest. After a while, when his buck had cooled down a bit, he climbed back up onto it and carried on towards Circle Valley.

Earth had come! He was happy happy like everyone, thinking

that all the cold and dark and fear would soon be over. But he felt sad for his friends who he'd left by their fire, waiting for the Johnfolk and their metal blades. It seemed cruel cruel that the two of them should have died less than half a waking before this news would have reached them.

🌿

Harry met a few more frightened people from Wide Forest, on their way over to Circle Valley. And then, after another half waking or so, he saw at last the headlanterns of the New Earthers' few woollybucks in the distance, on far side of a black emptiness where a valley of ice and rock was completely hidden in the darkness. And in their grey light, he saw what that guard and his mates had seen earlier: the shadowy shapes of many ringmen on the backs of their own thin New Earth bucks. There were more than a hundred of them, against his eight men.

He pulled off his headwrap, cupped his hands round his mouth.

'Hey! New Earthers!' His voice echoed round him against bare black rocks he couldn't see. 'My name is Leader Harry! I'm the son of David Strongheart!' He let the echo fade before carrying on. 'I've not come to fight you. I've come to talk!' He paused again, listening for any kind of answer from across far side of that pit of darkness. But apart from the echoes nothing came back. 'We have news! Important news! We have a message from Earth! A veekle has come down from the sky!' Again he waited. 'Can you hear me?' But there was still no reply from the ringmen who'd begun to make their way onto a narrow ridge at the top of that invisible valley.

Harry looked round at his men. 'You, David, and you, Mehmet, leave your spears behind and come with me. The rest of you, wait here.'

The three of them made their way down to the ridge that the Johnfolk had already reached. Presently Harry stopped and shouted out once again, and this time another voice called back.

'We've won the fight!' the voice shouted. 'The sons of John have won back Old Ground. Admit that! Give us Circle Valley, and we'll let you live.'

'You can come to Circle Valley. We promise not to fight you. We promise to let you leave.'

'That's not what I asked you for. Give us Circle Valley! Admit John has won! Accept the True Story!'

'Didn't you hear me? A veekle has come down from Earth! A new Gela has come! We've got a message from her for you.'

There was a short silence, and then a scornful laugh. 'That's a silly trick! A kid's trick. It shows how desperate you stonespears are.'

'Wait here,' Harry told the two guards.

He climbed down from his buck. He threw his own spear away into the snow, he pulled off the top part of his bodywrap so he was naked down to the waist in that freezing freezing air, and he held up the little black square that held the voice of Gaia inside it. He was a big man, as his dad had been in his young days, with a thick black beard and hair all over his body, halfway turned to grey.

'I wouldn't believe it myself if I was you,' he shouted out, 'but I have Gela's voice inside this thing, and if you let me come near you'll be able to hear it for yourself. You can shoot an arrow through me if I'm wrong.'

We saw Leader Harry sometimes back at Veeklehouse, and once he even passed through Michael's Place. Our own guard leader, Leader Hunter, had been showing his older brother round his ground, and they came through our little cluster on bucks draped in coloured fakeskin, with a bunch of guards riding behind them. Of course we knelt and bowed our heads as they rode past. These were high high men, the sons of Strongheart, and that's what high people expected. We knelt and bowed, and then, when they'd passed on, we went back to working for them. One quarter of all the starflowers we gathered in Michael's Place, a quarter of all the buckskins we scraped and cleaned, a quarter of the meat we cut up and dried, went to Leader Hunter, and I know the people up in Circle Valley had to do just the same for his brother Leader Harry. It was to provide for the guards to protect us, we low people were told, but we weren't stupid, we knew that what a guard leader gathered in from his clusters didn't just go to his guards. Lots of it was traded for fancy fakeskin wraps for the leader and all his shelterwomen and kids, and for bucks for them to ride wherever they went, and for the special food that was brought in for them from far away, and for those big big shelters of theirs, built round trees, where they could sit at ease, with helpers running round them.

We'd always grumbled about this, of course. Even Tom our cluster head grumbled, though he was proud proud of being one of David Strongheart's men. But at the same time we accepted that this was just how things were with high people. You worked and worked for them, and yet you had to behave as if it was you who had to be grateful to them, you who were gratefully receiving, and them who were kindly giving. For when we bowed to him, they would barely smile in return. They would just slightly slightly nod their heads, and perhaps if we were lucky, they would give that little lazy wave.

That was what Leader Hunter was like, that's what all the high men were like that I've ever heard of, and I'm sure Harry was no different. He wasn't an especially nice man. He wasn't especially good. He didn't think much about the feelings of his low people. He took whatever he wanted from them, even sometimes their daughters, if he had a fancy to it. (Could a low girl say no to a high man who was a son of David Strongheart? Of course not. Whatever he asked of her, she'd have to say yes, and pretend to be pleased about it as well.) And if any low person challenged him, whether they were right or wrong, he would have them beaten, or tied to a spiketree to burn their skin, the same as all the high men did with those they saw as troublemakers.

He was selfish, in other words. He acted like the story was all about him. He used other people like they were just starflowers or bucks or lumps of blackglass, not human beings like himself. And yet right now, standing there shivering in the pale light from the buck behind him, and his shadow stretched out in front of him over the snow, Leader Harry was brave brave. For he had stripped away everything that made him high, everything that made him more comfortable than other people, everything that made him safer, and he still walked towards our enemies.

I've thought about this a lot since I heard about it. I reckon we all live by stories, high people and low people. We all tell ourselves that what we do, we do for a good reason. 'I take things from the low people,' high men said, 'so I can feed and wrap the guards who protect them.' It wasn't just a story they told us, it was a story they told themselves. And each of us, high and low, half-believed it, and half-knew at the same time that it wasn't true. We all knew that the things they took didn't just go to the guards, and that anyway the guards were just our own men and our own sons, and the high men knew that too. We knew that the guards didn't really protect us, but protected the high people, and the high men knew that as well. Yet we all needed stories, them and us, we all needed something to tie things together, and so we all went along with those stories, half-believing them, believing them just enough to give ourselves a sense that the world we were in meant something, staying with each story no longer than we had to, and then moving on before it all toppled over or fell apart. It was as if all of us, high and low, were crossing a stream on wobbly stones, moving quickly from one to the next before we fell.

But right now it was different for Harry. He had a story to tell that he knew for certain was true. He knew the Johnfolk wouldn't believe it, any more than he would have believed it if they'd told it to him, but he had seen with his own eyes the veekle in Circle Clearing, and he had no doubts about it at all. And that made him strong strong. He wasn't standing on a wobbly stone just at that moment. He was standing on solid rock. It felt good good. Even the coldness of the Dark felt kind of good as it bit through to his bones. It told him he was right there in the world, with nothing left to hide behind.

'We were proud proud of him,' was what his guards said afterwards.

'You can shoot me if you want,' he called out, 'but I'm coming forward anyway, and you can see for yourself that I can't possibly hurt you.'

Forty-three

Gaia let me try on her ring. We were sitting outside the Earth people's shelter with Starlight and Clare. Little Suzie was sleeping beside Clare on a piece of woollybuck skin: her shoulder hadn't completely healed yet, of course, but all the heat had gone out of it. She wasn't sick any more, and Flame had gone out scavenging with the other grownups and older kids. Metty was asleep on my lap. Candy and two three other little kids were playing nearby with a couple of little dolls Dave had made for them from bone and buckskin.

'Let's pretend they get in the veekle and go flying off to Earth,' Candy said.

'No, that's boring,' said her friend Mehmet. 'Let's pretend a leopard comes for them, but they do for it with a spear.'

Earlier on, the three Earth people had opened up that old Screen with a kind of metal knife. All three of them had spent some time leaning over it, looking at what was inside and saying things to one another that I couldn't make sense of at all. Now Deep and Marius were poking round in it with some of their strange tools, still speaking to each other from time to time in words that I could hear, but could get no meaning from. Dave squatted nearby, whittling away at bits of bone with a stone knife. He was no good for hunting or scavenging.

After I'd tried the ring on my finger, I took it off and looked at the tiny letters inside. 'It's beautiful beautiful,' I said as I handed it back to Gaia.

'There are thousands just like it on Earth,' Gaia said. 'Back when Angela was growing up, it was a common thing for people to give their sons and daughters a coming-of-age ring when they were eighteen. It was a sort of... tradition – I guess you know that word? – but it was a tradition that grew up in one generation and then died out again in the next. Things got hard, I guess, and an awful lot of people were too worried about getting enough to eat and staying alive to bother with stuff like rings.' She slipped it back onto her finger. 'There were fancier ones than this, rings with... with shiny stones... but these two-metal ones were one of the commonest kinds. They were...' She paused, as the Earth people did when they came to a word or an idea they thought we wouldn't understand. 'They were quite easy to make, so ordinary people could get them. Lots of families still have them back home, tucked away somewhere.'

'Well, we've only got one here,' Starlight said, with a slight edge in her voice. 'There were... well, you'd call them *wars* about it. People were done for with spears, and tied to trees, and—'

'How strange. Wars over one cheep ring.'

Cheep meant easy to get, I found out, like a thing that you could have from a trader for only a stick or two.

'I guess in that first generation the only people on Eden were just a bunch of kids and two adults,' said Deep, without looking up from what he was doing inside the Screen. 'Imagine how they must have admired that ring on their mum's finger, when it was the only metal they'd ever seen. I can see how it became important to them.'

'I guess,' said Gaia, and then she smiled. 'You know what! I've just figured out something! One or two of the things you Eden guys say sound like how little kids speak on Earth. Like you say "*big* big" when we'd say *very* big. I guess that must have started at that same time.'

Of course we'd all noticed that new word *very* that the Earth people used, and many Eden people were already starting to copy

it. Of course they were. Earth speech sounded so smart and powerful – even high people's speech seemed dumb beside it – and it
made Eden folk feel a bit smarter and more powerful themselves
when they spoke in the same way.

'I reckon that might be how that double word thing started,'
Gaia said. 'Tommy and Gela spoke babytalk to their kids, like all
mums and dads do, even to one another, but in their case there were
no grownups round them to bring them back to talking like adults.'

Deep glanced uncomfortably at me and Clare. '*Not* that you're
saying that these guys talk like babies, of course, Gaia!'

Gaia was embarrassed. 'Oh no! Certainly not! I'm so sorry, you
guys. I didn't mean that at all!'

Starlight shrugged. 'Don't worry. We *are* babies compared to
you. We know that. And of course it was babyish to fight over a silly
thing like a ring. But we don't have starships and veekles, we don't
have cars, we don't have telly vijun and screens and lecky-trickity.
And so that ring—'

'Gela lost the ring, remember,' I interrupted her. The old story
suddenly seemed powerful powerful to me, here in the company
of these Earth people who were with us now, but would so soon be
gone again. It felt so powerful that I almost burst into tears. 'She
lost the ring and it was her last link to Earth. *That's* why it's important to us! If the stories are true, she cried and cried for wakings and
wakings, raging against Tommy, raging against the kids she'd had
with him, for stealing her from her mum and dad and everyone
she knew.'

Dave nodded. 'Yeah. The Big Row.'

'The Big Row?' asked Gaia. 'That's a story you all know?'

'Yeah, of course,' said Dave. 'We often tell it and we often act it
out.'

Gaia glanced at Deep and Marius. 'Wow! Think of that! A man
and a woman have a fight in front of their kids, and four hundred
years later their descendants are still acting it out!'

I'm sure she didn't mean to shame us, but I felt ashamed.

Probably we all did. Because, now that she'd pointed it out, that also seemed pretty babyish, the fact that we kept on acting out a little thing like that after all this time. After all, there must be arguments between men and women every waking, all over Eden.

But then Marius spoke, still bent over the Screen and his tools: 'I get that, actually,' he said slowly, like he wasn't just telling us something, but figuring it out for himself. 'My mum and dad used to fight a lot when I was little. It was horrible. Each time it felt like the whole world falling apart. Sometimes I'd lie on my bed and stick my fingers in my ears and mutter to myself so it would blot out the sound of their shouting. I had other people to turn to, though. I had my sister, and my friends, and my grandpa, and my aunt Hentie. But for those kids back at the beginning here on Eden, there *wasn't* anyone else. Tommy and Angela really *were* the whole world. It really *was* the world falling apart.'

Starlight shrugged. She wanted to get back to what she'd been talking about. 'Anyway, the reason I spoke of the fights over the ring is that I wanted you to understand how important Earth is to us, and how much even the smallest thing from Earth means to us. And because of that – I'm sorry to say it, but I'm not sure you Earth guys really understand this – because of that, every single little thing you say and do will change the whole story of Eden forever.'

This was such a different Starlight from the one I'd known when I was a kid. Back then, all she was interested in was having as much fun as she could. Now she was trying to speak for all of Eden.

'The truth is—' began Gaia.

'The truth is you didn't expect to find us here,' Starlight said. 'I know that. Your science told you it was impossible for the children of just one man and one woman to survive and carry on like this. But we *are* here, and we've been waiting for you for generations and generations. Most people here think you're going to take us all back to Earth, or bring all the good things you have on Earth across the sky to Eden. Many many people think you're Gela herself who's come back to—'

Gaia shook her head. 'Honestly, Head Woman, I've done my best to stop that. I keep telling folk I'm not Angela Young, that the only connection I have with Angela is that one of my ancestors was her sister, but no one seems to believe—'.

'Strongheart doesn't want to ask you this,' Starlight said. 'In fact Strongheart doesn't want to say *any* of this stuff to you, because he's so proud to be the one who was Head Guard when Earth came back, but you need to tell us: what can you really give us, and when are you going to leave?'

The Earth people looked at each other. Gaia drew breath.

'We can't take people back to Earth,' she said. 'Well, maybe one at most, but no more than that. And we haven't got anything to give you right now, apart from maybe fixing a few more people with the ... uh ... poison fever, as you call it, and maybe finding out what's in this screen. As for how long we'll be here, we can only stay for a few more days, because the starship is ... well, I guess you could say it's like a creature that starts growing old as soon as it's born. But we're finding out about Eden and how it works, and what the trees and animals are made of, and when we get all of that information back to Earth, then people there will be able to figure out ways to help you. New ways of feeding yourselves and keeping healthy and making you better when you're ill. New ways of using the stuff round you to make things. New tools. So next time some-one comes, they'll be able to give you things that will make your life easier and—'

'Next time?' asked Starlight. 'Are you sure there'll *be* another time?'

Again, Gaia looked at the other Earth people.

'I'm sure there will,' she said. 'It won't be any time soon, though, because we have to rebuild the whole starship and that ... well, like Marius explained before, by the time we've got all the stuff together, it could be ...'

'It could be fifty years,' Marius said, still bent over that screen, 'or even longer.'

I felt a terrible stab of grief. All these years we'd waited, all these generations, making circles on the ground, singing songs, making it okay for ourselves that Earth wasn't here by telling ourselves to be patient, and one waking it would come. And now it *had* come, but it would soon be gone again, and we'd be alone once more, scratching in the dirt, fighting over old stories. And when Earth came back, *if* it came back – even that didn't sound certain – it would most probably be too late for me. I wasn't exactly sure how old I was in years – we didn't count time that carefully out on the Grounds – but I reckoned I was well over thirty, and few people got past sixty seventy.

'One person can go with you?' I suddenly said. 'Is that what you said?'

Gaia looked at me, surprised.

'Yes, we figure we could take one.' She smiled. 'Why? Would you like it to be you? You were the first Eden person we saw, after all, you and Trueheart, and you've been a good friend to us.'

Those tears that had been so close to coming out before came pressing forwards again. I laid Metty on the ground beside me and stood up so I could walk a little way off and turn my face away. Would I like to get away from Dave's moaning and his hands feeling for me after every waking, like I was there to prove to him, over and over, that in spite of his clawfeet he was a man? Would I like to get away from his brother Tom sneaking up on me? Would I like to get away from scratching and scraping to find enough to eat, and then having to find still more to keep the Leader off our backs? Would I like to have my batface taken from me, that ugly face that made me feel like I should apologize to each new person I met? Gela's heart, of course I would. That would be like laying down a heavy heavy load that I carried every waking of my life.

But to say goodbye forever to my own kids? Well, I couldn't bear that. And I couldn't do it to them. I just couldn't.

Yes and anyway, I said to myself, who was I kidding? I'd never feel at home in that strange pale place. Whatever they did for my mouth and nose and teeth with their metal needles and knives, I'd still feel like a batface among those tall beautiful people, who knew so much. Beside them, I'd always be a foolish child.

Clare had come after me. She laid her hand on my arm.

'I'm alright,' I told her. 'It was a silly question Gaia asked, wasn't it? She knows I've got three kids.'

'Yes, and Dave would never manage without you.'

🌿

Later the Earth people went out in forest again with their strange tools that worked by lecky-trickity. (Yes, there really is such a thing, though the Earth people's name for it seemed to have changed. They say eleck-trissity. I guess words wear down more quickly when you use them all the time, like the edge of a stone knife.) They promised Strongheart they wouldn't go far, so he could call them back with horns if the New Earthers came to talk.

Forty-four

'**K**neel on the snow, stonespear!' commanded Luke Johnson. 'Kneel on the snow and bow your head. Show me you admit the fight is over.'

Shivering shivering, blue with cold, Harry half-glanced back towards his guards, and then knelt and bowed as he'd been asked. 'It *is* over,' he said. 'But not for the reason you think.'

We used to tell a story back on Knee Tree Grounds about John Redlantern, standing on the cliff by the crashed Veekle, trying to decide whether to keep Gela's ring or throw it out into the Pool. He told people afterwards that he heard the voices of people not yet born, calling out to him, arguing with one another about what he should do next. 'Throw it away!' some said. 'It'll only bring trouble.' 'Keep it,' said others, 'that ring is precious precious to everyone on Eden!'

When the story got to that part, we kids would start calling things out ourselves. 'Keep it!' some of us would shout. 'Toss it into the Pool!' the rest would yell. And then the grownups would point out to us that the voices John had heard were ours! *We* were the people not yet born, and we *were* still arguing about his decision, just as John had known we would.

It must have been the same for Leader Harry. He must have known that, whatever happened next, there would be stories in the future about this moment. A hundred Johnfolk facing just eight guards and one leader, the son of the Head Guard facing the son of the Headman, a guard leader kneeling half-naked in the snow with the voice from Earth inside a square of smooth black glass: well, Tom's dick, how could all of that *not* become a story?

Headmanson Luke rode forward on his blue-skinned buck, a ringman on a woollybuck riding beside him to give him the light of its headlantern. Luke suspected some kind of trick, though he couldn't figure out what it might be, and he had an arrow half-drawn on his bowstring.

Harry looked up at the Headmanson and showed him what he held in his hand. The glass glinted in the bucklight. One of Luke's ringmen shouted, 'Father! A blade!' and Luke fired his arrow at Leader Harry. It hit him in the belly. There was a silence, the kind of silence you only get up on the Dark, with no trees to pulse and hum. Harry felt for the shaft of the arrow with his left hand. He had a puzzled look on his face, as if he couldn't quite figure out what this thin hard thing might be that was suddenly sticking out of him.

Of course Harry's two guards, David and Mehmet, rushed forwards at once on their bucks, but they didn't get far. Straight away Luke's ringmen fired more arrows, not just one or two but dozens of them, and the two of them fell backwards off their bucks onto the snow. Now the other six guards came riding forwards too. The ringmen aimed their bows. In a couple of heartbeats all six would be dead as well. But then Harry yelled out. He was still alive, kneeling in the light of Luke's buck, with a big circle of red red snow all round him. And he yelled out not just to his own men but to everyone who was there.

'Gela's heart, *stop it*!' he yelled. 'Stop this nonsense, will you, and listen!'

And everyone did. There was something about the way this dying man spoke that pulled them up short, ringmen and guards both, Johnfolk and Davidfolk, even the Headmanson of New Earth. Everyone stopped and listened, and in the silence, the Headmanson and the ringmen who'd rode up beside him heard a woman's voice, small small, that seemed to be speaking from Leader Harry's hand.

'Hello Johnfolk,' it said, 'this is Gaia from Earth. Three of us have come in a starship. Please stop fighting now and come to meet us.'

Then Harry tipped forwards onto the bloody snow and the black square fell from his hand. Luke jumped down from his buck and picked it up. Almost at once it spoke again, startling him so much that he dropped it back onto the snow.

Luke stood there for a moment, looking down at it, then he turned towards his men, his face suddenly scared and desperate, almost like he was hoping they'd tell him what to do. Of course they said nothing. He couldn't even read anything in their faces, hidden away as they were by their buckskin headwraps. All he could see here or there was a glinting eye. After a couple of heartbeats he stooped down again and once more picked up the black square. He must have held it a different way this time because it remained silent. He tipped it back and forth in his hand. He sniffed at it. He turned round to his men again, as if he still hadn't given up on the hope they might know what to do next, but of course nothing came back to him from those rows and rows of blank buckskin masks. In New Earth, just as in the Davidfolk Ground, low people don't tell high people what they should do.

'You!' he called out to the six guards who were still alive. 'You guards! Come forwards and talk. We won't hurt you. Tell us what this thing is!' Of course the guards didn't move. They might just be ordinary guards, but they didn't take their orders from Johnfolk, whether high or low. 'Please!' called Luke. *'Please!* We won't hurt you! I promise you that.'

For a third time he turned back towards his men. He still had no idea what to do. He wasn't even sure what was happening.

Everything was so sudden, and so strange, and so dreadful that it was hard to believe that he was even there. But all the same, two things were becoming slowly clearer to him. The first thing was that a messenger had been sent to him by Earth, and he'd answered with an arrow. And the second was that, when stories were told about Headmanson Luke in generations to come, that would be the one thing he'd be remembered for. Long after everyone had forgotten his face, and the sound of his voice, long after anyone could remember what his friends and his family liked about him, or what he cared about, or what he was good at, people across Eden would remember that Headmanson Luke Johnson was the man who did for Earth's messenger.

The six guards looked at each other, exchanged nods, and came reluctantly forward. They climbed down from their bucks and squatted down to attend to their leader and their two mates, David and Mehmet. But all three were dead, each one in his own slowly spreading patch of bright red snow.

One of the guards stood up – he was a guy of forty fifty with a thick grey beard called Roger – and looked straight at Headmanson Luke. He knew that Luke was a high man, and he knew that Luke's ringmen could do for him at any moment, but he was too angry to kneel or bow or be polite. The dead guard David had been his younger brother.

'Leader Harry got down from his buck,' he said. 'He came forward on his own. He threw away his spear and pulled off his wrap. Tom's stinking dick, man, what *else* did he have to do to get you to listen to him?'

Luke held out the little square of glass. His hand was shaking.

'What is this thing?'

'I don't know its name but it's something from Earth. Surely you can see that for yourself? Earth has come back. Two tall men and a new Gela with black black skin. That's her voice inside that thing. Their veekle's sitting in Circle Clearing right now. It's alive, it moves, it gives out light and makes sounds. Lucky there were

Davidfolk there to meet them, wouldn't you say? Lucky we didn't all follow your Juicy John. If we'd all been skulking across the Pool there in New Earth, they'd have come and gone and never known anyone was still alive here in Eden.'

Forty-five

As the Earth people wandered about in forest, looking at animals and starflowers and trees, they ran into the Michael's Place folk who were out there scavenging. Trueheart was with the scavengers, but as soon as she saw the Earth folk there, with their science tools on their bike, she asked to go with them as she'd done before.

'Certainly not,' Tom hissed at her, too quietly for the Earth people to hear. 'I'm your dad, and I'm telling you to stay with us and help find food for your family.'

But Gaia called out that of course Trueheart could go with them, and so Trueheart ignored her dad a second time and ran over to Gaia and Marius and Deep.

Tom said nothing, but two three people described to me how the knuckles of his one hand turned white white round his spear.

Later, when Tom and the others came back to us with the few things they'd found to eat – small bony slinkers, bitter batmeat and stale seeds picked up, one by one, from the dirt – Tom growled to Clare that Trueheart was going to get what was coming to her when the Earth people had gone away.

'They don't seem to understand,' he complained. 'Okay, I know they come from Earth and I know they're high high people, but high people here in Eden would never come between a dad and his kid. They'd know whole of Eden works by each person knowing their place between high and low. They'd know there wouldn't even *be* high people if there weren't people in between.'

'She's a bad girl, your Trueheart,' said Flame. She'd become bolder lately, since we'd all felt sorry for her about Suzie. 'My dad would have beaten me hard hard if I'd behaved like that.'

Clare had been more friendly to Flame lately, but now she glared at Tom. Was he going to let his young shelterwoman speak to him like this, when she wasn't much older than Trueheart herself?

Not long afterwards, Trueheart came back with the Earth people. They unloaded a pile of things they'd gathered up – some wood, some wavyweed, a dead bat, a piece of rock, a whole bunch of tiny creepy-crawlies like ants and worms – and Gaia and Marius began to do *tests* on it all, as they called it, with their lecky-trickity tools. Trueheart watched and asked questions, trying with all her might to understand. Deep, meanwhile, picked up the Screen again and another set of tools, and carried on trying to find things inside it.

'We'll show some more pictures tomorr … I mean, next waking,' Gaia told me, 'and we'll talk to everyone about how long we can stay, and what Earth might be able to help them with. Your friend Starlight was quite right to ask about that. We can see we're making things difficult for everyone by not being clear.'

'You saved my sister's life,' Trueheart said. It was the first time I'd heard her speak of baby Suzie as her sister. 'And you're going to stop the fight with the Johnfolk. I don't call that making things diff—'

But at that moment an old woman began to screech from across the fence. 'Gela! Our Mother! You've come back for us!' She was standing among a group of nine ten people who'd just arrived from across the Dark. She was thin thin, and all she had on was one bit of fatbuck skin wrapped round her dry old belly, but she and her companions' faces were cracked in toothless smiles of delight to see the Earth people sitting there. So it was true! Just as they'd heard on the Dark! Earth had really come!

Gaia sighed, laid down the tool she was working with – it was like a tiny screen with a metal needle attached to it by a kind of string – and stood up to go over to the fence. We'd been through this scene many times now. The old woman and her friends laughed and clapped their hands as Gaia came near, tears running down their faces. They stretched their arms out to her over the fence. 'I never thought...' they would tell each other later. 'To think that I was alive when...' 'If only my old mum could have...'

Gaia touched the hands straining towards her, squeezing some of them, and stroking the cheeks of little ones that were held out to her over the fence. She looked so tall and strong, so beautiful and sure of herself, next to those funny shrivelled little Eden people in their rough skin wraps, that it was strange to think that she and them were even the same kind of creature.

'I'm not Gela,' she told them. 'I'm not Angela. Angela is here in the Burial Ground in Circle Valley, under that huge pile of stones. My name is Gaia, and my ancestor was Angela's sister, Candice.'

The people looked at each other. How strange and wonderful her Earth speech was. You could only make out the odd word, and yet somehow you knew you'd be able to figure it out, if only you listened long and hard enough.

'Candice?' crowed the old woman. 'Did you say Candice? My name's Candice too!'

'Hey!' called Deep. 'Gaia! Marius! Come and check this out! I think we're finally getting somewhere!'

Forty-six

I feel a bit sorry for Headmanson Luke when I think about that moment up there in the snow and the darkness. In front of him were three dead men and six angry guards. Behind were all those ringmen waiting for him to decide. He was young young – younger than me and Starlight were that first time we went to Veeklehouse – but he'd already made himself the fool of a story that all these watching men would take back to the Johnfolk and the Davidfolk both. He'd come across to Mainground to make his stern grey father proud, and bring some happiness to his mother Lucy. He'd come full of plans to help his friend Teacher Gerry bring the True Story of President to all the people of Eden. But now Teacher Gerry was dead and Luke had brought shame to his family and to all of New Earth. It would be hard for anyone to move forwards from a thing like that. But Luke was the Headmanson and he knew he must.

'Topmen,' he called, 'come talk to me.'

In New Earth they have a Headman instead of a Head Guard, chiefs instead of guard leaders, and topmen are the bosses of smaller groups of ringmen under the chiefs, much like the blokes they call groupmen in the guards. There were four of them there among his ringmen. They climbed down from their bucks and walked over to him, pulling off their headwraps, which up here on the Dark they wore instead of their metal masks.

'I'll take ten men with me, and carry on to Circle Valley to talk with the Headman.' Luke pointed to the oldest of the topmen. 'You can come with me, John. Pick out nine more to bring with us. You three can take the rest of the men back to Wide Forest and—'

'But, Father, you won't be safe with only—!'

'You can take the men back to Wide Forest, and give a message from me to our chiefs down there to stop fighting and go back with their men to Veeklehouse, David Water or Nob Head, wherever they first grounded. You can tell them what's happened, and tell them about this... this...' His voice became wobbly as he looked down at the little black square of glass and tried to figure out what to call it. 'You can tell them about this black thing.'

At that point, he must have touched whichever part of it made it speak, because right then Gaia's voice spoke out again, saying those exact same words in the exact same way:

'Hello Johnfolk, this is Gaia from Earth. Three of us have come in a starship. Please stop fighting now and come to meet us.'

The topmen hadn't heard it so clearly before. They started, they gasped, their mouths fell open, and at the same time their hearts opened too, and tears came to their eyes as they heard the clear, firm voice of a confident young woman, coming out of this tiny object as if she was actually there. Topman John fell straight to his knees and all three others followed him at once. For of course the Johnfolk looked up to Mother Gela no less than the Davidfolk, even if they heard her telling them completely different things.

How wretched it must have been for Luke Johnson, knowing he couldn't share in their joy that Earth had returned. Now he could only look forward with dread to his meeting with the woman whose voice was somehow held inside this piece of glass. But he didn't show those feelings. He'd managed to get back in control of himself. Whether he liked it or not, he had a place now in the story of whole of Eden and, like dead Leader Harry a short time ago, and like his many-greats grandfather John Redlantern, he knew that not only these men round him, but people not yet born, were watching him to see what he'd do next.

He turned to the six guards who were still alive. 'You heard what I've told my men. The fight is over. I'll come and meet the Earth people with your Headman, and they can decide which of us is right and which is wrong. I'd like to ask three of you to ride on to Wide Forest. Tell your leaders there from me that we won't fight them any more, and that, if they let us, all my men will go quietly back to the places we grounded and wait there until the Earth people have told us what to do. I'd like the rest of you to lead the way back to Circle Valley, so you can tell your big people when we get there, and your people we meet along the way, that this isn't a trick, that I've come to talk, just as the new Gela has asked, and that all of my ringmen except these ten have been told to go back to poolside.'

The six guards looked at each other, shrugged, and nodded. 'We can tell folk what happened here,' one of them said, 'and we can tell them what you've just said. But we can't speak for the high people. What they do is up to them.'

Luke Johnson looked down at the black square in his hand. If only he'd held back for one single heartbeat longer, he'd have heard the voice before he shot the arrow. 'Of course. All you can do is tell them what I said.'

He pulled his headwrap back on and climbed back up onto the slim blue-skinned buck he'd brought over from across the Pool. He made himself sit up straight straight on its back. He made himself lift his head up high, like his father Dixon would have done, or his mother Lucy, who'd had to live with so much sadness. Then he turned towards Circle Valley again while three of the guards rode out ahead of him, and Topman John and those ten ringmen gathered themselves behind him.

Forty-seven

Deep had found some more pictures of Earth, and now the Earth people were showing them on the screens in Circle Clearing. They were pictures of a place called London, a place they knew we'd have heard of, because it had been the home of Angela Young, and part of Old Family cluster was still named after it. More than a thousand thousand people lived in London now, Gaia told us – more than a *millyun* to use their word – which was surely many times more than lived in whole of Eden. But she said this was still much much less than used to live there.

The screens showed us a moving picture of rows and rows of houses with doors and black windholes, under that strange white sky. Pale pale pale: that was the word that kept coming to me. When we'd imagined the brightness of Earth we hadn't imagined it like this, because our brightness is always next to darkness, and it's darkness that makes the brightness shine out. Brightness next to other brightness is a different thing, just like a voice speaking in the humming forest is a different thing from a voice in the emptiness of Snowy Dark.

'Why are those houses in water?' someone called out.

'Lots of houses in London are,' Gaia said. 'It's the same in many sitties.' A sitty, we found out, was a giant cluster where many thousands lived. 'The water rose up when the ice melted. It was a hard time, and there were lots of fights between the people who'd been driven out of places and the people who still had homes. Whole areas of London had to be given up. These houses here are empty. No one lives in this part of London any more, but… oh here you are, look!… There are lots of birds there!'

A strange white creature flew out of one of the windholes. It rose up into the pale grey sky on long thin wings that were white as human bones. And, as it climbed up through the air, it suddenly gave out a cry, a strange lonely shrieking, which made us shiver, as if a skeleton had opened its jaws and wailed. We watched it in silence. We'd always been told that the animals of Earth were like people. We'd always understood that they had red blood, and a single heart, and eyes like human eyes, and that you could look into those eyes and see how they were feeling, just like you can with people. But this was nothing like a person, and it seemed to us far far stranger than any Eden creature.

I looked round at the hundreds of people who'd come to the clearing to see the pictures. It was easy to tell the people who'd come down into the Valley in the last couple of wakings because their eyes were full of tears at the sight of the veekle and the pictures from Earth. The people who'd been here long enough to see the pictures before were all watching with dry eyes. But new arrivals or not, no one seemed to know what to make of the white winged creature with its cold and lonely cry.

The Earth people looked out at us worriedly. They could tell there was a different mood in the clearing this time.

'We thought perhaps you'd like to see some pictures of yourselves,' said Gaia, and straight away the three screens showed forest of Circle Valley, and three little boys doing a silly dance.

'It's Davey!' someone shouted. 'It's Davey and Tom and Trueson!'

Now *this* was fun! We all cheered up at once, and soon everyone was laughing out loud.

Another picture appeared. 'Look! It's you, Lucy!' someone yelled out delightedly. 'No way!' a woman answered. 'No *way* is that me!' Her friends laughed at her. 'It is, you know! That's exactly what you're like!'

Another picture came, this time a moving one. 'Tom's dick! Look!' a man shouted. 'It's old Roger. I'd know that weird walk anywhere!'

Then came a picture that talked. 'You want me to speak? I... um... I don't know what to say,' said an old guy in a fancy wrap, looking shyly out of the screen. And everyone cheered because it was David Strongheart himself, but he didn't seem that scary or high when you saw him like that, not like the fierce leader who'd sent hundreds to their deaths, but more like a kind old granddad to us all.

There were more pictures of low people after that, each one greeted with delight by their friends and family. It went on for some time. Everyone was way way happier being shown what they already knew than they had been looking at those strange pale pictures from Earth. Even pictures of places delighted people.

'Hey, look! It's that bent tree over by Lava Blob!'

'Ha! I know that place! It's just this side of Cold Path Neck!'

'That's Longpool, isn't it? No, wait a minute, it's Greatpool, look! There's that bit of rock that sticks up on blueside.'

But at last the screens went black again.

'We've got an interesting thing to show you,' said Deep, his voice booming out from the veekle, 'a really special thing that we know you'll all want to see and hear, but first Gaia's got something to speak to you about.'

'I want you all to listen carefully,' said Gaia, speaking slowly slowly and carefully carefully. 'I want you all to understand what I'm going to say. I want to tell you first of all that I'm not your Gela, whatever some of you think. What we know of Gela back on Earth is that she came to Eden four hundred years ago and never came back. We don't know anything after that. We assumed she must have died here on Eden, but we didn't know until now that she'd had children and grandchildren. As far as we know she never came back to Earth, alive or dead, and all that's left of Gela is here on Eden.' She waited, watching our faces to see if she'd been understood. She'd managed to keep her voice strong and sure, but we could see in her eyes that she'd dreaded saying these things. 'I am *not* Gela,' she repeated. 'In fact I'm not even as closely related to Gela as all of you are. Half of every one of you comes from Gela. My only connection with her is that a tiny tiny part of me comes from Gela's twin sister, Candice.'

There was a silence across the whole clearing. The trees pulsed. The flutterbyes rustled and flicked round the lanternflowers. A starbird screeched in forest: a proper Eden bird with feet and hands and big flat eyes.

'That's the first thing we have to tell you,' said Deep, 'and the second is that, we're really sorry, but we can't take you back to Earth. It's just not possible. Any of you who have been inside the old landing veekle will know that there's only room inside it for a few people. It's only meant for three. I'm afraid there will never be a time when more than a few people can go back and forth between Earth and Eden. Even just to get three of us here took the work of tens of thousands of people for tens of years. When we go back to Earth – and that will be soon, I'm afraid – we'll work hard to get more people to come here again and help you with your lives, but no one is ever going to be able to carry you all back to Earth, though I know many of you have hoped for that for many many years.'

The Earth people looked out at us. You could see how hard this was for them, just the three of them facing so many many disappointed people. As for us Eden folk, well, I guess a lot of us had already half-figured out what they were telling us, but hearing them say it was a completely different thing. When you figure a thing out for yourself you can still hope you're wrong. They'd taken away any possibility of that.

'We're sorry,' said Deep. Right behind him, their veekle stood in the Circle of Stones that the Davidfolk had kept in readiness for it all these years. How many hundreds of copies of that Circle were there, I wondered, across whole of the Davidfolk Ground? How many times these last four hundred years had Davidfolk stood beside those circles and sang 'Come Tree Home'?

'*You're* sorry, are you?' a woman screamed out, her voice harsh with anger and loneliness and cold cold grief. I recognized her face. It was the woman called Treelight I'd stood next to in the line for dry meat, the one who'd lost eight of her nine sons to the ringmen's metal-tipped arrows. I remembered that brightness in her voice then as she told me she knew she'd see her boys again on Earth, that particular kind of brightness that people put in their voice when they're determined that they're going to be cheerful, no matter what, determined to believe that what they're saying is true.

Eight sons and their dad, all dead! But Treelight had told me how she'd made herself hold all that grief inside as she'd crossed Wide Forest and climbed up onto the Dark, so as to be able to look after the little kids, and comfort the oldies, and keep things going, along with the other women who'd lost their men as well. All the way across the Dark, she'd told me, she'd made herself push her dead boys out of her mind every time she began to think about them. But when she was coming down far side of the Dark into Circle Valley, she began to feel that she wasn't going to be able to manage it any more, that her grief would come bursting out of her no matter what. I can't carry on doing this, she thought. I've reached the end of it. I've got no strength left.

And just then, so she'd told me, right at the exact moment she was thinking she couldn't hold on any longer, Leader Harry and his eight men had come riding by on his way up to the Dark, calling out the news about the veekle that had come down in the Circle and the people inside it from Earth. Treelight had laughed with happiness, the other women too. They'd all laughed and shouted and sang. There was no need for grief any more, no need for loneliness! Hungry and tired as they were, they'd come down into forest of Circle Valley with cheerful cheerful hearts.

But now this! The end of hope. The end of those few precious wakings when she'd thought she might never have to face that huge awful icy grief that had been welling up inside of her.

'*You're* sorry, are you?' Treelight screamed. 'So what have *you* lost, eh? What have *you* had to give up? You'll be back on Earth in a few wakings, I guess, telling your friends about the funny Eden folk who don't have lecky-trickity, or starships, or pictures that can talk.'

All three Earth people stared at her with scared, shocked eyes.

Treelight was just one person, but there were *many* many who were like her. Most of the people there were hungry, and worrying how they'd keep their kids alive when Strongheart's stores ran out. Most of them had lost their homes. Many had seen friends done for by the Johnfolk. Most had men and newhair boys who were still in Wide Forest and could well be dead. Over and over, the mothers and fathers of guards had had to listen to stories about how our guards' glass-tipped spears were no match for the metal spears and arrows of the masked ringmen. Over and over they'd had to hear about what the ringmen did to the men they caught.

All these people had clung to the hope that the Earth people would save them somehow, take away from them the reasons for their fear and grief. It was like they'd been running from a leopard and for a little while had really thought they were going to escape it, but now suddenly they'd reached a high high cliff and they couldn't run any further. They had no choice but to stand and wait for that merciless creature to reach them.

I suppose if they'd thought about it, most people would have seen that this wasn't really the Earth people's fault, but right now the crowd wasn't in the mood for thinking. And people all round the clearing began to scream out in their bitterness and disappointment as that dark dark leopard of grief and fear began to gobble them up.

'It's alright for *you*, isn't it?'

'What did you come here for anyway?'

'You should have left us alone!'

'The slinkers! They just came here to make fun of us!'

Everyone was full of fear, everyone was full of rage. Kids picked it up at once. Candy had stood up to shout and laugh with the others when those pictures of Eden people began to appear on the screens, but now she came back to my lap again, pressing her cheek against my breasts and putting her thumb in her mouth as she watched and listened to the anger all round us. Fox had been standing apart from me with some friends, but now he came back too and squatted beside me, resting one hand on my knee, his face tense and pale.

In front of the Circle of Stones, guards tightened their grip round their spears. I don't think the Earth people would have lived if they hadn't been there.

'We're sorry we can't help you more right now,' Gaia called out, glancing at the two Earth men as she stepped forward, and holding her linkup near her mouth so the veekle would make her voice louder. 'We know you're disappointed and we can understand that. We would be too if—'

'Shut up, woman!' a man shouted out. 'We're sick sick of all of you!'

Gaia waited for the shouts and jeers to die down a bit. Someone threw a stone at one of the screens, and it fell from its pole to the ground.

'I'm sorry we can't give you everything you'd hoped for,' she said. 'But don't forget—'

'We don't want to hear your excuses!'

'—don't forget that we've asked the leaders of the Johnfolk to come and talk to us, and we're going to tell them to stop fighting you. That at least will help you, surely? I know many of you have had to come here across the mountains to get away from those ringmen, and we're going to try and make it possible for you to return.'

The shouting didn't stop but it died down a little. Being able to go back to our clusters would be better than starving here, even if our shelters had been burnt down, and even if the dead bodies of guards were lying rotting all round them. It wasn't what we'd hoped for when we sang songs round our circles of stones – Earth was supposed to rescue us from that sad hard life we'd lived in Wide Forest, not help us return to it – but it would still be better than what we had now.

'But now we've got that new thing to show you that Deep told you about,' Gaia said, speaking a bit too eagerly, like a grownup trying to distract a crying child. 'We've looked inside the old screen that used to belong to Angela, and we've managed to find some of the things she left there. There are bits missing, but if you listen you'll hear her voice, the real voice of your own precious Angela, the Mother of you all.'

No one was shouting now. We could hear the trees, we could hear the flip and flap of flutterbyes, we could hear the stream at the edge of the clearing, running over its stones. Then a loud crackly hissing sound came from the veekle, like the sound of a fire and the sound of a waterfall, all mixed up together.

A face appeared on the screens, blurred like it was in a fug, with little lines and sparks of white light that kept shooting out across it. We couldn't really see what the face looked like, but you could just make out human eyes in there, looking downwards at something inside the picture, and a human mouth moving.

And then a voice spoke, a young woman's voice. It was sometimes hard to make out what she said, through that crackling hissing sound, and yet we found her easier to understand than the Earth people in front of us, her speech more like our own.

'So…' she said, 'to sum up, we can't all go back together. That's obvious. The state the ship's in, those of us that do go back in it will most probably die anyway, but if we all try and go at once, we'll *all* die without any doubt at all.'

Forty-eight

The Crying Tree stood by itself at the bottom of that dim white bowl of snow, its lanterns shining out their pure white light, and a thin trail of steam rising upwards from its airholes. A strange little group rode along the ridge above it. The war was still going between guards and ringmen back in Wide Forest, but there were three guards and ten ringmen riding up there together, along with the Headmanson of New Earth. Under their head- and bodywraps, it would have been hard to tell which ones were the Davidfolk and which the Johnfolk.

Behind them came three bucks with corpses tied to their backs, their legs dangling down one side, their heads and arms down the other. The bodies had long since turned cold and hard, and they jolted stiffly as the bucks made their way over the uneven snow. One of the corpses was bare to the waist.

'I'm guessing that must be the tree where John saw the great-bat,' Luke Johnson said to the guard Roger. 'Though I guess you people might not know the story?'

'Of course we know that story. Mehmet was there, remember, Wise Mehmet who came back to David.'

'Wise Mehmet? Mother of Eden, is that really what you call that little slinker?'

'He was a good good man. It was down there by the tree that he first realized that he'd been wrong to follow Juicy John. It's a brave man that admits he's wrong.'

Luke would never have let one of his own ringmen talk to him like that before, never mind a guard of the Davidfolk, but now he just rode on in silence.

'It *does* take a brave man,' he finally said. 'You're right about that. Some of us are going to have to do that pretty soon, aren't we – admit we're wrong – now the Earth people are here to set us straight? And maybe all of us. Who knows what story this new Gela will have for us?'

'She came to us Davidfolk,' said Roger, 'not to you Johnfolk. Doesn't that tell you something?' He was full of tears. His brother's cold corpse was draped over one of the bucks behind them and he didn't care what he said. The only thing he had to be glad about right then was that Luke was miserable as well.

They carried on riding along the ridge above the Crying Tree.

'I'm far far away from my father's house in Edenheart,' Luke said after a bit. 'I've given up on the fight I've been preparing for since I was a kid. My best friend is dead, and I've shamed myself forever by doing for a man who was bringing me a message from Gela. And here I am on Snowy Dark, looking down on that tree from the old story, where John saw a giant slinker creeping towards a bat. Back home the teachers say that, in John's mind, the slinker was David Holeface and all the things that David stood for, and the bat was himself and everything that mattered to him. But I look at it now and I don't—'

'David Holeface! That's how you speak of Great David, is it? The man who worked and struggled all his life to make sure Family was ready for this time we're living in now.'

Luke waited for Roger to finish, allowed a few heartbeats of silence to pass, and then carried on with what he was saying.

'But now I look down at it, I don't see all that. I see Eden down there. That tree on its own, caring nothing for us, living its own life without even knowing we're here: that's Eden. And that bat John saw: that was us. *All* of us, I mean: Johnfolk, Davidfolk, Tinafolk, whatever. That bat was like all the people of Eden, trying to stand up tall and do our best to make our lives mean something in this lonely dark place that doesn't care about us. All these stupid dreams we have, all these big plans, all these stories we go on and on about all the time... It's like... It's like we have to keep on yammering away because we're afraid of shutting up, even for a moment, and noticing the silence all round us. Do you know what I mean?'

Roger didn't answer.

'My poor sweet Gerry, for instance,' Luke went on. 'He used to talk excitedly to me about President guiding the world, President speaking to him across the sky, President being the one that tells the story we're all of us in, every one of us: Johnfolk, Davidfolk, humans, bats, bucks. But *I've* never heard him, have you? Not if I'm really honest. I've never heard him once. Or Mother Gela either, for that matter. There's no one really speaking to us, no one reaching out to us, no one guiding us. And all the while the darkness is creeping towards us, out of airholes, out of cracks, out of little gaps, the darkness that truly belongs here as we never never will. It's all round us all the time, watching us, waiting, ready to lunge out at us when the moment is right. Do you know what I mean? Do you ever feel that way?'

Roger said nothing. Why should he listen to the self-pity of a man who'd caused his brother's death? Without saying a word, he rode on ahead to join the other two guards.

Forty-nine

It wasn't the voice of Gela as we'd imagined it. We'd imagined her as gentle gentle and wise wise. We'd thought of her as being so grownup that we would all still be children beside her, so that, even if we were grownups ourselves, even if we were old old old, she would comfort and look after us, forgive us the silly things we'd done and love us anyway. But this voice wasn't like that at all. It was angry and bitter, a sharp tough young woman used to getting her own way, maybe four five years older than Trueheart. It reminded me a bit of Starlight as she was way back when we were in Veekle-house together and she set out across the Pool.

'If some of us decide to stay here, they won't die,' the voice said, 'not if they're careful. We've established that you can eat the plants here and the meat as well. It's all absolutely disgusting, but you can eat it. We've even found a source of vittermin dee, which I guess is… well… *lucky*, though I can't say I feel very lucky right now. And…' There was a long pause. The head barely moved, the fire-waterfall crackled away, the lines and flashes kept flickering out onto the screens and disappearing again.

Then the woman's voice sighed. 'You don't have to know much about polly ticks to know there's not going to be much support back home for getting the other ship ready to come and fetch us. And that's assuming they haven't yet scrapped it, which Dixon reckons they may well have done, given the way things have been going. I mean, who's going to want to go to all that trouble, just for a couple of people on the far side of the glacksy, when there's so many needing help right there, in Merka, and Inglund and everywhere else? I mean, think of those millyuns flooded out of their homes in Chiner, and all those people in Mecksy Koh. Who's going to sacrifice millyuns for the sake of two? Our only hope is that they'll think this place might be useful to them in some way.' The woman gave a short little laugh. 'Though I really can't think *how*.'

There was another pause. Through that crackly fire-and-waterfall sound, we could just make out the sound of this stranger breathing.

'Dixon threw the idea out recently that it's possible the ship might go back on its own,' she said at last. 'That was news to me, and I asked him why the fuck we're talking about *anyone* going back, if that's the case? Why couldn't we *all* wait here while the ship goes home on its own and brings help? He said he didn't think there was much chance of help coming for us any time soon, even if the ship did get home to tell people where we are and what's happened. He's got kids, and feels he's got to do everything he can to be with them. Michael's got kids too, of course, and so has Mehmet. He showed me their pictures: four beautiful little kids, back home in Tirkee. Which is a shame, because I like Mehmet the best. He's funny. And kind too, I think. I don't know why, but I feel I could forgive Mehmet for stealing the starship and bringing me and Michael here. I could forgive him in a way that I don't think I could forgive Dixon and Tommy. I wish he could be the one to stay with me.'

We could faintly hear her sigh as her voice trailed off again, and then there was only the crackly waterfall sound for a bit.

'Whoever stayed here would have a long long wait,' she said after a while. It was strange how *close* her voice sounded when she started speaking after a long silence. It was like she was right next to you, murmuring into your ear. 'Maybe a whole lifetime. Maybe even . . .' Again there was a long pause. The waterfall hissed, the fire crackled. 'Maybe even forever.'

She paused for a few hearbeats and, when she spoke next, there was so much anger in her voice all of a sudden that it made me jump. '*Shit! Shit! Shit!*' she hissed, and you could hear her hitting out hard at something with her fist, as she made herself hold in her tears. 'Bloody fucking *shit*! Of all the bloody luck! And my life was going so well, too!'

Candy could hear the anger and it scared her. She pressed up against me, hiding her face in my breasts. I held her and Fox tightly and rocked them gently back and forth. The helplessness I could hear in Gela's voice was just like the helplessness I was feeling now myself. We too were trapped with nowhere to go. We too had no power to change things. Gela herself had been our one hope of there being something different out there somewhere, something more than life in dark dark Eden. We'd always known that Gela herself felt trapped and alone when she lived on Eden, so there was no surprise there, but it was hearing her voice, hearing that she was just an ordinary human being like us, that made our hope seem so empty and foolish. How could we ever have imagined this woman had come alive again on Earth? How could we ever have thought that she would guide us all home?

When Gela spoke again, her voice had changed once more. You could tell she was trying to make the best of things now, trying to find something to hang on to. 'But if one of the guys stayed with me,' she said, 'we could have kids, and that would be company at least, I guess, company and something to live for.'

The crackling hissing sound went on so long then that I began to wonder if the voice was going to come back at all.

'Admittedly that would make things kind of complicated,' she finally said, just when people were starting to get restless, 'if we did eventually get back home.' Then she laughed harshly. '*Kind of complicated!* What a fucking stupid pathetic thing to say! That would be *easy*! *This* is complicated.' There was another short pause, and in among the hissing and crackling we faintly heard a clicking sound, like some people make with their tongues against the roofs of their mouths when they're busy thinking: *tk–tk–tk*. 'There's always death, isn't there? On Earth, here, anywhere: death is always an option, it never lets you down. It'll come soon enough, anyway, and if push comes to shove, we always have the choice of bringing it sooner.' Again she laughed. 'Not that I ever will. I'll always want to know what happens next.'

Tk–tk–tk went her tongue.

'I mean, when you think about it, I'm no worse off than my ancestors, am I? When they were taken from Affricker in chanes, they didn't get to choose where they lived, did they, or who they had kids with? And there was no way they could ever hope to get home. Things look pretty bad for me, but I'm still better off than they were. At least I won't have guys beating me if I don't work hard enough… Or I bloody hope not anyway!… No, it really was much worse for them. And yet even so they still chose to live, didn't they? In spite of everything, they chose to carry on and see what happened next. Otherwise there'd be no me.'

The head on the screens moved. You could tell somehow that she was about to finish.

'Okay. I'm going to make the offer to all of them, though I know it'll be Tommy who says yes. Just my fucking luck. He's handsome, I'll give him that, he's got a beautiful body, but he's so… I don't know… He's such a *kid*… He's this world-famous astronaut, and he's never had to grow up. He thinks the whole story's all about him.'

The face vanished. The crackling and hissing stopped. The screens went black. We were back in Circle Clearing with the trees pulsing all round us. No one knew what to say. We were all kind of numb.

'That's the end of that bit,' said Marius, 'but there's another bit here from later on, from the time after the other three had gone, and only Angela and Tommy were still here.'

Fifty

Headmanson Luke rode forward to join Roger and the other two guards. They'd made it pretty clear they didn't want to talk to him but somehow he couldn't bring himself to leave them alone.

'So they came down in the Circle of Stones, did they, these people from Earth?'

'That's right,' said one of the guards. 'Smack in middle of it. Their veekle's sitting there right now.'

'I'm sure you know my ancestor John destroyed the Circle. He thought it was holding us back. He chucked the stones in a stream.'

Roger sighed. 'Well, we Davidfolk put them back again, didn't we?'

Luke rocked back and forth on his buck, like he was so anxious and agitated he just couldn't keep still.

'Do you know what we keep telling ourselves to do in New Earth?' he said. None of the guards answered him. They rode together side by side without even looking round at him, like he was just some stranger that was bothering them. They didn't want to speak to him and, in any case, they had no idea what he was talking about.

'We tell ourselves, *Become like Earth*!' Luke said. 'It's written in big letters on the wall of my father's house in Edenheart. It's written all over the place. And that's what we try and do. That's why our ground is called New Earth. That's how come we found metal, and figured out how to make windcatchers. That's why our spears and arrows are so much better than yours. Because every waking we work and work at learning new things so we can find our way back to all the knowledge and power that people have on Earth. We're even working at making lecky-trickity and jet planes. Did you know that? We have a competition every two hundredwakes, at a place called Winghouse, for the best plane. We already have guys who jump from the top of a high cliff with wings made of wood and buckskin and fly to far side of the valley. They just haven't figured out yet how to fly up again.'

One of the guards gave a quiet little snort of laughter.

'But we *will*,' said Luke. 'You can laugh, but we'll figure it out, believe me. Just as we figured out metal. I guess you'd have laughed if you could have watched our people searching for rocks waking after waking, breaking them up, heating one kind after another in hot hot fire, over and over and over. But we got there, didn't we? We found the one that gives us redmetal, and no one laughs at that.'

He pulled off his headwrap, showing his troubled face to the freezing freezing air, and rubbing the tired skin round his eyes.

'But never mind that now. What I'm trying to say is that we want nothing more than to be like Earth, to live up to what Earth achieved. And yet Earth came back to you and not to us! That's the part I can't understand. We Johnfolk try so hard to be true to Earth, but Earth came back to that same Circle of Stones that John wanted to destroy.'

The guards refused to speak. They'd set out with Leader Harry to bring this man back to Circle Valley, and that's what they were doing. No one had told them they had to talk to him.

'Yes,' Luke said, pulling his headwrap back on again, 'and we try to be true to Gela who's always helped us so much right from the beginning, and true to her father, President. My own mother wears Gela's ring on her finger, and teaches the small people what Gela wants from them. I don't think you guys even know that Gela led us to the ring not just once but two different times? John found it first, after it had been lost for generations. But not so long ago it was stolen from us by a woman from this side of the Pool. She took it right across Worldpool but *still* Gela brought it back to us. I mean, think about it! How could you explain that if Gela wasn't on our side? What other explanation could there be? And yet now she's come to your people and not to us. I just don't understand it.'

He took out the smooth black linkup from the pocket in his bodywrap and turned it over in his hand, his eyes glinting in the bucklight as he looked down at it through the holes in his headwrap. He'd figured out by now which part of it he had to touch if he wanted to make it speak, and he carefully avoided that part. The thing itself was proof enough that the Earth people were really here, without his having to listen to Gela's voice. And each time he heard her it felt like a reproach, not just for Harry's death but for many other things too.

He thought about the people they'd met on the Dark before Harry appeared. The guards his men had spiked up on their own spears, the little groups of desperate people whose bucks they'd chased away, and whose pots of embers they'd scattered across the snow. There was one group in particular that his men had told to run away. One of Luke's men had counted to fifty, while those poor terrified folk blundered off through the snow: old women, kids, newhairs, trying their best to run and help one another, with snow right up to their knees. Luke's ringmen had laughed loudly as they readied their arrows on their bows.

'I know what you're thinking,' he said, quickly so as to blot out the memory. 'You're thinking it's about time I admitted that the Davidfolk were right all along. Isn't that so? You're thinking we destroyed the Circle that Gela and Tommy laid, and we broke Gela's Family in two, and we stole Gela's ring from the rest of Family, and now, as if all that stuff wasn't bad enough, we've brought all this killing to Old Ground, and done for Gela's messenger as well. Is that right? Isn't that what you're thinking? Never mind that the ring keeps coming back to us. As far as you're concerned, everything points to us Johnfolk being the ones who are in the wrong.'

The three guards said nothing. They didn't even turn their heads towards him.

'Mother of Eden, guys!' Luke cried out. 'I don't care what you say! I don't care if you want to yell at me! But answer me at least!'

Fifty-one

'So, it's done now.'

From behind the loud crackling and hissing, the young woman's voice murmured into our ears like she was right there next to us. Lines and flashes appeared on the screens and vanished again.

'It's just me and Tommy here now. Him and me. We're everyone there is on Eden. He's already driving me nuts, but it seems we're stuck with each other. We gave them two months before we'd make up our minds that we were here for the long haul. Tommy figured that was how long it would take to get the other starship ready and bring it back to us, if the ship hadn't already been scrapped, and if Earth was interested enough to get right down to it. Those two months have gone.

'Of course, the other three may still have got back to Earth for all we know, but the odds were always against it. We just can't know what's happening out there, far away in the depths of this dreary black night sky that's always above us, but my agreement with Tommy was that at this point we'd start acting like this was going to be home for a good long time. Last night... No, wait, I am going to have to stop saying night and day... At the end of our *last waking time*, me and Tommy had sex. It wasn't exactly a promising situation. I don't love him. He *expects* women to love him at first sight because there were plenty of women on Earth to tell him he was godz gift, but he isn't my type at all, and I'm just *so* angry with him and the other two for trapping me here in the first place.'

She sighed. 'But then again, we're both lonely, and we're both scared, so I guess any kind of comfort is a plus. I bet my ancestors felt the same, back in J'maker. I bet there were times they turned to whoever they could reach.'

There was crackling and hissing for a while before she spoke again. 'And it was unprotected of course,' she said. 'I could be pregnant already for all I know, and if not now, then probably sometime not too far away. "It'll be tricky for the third generation," I said to Tommy as we lay there afterwards, "if no one has come from Earth." "What do you mean?" asked Tommy. "Oh come on, mate," I snapped at him, "it's not so hard to figure out! If no one comes from Earth, our kids are going to have to do to one another what you and me have just done, unless of course they'd prefer to die alone." "Jesus!" he said. "Did you have to completely spoil it?" "Wait a minute," I said. "Let's remind ourselves who spoiled it. Let's just think, shall we? That would be the ones who created this situation, wouldn't it? And – let me see – that would be Dixon Thorleye, wouldn't it? And Mehmet Haribey, of course, and – oh yes, I almost forgot! – Tommy Schneider, also known as *you*. The three arrogant idiots who stole the starship, the three who dragged me and Michael through the wormhole after them. I wonder if Michael got back, eh? I wonder if he saw his kids again? I somehow doubt it. He was a real family man, you know. He was about to leave the service so he could spend more time at home." Tommy just turned his back to me and pretended to go to sleep. Well, he can't very well walk out on me, can he? Or me on him.

'Anyway, we lay there back to back, near enough to one of those things that we've started to call trees to be able to feel some of its warmth. In the distance two of those booming creatures were calling out. *Hooom! Hooom! Hooom!* goes one, and then the other answers, *Aaaaah! Aaaaah! Aaaaah!* Michael gave them the name of *starbirds*. Not that they look much like birds – they have six limbs, for a start – but they fly, sort of, and they have those long scaly things that look vaguely like feathers, covered in glittery dots like stars. We lay there, back to back, listening to the starbirds, Tommy thinking his thoughts and me thinking mine.

'I don't know what was going on in Tommy's head – he doesn't talk much about that kind of thing – but I thought about the kids the two of us would have, and how this place would be their world. And about how, however horrible it might seem, and however much Tommy might prefer not to even think about it, they really might end up having kids with each other. I know that's not good, but I'm no doctor and I've got no real idea what kind of problems it will cause them. All I know is that, whatever happens, we'll just have to deal with it. If it kills us, it kills us. No point in fretting about it now.

'Then I got to thinking about what we'd tell the kids. They'd have no school, no media, no one else but us to learn things from. So what information did we need to give them? What would they really need to know? And I thought about all the shit we've had in the history of Earth. Idiots claiming that some mouldy old book was the truth about everything, and it was okay to do for people you didn't like, just because the book said so. Other idiots coming up with fancy arguments to say it's fine for white people to buy and sell black people, or men to stone women to death for having sex without their permission... All that shit, which even a child could see was just nonsense, that gets to be called the truth because it suits some bunch of people, almost always men, who've got a bit of power.

'And I thought, well, one good thing: we can start again here. We can set aside all of that, and teach our kids some sense. This is Eden after all. This is a new Eden. And then I thought, hang on a minute, this is Tommy Schneider we're talking about here, and he is *full* of shit. I mean, I guess we all are, to be honest, but he *really* is. There's no way I can rely on him not to pass on that old crap all over again. So then I decided to do two things. One, I'm going to do my best to come to an agreement with Tommy about the right things to teach our kids. Two, regardless of what we agree, I'm going to come up with a list of stuff that's obviously true but seems to keep being forgotten. That black people and white people are as good as each other, for instance. That women are as good as men. That having a lot of stuff doesn't make you more important than other people, or entitled to more stuff. That you need to watch out for guys who act like the story is all about them...'

I felt a kind of shiver go right down my back. There must have been women all round the clearing who felt the same. This was the Secret Story! This was the story that my aunt Sue had told me on Knee Tree Grounds and asked me not to tell anyone else until I had daughters or nieces of my own. Sue had been told it came from Gela herself. Mary had said that it was a lie, as all the shadow-speakers did. But the shadowspeakers were wrong, as it turned out, and Auntie Sue was right, because here it was now, the Secret Story, coming not from someone's mum or auntie, but right from Gela's own mouth.

I guess some of the guards and high people there must have known those words as well. And I guess a lot of other people, men and women, had heard enough about the Secret Story to kind of guess what it was they were hearing, for there was a new tension in the crowd. Bit by bit, the True Story of the Davidfolk was crumbling in front of us. As we strained to hear every one of Gela's words, some people glanced at one another, while others tried to avoid meeting anyone's eyes at all. I wanted to look round and see how Starlight was taking it, because of course she knew the Story too, but I decided I shouldn't.

'I'll make a list of all those things,' Gela's voice said through all that waterfall hissing and crackling, 'all those simple important things that ought just to be obvious but keep getting lost and buried, and then, if we have daughters, I'll pass it on to them and ask them to—'

'*That* isn't Mother Gela!'

It was the firm loud voice of a woman shouting from the back of the crowd, drowning out the rest of what Gela had to say, and dragging us all back to Circle Clearing, and the pulsing trees, and the people from Earth who would soon be gone again.

'*That* isn't Mother Gela! Why are we all listening to it as if it was? Tom's dick, people, doesn't anyone *recognize* these words she's saying?'

It was like we'd all been woken from a dream. We were ourselves again, we were back in our own lives, and right there in front of me was someone from *my* own life that I'd been avoiding for eight years. For the woman who'd called out was Mary the shadowspeaker.

Fifty-two

Mary had been thinking hard hard as she made her way across the Dark. While her guards and helpers rode sullenly behind her, wishing they could be with the cheerful crowd from Tall Tree they knew was following after, Mary had struggled and struggled in her mind.

How could half the old story be so right, she wondered – Earth would come back, a veekle would come down again in the Circle of Stones – if the other half was so wrong, the part about Gela reaching out and speaking to us through the stars? Mary always tried hard to be honest with herself, and she knew it no longer made any sense to say that Gela had been speaking to her, right up to that show in Tall Tree, if Gela herself had been on Eden right at that moment and Mary hadn't known. She felt a fool. She felt deep deep shame. She remembered times when she'd laughed at other people's ideas, and she knew quite well that she was the one who deserved to be laughed at now. She had given up many things to help the David-folk find meaning, but now the meaning was pouring out from her own life. It was like when you crack a jug of badjuice. You put your hand over the crack to keep the juice inside, but the crack is too big, the jug itself is falling apart, and the juice just comes streaming out anyway over your fingers and down onto the dirt.

But if it hadn't been Gela who'd spoken to her and kept her strong all these years, then who had it been? Mary kept reminding herself that it wasn't as if the whole story had been nonsense. Earth *had* come, just as she'd always said it would, and Gela *was* alive, just as she'd always told people, over and over, in all those little clusters, up and down between Rockway Edge and the White Streams.

'I must be patient,' Mary kept telling herself. 'I just have to wait for Gela to set me straight.' Gela was good and wise, and must surely know that Mary had done her best. She'd help Mary understand as Mary herself had helped so many others. She'd explain everything, and then it would all fit together again, just like it did before.

She remembered that her helpers and guards were behind her, and stopped to look round at them.

'You lot are quiet!' she called out, in the most cheerful voice she could manage. 'Cheer up! We're going to see Gela and the people from Earth. I'd have thought you'd be happy happy!' And she made herself laugh loudly, trying not to notice too much the lonely sound of her voice echoing back from bare rocks, hidden in the darkness above them.

'I guess you're worried that I may have got the story wrong? Is that right?'

They didn't answer, and of course she couldn't see their faces behind their buckskin headwraps.

'Well, look at me! *I'm* not worried. I know I've done my best. There are some things I obviously didn't understand properly, but I know our Mother can see how I've tried to help her, and I know she'll explain where I went wrong.'

But she still couldn't help wondering just *how* Gela was going to do that, and worrying about what the answer might be. In some ways, it might actually have been easier for Mary to have accepted that the whole story wasn't true than to accept that *part* of it was true but that she herself had been completely wrong about her own place in it. It might have been easier to accept that Gela was dead, and that no one would ever come from Earth, than it was to accept that Gela was alive and Gela had really come back to Eden, but that she'd never ever spoken to Mary.

A couple of wakings before Luke reached the same spot, she passed along the ridge above the Crying Tree. She thought of her ancestor Wise Mehmet, down next to that exact same tree more than two hundred years ago, beginning to face up to the fact that he'd made the wrong choice, followed the wrong man, believed in the wrong story.

But it was easy for him, she thought. He'd only been with John a short time. He was still young. No one was asking him to give up something he'd believed in all his life.

◆

She'd reached Old Family cluster just as the crowd was gathering in Circle Clearing to see that second show of pictures on the screens. There was the new veekle standing there in middle of Circle on its thin thin legs, just where the Davidfolk had always said it would be. There were the tall Earth people in their strange smooth wraps that seemed to be made out of some kind of soft metal. There was a beautiful woman with dark dark skin.

So it really was true! Poor Mary was trembling. Her mouth was dry. She didn't know what to feel or to think. She'd always said that Earth would come, she'd always told people they must get ready for it, but it turned out that she wasn't at all ready herself. She'd certainly never really thought she'd see Gela standing in front of her in her own lifetime, as alive and real as anyone she met as she travelled across the Davidfolk Ground.

Part of her was excited in the same way that we all felt excited at the beginning of all this – how can you not be excited when something happens right in front of you that you've been long- ing for all your life? – but for Mary it meant losing so so much. If you spent your life speaking for Mother Gela, what was left for you when Gela was here to speak for herself? Mary made herself notice her own jealousy. She made herself notice her own bitterness at the fact that Gela didn't spot her there, didn't call out to her: 'Hello

Mary, my old friend. I'm glad we can finally meet!' She realized that she was a complete stranger to Gela, just as Gela was a stranger to her.

Then the Earth people showed their pictures of London. I'd already seen the strange flat paleness of Earth, but it was the first time for Mary and I guess it was as disappointing for her as it was for most people. We'd all thought that when we saw Earth, it would be like when you see a dear familiar face from long ago. You might not have been able to picture that face in your mind any more – how long do you have to be apart from a person before you lose the trick of doing that? – but, as soon as you see that face, you remember it perfectly, like there's a gap inside you that only that one face can fill. Each of us had felt a hole inside that we thought was the same shape as Earth, and we'd assumed that when we saw Earth again it would fit into place at once. But that didn't happen. It was strange and unfamiliar, that's what Mary discovered, the same as we all had done, and it didn't bring back any memories at all.

And then the Earth people talked about troubles that had happened back there: the floods and the fights, and how people had been driven out of their houses, and how miles and miles of London now stood empty and crumbling. That was a shock for Mary. She'd always told people that everything was perfect on Earth, everything was safe.

And of course, after the Earth people had showed their pictures of Eden, the news came that changed everything all over again. This black woman was *not* Gela. She hadn't brought anything special with her. She couldn't take us back with her. She was just a woman from Earth who'd come to see what Eden was like. Mary was new to the Earth speech and must have found it hard hard to follow, but Gaia spoke slowly slowly for this part and Mary's mind was quick. She heard Gaia insist that she was *not* Gela. She heard Gaia say that the people of Eden were much closer to Gela than she was herself.

We're closer to Gela than they are, Mary repeated to herself in her mind, testing out the idea to see what came from it. Few people could think as quickly as she could. Few people were better at finding a new way of telling a story. And, when the Earth people made that crackly voice come out of that old screen, a question came into her mind. How could the Earth people possibly be sure that this was the voice of Gela? That screen had been in Circle Valley for four hundred years. We'd always known that it had once shown pictures that moved, and now we'd learned that it could also listen to people's voices and remember them. These three Earth people knew all about screens, so they'd managed to find this old voice and make it speak out again through the veekle. But how could they know whose voice this had been, when so many different people had held the screen and spoken in its presence?

Suddenly Mary felt her old power coming back. She'd believed Mother Gela would make things clear when she reached Circle Valley, and that's exactly what had happened! Our Mother hadn't let her down. Gela was speaking to her again and Mary's old certainty was beginning to return. The certainty that had filled her up so many times with grief and joy and rage! The certainty that made other people afraid of her! The certainty that gave her the strength to speak out, to name what she saw in front of her, to ride those powerful feelings like the kids back on Knee Tree Grounds rode the waves coming in from Deep Darkness!

'How could these Earth people know who this is?' she called out. 'All they can know is who she *says* she is. But we Eden folk know better than that, don't we? Many of you will recognize those words that voice spoke. And if you do, you'll know they were part of that silly lie that some foolish women whisper to their daughters, calling it the Secret Story, and claiming it comes from Mother Gela.'

Muttering and murmuring surged in the crowd, like a great wave rising.

'And what does that tell you, people?' Mary asked. 'Isn't it obvious what's happened? Isn't it obvious obvious? One of those silly women, long long ago, got hold of this Screen and spoke to it!'

Somewhere in the background that young woman's voice was still murmuring from the hissing crackly screens, but Mary's was the only voice that people were listening to now. She had one of the best-known faces in all of the Davidfolk Ground, much better known than even David Strongheart's, because she travelled more often than him, and visited places he'd never think of going. There'd be a few in the crowd who hadn't seen her before, but there'd always be someone nearby to tell them who she was. And everyone knew about Mary Shadowspeaker. Everyone knew she was honest and brave and smart.

Deep tried to interrupt her. 'But even if no one had used it at all, the bat-tree in that thing would only have lasted a few years at mo—' he began, but Mary was in full flow now, and she couldn't be stopped, not even when he had the veekle to make his voice boom out across whole clearing. People hissed at him to be quiet.

'Gela is still with us!' Mary called out. 'I can still hear her voice, the same as ever. She's telling me these Earth folk are just people like us, and the Earth they come from is just another place like Eden, with troubles and worries of its own. Well, this woman here told you that herself, didn't she? She showed us the houses in the water. She told us about the floods and the fights. It's a place just like Eden where trouble comes and people have to run from trouble. But that's not the Earth where our Mother waits for us! This woman said that too, remember? She told us they know nothing of Gela where she comes from. She said the last they heard of Gela was that she'd come here to Eden and died.'

She held us all now. Even the Earth people stood and watched her in amazement. How many people could have moved so quickly in their heads from that first bewildering, head-spinning moment of seeing the people from Earth, to where Mary was now? How many people would have had the courage to speak out as she was doing, with the veekle and the screens right there in front of us to prove how powerful and smart the Earth people were? But of course she was as smart as any of the Earth people, and she was brave and powerful too. In her own way, she was as powerful as anyone there. Even Strongheart, even Newjohn, even Starlight.

'We *know* our Mother's alive, don't we?' Mary said. 'We *know* she speaks to us. Because everyone hears her, don't they? Some faintly, some more loudly. We all hear her, and we all know she watches over us. We all know she calls out to our shadows when they're all alone in the cold forest between the stars. All that's still true, that hasn't changed one bit! All we've learned now is that she's not on the sad Earth that these three people come from. That's the one new thing we're finding out. I wished I'd listened better to our old stories about Earth, because then I'd have known that already. I wish I hadn't been so quick to dismiss them as children's tales. But let's not worry just now about what we didn't know and what we got wrong. Think about what we *do* know, and what hasn't changed at all. We *know* our Mother calls us back to her, don't we? We don't need anyone to tell us that. We know as a fact she calls us home. But it seems she's made a better Earth for us to return to, not an old home but a new one. And that's the place of warmth and light that we've always known was out there waiting for us, that's the place where we'll be safe forever.'

Some people were crying now, just like in her old shows. She was touching the disappointment we all felt, and the grief and the loneliness that had been creeping back over us, but she was touching the anger too. There were hundreds there, like that woman Treelight, whose hopes had been so raised up by the people from Earth that they thought grief itself had come to an end. The Earth people had smashed that hope, but they'd done much more than just smash it. They'd taken away the comfort as well of our old stories and our circles and our songs. It was true those things had all been wobbly stones. It was true they hadn't been strong enough to take our grief away from us, but they'd still helped us to bear grief and get through it. And, until Mary spoke, it had seemed that we were going to lose them now as well, with that ordinary young woman's voice, still murmuring away in the background, slowly destroying what little was left of the Davidfolk's True Story.

So it felt good good to hear Mary still standing up for it. Everyone was on her side. Everyone was angry angry angry with the people from Earth.

'Yeah, you tell them, shadowspeaker!' some guy shouted out. 'These Earth folk don't know everything, whatever they try and tell us!'

'They don't know *anything*, you mean!' a woman answered him. 'They don't know anything that's any good to us.'

There were shouts and jeers after that, and harsh angry laughs, and once again Treelight called out, the one who'd lost her eight sons and her man to the Johnfolk over in Wide Forest.

'They're *useless*!' she yelled. 'They're useless useless. And they're cruel too. Our boys are dead and we're hungry and scared, and what do they bring us? Pictures and voices inside a screen! Things you can't even touch. Things that just make us smaller and lonelier than we ever were before.'

'Well, we tried to...' began Gaia, but shouts and jeers stopped her from going on. And then, for a long time, no one spoke at all, and the crowd just roared on its own.

Poor Gaia, poor Deep, poor Marius: just three of them, far away from home, facing hundreds of angry Eden folk. They could feel the depth of the rage round them, of course they could. And, for all their linkups and lecky-trickity and bikes, they were just people, made of flesh like we were. Spears and arrows would do for them as easily as they'd do for us.

Gaia hadn't been able to quiet the crowd, but when Mary held up her hands to ask to be allowed to speak, everyone stopped shouting at once. Even the voice and the crackling from the screens had gone silent. I guess one of the Earth people had stopped it.

'There's no need to take it out on these Earth people,' Mary said. 'From what I've seen of them, it doesn't seem to me that they meant us harm. And, okay, they've told us they can't take us with them, but do we really need to be sad about that? I mean, would we even want to go to that sad watery world they just showed us? I don't think so, do you?'

Lots of people shouted out: 'No! No! No!' at that. Who cared about that pale place with its cold trees and its stupid shouting animals?

'And what we mustn't ever forget,' Mary said, 'is that, even when they've gone, we will *not* be left on our own. Because we still have Gela. Look inside yourselves and you'll see you already know that without me even telling you. We'll still always have Gela. And, if only we listen to her, we'll always have the true home she's keeping for us, where all our troubles will end.'

There was another big roaring cheer. It wasn't a happy cheer, it was still angry angry, but it was proud proud as well. It was like the Davidfolk were telling the people from Earth that they could do what they liked, because we hadn't needed them anyway.

But behind us, Strongheart was rising unsteadily to his feet, signalling to his horn man to blow and make us quiet.

'That's enough now!' the old man called out. 'This meeting is over. We mustn't be rude to our visitors from Earth. They've come to help us. They've come to stop the fight with the—'

He was the Head Guard, the Head of True Family, the most powerful man in all of Eden, a man that people would kneel and bow in front of if he ever came near them, a man that, if he asked for silence, would normally get silence at once. But now the people in the crowd didn't let him finish. Mary had found her way, as she always did, to people's deepest longings and fears, and it was like when a stream floods over its banks, or a jug full of juice is smashed on the ground. You can't put it back, you can't fix it together again. No one was interested in what that old man had to say.

'Gela! Gela! Gela!' part of the crowd began to chant, and then Mary started singing 'Come Tree Row' in her loud strong voice, and the chanting faded down as we all joined in. We sang it through again and again, round and round, so as to come again and again to that place at the end of the song where it reaches its home. And when Gaia's voice finally boomed out from the veekle, asking if she could say a few more words, people shouted angrily at her to shut up and let us sing.

'You've got nothing to give us!' a man shouted out.

'Yeah,' another man called out, 'you're useless. Go on back to Earth and leave us alone.'

'Yeah, go back to Earth, why don't you?' a woman echoed. 'Why can't you just bloody go?' More folk took that up until it became another chant: 'Go! Go! Go!' And then some of the newhairs began to pick up stones and throw them, so that the Earth people had to hold their arms in front of their faces to protect themselves.

Strongheart told his guards to empty the clearing. Mary tried to call out that we should leave the Earth people alone, but by then it seemed that even she couldn't control what she'd set loose. The shouting and stones kept coming until suddenly those lights shone out from the veekle, with a brightness we hadn't seen since it first came down from the sky, a brightness that filled up forest, making everything pale, and covering the ground under the trees with long black shadows, like fingers of darkness pointing out accusingly from the shining veekle. The light hurt our eyes so that we had to turn away from it and, as we did, we saw each other, the blemishes on our skins, the deep tired lines in our faces, and we saw how the lanterns on the trees, which were normally the light of Eden, were drained of any light at all by the brightness all round them, and were just pale shapes dangling from the branches. It was as if dimness had been a wrap round us, keeping us warm, and now it had suddenly been stripped away.

We let the guards drive us out of the clearing, but before I left I looked back and saw Mary still standing there, still looking in the direction of the veekle, her fingers like a cage in front of her eyes, like she was trying to face out those brilliant lights and make out what was behind.

Fifty-three

When I tell you things that happened when I wasn't there, I rely on what people who *were* there told me or what they told other people. Starlight told me things that happened in Strongheart's big shelter, for example, and I heard about Leader Harry's death from the stories passed round by the three guards who came back. It's tricky because people always hold things back, or hear what they want to hear, or tell the story in a way that makes better sense to them than how they heard it themselves. I've heard several different stories about how Leader Harry died, for instance. I've told you the one I've heard most often, but there are those who say it was Luke himself who called out 'Blade!' and the guy on the woolly-buck next to him that shot the arrow, and some say Luke just shot the leader because he wanted to, and no one shouted 'Blade!' at all. I guess if I could speak to Luke or some of his ringmen, I might hear other stories again. Maybe they'd say there really *was* a shiny blade in Harry's hand. It's not impossible. Our guards still carried blackglass spears back then, but their leaders all had metal knives. And anyway, blackglass can shine in the light.

When the story isn't certain – and it almost never is – all I can do is think about the people and the situation they were in, and figure out for myself what makes most sense. I work out, as best I can, how things would most likely have unfolded and connected together, and make the best guess I can as to how it must have been.

I might be wrong – I'm sure I *am* wrong sometimes – but I figure that if we only ever told stories we could be completely certain of, then there'd be no stories at all. I mean, never mind other people, we can't even be sure of our own memories.

I met Headmanson Luke that one time in Wide Forest when his men surrounded us as we were running away from Michael's Place. I saw him again for a short time when he came down into Circle Valley with Harry's body. I also listened to the stories that were passed round by the guards that came with him down from the Dark. Yes, and I also met his dad long ago, that first time me and Starlight went to Veeklehouse: Chief Dixon as he was then, that cold, proud man, who later did for Greenstone and became Headman of New Earth. Starlight had to deal with Chief Dixon when she was in New Earth – if he'd had his way, she'd have been thrown into the fire with Greenstone – and she met Luke's sister and his mother Lucy, whose own dad and brothers had been thrown into that fire themselves by Greenstone's dad. Luke would only have been a kid when she was over there, and Starlight says she must have met him, but can't remember it. She would soon meet him again, though. She'd meet him in Strongheart's shelter in Old Family cluster, and she'd tell me what happened there. It's from all those things that I've got a sense of that young man, and what was in his mind.

When the light flashed out from the veekle, Luke had just reached the place on David's Path where you can look down into Circle Valley. He saw forest round the distant clearing fill with brilliant light, far brighter than anything he'd ever seen, even in the shining caves of New Earth, and he saw how the smoke that rose from the many fires of Old Family cluster, which had been a dull orange smear against the stars, suddenly shone white against the black black sky.

His heart filled with dread. He knew this was the pure pure light

of Earth pouring out from the Circle of Stones into the darkness of
Eden. He knew the Davidfolk had always claimed that their Circle
was the place where Earth would return. He knew his own many-
greats grandfather John Redlantern had denied that claim when
he destroyed the Circle, broke up Family, and brought killing into
the world. But now here he was, Luke Johnson, the many-greats
grandson of John, who had come across the water to destroy the
Davidfolk, being summoned back to the Circle by Mother Gela.
She'd sent the message by the many-greats grandson of Great
David. And he was riding down to meet her with yet more blood
on his hands.

Gela was the gentle Mother of all of Eden. The Johnfolk believed
that no less than the Davidfolk, but Luke knew better than many
that mothers had another side. His own mother had seen her dad
and her brother thrown down into that fire by her uncle Firehand,
and she was full of bitterness and rage. That white light in the distance didn't seem gentle to Luke. It didn't seem kind. It seemed to
him to be a sign that Gela already knew what he'd done. It felt to
him like it was searching for him through the trees and that nothing could escape it in the end. He thought that, when that light
finally found him, it would shine right through him and into the
darkest and most hidden parts of his mind. His mouth was dry dry
as he called out to those three guards who kept refusing to talk to
him. 'What *is* that light? How do they make it?'

'How would we know?' the guard called Roger answered with a
shrug. 'It comes from their veekle. I guess it's the light of the sun.
We know the Earth people can carry pictures and voices from one
place to another, so I suppose they've got a way of carrying that
with them as well.'

Luke yanked off his headwrap, suddenly maddened by the stuff-
iness and the smell of it, and, as his buck began to pick its way down
the slope, he felt the cold cold air of the Dark against his face. 'The
light of the sun,' he said, running his tongue round his dry lips.
'Yes, I guess it must be. They do say that sunlight is pure pure white.

Mother of Eden, imagine that! They can gather the light from a star and bring it down to the ground, as we might gather a jug of water from a pool.'

Roger didn't answer him, but one of the others gave a harsh laugh and spoke not to Luke but to Roger and their mate. 'I bet he wishes he hadn't messed with people who can do things like that.'

'Never mind that,' said Roger. 'I bet he wishes he hadn't messed with the Davidfolk.'

Behind him, Luke's own ringmen were silent.

Fifty-four

It was different this time when we walked back to the Earth people's shelter with them. People crowded round them, and, while there were still some who just wanted to stare at them or hear them speak, there were many who yelled at them that they should go.

'Why bother to come here at all,' a woman called out, 'if you've got nothing to bring us, and you can't take us back? Why come here and upset us for no reason? It's just cruel, that's what it is, it's just bloody cruel!'

Other people shouted angrily in agreement.

'We didn't mean to upset anybody,' Gaia said, when she could make herself heard. 'We didn't even think there was anyone here.'

'In other words,' another woman shouted, 'you waited to come here till you thought we'd all have died!'

'We should take that red box off them,' a man called out. 'It's the only thing they've got that's any use.'

Even when we were back inside our fence it didn't finish, though we had guards with spears round us to keep people from coming near. Someone hurled something heavy that landed beside us with a soft thud. It was a big stinking turd. 'Thanks for nothing, Earth people,' shouted the young guy who'd thrown it, before the guards chased him away. 'I'm going to find that shadowspeaker,' he called out as he ran off. 'At least she talks some sense.'

'We need to go,' Deep said. 'This is dangerous.'

Gaia nodded. 'Yes. We need to go now. We're already causing a food problem, and if we stay any longer one of us or one of them is going to get killed.'

'Now?' I said. '*Really* now, you mean?' It was one thing to know that they had to go soon and we'd have to go back to our old life, without screens and metal needles and bikes and the beautiful tall Earth people, but it was another to think it was going to happen this same waking. And nothing had been settled, of course. Everything had been turned upside down, but nothing had been sorted out. 'But what about that message you sent across the Dark? Aren't you going to wait for the Johnfolk to come?'

The Earth people looked at each other. We all watched them anxiously. Clare had tears running down her face. So did Kate. Tom and Dave were frowning. The Earth people troubled them, and Dave didn't like the way they took my attention away from him and from the kids, but all the same, I guess they still felt the same sense of loss. Trueheart, as she often did, sat a little way back, not exactly a grownup, but not a kid either. She was trying hard not to show her feelings but her eyes too had filled with tears.

'We can't wait for the Johnfolk,' Marius said. 'We don't even know if they're coming, or how long they'll be. We can't take the risk of any more trouble.'

Gaia nodded and stood up. There were tears in her eyes too. 'Okay,' she said. 'Let's start loading up the veekle now.'

I stood up myself. It was awful to think that this strange and wonderful time was almost over. 'At least you'll have memories,' people say when things come to an end, but I'd already learned what thin and empty things memories are, and how little comfort they give. Memories of people and happy times don't fill up your heart, I don't think, any more than memories of food can fill up your belly. They're just empty holes that happen to be the same shape as the real things that are lost and gone. 'Well, you'll want to say goodbye to Strongheart and the other big people, won't you?' I asked. 'Strongheart and Starlight and Headman Newjohn?'

'We'll see them after we've loaded up,' Gaia decided. 'Can you guys help us carry our things back to the veekle?'

They had boxes of tools, and screens, and guns, and other things whose names I'd not yet learned, and it took five six of us to carry everything. Even Candy was given one little tool to carry. Fox carried his brother Metty, Dave hobbling painfully beside them, along with a couple of guards. As we walked back to Circle Clearing, people followed us, quite quietly this time, sensing that something new was about to happen.

In front of the veekle, Gaia lifted one of those little black squares, the things that the Earth people called linkups, and straight away the veekle came to life, like some huge animal waking from a sleep. It moved slightly on its legs and little lights flickered as it made that soft beeping sound.

'Lower the steps,' Gaia told it.

At once, with a soft whirring sound, the metal square folded down from underneath it so the veekle could put down the ladder. More light poured down from that mysterious inner cave where none of us had been. We all stared up longingly, and Deep laughed. 'Come and have a look inside if you like.'

'It's a bit small for all of you at once,' said Gaia. 'You'd better take turns. Angie and Trueheart first, I reckon, seeing as you were the first people we saw in Eden.'

Trueheart nodded and headed straight up the steps. I hesitated. I don't know why. 'Come on, Angie dear,' Gaia said. 'It won't hurt you.' So I followed Trueheart. Of course I half-knew what to expect from the other veekle by the Pool, but that was an old dead thing, a rotted corpse, while every part of this veekle was alive. Little lights shone and flickered. Pictures and writing moved across screens. It was like a kind of tiny forest in there, with its own shining lanterns and bright pools and animals darting about, but this was a forest that people had made.

Gaia pointed things out to us. 'This tells us how high up we are ... That shows us which way we're facing ... When we're flying,

those lights there help us to see whether we're tipping forwards or
back…'

The lanterns in this forest didn't feed flutterbyes, or grow into
fruit. They were only there to tell people things, to help them
understand the world, to help them see and hear and touch things
beyond the reach of their own eyes and ears and fingers. So,
although it was like a forest, it was also like being inside a person's
mind. It was a forest of meaning. I saw Trueheart looking at it in
delight and wonder, trying to take it all in and store it in her head,
so she'd have something to feed herself with for the rest of her life.

'You people understand *so* so much,' I said to Gaia, 'and we
understand so so little.'

Gaia came to stand between me and Trueheart, taking each of
us by the arm.

'We know a lot, but maybe not as much as you think. People on
Earth have dug down deeper and deeper into smaller and smaller
parts of things than you've been able to do here, and further out
into time and space. Or some Earth people have, anyway. A few.
Most of us can't follow them even half the way. I've no idea how
this veekle works, for instance, and nor does Deep. But the thing
you should remember, Angie, is that even for the smartest people,
however far they get, the mystery's still always there, beyond their
reach, just as it is for you. And it's not because they're not smart
enough, it's because it goes on forever. Isn't that so, Marius? There's
no bottom, no end. However many questions we answer, there are
always new questions beyond.'

Marius looked up. He was putting a box of tools away somewhere, through a kind of small metal door.

'Well, I guess, although—'

But Gaia didn't let him finish. 'And you know there are lots of
questions you can't answer in that kind of way at all. Like… like
what it's like to be inside the mind of another person, or how we
should live our lives. In the end, all there is in the world is… well…
this.'

She gestured with her hand through that bowl of clear glass that sat on top of the veekle, and out into forest. There was a bunch of whitelantern trees out there, with a couple of redlanterns among them, steam rising here and there from their airholes. The trees round the Circle were pruned to make the lanternflowers grow thickly and flutterbyes were dancing in all that white and pink treelight, while a single jewel bat was swerving and looping through them, grabbing out at them with its little hands as they darted out of its way.

I couldn't really see what Gaia meant, so I turned back to admire the shining screens.

We came out again, and Gaia invited the other Michael's Place people to come inside two at a time. Flame was squeaking like a little kid, just like my Fox and Candy. Tom and Dave and Davidson were tense and stiff, but you could see that even they couldn't wait to get inside. No one seemed to notice or mind that they were stepping inside the Circle of Stones.

Meanwhile, more people were gathering in the clearing.

'Yeah, go on. Run off back to Earth, why don't you?' someone shouted. A stone came flying and hit Deep on the head. 'You're no use to us here.'

With a kind of hurt smile, Deep felt where he'd been hit and looked at the red blood on his hand. Guards shook their spears and shouted out to leave the Earth people alone.

Just as Gaia came outside again with the last of the Michael's Place folk, Strongheart hobbled into the clearing, supported by his shelterwomen Jane and Flowerlight, and followed by Starlight and Newjohn, and four five other high people.

'You're leaving us so soon?' the old man quavered. 'But you've only just come!'

'People are unhappy with us because we haven't brought

anything for them,' Gaia told him. 'The longer we stay, the unhappier they'll be. And of course, all the time we're here, more people will keep coming to see us, eating up all your stores of food, until there's none left.'

'People will come here anyway to get away from the New Earthers in Wide Forest,' Strongheart said, his whole face all creased up with worry. 'I thought you were going to stay and help us stop the fight with the Johnfolk.'

'We can't wait that long,' Deep told him, dabbing at the cut on his head with a kind of fakeskin he carried with him. 'But you can tell them from us that their story isn't any truer than yours.'

'I'll put some more words in a linkup for you,' Gaia said. 'And I'll give you this as well.' She took the ring from her finger and handed it to the old man. 'If the fight really has been over a ring like this, you can have this one, and let the Johnfolk keep theirs. I promise you, they're both exactly the same, except only for the name inside. The other one was Gela's ring, and this one belonged to her sister. They're both just as good.'

'Go on, you useless lot, just *go*!' screamed a young woman, and another stone was thrown, bouncing off the veekle with a strange hollow sound.

'I want to go with you,' said Trueheart suddenly. You could see she herself was shocked by what she'd said, terrified by her own choice. Her face was pale and she was trembling all over. 'You said I could be as smart as anyone on Earth, Marius. I want to come with you and learn the things you know.'

Clare stared at her in horror. 'What?' she whispered. 'What?' And then she began to shout. 'You can't, you silly girl! You *can't*! They might not come back again for fifty years! We'd never see you again!'

Trueheart was shaking so violently she could hardly speak, and her little sisters began to scream. 'I love you all,' Trueheart said. 'Mum, Dad, all of you. I don't *want* to say goodbye to you, but if I stay what can Eden offer me? Dad would find me some guy in a year or two, I guess, some other batface, perhaps. Or maybe one of his old guard mates will have some slowhead son who needs taking off his hands, and Dad will give me to him as a favour. Whoever it is, I'll be his shelterwoman and have his kids and spend the rest of my wakings putting food in their mouths and washing their bums, even though no one really wants a batface, and—'

'How can you say that!' roared Clare, running forwards and grabbing her by the shoulders. 'How *dare* you say that, Trueheart!' She shook her daughter violently as she spoke. 'How *dare* you say that, when you *know* we've loved and cared for you just as much as all the others.' She looked round for Tom. 'Go on, Tom! Gela's tits, man! You're her dad. *You* tell her!'

Tom didn't know what to say. 'I...' he began, 'we—'

'No man or woman chooses a batface to be with if they could have someone else,' persisted Trueheart, enduring her mother's leopard grip on her shoulders. She looked at me. 'I'm sorry, Angie, but it's true, isn't it?'

I was about to answer, but she carried on. 'It's not fair, but it's true. A low person, a batface, a woman. If I stay on Eden there's no way I'm going to be anything other than low low low.'

'Nothing wrong with being a low person,' her dad said. 'There'd be no high people without the—'

But Trueheart cut right across him. 'I'm smart. You all know I am, but what use is being smart if all you're going to do all your life is look after babies and grind up starflower seeds?'

'It should be a high person that goes,' said Strongheart suddenly.

It was weird, we Michael's Place people had quite forgotten that the Head Guard of all the Davidfolk was right behind us. And of course it wasn't only him that was there. The Heads of the two other parts of Mainground were there too: Newjohn and Starlight. We were among the highest people in all of Eden. Only Headman Dixon was missing.

Headman Newjohn laughed. 'I don't think what we call high and low means much to people from Earth,' he said. 'I reckon to them, we must all of us seem pretty much like kids playing a game among the trees.'

'It's up to her of course,' Marius said. 'But I can't think of anyone more suited to come with us than Trueheart. She really is one of the smartest people I've ever met.'

'Yes, and you Eden folk could do with having one of your people on Earth, Head Guard,' Deep pointed out to Strongheart, as he dabbed at his still bleeding head. 'You need someone there who can help us figure out how best to help you when we visit again.'

'Yes,' said Gaia. 'But what Clare says is true. Whoever comes, it'll most likely mean saying goodbye forever. Or for thirty forty years at least.'

'I'm going,' said Trueheart simply. There were red marks on her shoulders from her mother's grip, and in two three places Clare's nails had broken her skin.

The Earth people looked at one another. Clare wept. Trueheart's younger sisters, Sue and Starflower, clung tightly to Trueheart's arms, like they simply wouldn't let her go. Trueheart endured this too. Tom stood there trembling, his face half-angry and half just bewildered and scared.

'Well, if that's agreed,' Gaia said, 'we'd better get your things.'

Things? None of us knew what she meant. Did Gaia think Trueheart had boxes full of tools as she did? Trueheart had nothing, of course, none of us had anything more than a few skin wraps, and maybe the odd bone tool, or ring made of wood or stone. What good would such things be on Earth?

'I've... I've got a little doll in our shelter,' Trueheart started to say, and then she began to cry. 'Dad made it for me out of wood and bone, and Mum made a tiny wrap for it out of fakeskin. It will help me to remember you all, when I'm...'

She couldn't bring herself to finish what she was going to say. But her sister Starflower glanced across at her dad and, when he nodded, released Trueheart's arm and ran to fetch the doll.

'Why are you crying, Mum?' Candy asked me.

'Trueheart's going to Earth, dear, and we're going to have to say goodbye.'

Candy laughed. 'That's silly, Mum. Of course she can't go there. That's only a place in a story.'

❦

We were nearly at the end of it. Trueheart took her doll and climbed inside the veekle with the three Earth people. The metal door shut, the lights shone out, and that whining sound started up somewhere deep inside the veekle's body that Trueheart and I had once heard and not been able to figure out what it was. It was quiet at first but quickly grew louder.

We saw four faces looking out at us from that glass bowl on the top of it. A few people threw stones and shouted: 'Go home!', 'We don't want you!', 'What use are you to us?', but there was grief in every single face all the same. I'm sure that everyone there who was old enough to understand, even the ones who were shouting, felt pretty much as I did when they saw the veekle lifting up from the ground and rising up into the black black sky. It was like the insides had been scooped out of me, and someone had put in their place a bit of that cold emptiness that lies between the stars. It didn't matter whether the Earth people had brought anything for us or not. They'd still come from Earth.

And now all that was left was the Eden we'd known since we were born, the Eden where we had to work so hard, the Eden where our worries were, and our deadly enemies, the Eden that was the home of all the problems and threats that faced us every single waking. The Earth people had shown us light, but we were still where we'd always been, in dark dark Eden.

Part III

Part III

Fifty-five

Starlight wanted me to go back with her to Half Sky, but Dave flatly refused to go to the Women's Ground, or to let me take our kids there, and all the Michael's Place people backed him up. I'll go there one waking. I'd like to see my family again, and all the people from Knee Tree Grounds. It's a long way off, though, and to be honest I'm a bit scared. Not of the travelling or of crossing the Dark – I'm used to that – but of what I'll find there and how I'll feel. Because one thing the visit from Earth has shown me is that when you long and long for a thing, and then it finally happens, it's going to be different from what you expect.

The Earth people coming wasn't what we expected because it wasn't the end of the story. Our old story just stopped working. But straight away a whole lot of new stories started up and spread out across Mainground. You can meet people these wakings who believe Mother Gela came and was driven away. You can meet others who say that bad people came from Earth and tried to trick us by pretending to be Mother Gela. There are even some who say that Gaia and Deep and Marius didn't come from Earth at all, but from some other place, and that the real Earth will still come one waking if we're good. After all, if Earth could find our dark Eden among all the stars of the glacksy, why shouldn't they have found another world as well, somewhere else in the sky, like the Johnfolk found their New Earth across the water?

Speaking of New Earth, I don't know what stories they tell over there these wakings, so far away from Circle Valley, but I think it's quite possible that people there don't know that anyone came or that anything happened at all. And I'm fairly sure that, if they *have* heard any stories, they'll have been told it was all a trick played by the Davidfolk.

A long waking after the veekle had disappeared into the sky, Head-manson Luke reached Old Family cluster, bringing the bodies of Leader Harry and those two guards, David and Mehmet. As he'd rode through forest of Circle Valley, he'd passed groups of excited people from the High Valleys who'd come to see Mother Gela. The three guards in front shouted out to them not to be afraid, the ringmen hadn't come to fight, but to talk to Gela. Standing warily back from the path, the people watched the ringmen ride by on their strange blue bucks, the high young man in front in his fancy wraps, with his blank face staring straight ahead, and the three dead men that followed behind, cold and stiff, draped over the backs of woollybucks.

Luke came straight to Strongheart's big shelter, where the Head Guard sat with Starlight and Newjohn. (The three of them had run out of things to say to each other by then, and spent a lot of time talking with their own people, and sending messages back to their own grounds, while they waited for news from Wide Forest. Starlight told me that she and Newjohn sometimes played chess. He was a pretty good player apparently, though she beat him more times than not.)

Old Strongheart howled with grief when he saw the body of his second oldest son, kneeling and throwing himself over it to kiss, over and over, its cold cold cheeks. Leader Harry's corpse had long since gone completely rigid. The mouth was fixed open, the eyes dried and shrunken in their sockets, and, because it had been carried over the back of a buck with its arms hanging down one side and its legs the other, it was stuck in that position, lying on the ground on its side with its arms extended upwards and its legs straight, its head facing its knees, as if poor Harry had been frozen solid in middle of trying to touch his toes. 'I should have died,' the old man wailed, 'not you, my boy. It should have been me.'

Harry was no boy really, of course. In fact he was a grandfather himself, many times over. Jane and Flowerlight knelt beside him, Strongheart's two young shelterwomen, stroking his back and making soothing sounds.

Luke watched all this, appalled. When that arrow had done for his friend Gerry, his feelings for the Davidfolk had turned to pure hate. But all that had changed since he'd heard Gaia's voice in the linkup – Gerry would never have died, after all, if the Johnfolk in their pride hadn't crossed the water – and now he blamed himself, not just for Harry's death, but for Gerry's as well, and many others too. He knelt down beside the old man.

'Forgive me, Father,' he whispered. 'Forgive me. I know how it hurts, and if only I could undo what I did, I would, even if it meant giving up my own stupid life.'

Strongheart showed no sign that he'd even heard him, his tear-stained face pressed against the cold stiff shoulder of his son, so Luke lowered his own face right down until it was on a level with the old man's. 'I'm so sorry, Father. We thought he had a knife, but he was just trying to…'

All the shame and grief of the last few wakings came welling up inside him, and his own tears began to run down his face, only a matter of inches away from the old man's but also from the two shelterwomen's, who'd laid their own heads next to Strongheart's. Jane, the younger of the two, caught Luke's eye, and he wondered for a moment if she might help him reach out to the old man. But she gave Luke such a look of pure pure hate that he quickly looked away from her.

'I've told all my men to stop fighting, Father,' Luke said.

'I told them to stop fighting and go back to the places they grounded on the poolside: Veeklehouse, Nob Head and David Water. I want to stop the killing.'

When Strongheart still didn't respond, Luke lifted his head and looked round Strongheart's shelter for someone else who might help him get through to the old Head Guard. Two of his ring-men had come in with him and now stood uncomfortably nearby, watched by twenty thirty guards, but they were no use to Luke now, and the only other face he found that wasn't a stranger's was the face of Newjohn, who'd once crossed the Pool to meet Luke's dad Dixon, his fellow Headman. Dixon didn't like Newjohn. 'I don't trust him one bit,' he'd told Luke. 'He's one of the Davidfolk at heart. He pretends to be one of us when it suits him, but then he cosies up to Strongheart again as soon as our backs are turned. In fact I don't trust any of those Brown River people. Even their stories are more like the Davidfolk's than ours. The only true Johnfolk are the ones that followed John across the Pool.'

The fact that Newjohn had been here, deep inside the Davidfolk Ground, when Johnfolk and Davidfolk were fighting one another over in Wide Forest, seemed to back up what his father had said, but Luke wasn't certain of anything any more. Maybe Newjohn had been right to try and heal that deep deep wound that divided the people of Eden?

'Headman Newjohn...' Luke began, climbing back to his feet and bowing. Then he broke off. Something was missing surely? He looked again round the wide space of the shelter. 'But where is our Mother? Where are the people from Earth?'

'They've gone,' said Newjohn with a shrug.

Luke felt inside himself that same sudden emptiness that I'd felt myself only a waking before.

'They've gone? Not far away, though, I guess?'

'Yes. Back to Earth.'

'But the message... The voice inside this... this...' He took the black linkup out of a pocket in his wrap. 'Gela's voice, inside this...

this thing here. She told me to come here and meet her.'

'They were here in Circle Valley,' said Strongheart, without looking up from his dead son, 'but they had to go. They went back up into the sky over a waking ago.'

Something shifted inside Luke. Up to that point he'd been willing to admit that he had been wrong, that everything was his fault, and even maybe that the Johnfolk themselves had been in the wrong all these years in their argument with the Davidfolk, but now, all at once, a new, suspicious mood took hold of him. It was a bit like the moment when a tubeslinker suddenly pulls right back inside the airhole of a tree – *snap!* – when it's been reaching right out, as far as it can go without toppling over, and swaying from side to side in the lanternlight.

'If they'd really asked me to come here, why would they go before I came? You'd have told them when they sent the message how far away I was, and how long it would take me to get here. And I came faster than you could have expected because you couldn't have known I was already up on the Dark.'

'It's no good asking *us* why they went, Headmanson,' Newjohn said. 'They're people from Earth. They make their own decisions.'

Luke glanced down at Strongheart, who was still kneeling by his son's body on the packed dirt of his shelter floor, but was beginning to struggle back up to his feet with the help of his two shelter-women. Then he looked back at Newjohn. Luke's eyes narrowed as he considered the Headman of the Brown River Ground. No wonder his dad hadn't trusted this guy, with his cunning pointy face.

'Tom's stinking dick,' he hissed. 'This is a trick, isn't it? Gela was never here. Earth never came. Of course not. It was just a trick to get me to stop the fight!'

'Oh come on, Headmanson,' snorted Newjohn. 'Look at what you've got in your hand, boy! Surely you can see that comes from Earth? Surely it's obvious that no one in Eden could make a piece of glass that can talk?'

Luke looked down at the linkup. Of course it was obvious it came from Earth. And he'd seen the light as well, of course, the light of Earth's sun, as that guard Roger had described it, shining out accusingly from the Circle as he stood looking down from the Dark. He hadn't seen the veekle rising up into the sky, because by that time he and the men with him were under the trees, but he had seen the light that the veekle made, and he knew that there was no light like it on Eden.

'They gave me this ring,' Strongheart said, and he showed Luke a metal ring that was identical in every way to the one his mother wore on her finger. As everyone knew on both sides of the Pool, except perhaps a few Hiding People, there'd only ever been one such ring on Eden, and it could only have been made on Earth. There was metal on Eden, but it was red, and it stained your fingers green if you wore it as a ring for too long. This one was made of two metals, just like his mother's, one yellow and one white. 'It belonged to Gela's sister,' Strongheart said, his voice flat and his face grey and indifferent with grief. He was a frail frail old man now, close close to death.

'And of course you've got that new message too, Head Guard,' Newjohn gently prompted him. 'You've got that new message for the Headmanson to hear.'

'Oh yes, I…' Strongheart fumbled in his wrap with trembly hands and took out another smooth black linkup. 'By the way,' he said suddenly, a little of his old strength and power returning for a moment to his voice, 'they told us that President was *not* Gela's dad. It was a man, it's true, but Gela never even met him, and it wasn't President that called the Three Men down from the sky.'

He fiddled round awkwardly with the square of glass until suddenly a woman's voice came out of it. Luke recognized it at once as being the same voice that had spoken from the linkup he still held in his hand, but he refused to listen to what it had to say. It was going to be *so* much easier for him if he didn't believe that Earth had come. That way he wouldn't have to go on carrying the awful burden of shame and guilt that had been with him ever since Harry's death. He wouldn't have to spend the rest of his life being the one who'd done for the messenger from Earth. He wouldn't even have to wonder whether the Davidfolk were right after all about John Redlantern and the Johnfolk, and whether he'd brought his friend Gerry across the Pool to die for no good reason at all.

'Put that away,' Luke said, while Gaia's voice was still speaking to him. 'I'm not interested in your tricks. We've always known you have old things from Earth here in Circle Valley. We've always known that some of those old things could talk or show pictures or give out light. You've just used some of them to fool me.'

Starlight stepped in now. 'Oh come on, you idiot! Use your head! You can see these things are bright and new. The Mementoes that were here before are so old that they're crumbling away, and none of them *do* anything at all. The Head Guard can show them to you now if you don't believe me.'

Luke hadn't spotted Starlight before. He'd vaguely noticed that there were high women in the shelter as well as women helpers, but women in New Earth played no part in the kind of talk that was going on now, and he'd paid them no attention. Now he'd seen Starlight, though, he recognized her at once. She might not remember meeting Headman Dixon's little boy when she was over there, because she'd been too busy watching Luke's dad Dixon and his mother Lucy – when a leopard's singing to you, as people say, you don't look at the flowers! – but the little boy remembered *her* alright, even after more than ten years.

'The fishing girl!' he hissed. 'The slinker who tried to steal our ring. So she's still alive, is she? Now I *know* this is all a trick!'

And not only that. He knew for certain again that he was in the right. After wakings of doubt and shame, he knew once more that he was one of the good guys in the story of Eden. He knew that the Johnfolk were the true followers of President and Mother Gela, and these people round him were the cowardly slinkers who'd followed the Holeface back at the time of Breakup. All his guilt had gone.

Fifty-six

I went to find Mary. It was too late to get her to meet the people from Earth, which I would have liked her to do, but, scared though I was to meet her, I thought I should still tell her something about what I'd learned about them. She was a powerful person and would have a lot of say in how this story was told from now on.

After she'd shouted at the Earth people, the guards told her she must leave the cluster and not come back while the Earth people were still there. But everyone seemed to know where she was, camping beside a pool with her two helpers and her guards, a mile or so out in forest, saying what she thought to anyone who came to see her. I got a young batface boy to take me there for half a stick.

When I arrived she was sitting with her back to me with her feet in the pool. It was such a familiar sight – that strong solid body, that big square head – that it was hard to believe that eight years had gone by since she'd ordered me out of her sight. I was terrified. But I asked myself what was the worst that could happen? It wasn't like she'd do for me, was it? It wasn't like she'd even hit me. At most, she'd be angry with me again and tell me she didn't want to see me. I could get over that.

I gave the boy his half stick, and told him I could find my own way back, then I walked forwards. She still hadn't noticed me, still just peacefully sat there waggling her big feet in the water. In between shows, she'd always liked to spend time alone with her own thoughts, sorting things out and joining them together.

'Mary?'

It took her a moment to recognize me, but when she did, it wasn't what I was expecting at all.

'Angie!' she cried, and her whole face lit up with pleasure as she scrambled to her feet. 'Oh Angie, I thought I might never see you again!'

She wanted to hug me, I could see, but she wasn't sure if she should, so I kind of half-opened my arms to let her know it was okay, and straight away she rushed forwards and held me tightly. I didn't know what to say and, anyway, she hadn't left me a lot of breath to speak with.

'Well, it *was* you that sent me away, Mary!' I gasped out.

'I know, I know, and I was so so wrong. I knew that almost at once, and all this time I've been hoping hoping that I'd see you so I could tell you so and say I'm sorry.'

Mary called out to her helpers and guards. 'Janey, Brightness, Davey, Met, this is Angie, that old helper of mine I often talk about. The one who came from that little grounds out in the Pool by Nob Head.'

The helpers and guards nodded to me without smiling, not quite as pleased to see me as Mary was, but Mary ignored that, taking my arm and leading me away from them into forest.

'I'm so sorry for what I did, Angie.'

I shrugged. 'I guess you were disappointed. After all your teaching and all the encouragement you gave me, I still couldn't hear our Mother.'

'If you couldn't hear her, you couldn't hear her. There was no reason for me to get angry with you. The only thing that might achieve was to make you pretend you could hear her so as to please me, and what would be the point of that? Not that you'd have done that anyway, Angie. You're way too honest.'

I smiled. 'Well, I did think about it.'

Mary stopped and turned to face me. We were passing under

some yellowlantern trees. She held my shoulders and studied my face in their light. When you're a batface it isn't often that someone looks into your face for so long and seems so pleased to do it. It felt pretty good.

I smiled. 'Why *were* you so angry, Mary? You accused me of thinking I was better than you, but you really couldn't have been more wrong! All the time I was with you – more than two years – I always thought you were *way* way better than me.'

She released my shoulders and turned away from me. She was ashamed, I realized. Mary, who was always so strong and so certain, was too ashamed to hold my gaze.

'I guess there's always doubt,' she said. 'Always doubt about everything: Is it really true? Am I just imagining it? Am I just making it up? Am I just saying what people want me to hear? When I first stood in the Circle myself, I was with a speaker called Firespark. To tell the truth, I wasn't sure if I'd really heard Gela, but partly because I was afraid of Firespark and partly because I wanted so much to be a speaker in my own right, I told her that I'd definitely heard our Mother. It wasn't for a long time, not until after I'd left Firespark and set out on my own, that I really felt confident that Gela was speaking to me. But even then, there were still sometimes moments when I...well...doubted. But I pushed the doubts away. I told myself they were weak. Well, you can doubt anything, can't you? You can doubt you love someone. You can doubt that anything matters at all. If you wait to be completely completely certain, you'll never believe anything, that's what I always told myself. A strong person makes up her mind and then sticks to it.'

She began to walk again, and I followed her. We moved from under the yellowlantern trees into the blue light of a couple of spiketrees. *Hmmmph hmmmph hmmmph* they went as they pumped up their boiling sap from down in the fires of Underworld. Even six seven yards away from them I could feel the heat of their trunks against my skin.

'Like leopard hunters,' Mary said. 'That's how I always explained it to myself. If they allow themselves to doubt at the last moment, if they hesitate or change their minds about what they're going to do, then they're dead. And if they allowed themselves to doubt before they even started, well then, they'd never go after leopards at all. They'd hunt bucks instead, or gather starflowers.'

'Well, it *is* brave to take a story and stick to it. You're a brave person, Mary. That's why people come to hear you. They *know* you believe what you say. They know you won't waver. That's why I wanted to be with you too.'

Mary nodded, but she'd spotted a groundrat ahead of us, and she held out her hand in front of me to tell me to be quiet, so she could creep up on it. We were always on the lookout for food in Circle Valley. But the rat ran off, and she relaxed and carried on.

'But you were always so honest, Angie, always so straight with me, always on the lookout for ways in which the True Story might be bent or broken by other things, like what the high people wanted, or what would make my life easier. Remember how you used to ask me about that, again and again? Was I just saying what the high people wanted me to say? Why did Gela only tell off the low people? So when you said you couldn't hear Gela, part of me was angry with you for not having the guts to believe, but another part of me was afraid that you actually had more guts than I did. Because it would have been much easier for you, wouldn't it, to tell me you'd heard Gela than to tell me you hadn't? Just as it was easier for me to say to old Firespark that I'd heard our Mother, and have her hug me and tell me what a clever girl I was.'

We came to a little stream. The shining wavyweed under the water made it into a kind of smooth, glowing path, winding through the criss-cross pattern of light and shadow under the trees. Without even thinking about it, we both peered down into the water for fish.

'I thought about all this all over again,' Mary said, 'when I heard the news about these people from Earth. It made me doubt everything. It made me wonder if I'd been completely wrong all my life, claiming to hear the voice of Gela, and then not even knowing it when she was right here in Eden. And it made me think about you, and the courage you'd shown by not saying something was true unless you were sure. And—'

I put my fingers over her lips to make her stop. 'Listen, Mary. I *did* hear our Mother in the Circle, but I didn't like what she was saying to me, so I pretended to myself I didn't. Not so brave at all, I'm afraid.'

Mary looked at me. Her face was more lined than I remembered, but those small sharp eyes were so familiar as they searched me, so familiar and also so dear. 'So... So can I ask what she said to you?'

'There were things I was hiding from you. She told me I shouldn't keep them secret.' I hesitated for a moment, but it didn't seem so hard any more to tell her those things that I'd been so afraid to speak of before. 'I was hiding the fact that my best friend went over to the Johnfolk across the water. And that she wore Gela's ring on her finger, and spoke the Secret Story out loud. I was hiding the fact that I was proud of her. I was hiding that I knew the Secret Story myself.'

'Oh that stupid story,' Mary snorted, waving the thing away with a sweep of her hand.

'Listen, Mary, I got to know those Earth people. You were quite right back in the clearing, they *are* just people. But they aren't *bad* people, and they didn't come here on purpose to trick us. The truth is, Mary, they didn't expect to find us at all. They assumed people wouldn't have survived here. They just came here to look at the animals and the trees. Don't ask me why. It's something called *science*. But listen, Mary, that voice from the screens telling the Secret Story. It *was* Gela. The life in those screens comes from a thing called a bat-tree – I guess because it's like a living tree that life comes flying out from – and the Earth people told me that a bat-tree of that kind only lasts five years at most. And that's only if you don't use the screen at all. If you use it a lot, it doesn't even live half that long. So if you think about it, even if it was only used that one time when the voice was put inside it, there would only have been one grownup woman on Eden when that screen died, and that woman was Gela.'

Mary picked up a stick and pushed the wavyweed about in the water like you do when you're looking to see if any fish are hiding underneath, though I doubt she'd have noticed right then even if there was a whole bunch of them. Forest hummed all round us. Not far away the stream trickled down a sparkly little waterfall into a pool.

'I've got so many things wrong, Angie, haven't I? How many women have had a beating from the guards over the years because I got it out in the open that they'd told that Secret Story?'

'Certainly quite a few when I was with you.'

Mary nodded. 'Do you remember when we went to the White Streams? There was an old woman down there who asked about those stories you hear about fights on Earth – the white people and the black people, the Germ Men and the Juice – and I told her they were just silly children's tales.'

'Well, like you say yourself, Mary, if you wait to be quite certain you're completely right, you'll wait forever, and never do anything at all. People come to hear you because you've got the guts to believe in something. Of course sometimes you're wrong, but then you think again. I didn't like how you made the poor Earth folk look bad, but… well, you were trying to make sense of things – I could see that – and helping us make sense of them as well.'

She studied my face doubtfully. 'Was I?'

I couldn't believe that Mary – strong fierce Mary – was asking me to reassure her.

'I think so. I think that's what you do. Most of the time, anyway.'

She smiled. 'Gela's heart, Angie, I do love you! It's so good to see you again. I've missed our talks so much.'

Fifty-seven

'Come on, men!' Luke said. 'We're not staying here with the fishing girl!'

He turned towards the door of Strongheart's shelter, and the two ringmen hurried to follow him out. David Strongheart had sunk down again over the stiff bent body of his dead son, and seemed quite ready just to let Luke go. And seeing that Newjohn wasn't going to step in against the son of his fellow Headman, Starlight decided to take charge.

'Stop them, guards!' she bellowed. My old friend was nothing to do with the Davidfolk Ground. She wasn't born there, she didn't live there now, and before this time in Circle Valley, the only Davidfolk places she'd even visited were Nob Head on our trading trips from Knee Tree Grounds, and Veeklehouse on that one single occasion. But never mind that: she spoke so firmly that Strongheart's guards rushed to do as she said, blocking the way to the door of the shelter and surrounding Headmanson Luke and his two men.

'Here's my suggestion, Head Guard,' Starlight said to Strongheart. 'You hold Luke here, and you make him tell his men on poolside to hand over all their metal spears and arrows and knives, and all their metal masks, and get onto their boats, and disappear over World's Edge. That way you'll take away the advantage they have, and they'll know there's no point in trying to come straight back over again and take over your ground again.'

Starlight knew that it had taken New Earth years to gather together the metal they used for all those arrows and spears and masks. Just to make a couple of arrowheads, she told me, it took a pile of green rock the weight of a tree trunk, which had to be dug out of the ground, and broken up into little pieces, and heated in a big clay oven, many times hotter than any oven we'd ever seen on this side of the pool.

'Let one boat stay back for Headmanson Luke,' Starlight suggested, 'and when you're sure that all the rest have gone, let him follow them back over to New Earth.'

Still on the floor, Strongheart nodded, while his two young shelterwomen stared at Starlight with a mixture of puzzlement, jealousy, hate and admiration. No high woman of the Davidfolk would ever take charge of guards as she had done, or get involved in a fight between two grounds. Their job was to look after the high men, and to help bind together the families of the different guard leaders by being sent from one family to join another.

'I'm not accepting that,' Luke said, realizing he was about to be the fool of the story all over again, even if it was a different story. He couldn't bring himself to look at Starlight, and it seemed silly to speak to the frail griefstricken old man on the floor, so he spoke to Newjohn. 'Ringmen don't go skulking back across the water without their spears, least of all when they're winning, as you know quite well they *were* doing, until I sent them back to poolside. Do for me if you want, but I'm not telling my men to throw down their spears.'

Newjohn gave a sort of shrug, as if to say it was nothing to do with him. But the truth was that he was kind of trapped too. There was no way now that he could take the side of the New Earthers.

'So what's going to happen then, Headmanson Luke?' Starlight asked. 'Let's think about it, shall we? You can't get a message to your men, whether you're alive or dead, and they're divided into three separate parts, spread out along poolside, that can't speak to one another. I guess they'll wait where they are, as you've told them to do, until they start to get seriously hungry, and then they'll have to make up their own minds what to do. But it won't be like when they first grounded. This time they'll have guards all round them who are good and ready for them. You might have done for Leader Harry, but his big brother Mehmet is over there now to organize things, along with Leader Hunter. And they're not boys like you, Headmanson Luke, they're grown men with grandchildren. And they've got all of Wide Forest back again to feed their men, and all the Davidfolk to support them. Your men might have been stronger when they were all working together, but things are different now.'

She'd always worried that by going over to New Earth and stirring things up, she'd brought forward the waking that the ringmen would come across the water, but she'd more than made up for that now. 'Of course now I've got to worry about the power of the Davidfolk,' she told me later, 'and the threat they pose to Half Sky.' But that was a problem for another waking. Stories do not end, this is what we've learned. There's always another bit to come.

Luke glanced guiltily at his two ringmen, and then turned back to Newjohn.

'Okay,' he said, 'I'll send a message to my men by the Pool.'

He had a long time ahead of him in Circle Valley. A long time not to hear all the stories about the Earth people, and the pictures of Earth, and the voice of Gela, and the veekle that was alive. A long time not to think about the ring that Strongheart now wore on his little finger. Some stories are hard hard work to keep on believing in, but he worked away at it anyway.

And eventually, over beside Worldpool, in Veeklehouse and Nob Head and David Water, the ringmen piled their spears and masks in great heaps, pushed their boats out and began the hard hard work of paddling back out against the wind into the bright water where my Candy had first seen them coming with her sharp sharp eyes.

And finally Luke was allowed to follow them, out into the bright water and on into Deep Darkness where the great waves rise and fall unseen, as they've done since long before any human being ever heard of Eden.

Fifty-eight

I'm a shadowspeaker now. I went back into the Circle and heard the voice of our Mother. It's completely different from the voice that the Earth people found inside those screens. That Gela was just a woman, like Jeff Redlantern used to say; she was just a woman from Earth and Earth is just a place, even though she was the mother of all of us here on Eden. The Mother that me and Mary hear doesn't speak in words. Words would never be enough for her. She speaks in feelings, and pictures, and whole big ideas that come suddenly into your mind.

You can't always be sure that you've heard her right, and of course sometimes you wonder if you've really heard her at all. But it's like the bits of this story I've told you that are about times where I wasn't there and can't be absolutely sure about. I could have missed them out completely, and given you a story with all kinds of holes in it, but I decided to figure out what happened as best I could, even at the risk of getting some things wrong. What else are we going to do? We don't have science to tell us things like they have on Earth, and if we only spoke about what we were certain of, we'd hardly say anything at all. But people still need stories to make sense of their lives, and clever Mary has figured out a new kind of, story that fits with what we know now and yet still lets the Davidfolk carry on drawing their circles and singing 'Come Tree Row', even though Earth has been and gone. It even lets those crazy brave boys up at Rockway Edge carry on burning their backs on spiketrees and showing off their horrible scars.

I travel round the Davidfolk Ground with Mary like I did before, back and forth, rockway to alpway, peckway to blueway. Candy and Metty come with me, but Fox prefers to stay with his dad and his friends. I don't like to think about it too much but I guess one waking Candy may decide she prefers that too, even though she tells me now that she never will, and that when she's a grownup she'll be a shadowspeaker like me and Auntie Mary. Metty, I'm pretty sure, will want to stay behind when he's older. Children like to have friends round them to grow up with, not just their mum and an old shadowspeaker and a couple of guards, and no one to play with but strangers' children who tend to keep their distance from the shadowspeaker's kids.

Every Virsry time, we go back to Veeklehouse and I spend a hundred wakings in Michael's Place. That's part of the deal I made with Dave and Tom. I hate leaving Fox when the hundred wakings are up – it feels like tearing out my heart – and I hate how distant he is at first when I return, each time a little more distant than the last. Dave mutters that it's a funny kind of mum who can walk away from one of her kids for two hundred wakings at a time, and take her other kids away from their dad, and I do feel badly about it myself. But I know my kids are proud of me – the older two, anyway: Metty's not really big enough for that – and I kind of hope my example will help them see that, if they don't want, they don't have to be exactly like the other people in Michael's Place.

I'm sure Dave misses Candy and Metty like I miss Fox, but a big part of why he hates me going away is that it makes him feel ashamed. It shames him that, though he's told me I shouldn't go and that I shouldn't take the little ones with me, I still *do* go and still *do* take them, and he and his brother Tom don't feel able to stop me. They know that Mary is the most powerful shadowspeaker in all the Davidfolk Ground. They know that my old friend Starlight has become a friend of Head Guard Mehmet since she helped his old dad get rid of the Johnfolk, and that she comes over the Blue

Mountains each year to share the Virsry with him in Circle Valley. They know that I'm known myself across the Davidfolk Ground as the one who made friends with the dark-skinned woman who came in a veekle from Earth. And all those things give me power.

Being a shadowspeaker gives me power as well, of course. It makes me into a kind of high person, in a way, far more so than I would have ever been if I'd gone with Starlight to Half Sky, or with Gaia to Earth. And that's one of the things I like about it, if I'm honest. I like being well known, I've found out, and I like being looked up to. Come to that, I don't mind the presents people give us either. They're not my reason for being a shadowspeaker, but I do like them, and they certainly help me to smooth things over with the people at Michael's Place. It's easier to get past that awkwardness when I go back there if I can bring a metal knife for Dave, or a necklace for Clare, or a handful of sticks for Tom.

We don't pass on messages from dead people in our shows any more, and we don't pretend we know where our Mother is exactly, or what the place is like that she's calling us to: we just call it the true home, and say the Circle is the sign of it. After all, like Gaia said, even for the Earth people everything they know is only a little patch of light with mystery all round it. Mary admits that she was wrong to say that Earth was our true home. She says that out loud in our shows. Earth is just a place, she says, a faraway place, where our many-greats grandparents used to live. Which is pretty much what Jeff Redlantern used to say, if our old Knee Tree stories are true, but I tend not to point that out to her.

Mary doesn't go on about the Johnfolk being bad any more either. She knows that sometimes other people hear our Mother saying different things, and sometimes they may be right and her wrong. We don't let the high people tell us what to say either, and I guess one waking that's going to get us in trouble: that and the fact that we regularly say things that come from the Secret Story, not because Gela said them, but because, like she said, they're obviously true. But the high people are grateful to us for helping people feel okay about the fact that Earth has come and gone again, and so, for the moment, they let us alone.

After we've done a show and settled down the kids, me and Mary like to sit up and talk. I've often said how smart Mary is, and how smart Starlight and Trueheart are, but lately I've come to see that I'm pretty smart myself. I notice things that most people don't bother with, and I have a need inside me to think about the world round me and try and figure it out, much as bats have a need to fly, or little kids have a need inside them to shout and run round. Me and Mary talk a lot about true home and whether it's a place you can touch or see, or whether it's more like a feeling or an idea. Mary wants it to be a place. She wants that so much that, if anyone can do such a thing, she'll make it true just by believing it. I'm not so sure, but I figure that even the idea of home *is* a kind of home, and that when you really feel at home, like at the end of 'Come Tree Row', then home is where you really are, whether you're on dark dark Eden or pale pale Earth.

And one thing I've found out is that I feel at home with Mary and she feels at home with me. We kiss and cuddle sometimes now as well, and give each other some pleasure in that way. 'You used to think I was too ugly for this, didn't you?' I sometimes say to her, and she just laughs and says, 'Well, you *are* ugly, Angie. You are ugly ugly. But I can't help loving you anyway.' Funnily enough I kind of like that. It feels more comfortable somehow, more secure, than when she told me that first time I was beautiful. It's not so hard to live up to, I guess.

None of that changes the fact that the most perfect moment in all my life was when the veekle came down in front of me in Circle Clearing and I met Gaia. I dream about it often. She comes back and speaks to me, her voice close close, like Gela's voice speaking from those screens.

I also dream often about Trueheart, good brave Trueheart, far far away across the stars, walking and talking in that strange pale place with its drowned houses and its sky that's sometimes white and sometimes pink and sometimes black like ours. Every single waking, I remind myself that she really is there on Earth right at this moment, alive and seeing and breathing: someone I know, someone I've held in my arms, a daughter of Eden like me. It makes Earth seem much much nearer and Eden seem much less alone. (And we really *aren't* so alone, are we – we really aren't – now we're certain that Earth knows where to find us?) I often stop and wonder what Trueheart's doing there right now, and whether she understands science yet as well as Marius, and if I'd even know her with that new face that the Earth people will have sewn for her with those fine metal needles of theirs. I won't ever see her again, I'm sure, and nor will her mum and dad, but I like to think her sisters and brothers will, and so will my own kids.

Gaia gave me a present just before she went away. She gave it to me when no one else was looking, and suggested I keep it to myself. It's a linkup, one of those black squares of glass. It's got some of her words in it, thoughts she spoke into it during her time on Eden, and some pictures of Earth, and it's got all the crackling hissing words they managed to find in that old screen. Gaia told me the bat-tree inside it is stronger than the one in the screen, and might last as long as six seven years if I make sure only to use the linkup just one waking every year. So me and Mary have a little tradition that we settle down to listen to it once each year as we draw near to Veeklehouse just before the Virsry time. One waking, we know, we'll try it and nothing will happen. The tiny tree inside it will have died and gone cold, and the little bats of lecky-trickity won't come darting out from it any more. That's going to be sad, like saying goodbye to Earth a second time, a bit like Gela losing her ring. But even then I'll still have a silent square of glass to prove to myself that I really did meet that woman who came from Earth.

When we settle down to listen to it, we take it in turns to pick things we want to see or hear. Mary's sad and angry with herself that she lost the chance to meet the Earth people, so she usually picks some of Gaia's words, but my own favourite part are the words the Earth people found inside that old screen in Circle Valley. Angela speaks most of them, but the last time we listened, we found a little bit where Tommy spoke as well. People don't talk about him so much as they do about her – somehow or other we've never had difficulty in his case with remembering he *was* just a person – but as me and Mary sat there side by side in the humming, shining forest, it was kind of nice to hear the two of them together, the first two people in Eden, sitting and talking just like us.

When Tommy speaks, him and Gela have been listening to starbirds calling out to each other in the distance. *Hooom! Hooom! Hooom!* From inside our little square of glass, me and Mary could still just hear that bird from four hundred years ago, faintly faintly, behind all the crackling and hissing. And then, even more faintly, we heard another one answering it back in the way that starbirds do: *Aaaaah! Aaaaah! Aaaaah!* It was so familiar and yet so strange at the same time that it made us both laugh. I don't know how long a starbird can live if no one does for it – how would you begin to find out? – but I guess those two birds we could hear are long since dead, so that all that remains of them now are those calls inside our little square of glass. When the bat-tree dies, they really will be gone for good.

We were listening for the first bird to call out again, when suddenly Tommy spoke. 'They don't give a damn, those starbirds, do they?' he said. 'They don't even notice that great wheel burning up there in the sky. They don't give it a moment's thought.'

'No, they don't,' said Gela. 'You're right. This Eden, this dark Eden, it's just life to them, isn't it? It's just the way things happen to be.'

And then a real starbird cried out right next to us, so loud that it made us jump. *Hooom! Hooom! Hooom!* said the starbird, and straight away, maybe a hundred yards off, another one answered: *Aaaaah! Aaaaah! Aaaaah!*